T0265891

THE
EMPUSIUM

ALSO BY OLGA TOKARCZUK

TRANSLATED BY ANTONIA LLOYD-JONES

Drive Your Plow Over the Bones of the Dead

TRANSLATED BY JENNIFER CROFT

Flights
The Books of Jacob

THE
EMPUSIUM

A Health Resort
Horror Story

Olga Tokarczuk

TRANSLATED BY

Antonia Lloyd-Jones

RIVERHEAD BOOKS

NEW YORK

2024

RIVERHEAD BOOKS
An imprint of Penguin Random House LLC
penguinrandomhouse.com

This book has been published with the support of the ©POLAND Translation Program.

Images from the collection of the author.

Library of Congress Cataloging-in-Publication Data
Names: Tokarczuk, Olga, 1962– author. | Lloyd-Jones, Antonia, translator.
Title: The empusium : a health resort horror story / Olga Tokarczuk ; translated by Antonia
Lloyd-Jones. Other titles: Empuzjon. English
Description: New York : Riverhead Books, 2024. |
Identifiers: LCCN 2024010569 (print) | LCCN 2024010570 (ebook) | ISBN 9780593712948
(hardcover) | ISBN 9780593854082 | ISBN 9780593712962 (ebook)
Subjects: LCSH: Tuberculosis—Patients—Fiction. | Sanatoriums—Poland—
Sokołowsko—Fiction. | LCGFT: Historical fiction. | Novels.
Classification: LCC PG7179.O37 E6713 2024 (print) | LCC PG7179.O37 (ebook) |
DDC 891.8/538—dc23/eng/20240525
LC record available at https://lccn.loc.gov/2024010569
LC ebook record available at https://lccn.loc.gov/2024010570

International edition ISBN: 9780593854082

Printed in the United States of America
1st Printing

Book design by Alexis Farabaugh

Every day things happen in the world that can't
be explained by any law of things we know. Every day
they're mentioned and forgotten, and the same mystery that
brought them takes them away, transforming their secret into
oblivion. Such is the law by which things that can't be explained
must be forgotten. The visible world goes on as usual in the
broad daylight. Otherness watches us from the shadows.

FERNANDO PESSOA, *THE BOOK OF DISQUIET*,
TRANSLATED BY RICHARD ZENITH

Characters

Mieczysław (Mieczyś) Wojnicz
A student of hydroengineering
and sewage systems, from Lwów

Longin Lukas
A Catholic traditionalist,
gymnasium teacher, from Königsberg

August August
A socialist-humanist, classical
philologist and writer, from Vienna

Walter Frommer
A theosophist and privy counselor, from Breslau

Thilo von Hahn
A student of the Beaux-Arts and
connoisseur of the landscape, from Berlin

Dr. Semperweiss
A psychoanalyzing doctor, from Waldenburg

Wilhelm (Willi) Opitz
Proprietor of the Guesthouse for Gentlemen in
Görbersdorf, whose uncle served in the Swiss Guard

Raimund
Opitz's young assistant

György
A philosopher, from Berlin

AND

Frau Weber and Frau Brecht

Gliceria

Herri met de Bles

Klara Opitz, wife of Wilhelm

Sydonia Patek

Frau Large Hat

Tomášek

Saint Emerentia

The Tuntschi

Tharcoal burners

Nameless inhabitants of
the walls, floors and ceilings

THE
EMPUSIUM

THE GUESTHOUSE
FOR GENTLEMEN

The view is obscured by clouds of steam from the locomotive that trail along the platform. To see everything we must look beneath them, let ourselves be momentarily blinded by the gray haze, until the vision that emerges after this trial run is sharp, incisive and all-seeing.

Then we shall catch sight of the platform flagstones, squares overgrown with the stalks of feeble little plants—a space trying at any cost to keep order and symmetry.

Soon after, a left shoe appears on them, brown, leather, not brandnew, and is immediately joined by a second, right shoe; this one looks even shabbier—its toe is rather scuffed, and there are some lighter patches on the upper. For a moment the shoes stand still, indecisively, but then the left one advances. This movement briefly exposes a black cotton sock beneath a trouser leg. Black recurs in the tails of an unbuttoned wool coat; the day is warm. A small hand, pale and bloodless, holds a brown leather suitcase; the weight has caused the veins to tense, and now they indicate their source, somewhere deep inside the bowels of the sleeve. Under the coat we glimpse a flannel jacket of rather poor quality, slightly crumpled by the long journey and marked by tiny bright dots of some nonspecific impurity—the world's chaff. The white collar of a shirt is visible too, the button-on kind, evidently changed quite recently, because its whiteness is fresher than the white of the actual shirt and contrasts with the sallow tone of the traveler's face. Pale eyes, eyebrows and eyelashes make this face look unhealthy. Against the deep red of the western sky the whole figure gives the unsettling impression of having arrived here, in these melancholy mountains, from the world beyond.

The new arrival walks toward the main hall of the station, surprisingly large for this highland region, along with the other passengers, but unlike them walks unhurriedly, perhaps reluctantly, and is not greeted or met by anyone. Putting the suitcase down on the worn tiled floor, the traveler pulls on a pair of quilted gloves. One of them, on the right hand, is soon curled and put to the mouth to receive a volley of short, dry coughs.

The young person stoops and searches for a pocket handkerchief. The fingers alight on the spot where a passport is hidden beneath the fabric of the coat. If we focus our attention on it, we shall see the fanciful handwriting of a Galician official, who has carefully filled in the fields on the document as follows: Mieczysław Wojnicz, Catholic, student at Lwów Polytechnic, born 1889, eyes blue, height average, face round, hair fair.

The said Wojnicz is now heading for the main station hall in Dittersbach, a small town near Waldenburg. As he walks hesitantly across this tall, gloomy space, where an echo is sure to inhabit the top cornices, he can sense someone's eyes scrutinizing him from behind the ticket windows in the waiting room. Wojnicz checks the time on a large clock—it is late, his was the last train from Breslau—then, after a moment's dithering, goes out in front of the station building, where at once he is enfolded in the broad embrace of the ragged mountain horizon.

It is mid-September, but here, as the newcomer notices to his amazement, the summer is already long over and the first fallen leaves are lying on the ground. The past few days must have been rainy, because a light mist still fills most of the landscape, making an exception only for the dark lines of streams. Wojnicz's lungs feel the high altitude, which is good for his enfeebled body. He stands on the station steps, suspiciously eyeing the thin leather soles of his shoes; he will have to think about winter boots. In Lwów the asters and zinnias are still flowering, and no one has thought about the autumn yet. But here the tall horizon makes it darker, and the colors seem more garish, almost vulgar. Just then he is overcome by a familiar sense of sadness, typical of those convinced of their own impending death. The world around him feels like stage scenery painted on a paper screen, as if he could stick a finger into this monumental landscape and drill a hole in it leading straight to nothingness. And as if nothingness will start pouring out of there in a flood, and will catch him up too, grab him by the throat. He has to shake his head to be rid of this image. It shatters into droplets and falls onto the leaves. Luckily an ungainly vehicle resembling a britzka comes rolling along the road toward him. In it sits a slim, freckled boy wearing a strange outfit, reminiscent of a military jacket of obscure provenance—not like a Prussian uniform, which would be understandable in this place—and a military forage cap, fancifully tilted on his head. Without a word he stops in front of Wojnicz and, muttering something, takes his luggage.

"How are you, my good fellow?" asks Wojnicz politely in schoolboy

German, but he waits in vain for an answer; the boy pulls his cap low and impatiently points to a seat for him in the britzka.

And at once they move off. First through the town over cobblestones, then along a road that in the falling darkness takes them through forest, on a winding track between steep mountain slopes. They are accompanied by the constant murmur of a nearby stream and its smell, which unsettles Wojnicz badly: the odor of damp brush, rotting leaves, eternally wet stones and water. In an attempt to establish contact he asks the driver questions, how long will their journey be, for example, how did he recognize him at the station, what is his name, but the boy remains silent and does not even glance at him. A gas lantern placed on the boy's right side partly illuminates his face, which in profile resembles the snout of a highland rodent, a marmot, and Wojnicz figures he must be either deaf or insolent.

After about three quarters of an hour, they emerge from the shadow of the forest onto an unexpected plateau between the wooded mountains. The sky is fading, but that tall, imposing horizon, still visible, brings a lump to the throat of any new arrival from the lowlands.

"Görbersdorf," says the driver suddenly, in an unexpectedly shrill, boyish tone.

But Wojnicz can see nothing beyond a dense wall of darkness that is heedlessly breaking free of the mountainsides in whole sheets. Once his eyes have grown used to it, a viaduct suddenly looms before them, under which they drive into a village; beyond it, the vast bulk of a redbrick edifice comes into sight, followed by other, smaller buildings, a street, and even two gas lamps. The brick edifice proves colossal as it emerges from the darkness, and the motion of the vehicle picks out rows of illuminated windows. The light in them is dingy yellow. Wojnicz cannot tear his eyes from this sudden, triumphal vision, and he looks back at it for a long time, until it sinks into the darkness like a huge steamship.

Now the britzka turns into a narrow side road along the stream and crosses a small bridge, on which the wheels raise a noise like the sound of gunfire. At last it stops outside a sizable wooden building with very strange architecture that brings to mind a matchstick house—there are so many verandas, balconies and terraces. A pleasant light glows in the windows. Under the first-floor windows there is a beautiful sign in Gothic script carved out of thick tin:

Gästehaus für Herren

With relief, Wojnicz alights from the britzka and fills his lungs with a mighty gulp of this new air, which is said to cure the most critical cases. But perhaps he does it too soon, because at once such an acute coughing fit assails him that he must lean against the balustrade of the bridge. As he coughs, he feels a chill and the nasty, slippery texture of rotten wood, and the positive first impression evaporates. Unable to restrain the violent spasms of his diaphragm, he is seized by overwhelming fear—that he is about to choke, that this will be his final attack. He tries to ward off panic, just as Dr. Sokołowski has advised him, by thinking of a meadow full of flowers, of warm sunshine. He makes a great effort, though his eyes are watering and his face is flushed. He thinks he is about to cough up his soul.

But then he feels a grip on his shoulder, and a tall, well-built man with gray-speckled hair offers his hand. Through his tears, Wojnicz sees a pink, healthy face.

"Come along, my fellow. Let's pull ourselves together," says the man confidently, with a broad smile that makes the visitor—though worn out by all the coughing—feel like huddling up to him and letting himself be taken off to bed like a child. Oh yes, indeed. A child. To bed. In some confusion, he throws his arms around the man's neck and lets himself be led through a hallway smelling of spruce smoke and up some stairs softly carpeted with a runner. All this prompts a remote association with wrestling, with a male sport in which hard bodies press against each other, rub and strike one another, though not to do each other harm, but quite the opposite, to show each other tenderness and affection under the guise of combat. He surrenders to the strong hands and allows himself to be guided to a room upstairs, to be seated on the bed and divested of his overcoat and sweater.

Wilhelm Opitz—for so the man introduces himself, pointing a finger at his chest—covers him with a woolen rug, and from hands that appear briefly in the doorway receives a mug of hot, tasty broth. While Wojnicz drinks it in small sips, Wilhelm Opitz raises his finger (Wojnicz is realizing what an essential part of Wilhelm that finger is) and says in soft, slightly comical German: "I wrote to Professor Sokołowski that you should take a break in Breslau. It is too long and tiring a journey. I said so."

The broth floods Wojnicz's body with warmth, and the poor boy is unaware of the moment when he falls asleep. We shall keep him company awhile longer, listen to his calm breathing—we are pleased that his lungs have settled down.

Now our attention turns to a streak of light as thin as a blade that falls into the room from the corridor and stops on the porcelain chamber pot underneath the bed. We are drawn to the cracks between the floorboards—and there we disappear.

At a quarter to seven, Wojnicz was awoken by the sound of a bugle, thanks to which it took him a while to work out where he was. The tune it was playing sounded off-key, which amused him and put him in a good mood. It seemed familiar, in the way that applies to things so simple as to be brilliant—as though they have existed forever, and always will.

Mieczysław Wojnicz was afflicted by various conditions best understood not by him but by his father, January Wojnicz, a retired civil servant and landowner. He managed these disorders with great competence, gravity and tact, treating the property entrusted to him in the figure of his son with great responsibility and—it was plain to see—love, albeit devoid of any sentimentality or any of the "female emotions" that he so abhorred.

One of these afflictions, which had to some extent been shaped by the father, was the son's exaggerated fear of being spied on. Young Wojnicz devoted much attention to the gaze of others, constantly checking to see if someone's eyes were following him from around a corner, from an angle, through a window in which a curtain had twitched, or through a keyhole. The father's caution and suspicion had given rise to the son's obsession. He felt as if another person's gaze were something sticky that adhered to him like the soft, hideous oral cavity of a leech. And so, in every room where he was to spend the night, he carefully examined the curtains, blocked the keyhole with a ball of paper, checked for holes in the wall and chinks between the floorboards, even peeked behind the pictures. After all, at guesthouses and hotels peeping was not entirely unlikely—one time, when he and his father had stopped at a hotel during one of their health-related visits to a specialist in Warsaw, the young Wojnicz had discovered a neat hole in the wall, clumsily disguised by the rich pattern of the wallpaper, so naturally he had glued it up with a lump of bread; next morning when he tried to investigate who might be watching the guests and from where, he discovered that the servants' stairwell, used by hotel staff, was on the other side of the wall. Aha! So he wasn't being paranoid. People do spy on each other. They love to watch another person while he is unaware of it. They love to judge and compare. Those who are observed in this way are defenseless—unwitting, helpless victims.

Once awake, Wojnicz immediately set about writing a message to his father to reassure him. It was a matter of a few simple words, yet he didn't find it easy; his forearm felt numb and weak. So he focused all his attention on his hand, as it ran the pencil tip across a sheet of cream-colored paper in a leather-bound notebook. We find this movement fascinating, we like it. It reminds us of the winding lines and spiral flourishes that earthworms bore underground, and that weevils carve into tree trunks. Wojnicz sat in bed, propped up on two mighty pillows. Before him lay a clever piece of furniture, something like a small table with no legs. Its underside consisted of a pillow stuffed with peas, allowing it to rest easily on the knees of the person writing.

First, two figures appeared, forming *13*, then a straight line and a cross, *IX*, and after it another four figures taking shape as *1913*. Then from the flourishes the name *Görbersdorf* appeared, underlined several times. The umlaut was treated with special reverence. The pencil continued to move evenly and persistently across the paper, the graphite creaking as the paper sagged beneath the round shapes of the letters.

The room was modest, but comfortably furnished. Two windows looked onto the street and the stream in front of the house, but the view was obscured by some crocheted curtains. Under one of the windows stood a small round table and two upholstered chairs, comfortable but rather shabby—a cozy corner for reading, if one so wished. To the left of the door stood the bed, with a beautifully carved wooden head-board, and next to it a wardrobe. There was a small dressing table to the right of the door. The walls were covered with fabric paper in broad light blue stripes, which made the room look taller and more spacious than it really was. On the wall hung prints from exotic parts: a down of hares and a pack of hyenas.

Writing in Polish, Wojnicz briefly described his impressions of the journey, converting 1,900 feet into meters (it came out at almost 600), and transferred these figures onto a rough map illustrating his journey from Lwów. His commentaries were mainly about the meals he had eaten on the way. Next to *Wrocław/Breslau* he wrote: *Pumpkin soup, followed by puree with lardons, cabbage and a cutlet exactly like our pork chops. For dessert, a vanilla pudding with meringue and blackberry compote, very tasty.* Underneath he added: *Price: 5 marks.* He had promised his father he would send him a few words each day, preferably about his state of health, but he didn't really know how he was feeling, so he chose instead to send menus or geographical information.

There was a soft knock at the door, and before he had time to say "Come in," a leather boot had wedged its way into the gap between the frame and the door, gently opening it; next the black pleats of a skirt appeared, the lacy edge of an apron, and a breakfast tray, which was soon standing on the little table. The boots, lace and apron vanished as quickly as they had appeared, and the bewildered Wojnicz merely managed to pull his rug over himself, stammer a greeting and say thank you. He was so hungry that he was interested only in the food.

He recorded it at once in his jotter: hard-boiled eggs, two, in lovely faience cups, covered with little hen-shaped hats, slices of smoked sheep's milk cheese garnished with parsley, balls of the yellowest butter served on a horseradish leaf, a small bowl of fragrant lard with a little knife for spreading it, a radish cut into slices, a basket filled with bread rolls of various kinds, light and dark, morello cherry jam in a glass dish, a mug of thick cocoa and a small jug of coffee.

At the end of the next sentence, the notebook banged shut, and Wojnicz delighted in eating everything that was on the tray. Then, invigorated by the meal, he got up. With the rug around his shoulders, he tottered to his suitcase, extracted a neatly folded set of underclothes, and set about his ablutions. As he was drying his face on a towel imbued with the scent of pine that pervaded the guesthouse, a vivid image appeared before his eyes, of his family's house in the country, and of underclothes drying in the attic in winter, when it was pouring outside and Gliceria took them up there in pails. He could clearly see the attic, always full of dust, and the view from its small windows known as bull's-eyes—the image of fields and a small park—and the acrid smell of rotting tomato stalks, sweet corn and beans on poles. And by the laws of some inexplicable synesthesia this image changed into a physical sensation: the coarseness of fabric, the stiffness of collars, the angularity of freshly pressed trousers and the pinch of a hard leather belt. And it was there, in the attic, as soon as he could, whenever he was alone and out of the reach of his father's discipline, that he undressed entirely; he would wrap his naked body in a satin tablecloth edged with a soft fringe and, feeling how blissfully it brushed against his thighs and calves, he would think how wonderful it would be if people could go about in tablecloth tunics, like the ancient Greeks. But now, with the memory of that satin toga, he dressed and was pleased to feel strong and rested at last.

We are witnesses as the clothing appears in layers on his slender body, until finally his figure, entirely different from yesterday's, coughing and ashen-faced, stands with a hand on the doorknob, eyes closed, imagining how it would appear to the eyes of someone who might now be observing it. It looks good—a slender young man with fair hair and subtle features in formal gray trousers and a brown woolen jacket. Moments later, he resolutely opens the door.

No, we do not regard it as an obsession, at most as innocent oversensitivity. People should get used to the fact that they are being watched.

At about ten o'clock Wojnicz went downstairs, ahead of his appointment to be examined at the Kurhaus.

The whole house was in semidarkness, because the windows were small and few, as was typical of highland architecture. Here there was an oval table covered with a thick, patterned cloth, a sofa and several chairs, while against the wall stood an upright piano, rarely used, judging by the isolated fingerprints on its glossy lid and the wad of yellowing musical scores. A small shelf hanging beside it was full of books about the region, the local ski trails and sights. In a huge glass-fronted sideboard a beautiful porcelain dinner service was on display, white with sentimental scenes of shepherds and sheep in cobalt blue.

"*Gemütlich*," Wojnicz whispered to himself, pleased to have remembered a German word that he particularly liked. That word was missing from his language. Cozy? Nice?

The words of Dr. Sokołowski came back to him too, from the days when he had first treated Wojnicz and started to tackle his apathy— that life should be made appetizing. Yes, *appetizing*, that was a better word than *gemütlich*, thought Wojnicz, for it could refer not only to space, but to everything else as well—to someone's voice, to a way of speaking, of sitting in an armchair, or tying a scarf around one's neck, to the way cakes were arranged on a plate. He ran a finger over the olive-green velvet tablecloth, and it was some minutes before he noticed, to his horror, a thin man sitting in an armchair by the window. He had distinctive, birdlike features, and a pair of wire-rimmed spectacles on his prominent nose. He was wreathed in a cloud of cigarette smoke. In Wojnicz's confusion, his hand bounced off the velvet as if scalded and vanished in the embrace of its partner. Equally disconcerted by this discovery of his solitude, the man stood and introduced himself quite officially, in German, with a strange Silesian accent: "Walter Frommer. From Breslau."

Wojnicz slowly and clearly pronounced his own first name and surname, in the hope that the other would remember them: "Mi-*etchy*-swuff *Voy*-nitch." In their brief conversation, Frommer informed him that he was treated in Görbersdorf regularly, and had been there for the better part of three years. He returned to Breslau at intervals, but there his condition immediately worsened.

"You see, the city of Breslau lies on water. In spring, swarms of mosquitoes hover above the buildings, small but extremely venomous, and people suffer from rheumatism. In summer it's impossible to sit out in the garden, so government officials are posted there for only a few years before they move on to better places. Breslau is a transitional city." A sorrowful note appeared in his voice, as though he sympathized with the city. "It's because of the omnipresent water, it creeps in everywhere . . . I tolerate it poorly." He began to cough. "Oh, you see, at the very thought of it I cough."

Wojnicz looked away toward the window, just as a jolly company walked past outside, bursting into occasional laughter. He thought the people were laughing in Polish, though he couldn't quite explain this impression. From afar their words were inaudible.

"Are you preparing for a transfer to the Kurhaus too?" he asked Frommer.

He thought this question might raise a faint smile on the face of his interlocutor, but the man took it seriously.

"God forbid," he said, bristling. "There are too many people there. You can't see anything from there. You won't find anything out. Life in a crowd is worse than prison."

So by now Wojnicz had a fairly well-formed opinion on the topic of Walter Frommer—he was an oddball.

He was apparently equally bashful, because they stood facing each other in awkward silence, while each waited for the other to utter some conventional remark. They were saved from this deadlock by Wilhelm Opitz.

"I hope I am not disturbing you in the heat of conversation," said the proprietor, and Wojnicz wondered briefly if he were mocking them, or if he were quite so unobservant. But Wilhelm took him by the arm with a strong grip and led him toward the exit.

"Excuse me, but I must pass this young person into the attentive care of Dr. Semperweiss. Our guest arrived here in a pitiful state."

Frommer muttered something indistinct, then went back to the window and sat down in exactly the same position as before, as if he had a permanent job there as a smoking piece of furniture.

"Dr. Frommer is a little odd, but he's a respectable person. Like everyone at my guesthouse," said Wilhelm in his dialect, the sound of which Wojnicz found more and more to his liking, once they were standing on the front steps. "Raimund will take you to Dr. Semperweiss. Watch out for him, he doesn't like people from the East. He doesn't like people in general. It's a great loss that there's no one here like Dr. Brehmer," he added pensively, at the little bridge.

Wojnicz watched as the mist formed strange streaks and floated upward like smoke.

"Perhaps you know Dr. Sokołowski?" he asked.

Wilhelm's face brightened and became animated.

"Of course, I knew him as a child. He was friendly with my father, who worked for him. All of us here work for the Kurhaus. How is he keeping?"

Wojnicz did not know how to answer that. All he knew was that Sokołowski worked at a Warsaw clinic and gave occasional lectures in Lwów. His father had taken him for a consultation on one of Sokołowski's visits to the city. It was thanks to him that Wojnicz had ended up here.

"Is he still as slim?" asked Willi.

Slim? No, he was not. Professor Sokołowski was a stout, stocky man. But Wojnicz did not have to answer this surprising question, because out of the trails of mist emerged yesterday's teenage coachman, whom Willi greeted with a light cuff on the head, a gesture the boy seemed to take as entirely natural and friendly.

Wojnicz and Raimund walked along the stream toward the center of the village, Raimund eagerly relating something, but in such a strange dialect that Wojnicz understood little. He observed with interest the fine houses along the road, and the laborers who were mending the electrical traction. Raimund asked Wojnicz if he knew what electricity was.

They bowed to two elderly women in wide skirts who were sitting on a bench outside one of the houses.

"Frau Weber and Frau Brecht," said Raimund with an ironical smile, and this Wojnicz did understand.

Soon the boy proudly pointed at Dr. Brehmer's sanatorium, the building that Wojnicz had glimpsed the night before, but now it seemed even more impressive, especially as the mist had almost vanished and somewhere high over the valley the September sun was shining lavishly.

Raimund led Wojnicz to a door in a wide corridor, then disappeared. Wojnicz was received by a nurse with red swellings beneath her eyes. A polite smile briefly shielded her large, yellow teeth, which matched the tarnished gold-plated watch on a chain pinned to her apron. Above the breast pocket, her name was embroidered: *Sydonia Patek*.

Wojnicz had to sit in the waiting room until the doctor came back from his rounds. His fingers reached for the illustrated periodicals provided for the patients, but his eyes found no reassurance in them: They could not focus on the Gothic script. But to his surprise, he found a newssheet in Polish, and his gaze immediately relaxed on seeing words in his mother tongue:

> **In Prussian Silesia, a quarter of a mile from the Czech border and eleven miles southwest of Breslau, in a long valley stretching from east to west between Riesengebirge and Adlergebirge, located in Waldenburg County on the Stein, we find the charming village of Görbersdorf, famous for decades as a mountain resort for those with chest complaints.**
>
> **Görbersdorf is situated at 570 meters above sea level, in a zone known to medical science as "consumption free." The mountains surrounding it reach 900 meters. They shield the village and its medical facilities from the winds; hence in Görbersdorf a stillness of the air prevails that is rare in any valley.**

He did not read on, but folded the brochure in half and shoved it into his pocket. Now his attention was drawn by a glass-fronted display case, in which stood a human torso made of wood. With no head, arms or legs, but an open chest and belly, it showed the internal organs painted in different colors. Wojnicz went up to examine its lungs. They were smooth and clean, polished, shining with varnish. They looked like the fleshy petals of an enormous flower, or fungi growing on the bark of a tree. How perfectly they fitted the proportions of the chest, how well their shape harmonized with the rib cage. He took a close look at them, trying to peek under the pointed corners where they joined other, coiled organs in various colors. Perhaps he was hoping to find something that he had not seen before, solutions to the mystery of why he was sick and others were not. If so, he was disappointed.

As he returned to his seat, he was seized by a familiar anxiety, a tension that always stirred the same physical reaction—he broke into a sweat. He would have to undress and expose his body to the gaze of a stranger. And panic: How would he hide his shameful affliction from the doctor? What would he have to say to avoid all those issues that he found so sensitive? How was he to escape? He had practiced it so many times before.

Dr. Semperweiss entered the waiting room at a rapid pace, the tails of his white gown flapping behind him. Without even glancing at Wojnicz, he gestured for him to rise. Almost at a trot, Wojnicz followed him into a large consulting room with an immense window, glass-walled cabinets, all sorts of medical equipment and some strange-looking armchairs. Somehow Wojnicz was not surprised to see a shotgun leaning against the doctor's desk—a large one, not a hunting rifle but more like a Winchester, with a finely polished butt. Without turning around, the doctor told him to sit down, which made Wojnicz feel safely hidden behind the desk, as in a trench.

He handed the doctor a letter of referral from Professor Sokołowski, but Semperweiss, hardly casting an eye at it, was clearly more interested in the body sitting before him. The young man was discomfited by the way the doctor was looking at him, as if he could not see Mieczysław Wojnicz, a patient from faraway Lwów, but just his body, a mechanical object. First he unabashedly pulled back Wojnicz's eyelid and inspected the color of the mucous membranes and the eyeball. Then he ran his eyes from chin to temple, and finally told him to strip to the waist so that he could examine his chest. He began to press the patient's nipples with a finger.

"Slightly enlarged, as are the lymph nodes," he said. "Is that always the case for you?"

"For several years," replied Wojnicz, intimidated.

Holding him by the chin, the doctor drew a finger over his feeble, patchy two-day stubble. He scrupulously palpated the lymph nodes, and then his bold fingers percussed the back, extracting a hollow sound, a rumble as if from underground. He did it very carefully, centimeter by centimeter, like a sapper in search of a hidden bomb. All this took half an hour, until finally the doctor sighed and told him to get dressed. Only now did he reach for the letter. Glancing over the metal frames of his glasses, he said: "Phthisis." It sounded as though he had whistled. "Tuberculosis, consumption, or as it is fashionable to say nowadays: Morbus Koch. You know all this, young man, don't you?"

As Wojnicz did up his shirt buttons, he nodded in the affirmative.

"Not very advanced, to be clear. Just a touch, a little grain of something. 'Phthisis' means decay, did you know?" He pronounced this word, *Zerfall*, with distinct enjoyment, rolling the *r*. "But here we can deal with decay."

"Yes, Dr. Brehmer's method—" Wojnicz began, but the doctor impatiently stood up and waved a raised hand.

"Oh yes, Brehmer noticed that traveling to Italy with consumption makes no sense at all. Only the mountain air can really cure it. Like the air here. Have you seen?" The doctor went to the window and stood there for a while, lost in thought. "We're in a basin," he said, making exaggerated circles with his hand, as if wanting to drive home to his listener the nature of the phenomenon. "Beneath us there's a large underground lake, thanks to which it's warmer here than elsewhere. This air is rich in oxygen, but there's no wind. Lung diseases and epidemics have never been known to the local population, would you believe it? Nobody here has ever had a lung complaint. On top of that, the altitude is within the essential range for treating lung diseases, because it does not unduly accelerate the work of the heart, which happens in places higher than nine hundred meters above sea level. Fir trees grow here, filling the air with ozone, and ozone plays a key role in renewing the blood and the entire organism. Merely breathing will stop the process of decay in your young lungs. Every breath is curative. Just imagine that with every breath you take, pure light flows into your lungs." The doctor was looking at Wojnicz through his spectacles, which enlarged his dark eyes in an unsettling way. "And we have other attractions too. You simply have to submit, to yield to the treatment regime. Feel as you would in the army."

He nodded out of the window at the patients strolling in the park.

"Those are your comrades in arms."

Suddenly Wojnicz realized that he would never grow fond of this doctor. He remembered kind, gentle Dr. Sokołowski.

"It's all clear to me, Doctor," he replied, pulling down his shirt cuffs. "I'd just like to know if I have a chance."

"Of course you have a chance. Otherwise you wouldn't have come here, young man. You wouldn't have dared to come here without feeling that you had a chance. You'd have suffered quietly in the East. It's flat there, isn't it?"

Wojnicz learned many curious facts about the brilliant Dr. Brehmer.

He had bought the village of Görbersdorf and the entire neighborhood, including more than a hundred hectares of forest and land, to
found this sanatorium. Long before, Brehmer had noticed that the
results of autopsies and examinations of patients suffering from tuberculosis always showed a disproportion between the heart and the
lungs—their lungs were relatively large and their hearts small, with
thin, fragile walls. No one had paid particular attention to this coin-
cidence before, and no one had come up with the idea of connecting it with the etiology of tuberculosis. But it seemed obvious that a
small, weak heart led to more sluggish blood circulation, and as a result to chronic ischemia of the lungs and pulmonary epithelium. The
consequence of this was consumption. Brehmer had also studied the
geographical distribution of the illness's occurrence, and this had
confirmed his belief regarding the aforementioned etiology. From
travelers' accounts it emerged that there were places and regions where
tuberculosis did not feature: the higher mountains in all climatic zones,
Iceland, the Faroe Islands and the steppes of Kirghizia.

First, the special features of the alpine climate were decisive here.
Lower atmospheric pressure meant that the organism reacted to it with
increased cardiac activity, as a means of defending itself against a lack
of oxygen—this led to faster metabolism and a higher body temperature. Lifestyle and diet were important too: plenty of food, especially
fat, kumis with alcohol content, and hard physical labor.

An accelerated heart rate caused an increase in the size of the myo-
cardium, and the organ developed strong musculature; in inhabitants
of the aforementioned regions this often led to cardiac hypertrophy,
and thus to the opposite of the phenomenon observed in tuberculosis
sufferers.

"My dear young man," said Dr. Semperweiss to conclude his lecture, "this is our entire prescription. In Central Europe, the consumption-free zone begins at an altitude of roughly four hundred and fifty meters. On top of that, there's the consistent supervision of a physician who regulates the diet. And also exercise in the fresh air. Nature itself cures us."

The doctor took out a sheet of paper and wrote down his recommendations point by point, while commenting on them in a rather bored tone. "For at least six weeks, ideally several months: Walks tailored to the patient, on routes of varying gradients, with benches to rest on at short intervals along the way to avoid tiring oneself. Moderate treatment with cold water. And that will help you. Moderation in medicaments. In case of a severe cough, I recommend restraining the cough as much as possible, and if it cannot be restrained, you should take tiny sips of cold water or soda water with hot milk. Should there be bleeding from the lungs, which God forbid, we apply small ice packs to the heart and lungs, and give morphine injections. For acute attacks, with breathlessness and swooning, first we provide a strong stimulant—champagne, for instance. Yes, do not be afraid of champagne, or of alcohol in general. But categorically only in small quantities—drunkenness is strictly forbidden! In case of fever, first one measures the temperature every two hours, for confirmation. Night sweats are effectively combated by taking milk in the evening with two or three teaspoonfuls of brandy or liqueur. Sister Sydonia Patek will explain and show you everything."

Throughout this speech he continued to note down his recommendations. Wojnicz was amazed that he was capable of doing these two things simultaneously.

"You are living at Herr Opitz's house, am I right? Every day you will come to the Kurhaus for treatment and rest cures, and as soon as a place is free at the sanatorium, I shall let you know. Everything is fluid here, fluid," he stressed. "For now, Herr Opitz's guesthouse is just as good for your health as this place, or Dr. Römpler's sanatorium, and the daily short walks will add color to your cheeks."

Semperweiss got up energetically and handed Wojnicz the sheet of recommendations. And it was all over—he had been admitted.

Now he was sitting in the waiting room while the ugly nurse prepared him a treatment diary and other necessary documents. He pulled the folded leaflet from his pocket and finished reading:

> **In general one should recognize that with regard to therapy, a sojourn in places including Merano in the Tyrol, Görbersdorf in Silesia, or Davos in Switzerland (modeled on Görbersdorf) is considered the most effective cure to date. Dr. Römpler's sanatorium, founded in 1875, is situated virtually at the foot of the mountains and consists of a suitable number of buildings in the form of elegant villas. A water system 1,140 meters in length brings crystal-clear spring water down from the mountain to the sanatorium, and thus the water gushes straight from porphyritic rocks to the tastefully furnished bathing rooms of the shower building.**
>
> **The patients have no lack of occupations and entertainments. The cure itself, including meals, etc., takes up a large part of the day, but the charming locality of Görbersdorf offers a wide variety of excursions. The aim of the cure is for the patient to endeavor to combat his own illness. By strengthening the organism, one increases its immunity. By this means, the development of the illness is first halted, then gradually the complaint recedes and good health returns.**

Through regular exercise, the affected lungs learn to perform correctly, and the fresh mountain air stimulates the functions of the heart. The results of a cure at Görbersdorf can be rated among the most favorable. Almost 75% of patients return to good health.

It would be marvelous to think that he belonged to that 75 percent.

2.

SCHWÄRMEREI

Wojnicz returned to the guesthouse with the small notebook in which from now on his treatment history was to be recorded, and considered what Dr. Semperweiss had told him. The most important feature of the cure was the regimen. One got up early, very early in the morning, took one's temperature, and noted it down. Before breakfast, which was eaten between seven and eight, gymnastics were obligatory, then after breakfast a walk, and perhaps baths as well, according to Father Kneipp's method, and other procedures. The walks were along a fixed route. There was a midmorning snack at ten—always fresh bread and butter, with milk. Then a rest cure on one of the many terraces. Lunch between twelve thirty and one thirty (soup with meat, a substantial meat dish with vegetables, then dessert and compote; on Sundays, instead of compote, a cake or other sweet made with flour was served). After lunch, coffee was de rigueur, in the winter garden or in one of the pavilions. Then came another rest cure, followed by another walk, but the afternoon route had to be

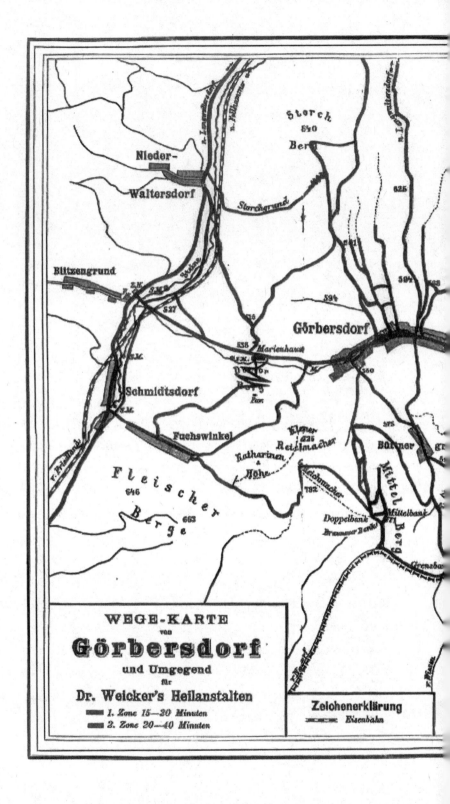

WEGE-KARTE
von
Görbersdorf
und Umgegend
für
Dr. Weicker's Heilanstalten

▬▬ 1. Zone 15—30 Minuten
▬▬ 2. Zone 20—40 Minuten

Zeichenerklärung

╌╌╌ Eisenbahn

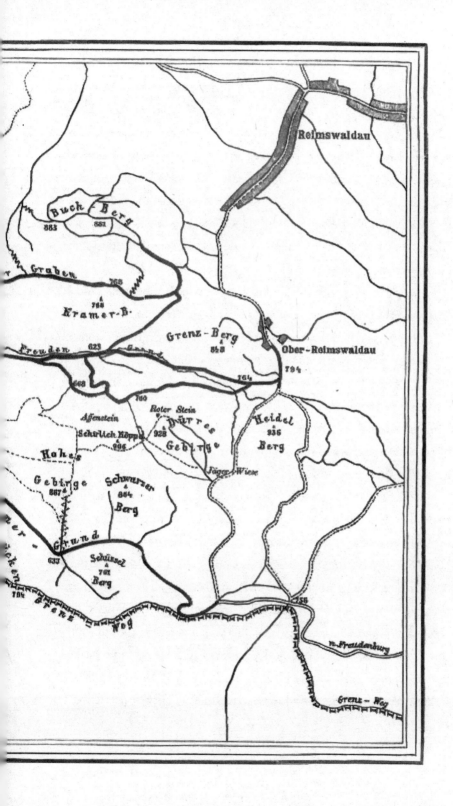

different from the morning one. Afternoon tea was at about four or four thirty, and supper at seven—a hot dish of meat and potatoes, with a required glass of milk. At night the thermometer was used again, and a few sentences were added to the notebook to record one's mental and physical states. Plenty of sleep. No excitement. Good, substantial food. Lots of meat, milk and sheep's milk cheese. Wojnicz decided on lunches and breakfasts at the Kurhaus; he would eat supper at the Guesthouse for Gentlemen. So he was advised. Once he moved into the Kurhaus, he would take all his meals there. The guests were summoned to them by the sound of a bugle.

He was bursting with exhilaration and good intentions, the kind of euphoria that heralds a fresh start, the moment when one cuts oneself off from the past and forgets about it. Now even the austere, ironical Dr. Semperweiss seemed to him a harbinger of change.

As he walked, he tried to memorize the relative locations of the various houses and guesthouses. He inspected the rather bizarre astronomical observatory, where apparently Dr. Brehmer had studied the effect of the cosmos and the weather on treating tuberculosis. Then he reached an imposing edifice called the Villa Rosa and turned back.

A full, golden September sun was shining. Mieczysław Wojnicz strode firmly in the middle of the large flat stones that paved the road.

The two elderly women were still sitting on the bench outside their house, silently shelling broad beans, snapping the dry pods open. Suddenly a bean sprang from one of their wrinkled hands and landed just ahead of Wojnicz's shoe. He picked it up carefully in two fingers and was going to return it to its owners, but for some reason they abruptly rose from the bench, picked up their bowls and baskets, and vanished into the house, their glossy black skirts flashing in the sunlight. Oh well, never mind. Wojnicz wiped the brown bean against his sleeve; it looked perfect. He tossed it in the air and caught it. Not knowing what to do with it, he put it in his pocket.

He found the guesthouse door wide open, which surprised him, and then he noticed a little prayer book on the ground in front of it, tossed into a puddle. The cream-colored pages were already soaked with dirty water. He picked it up and went inside, full of sudden anxiety.

The sitting room downstairs was empty—the other residents must all have been at their treatments. He placed the mud-stained prayer book on a small table and was about to head upstairs when his attention was drawn to the half-open door to the dining room, and beyond it a pair of boots—on the table, somehow familiar. Without thinking, as if hypnotized, he went up to the door and pushed it, to take a closer look inside.

The boots were at one end of a long bundle of imprecise shape, which turned out to be a human body. It was lying on the table at which the meals were eaten. It looked well wrapped in rolls of material—it seemed to be wearing a large number of skirts, shirts, bodices and capes. Wojnicz had never seen any woman so close and so still before; they always flitted past, in constant motion, so that it was impossible to focus attention on them and take in all the details. But here before him lay a woman's body, without doubt a dead one. He looked at the black lace-up boots protruding from under the skirts and petticoats. The latter were trimmed with embroidery, but the lace was already rather faded, and its edges were frayed. The shoelaces had been tied with great care in a double bow; how strange that someone who had laced their boots so precisely that very morning was dead by the afternoon. The top skirt, made of slightly shiny material in thin black-and-gray stripes, was neatly arranged. Above was a close-fitting jacket made of dark, almost black cloth, done up with round buttons, like the ones Polish priests had on their cassocks. A rather crumpled white shirt was sticking out from underneath it; a button hung by a thread, and the collar was pulled up to the chin, but carelessly enough for Wojnicz to notice a dark blue-and-red mark on the neck, shocking against the white skin.

Finally he had to do it—look higher, at the face. To his horror he saw the eyes, only half-closed, with a fine strip of eyeball shining under the lashes. The twisted head was turned toward him, as if wanting to make a confession. On the narrow lips, already rather blue, he noticed the trace of a smile. It seemed totally out of place, as if ironical. The tips of the teeth, quite dry, were just showing under the upper lip. And he also saw that the face was coated in fine, fair fuzz, like down.

He stood petrified, barely breathing.

He had immediately recognized that this was the woman who had brought him his breakfast that morning. At the time, he had only noticed the boot that opened the door and some ample curves hugged by a bodice, nothing more. Only now, after death, could she be seen in her entirety.

"She hanged herself," said Willi Opitz, standing in the doorway.

Wojnicz shuddered, horrified by the proprietor's low, resonant voice. The tone in which Opitz delivered this announcement made it sound like the confirmation of an act of criminal negligence, an unacceptable event. But his voice was shaking.

"Don't upset yourself. The people from the mortuary will be here any moment, and they'll take the body away. Raimund has run to fetch them."

Wojnicz did not know what to say. His tongue was bone dry, and his throat felt tight.

"When did it happen?" he asked.

"When? Just now, well, an hour ago. I went upstairs when she didn't come down to collect the vegetables from the supplier. She was hanging there. I cut her down. Go to your room, boy. Ah, here they are from the mortuary."

"She brought my breakfast this morning," said Wojnicz, with audible emotion in his voice. "She was your servant, wasn't she?"

"Oh, no, no. That's my wife."

Opitz waved a hand, as if shooing away a wasp, and opened the door for the gloomy mortuary workers, who began to talk to him quietly in dialect. Wojnicz withdrew from the dining room. As he hurried up the stairs, he could hear their stifled voices, but he couldn't understand what they were saying. The entire conversation sounded like the mutterings of people who do not need words to communicate.

Wojnicz sat down in a russet armchair decorated with a crocheted headrest. He was badly shaken. It was strange, it had not occurred to him that nice Willi Opitz had a wife. He should have known that men usually have wives who, without always being visible, support the family business from the kitchen or the laundry. Preoccupied by his journey and his illness, he had not even noticed her. And now she was dead.

Suddenly he was flooded by a wave of memories, because somehow this dead woman reminded him of his nanny. She existed in his memory as a blurred figure, always veiled by something, out of focus, on the run, a long, thin streak. But he used to play with her, he used to see her hands, and the wrinkled skin on them. He would grip that skin between his thumb and forefinger, pretending to be a goose (they used to call it tweaking), and in doing so he would smooth out her hands until they became almost young. He used to fantasize that if he could figure out how to smooth all of Gliceria (this bizarre name was very popular in those days among the peasants in the Lwów region), to tighten up her outer form, maybe he would succeed in saving his nanny from old age. But he couldn't. Gliceria was always old, and she would grow even older. It became harder and harder for her to carry out her duties—to launder, cook, iron and clean—and she left when he was seven years old, having seen him through to school age. By then, his father had decided that she was no longer needed in any case; a boarding school would replace her. Once he had established all the terms with the headmaster, Mr. Szuman, he handed the boy over to him. Unfortunately, Mieczyś (as he was known to his father and his uncle in those days) did not stay at this institution for long, for reasons that with friends his father would refer to as "sensitivity" and "an inability to conform," which for the boy meant total humiliation, and for the father a desperate attempt to make sense of the whole disappointing situation.

Proving the old saying "There is no evil that does not bring good," Mieczyś was taught at home by a full-time tutor, first one, then a second, and a third, which cost his father a lot of money and anxiety, because teachers were the most chimeric species in existence—nothing pleased them, and they were always finding something to complain about.

His father believed that blame for both national disasters and educational failures lay with a soft upbringing that encouraged girlishness, mawkishness and passivity, nowadays fashionably termed *individualism*. He did not approve. What counted were manliness, energy, social work for the public good, rationalism, pragmatism. He was especially fond of the word *pragmatism*.

He was a man of fifty plus, with dark hair almost without any gray, and thick stubble; he shaved with great tenacity, leaving only his magnificent mustache, which in the past he had cared for and curled with the use of a pomade, the base ingredient of which was tallow. As a result,

Mieczysław retained a childhood association of the smell of rancid fat with his father; it was his second, aromatic skin. Yet several years ago his father had stopped curling his mustache, and his only remaining cosmetic practice was to splash his cheeks with English Bay Rum aftershave. He was a *splendid* man, as they said in Lwów, handsome and dignified. Senior Engineer Wojnicz could easily have made a good second marriage, but he had lost all interest in women, as though the death of his wife had permanently destroyed his trust in the fairer sex—as if he felt cheated by it, or even disgraced. She had given birth and promptly died! What a nerve! Or perhaps no other woman could compare with the mysterious young lady from Brzeżany, the only daughter of a notary who was himself a widower.

The older Wojnicz's mother had passed away prematurely too. There was something wrong with these mothers; it was as if they did a terribly dangerous job, risking their lives in their boudoirs and bedrooms, tangled in lace, leading a lethal existence among the bedclothes and the copper pans, among the towels, powders and stacks of menus for every day of the year. In Mieczysław Wojnicz's family world, the women had vague, short, dangerous lives, and then they died, remaining in people's memories as fleeting shapes without contour. They were reduced to a remote, unclear impulse placed in the universe only temporarily, for the sole purpose of its biological consequences.

In the name of Mieczysław's education and appropriately masculine upbringing, his father had decided to sell some of the land and property his wife had left him and to buy a bright, comfortable apartment in Lwów. He took Gliceria with him, to serve as cook, maid and nanny—from then on, as befitted a respectable though incomplete family, they became citizens of Lwów.

It was a good decision. By investing his money in modernity, he behaved very pragmatically and in fact gained many advantages from living in the city. His new business interests picked up; it was easier to take care of them on the spot than from sluggish, provincial Galicia, where every trip to the city was like a voyage across the ocean. January Wojnicz was an enterprising, courageous man. He put some of the money from the property he had sold into a small apartment house and a brickyard in a village near Brzeżany, and he placed the rest in shares in the Galician railway; altogether this provided him with a tidy income, easily enough to support himself and his son in perfectly decent style. He was sensible and cautious, bordering on stingy. On the rare occasions when he bought an object, it was always of the best quality.

Naturally, attempts were made to marry him off for a second time, but in January Wojnicz's mind his late wife had become such a unique, perfect creature that no woman on earth could be more than a poor shadow of her, a figure unworthy of attention or even annoying, as if she were clumsily trying to imitate that wondrous creature.

As a result, the only woman whom Mieczysław Wojnicz remembered having seen up close and in detail was Gliceria. She had mothered him a bit, at least in the kitchen, supplying him with tasty morsels, but as her power did not extend beyond the thresholds of the other rooms, it was only there that little Mieczyś was pampered. She tried to compensate him for the loss of his mother by pouring a little buckwheat honey onto his plate, or by cutting the crunchy heel off the loaf of bread and thickly spreading it with fresh butter. Food always had good associations for him.

He received these manifestations of warm feelings with a gratitude that might have had the chance of developing into affection and love, but his father would not allow that. He treated Gliceria as nothing more than a servant, never with familiarity, and was full of mistrust toward this plump, elderly woman, hidden among skirts, flounces and bonnets. He despised her corpulence and, suspecting her of stealing food, paid her less than he should have.

Gliceria was succeeded by Józef. He usually made pierogis, and fried fish bought at the market. On Sundays father and son went out to a restaurant on Trybunalska Street, where they had a ritual lunch consisting of soup, a main course and dessert—and for the father an alcoholic drink and coffee—to persuade themselves that one can get by without women and incompetent cooks.

When Mieczysław Wojnicz saw the dead body on the dining room table, Gliceria came back to him in all the forms and details that constitute the essence of a woman, such as pleats, wrinkles, frills, bodices, yokes and lace—the entire heathen world of materials designed to cover the female body. In this lifeless human bundle lying on the table, he recognized something of his childhood and of his mother, but above all his Gliceria, long after she had left their house in tears, resenting January Wojnicz for his insults and groundless accusations.

Troubled and anxious as he listened to the shuffling and murmuring below, Wojnicz decided to slip out of this house that was now the site of a violent death. He managed to pass through the sitting room unnoticed, and once outside he set off with relief on a long walk, determined to avoid returning to the guesthouse too soon.

But there were not many walking trails in Görbersdorf itself, apart from the route traced by the patients along a promenade leading uphill from the sanatorium. Following it, one passed an attractive little wooden church, and beyond it several rather grand houses rising the length of the main street, each with its name inscribed in fancy letters above the front door: Villa Elise, Villa Schweiz, Villa Adelheid, and so on.

At the church, the road forked. One could turn right and walk across a park next to a small pump room, to reach a tiny Orthodox church. It had been built recently, evidently for the Russian patients, whom Wojnicz had already noticed, as their ostentatious wealth and irritating loudness made them conspicuous. Beyond this church there were two ponds where swans swam idly, then there were several more villas along the road, and a smart restaurant. He would gladly have stopped for a glass of lemonade, but having spotted the stiff Frommer inside, he did a rapid about-face. Past the restaurant rose a steep, wooded slope, casting an infinite damp, dense shadow on the church and the ponds.

The road straight ahead—which, after turning around, our Wojnicz eventually chose—continued uphill, crossing a winding stream several times on little bridges, and then on boardwalks. The houses grew smaller, as if a law were in force that stated "the higher up, the smaller and simpler." The last house was an impressive lodge built of logs, home to an elderly couple. In their small garden they had a little windmill and some miniature birds and domestic animals carved of wood. All the walkers stopped here to rest and inspect this menagerie before continuing the steep climb into the dark realm of the forest. Here the well-trodden path changed into a narrow, stony road, along which drove the occasional wooden cart harnessed to horned cattle bringing down either timber or piles of charcoal of a marvelous dark brown hue.

Wojnicz walked along, admiring the rich facades of the houses. Once he was acquainted with all of them, he set about collecting the early fallen leaves. The first to go red were sycamore maples, which were abundant here, and several tulip trees. Wojnicz was so absorbed in looking for the most beautifully colored leaves that he forgot about what had happened at the Guesthouse for Gentlemen. We have not yet mentioned the herbal that still lay in his suitcase but would soon gain a permanent home on his bedside table, to be studied often. Wojnicz in-

stantly resolved to collect the leaves of the local trees—colors as striking as these were only to be found in the mountains. Of course some
species occurred in Lwów too, including the maple (the master of
chameleon-like color change) and even the beech, whose boundaries
match the limits of the extraordinary expanse known as Europe; perhaps it should feature in its coat of arms, were it ever to have one. The
other plants had withered and finished blooming by now; clearly the
only additions to Wojnicz's herbal would be tree leaves. The ritual of
the fall had started, as if the proximity of death activated reserves of
extraordinary energy in these trees that, instead of continuing to support life, allowed them to celebrate dying.

Supper is very late that day.

Dusk has long since fallen. In the dining room the only light shining is an electric bulb above the table, in a transparent shade, at the
bottom of which we can see a dead insect. Its yellow glow is falling
onto the embroidered linen cloth covering the table. The needlework is
old and faded, depicting sprays of ripe elderberries. In the lamplight
white plates shimmer, and forks and knives glitter.

As we know, however, the most interesting things are always in the
shadows, in the invisible.

So here beneath the table there are five pairs of feet, and soon a sixth
will appear. Each wears shoes. The first is familiar to us—it is the same
wretched pair that appeared yesterday at the station, leather loafers on
thin soles; now they are resting politely side by side without moving.
To their left we find the exact opposite, a pair of restless shoes, black
with white toes, which seem more urban, completely out of place in the

mountains, as if taken straight from an art gallery or an arcade; in fact, their elegance is badly eroded, but we like the nonstop movement of the feet inside them, as the heels go up and down by turns. Next there is a pair of leather boots, beautifully polished and laced above the ankle. Their immaculate surface reflects small, blurred spots of light from the sitting room, light in exile. Their toes are touching each other childishly. In the empty place farther to the left a pair of clogs will appear shortly, and a pair of feet in thick woolen socks will slide out of them, abandoning their coffin-like footwear to play with each other, rub together, tread on one another. Next we see a sad slip-on boot with no laces. There is a skinny ankle sunk in it, clad in a handmade sock. The other boot is resting on someone's knee; under the table a slender hand is stroking it with pale fingernails that look phosphorescent in the gloom. Poor little hand, poor skinny bones and milk-white fingernails. The next pair are smart leather oxfords, with large feet in woolen socks inside them. One of them sits there quietly while the other raps against the floor unrhythmically, as if angry.

Wojnicz introduced himself to everyone curtly, because he felt that the solemnity of the moment did not allow for more. He also endeavored not to give his companions reason to accost him. The presentation was over and done with, and now Raimund was handing out plates of boiled beef. To Mieczysław's left sat Herr August—August August; in a surge of anarchical humor, his parents had given him a first name the same as his surname. He was a professor of Latin and Greek, a man of surprisingly northern features for someone born in Jassy in Romania. His hair was oiled with brilliantine, his hands were manicured and he wore a respectable light gray frock coat and a willow-green foulard. His light stubble was already in need of a razor; perhaps today's disruption had prevented the professor from shaving. The next seat was occupied by that stiff Breslauer, Walter Frommer, buttoned up to the neck and wearing a monocle. Now and then he took out a snow-white hand-kerchief with an embroidered monogram and wiped his perspiring brow. The light flush on his pale cheeks testified to a fever, or maybe not—perhaps Herr Frommer was simply perturbed by the situation. As he did not eat meat, there was a small mound of buttered potatoes on his plate, the only one already filled, with a fried egg gaily shining beside it.

Next to Frommer stood the chair of the proprietor, Willi Opitz—still empty. They were waiting for him, unsure how his mourning would manifest itself. Farther on sat Thilo von Hahn, a student from Berlin, very thin and pale. Like Frommer's, his high, bulging forehead was covered in beads of sweat. His eyes were glassy with fever, and they seemed to reflect everything they saw. The boy was gazing at the slice of meat on his plate as though it were not a piece of food but something from outer space that had shown up here moments before, by way of a magical trick. From time to time Thilo cast a hopeful glance at Wojnicz, suggesting a generational familiarity. Mieczysław was not entirely sure how to respond to it. He turned his gaze aside, onto a good-looking man with a shock of white hair, whom he at once mentally named the Grizzled Lion—this was Longin Lukas from Königsberg, who described himself as a "gentleman," drawing in his cheeks as if he were a taster in the process of sampling a rather unusual wine of unknown origin. He was nice to look at—the picture of health, well-built, with a full, manly chest, which made it hard to believe he could be sick. It was also difficult to define his age. He was wearing an English tweed jacket and a gray wool hand-knitted pullover, both looking as if they had seen better days.

At last Willi Opitz appeared in the doorway. He looked at the assembled company without a word, which intensified the drama of the moment, and then he turned his gaze to the very center of the table, where only a few hours ago the body of Frau Opitz had been lying.

"Gentlemen, I must officially inform you of the death . . . of the death of my wife. I know that the manner . . . the circumstances . . ."

They all stood up, and for the time being the scraping of chairs drowned the proprietor's words. Herr August was the first to approach him to offer his condolences: "Our deepest sympathies. Shocking!" He paused, as though to illustrate the inexpressibility of his own emotions, and then banally added: "But as you know, life must go on."

Each man went up to him in turn, shook his hand and repeated similar remarks in various configurations.

"I was going to dine on my own," said Opitz, "but please allow me to stay with you, gentlemen—that will be a form of support for me, encouragement. Do you have any objection to being joined by a widower?" Here he smiled weakly; it was plainly an attempt at a joke. "Unfortunately, Raimund has had to see to the supper today, I hope it is edible."

Once they had sat down, for a while silence reigned, broken only by the clearing of throats, the gentle creaking of chairs and the sound of the dishes of meat and potatoes being passed along.

"Well, this is a sorrowful moment, yet I will say it: we shall never know what women want," said Lukas philosophically, and set about cutting up his meat.

Wojnicz regarded this comment on the matter as being too brusque.

The meat was extremely tough; Raimund had prepared a makeshift supper at high speed, which was no surprise under the circumstances. The guests would have been willing to limit themselves to bread and cheese that evening, or to go and eat at the sanatorium restaurant. But Willi was a very conscientious host and had given instructions regarding the evening meal.

They ate in silence, rather shaken by what had happened. They did not go beyond "thank you," "please" and some indistinct grunting. It seemed that only Wojnicz, having returned from the Kurhaus prematurely, was aware of the fact that they were dining at the very table on which a body had been lying that afternoon. This was probably why he could not force himself to pick up his knife and fork. His obliging neighbor, the genial Herr August, had already put a slice of meat onto Wojnicz's plate, and had even poured sauce over it. But Mieczysław had a different image before his eyes—his plate was standing in the exact spot where the proprietor's wife's leg had been lying. Rolls of fabric, a stocking, skin, muscles.

Herr August had a natural tendency to forget anything unpleasant quickly; what is more, the sight of the meat had visibly restored his good mood. As he did battle with it on his plate, he was the first to speak.

"I believe, my dear friend," he said, addressing Opitz, "that we have no reason to feel guilty for failing to restrain the person from . . . for not having prevented . . . They say that only when we remain in the rational sphere can we act rationally. Wherever another person's motivations elude reason, we have no resort but to keep calm."

"Thank you, Professor. You have put it well," said Willi Opitz, mashing potatoes with his fork.

"I can console you, gentlemen. Scientific research has demonstrated that the female brain functions entirely differently, and even has a different structure," said Walter Frommer. "Above all it is a question of size, and also the convexity of different spheres. Where the will is located in men, in women we have desire. Where men have an understanding of numbers and structures in general, in women there is motherhood—"

"It's true, the female brain is quite simply smaller, and there's no denying it when objective research has proved it," interrupted the Grizzled Lion authoritatively, his mouth full of food.

"À propos, sometimes when we address a woman," continued the buttoned-up Walter Frommer, "we might gain the impression that she replies sensibly and thinks as we do. But that is an illusion. They imitate"—he placed special emphasis on the word *imitate*—"our way of communicating, and one cannot deny that some of them are very good at it."

"So they imitate . . . ," said Opitz hesitantly, as if thinking of something very specific.

"They don't even know they're pretending. It's an instinct, a reflex."

For a while the men chewed the tough meat in silence. Wojnicz would have loved to spit it out, but that wasn't appropriate. He forced himself to swallow it.

"Dear Herr Opitz," said August August, and Wojnicz was terrified he was about to raise a toast, "my dear fellow, we are racked by ignorance. Without wishing to be indelicate, may I say, on behalf of us all, that it would be easier for us if you were to tell us what happened. I hope this is not a discourteous request."

"I agree with you," put in the Grizzled Lion from Königsberg, raising a chunk of meat on his fork. "Anxiety is the fruit of ignorance. Well, let us be men, and let us tell ourselves the truth directly, however dreadful it may be," he added.

"What prompted her to commit this terrible act?" August continued. "I saw her only yesterday, and today she is gone."

A hush fell; Willi Opitz's face was not visible, because he had dropped his head and, fixing his gaze on his plate, was digging in the potatoes with his fork.

"I don't know," he replied a few minutes later, a note of helplessness in his voice bidding his listeners to believe what he was saying. "I simply don't know." He looked up at them, and Wojnicz could have sworn there were tears glittering in his eyes. "Perhaps she was homesick for her family? She was from the Czech lands."

He turned around on his chair and pointed a hand at the windows, where somewhere beyond the mountains lay the Czech lands.

A longer hush fell, with holes torn in it by the unpleasant sound of forks scraping against china as they continued to wrestle with the undercooked meat.

"We cannot regard the act of a woman as entirely conscious," said Frommer. "Female psychology has proved that a woman is at once a subject and an object, and so her choices can be only partly conscious."

Like Wojnicz, Lukas could not cope with the meat; to distract attention from the fact that he was putting down his knife and fork, he tried to finish the supper on a mild note.

"Women are more fragile and sensitive by nature," he said, "which is why they're easily inclined toward ill-considered acts."

"After everything that has happened here . . . ," began Frommer, but he did not finish, as if he had forgotten in midsentence what he was going to say.

They waited for him to continue, but when nothing followed these first words, they went back to chewing the tough meat in silence. Wojnicz wanted to ask about this and that but, gagged by the piece he had in his mouth, he could not speak. Finally, he managed to spit the meat into a handkerchief furtively and hide it in his pocket while the diners' attention was turned toward Opitz, who, after the meal—as Raimund clumsily gathered the plates, jostling a carafe of water in the process and dropping cutlery on the floor—fetched his own homemade liqueur from the sideboard. The very sight of it eased the tension to a palpable degree.

"Our new guest isn't familiar with this yet," Opitz said, turning to

Wojnicz. "I'm sure you have nothing like it in the East. This is our Schwärmerei."

"Dr. Semperweiss recommends it for the lungs," explained the Grizzled Lion, pursing his lips as if preparing to taste the drink.

Dark liquid was poured into some green shot glasses.

The liqueur tasted truly exotic—it was sweet and bitter all at once, and also sharp, like the famous Sieben-Kräuter, with a hint of moss, the forest, suggestive of logs in a cellar and slightly moldy apples. And something very strange too, which Wojnicz could not put into words, though he thought he had the way to describe it on the tip of his tongue.

The liqueur set everyone's thoughts on the right tracks, and the conversation turned quite naturally to the regular activities that Opitz organized for the patients each afternoon following their treatments. The proprietor solemnly promised to find a woman to cook as soon as possible, but until then, if they were disappointed with Raimund's culinary skills ("Ah, no, no," their not very vocal denials could be heard, "on the contrary, it was very good"), they could always dine at the Kurhaus. It would be much more costly, but he could honestly recommend the cooking there, none was better in the entire neighborhood.

He also promised that after the funeral, when all this unpleasantness was over, they would go on an outing to one of the peaks, to Hohe Heide, where the patients would see the major attraction of these parts: the Windlöcher (here Frommer raised a hand to his lips, to hide—or pretend to hide—a yawn). Some would be going for a second time, but nobody protested. The Grizzled Lion of Königsberg and Herr August began to argue about the origin of this geological phenomenon: were these strange caves the result of volcanic processes or weathering of the rocks? Wojnicz noticed that Thilo rolled his eyes in boredom, then got up from the table and curtly took his leave. As he did so, he smiled faintly and cast Mieczysław a knowing wink. Once he had left the room, Wojnicz was given an extra glass of liqueur along with Opitz's ambiguous comment, to the effect that the young needed more, because it helped them to indulge in various enjoyments.

"As rational people capable of enduring the adversities of fate with your heads held high, gentlemen, you should have no concerns that a sudden death is going to change your plans. Life must go on," he said.

It was hard to come to terms with the fact that they were sitting at the same table on which a dead body had lain a few hours ago, chatting and sipping a liqueur with the lovely name Schwärmerei, thought the mildly intoxicated Wojnicz, returning to his own reflections. Indeed, the entire dining room looked different now, illuminated by the electric lamp suspended above the table. And although this light was sullied by darkness, fuzzy, as if weary, the room looked larger and seemed to stretch farther into the depths of the velvety gloom, in all directions.

"So is it impossible to turn a woman back from the self-destructive path of mental illness?" asked Willi Opitz, the recent widower, in a melancholy tone.

Wojnicz thought there was an echo in the dining room, because the Grizzled Lion's answer reverberated as if he were talking into a well.

"In a man, a strong will can help him to combat the temptations of madness, but women are almost entirely devoid of it, and thus have no weapon for the fight."

Wojnicz's head was starting to spin. The electric light, to which he was not yet accustomed, seemed to cast a distinctive shadow, different from the ones he knew. Not the ordinary kind cast by the light of an oil lamp, as used at home—this shadow was ragged, unsteady, it seemed to flicker on the edge of his field of vision; Wojnicz felt as though something were moving close to the floor and then slipping under the sideboard, but whenever he turned his gaze in that direction, everything looked normal. He drank another glass of liqueur and realized that everyone had started to talk louder and to gesticulate, including Herr August. He had put the fingers of his two hands together and was now pecking the air with the beak they formed, while arguing heatedly with Lukas. But Wojnicz noticed to his amazement that the man's fingernails were livid blue, as if he had stained them with ink and then tried to wash it off.

Wojnicz was eager to join their extremely interesting discussion about the decline of the West, in which Lukas and August took the lead, while Frommer commented concisely on their statements, always to the point. But he was seized by the weakness of timidity, on top of which he felt his temperature rising again. So he merely sat and sighed, shifting his gaze from one man to another.

And now we shall leave them here, debating around a table covered with an ominously patterned cloth, we shall leave them, to vacate the house via the chimney or the chinks between the slate roof tiles—and then gaze from afar, from above. It has started to rain, droplets are flowing down the roof and forming transparent, shining lace before dripping onto the ground, teasing it, making it itch, carving little hollows, then gathering hesitantly into little rivulets to seek a course among the stones, under a clump of grass, beside a root, and finally down the path trodden by patient animals.

But we shall return.

3

PHEASANT DISTANCE

H e left the table with relief, unable to ward off the nasty feeling that they were isolated here, that they had landed in Görbersdorf like a unit cut off from a great army, under siege. And although there were no gun barrels in sight, or signs of the presence of devious secret agents, Wojnicz felt as if he had unwittingly ended up in a war of some kind. Who was fighting whom he had no idea, because everyone here seemed occupied by the same thing—struggling against consumption, trying to lower their fever, strengthening their body, providing mutual encouragement, putting themselves in order after the anarchic reign of illness.

Before reaching his room, Wojnicz stopped awhile, intrigued by some strange noises that seemed to be coming from the attic. He had heard them the night before, but, being half asleep and too tired to investigate, he had ignored them. Now he could hear gentle scratching again, and a sort of gurgle. He decided to ask Opitz what it could be when the opportunity arose. He was just heading for his room when a door suddenly opened and a pair of hands grabbed him by the sleeve and pulled him inside. He was so surprised that he didn't resist at all.

There before him stood Thilo von Hahn, small, panting, in neat, expensive pajamas, as if he were about to get into bed. Darkness reigned in this corner room; the windows were veiled by curtains and also covered with gray artist's canvas. Only a third window was exposed, letting the lamplight from the street fall onto some canvas stretchers turned away from the door. The room smelled of oil paint, turpentine and something like perfume, something subtle and light, possibly soap scented with flowers of some kind.

"What do you say to some licorice?" asked von Hahn in a whisper.

There were dark rings around his pale blue eyes, and they looked glassy. The reflection of the light from the window in them, split in four by muntins, made it look—it occurred to Wojnicz—as if the boy had crosses in his eyes.

"Licorice?" said Wojnicz in amazement. He'd have sooner expected vodka.

"Or not. Why should Willi find out you're in my room? Shush, quiet." He put a finger to his lips.

Wojnicz could tell that Thilo had a fever; the hand clinging to his sleeve was trembling slightly. He gently tried to release himself from the grip.

"Do sit down," said Thilo more calmly, as though suddenly aware that he had given Mieczysław a shock, and let go of his sleeve.

They sat down, Wojnicz in the only armchair and Thilo on the bed.

"I don't know how to broach this matter without sounding like someone who has trouble with his nerves. But I can tell you, my friend, you've ended up in a nasty place. There's always someone dying here."

"Well, of course, we're at a sanatorium. Chest and throat complaints are hard to cure."

"That's not what I meant. She didn't hang herself, you know."

"What are you saying?" Wojnicz was disturbed at this, because he had taken a liking to Thilo.

"People get murdered here."

The crosses had vanished from Thilo's eyes, but they still looked glassy and blurred, probably due to his fever.

"Who would have done that?" asked Wojnicz cautiously.

"That's not what I'm talking about. Not that poor little woman. I'm talking in general," said Thilo, making a vague, circular gesture, as if by "in general" he meant everywhere. "It's hard to explain, it's all interconnected. People die here. Strange things have been happening ever since I arrived." He spoke with difficulty, as if consciously having to control his own breathing. "This place is cursed. There's a strange acceptance of these deaths. It keeps recurring."

"Here, in Görbersdorf?" asked Wojnicz incredulously. He felt sorry for Thilo; he had been hoping for a not too intense but reasonably close relationship, something like friendship. "Women get hanged?"

"Oh, no, I'm not talking about Frau Opitz. Every year a man dies here, sometimes two. Ripped to pieces in the forest."

Thilo nodded, clearly pleased with the effect his words had produced.

Wojnicz felt uneasy. The pattern on the wallpaper suddenly seemed suggestive, full of faces and eyes fixed on the two of them. He shook his head.

"The newspapers would have written about it, and everyone would be talking about it. We're not living in the desert."

"They cover it up. I know what you're thinking. You think I'm a madman, don't you? Mentally ill. Ask Opitz. Ask them. You'll see how they lose countenance."

Wojnicz denied it, and was instantly perplexed by his own lie. Yes, he did think Thilo was a madman, or at least delirious because of his fever.

"Say what you like, but I'm not a madman," said poor Thilo, and leaned back on the bed as though intending to lie down.

A tense silence fell, and then Thilo brought out a box of brand-name chocolates.

"Have one," he said, as if to apologize to his guest.

"Have you been here for long?" asked Wojnicz, to drop the awkward subject.

"Since last autumn. My condition worsened when the academic year began. In the summer I felt fine. I was sure I'd come out healthy, but somehow I'm still weak. There's so much I'd like to do, but I can't even read. Not to mention paint. It's a wretched life."

Wojnicz could not resist looking at the canvas stretchers scattered all over the room, and at the sketches and prints pinned to the walls. Thilo had converted his bedroom into a studio.

"Are you studying painting?" he asked hesitantly.

Thilo lay down comfortably on the bed. He propped his head on his elbow and drew up his knees.

"Art history. I work on landscapes."

Wojnicz had no idea what to say. Certainly not that he was studying hydroengineering and sewage systems.

"There's something strange going on," said Thilo, returning to his earlier topic. "There's some force that makes . . . I don't really know how to put it. They find mutilated bodies in the forest. Opitz's cousins. They're all cousins here. They're called Fischer, Tilch or Opitz."

"How do you know all this?"

"I saw the murder victim last year. When his body was brought into the village. In pieces."

Wojnicz looked at him dubiously.

"Yes indeed. In pieces," he repeated. "I don't think all of them were found."

"You saw the body?!"

"They brought it into the village at dawn in a blanket."

Wojnicz didn't believe him. He felt a sort of distaste, weariness and disappointment, because he had imagined that, as his contemporary, Thilo was going to be a sort of comrade for him. He thought he was going to tell Thilo what he had seen in the dining room, about the body on the table. He might even have told him about Gliceria or his father, but now he had lost the urge, on top of which he was feeling the strange effect of the Schwärmerei—it was physically overpowering, but also intensified one's thinking. It was as if his thoughts were a flock of sheep running off in random directions.

"Thilo, I'm going now. I think I'm getting a fever too." He stood up and headed for the door.

Thilo opened his eyes and raised himself on his elbow.

"Don't go yet," he said.

Wojnicz went back and sat on the edge of the bed.

"Don't think about such things. They're just made-up stories. We're safe here, each fighting our own illness," he said.

"Do you know what is the most common mistake people make when they're in danger? Each one thinks their life is unique, and that death doesn't affect them. No one believes in their own death. Do you think I believe in my own death?" said Thilo, and fell back against the pillow.

Wojnicz gave no reply. He was exhausted. As he was attempting to get up and leave, Thilo leaned toward him and said: "Watch out for them, especially Opitz, he's a cunning fellow. He beat that wife of his, he treated her like dirt. I think he killed her, then hanged her. Or forced her to hang herself."

Wojnicz blinked; he preferred not to think about it. Thilo should get some solid sleep. He'd have given anything to be lying in his own bed now, but still he protested: "I don't believe you. Did no one go to the police with that?"

"That's how it is with the wives. No one here's particularly bothered about them. I am a patient here. I myself am barely alive," said Thilo, and shrugged.

Wojnicz put a chocolate in his mouth. It turned out to be filled with marzipan, silky and soft, and at that moment he remembered what else the Schwärmerei tasted of—it was the smell of a dog's paws. He smiled to himself at the memory of the dog he'd had in childhood. When still a young pup, it had chewed the rug in his father's study, after which it was forbidden to enter the house; later on, when they moved to the city, the dog had remained in the countryside.

Now Wojnicz asked about Lukas and August, having realized the situation was ripe for gossip.

"A fine pair of rascals," replied Thilo animatedly.

Clearly he liked to talk about others. He claimed that neither of them had any money, and they were here at the mercy of their families, in August's case a sister, and in Lukas's probably a daughter. Sometimes Lukas seemed to be such a suspicious character that Thilo was sure he must be a Russian spy, sent here for medical treatment. Apparently he was not called Lukas at all, but Łukasiewicz, and he was at least a half compatriot of Wojnicz.

Thilo also believed that not everyone here was really ill; some of them were just pretending, in order to escape from life or to hide away. He waited for his words to take effect, and then he warned Wojnicz against August.

"What can I say to you? The man's a bloodsucker."

Mieczysław tried to find out what he meant, but Thilo had already moved on to Frommer. Frommer turned out to be a theosophist and spiritualist who saw ghosts everywhere. Lukas had told him that Frommer was very ill, but Thilo owned that he had never seen him coughing. Frommer came here regularly for several weeks, then went back to his damp city of Breslau, whence he returned again a few weeks later, relaxed and well rested. It was hard to figure him out, and Thilo did not trust him, but even so he preferred his eccentric company to Lukas's sinister importunity or August's pretentiousness.

"So he reminds you too of a little lead soldier, so stiff, ready for every summons from the world beyond. And that collar. Who wears collars like that?"

Yes, who wore collars like that? But Wojnicz had the strange feeling that Thilo was trying to tell him something else entirely, something that had nothing at all to do with the men at the guesthouse or with the death of Frau Opitz. He was giving him a penetrating look, a touch ironic and a touch expectant, as if willing Wojnicz to guess something. But as Wojnicz appeared not to understand what he meant, Thilo stretched and yawned.

"I think he's an opium addict. Sometimes he has such a misty gaze," he said.

Just then they heard a gentle knock at the door, and Thilo glanced at Wojnicz as if to say: *Ah, you see?* They saw Opitz's head.

"Everything all right?" asked the head.

"Yes, yes, we're just going to bed," said Thilo in a feeble voice. "I wanted Herr Wojnicz to close my window. It's jammed."

"I'm just leaving," said Mieczysław, and took the opportunity to slip out of the sick boy's room. He felt he'd had enough thrills and gossip for today.

"Oh, yes," said Opitz. "I'll send Raimund up tomorrow. Go to sleep."

As Wojnicz stood in the doorway, Thilo cast him another meaning-ful look, and merely by moving his lips he sent him a message: *They're keeping an eye on me!*

Opitz had gone upstairs to his own room; for a while, Wojnicz stopped and listened, trying to tell where the faint sound that had in-trigued him earlier was coming from, that gurgling or soft knocking or barely audible shuffling.

Suddenly it all felt extremely unreal, and he found himself wonder-ing whether he had already fallen asleep, and Thilo and all the others were just figures in a dream. The mutilated bodies in the forest and the wife-beating Opitz. He wiped his brow helplessly, as though he were reading a totally absurd book, of which he understood only individual words but not sentences. Perhaps he had a fever too? Yes, he definitely had a slightly raised temperature, he could hear that distinctive soft ringing in his ears. Maybe he was hallucinating.

Yet he could still see the woman's body lying on the table before him, and Wilhelm Opitz smoothing the folds of her skirt, then telling the shocked Mieczysław: "Go to your room, boy." He was also think-ing: And what now? What will happen? Will the police come? Where have they taken the body? And that it was unpleasant to live in a place where someone has died (though there is probably no place where no one has ever died—the world has existed for long enough by now). But what astonished him the most was how easily one could come to terms with another person's death. How simple it was. Especially here in Görbersdorf, where people were always dying.

Then Dr. Semperweiss's gun appeared before his eyes, leaning against the desk, and it brought back images of the time when his fa-ther and uncle had taught him to shoot. They hunted pheasants, strange birds that burst out from underfoot and flew heavily into the air with a whir. Their ungainliness was annoying; it prompted one to think them to blame for their own deaths. It was not hard to shoot them, and his uncle often succeeded. But Mieczyś was quite recalcitrant about killing them, and always aimed a centimeter to the left—a minor deception, "pheasant distance" as he called it—an action that neither his uncle nor his father ever noticed, preferring to call the shot "abortive." Pheasant distance was a defiance strategy similar to reticence, vanishing at the relevant moment or moving out of sight. Mieczysław appeared to take part in the game imposed on him but found a way of escaping it. A slight shift of the sights, imperceptible to others, thwarted the whole performance.

He opened his bedroom door and was met by the calming scent of coal tar soap, a supply of which his father had bought him just before his departure. His mind now turned in a different direction. He realized that he had more important things to consider than Thilo's conspiracy theories. Should he transfer to the Kurhaus entirely, meals and all? Did he have enough money budgeted? His thoughts flew into the near future, beyond the limits of the night, to the bright dawn of tomorrow. He was worried he didn't have the right bathing trunks, what would happen when he had to strip naked, and whether he could cope with the long rest cures. And what sort of surprise prepared by Opitz lay ahead of them when they took their walk into the mountains. Would his shoes withstand the hike? Perhaps he should write to his father to say he must buy new ones, but that was a major expense.

All these matters absorbed his mind, drawing the world inside, into the large, chaotic space that each of us carries within like an invisible piece of luggage that we drag after us all our lives, without knowing why. Our true self.

4

CHEST AND THROAT
COMPLAINTS

everal beautiful, quite summery days went by, which Wojnicz devoted to getting used to the new course of his life. He liked everything here, the order and punctuality, the professionalism and calm. People took their ailments seriously but did their best to live normally. And on the whole they were ordinary, which made them appear friendly. They wanted to live in the same way as others, they liked the same things, wore almost the same jackets and identical Panama hats. They behaved correctly, and knew moderation in all things. They had decent beds and clean sheets. They dreamed of ordinary matters: that they would recover, have long lives and live to see their grandchildren, and that the money they had saved would prove useful in their old age. They solemnly bought cakes at the patisserie and earnestly read the news in the papers. Yes, this was the "appetizing" atmosphere Wojnicz had been looking for.

There was no cemetery in Görbersdorf, as Wojnicz learned to his considerable surprise. So many people lived here! And so many people died here, yet their deaths seemed to pass hygienically and unnoticed, tactfully conforming to the rhythm of local life, like a thrifty house-wife who always manages to dispose of the rubbish and leftovers with grace.

So said Herr August, who was walking along the promenade, flour-ishing a bamboo cane, when Mieczysław chanced to run into him, too late to bypass him without being seen, so like it or not, he had bowed and joined him. Now he was trying to adjust his pace to August's slow, rather ceremonial step, which was causing him considerable discom-fort. It occurred to him that in future he should walk along the out-skirts of the village lest he bump into someone he knew. But he had decided to take advantage of this encounter to learn more about the dreadful death of Frau Opitz—dreadful to him, even if no one else seemed particularly concerned about it.

Herr August grabbed him by the elbow and steered him toward a pretty little bench a short way from the main path, at the foot of the church standing on a hillock. Wojnicz was afraid he was about to hear a lecture, but by now there was no way to escape it.

"You see, sir, the Truth with a capital *T* always relies on the threat of cutting off anything that extends beyond its boundaries. No fringes, none at all. Behind the Truth hides violence," said August once they had sat down. He gave Wojnicz a piercing, not to say meaningful look. "Do not demand the Truth. It's a waste of your young time."

Here he broke off abruptly.

"Please keep very still for a moment!" he cried, and removed from Wojnicz's arm an enormous green insect that looked like a cross be-tween a grasshopper and a crab, then placed it on his palm and held it out to the youth, so that he could admire the full splendor of this bizarre creature, which prompted both curiosity and repulsion. As Wojnicz was almost instinctively leaning forward to take a closer look, August shouted *"Waaaa!,"* which gave Mieczysław a real fright. Unpleasantly surprised and disgusted by this joke, he merely responded with a grunt.

Quite pleased with himself, August explained to him that Görbersdorf was the most northerly place in this part of Europe where praying mantises appeared, thanks to the configuration of the terrain, the temperature and the lack of wind. He began to draw a map of Europe in the sand with his bamboo cane, which, to tell the truth, Wojnicz did not follow.

"Please look and see what a great distance these poor creatures must travel, all the way from the Mediterranean basin. That is where everything comes to us from, my dear fellow. Both the beautiful and the ugly," he said with a meaningful smile.

Soon they stood up and headed toward the Kurhaus, passing Frau Weber and Frau Brecht, who were sitting outside their house, this time with their arms folded, as if warming themselves in the last rays of the sun. Wojnicz noticed that one had very swollen legs, squashed into specially made, rather scruffy footwear, while the other was so ugly as to be fascinating. Her drooping lower lip made her look like an ancient sculpture depicting some sort of creature from Hades. Noticing that Wojnicz was looking at them, August added in a hushed tone: "Apparently there is a third, but she never comes outside, and no one has actually seen her for years."

Wojnicz glanced at him in disbelief, and August winked. As they walked on, August regaled Mieczysław with his reflections, which he referred to as "peripatetic conversations," though in fact he did all the talking. Wojnicz did not deny that these lectures were very interesting, but he could not focus on them, because he was avidly observing the patients passing by, especially the ladies, who were beautifully dressed and wearing ridiculous hats.

"Oh yes, my dear boy," opined August, "each of us reaches the set upper limit of his personal potential, and thereafter ceases to develop. That is the basis of old age, this incapacity for change. We stop on our own journey. It happens to some people in midlife, and to others as soon as they finish their education. Yet others go on developing into ripe old age, right up to death in fact, but they are a rarity."

He became pensive, as if about to add something, then he fell silent as a group of young people passed them, talking in Polish. Wojnicz dropped his gaze and pretended he couldn't understand them. Perhaps for this reason August blithely continued: "Some are vaguely aware that they have stopped developing, do you know? They feel unwell in this confinement, for them it is stagnation; they are drawn into the past, as if trying to find something stimulating there, ha ha. That is when a man starts to be interested in his own family, to draw genea-logical trees and spend Sunday afternoons examining photographs, as if his miserable existence were to spill into a greater, family form."

Indeed, there was plenty of truth in what August was saying. His father and his uncle, thought Wojnicz, had certainly stopped develop-ing by now. They did and said the same things all the time, as if trapped on a treadmill, unconscious of its limits. He started thinking about other people, but chiefly about himself: Had he already got stuck for good, or was there still movement in him?

"But you see, sir, women develop in another way. Their psyche simply functions differently from the male one—our pattern of devel-opment does not apply to them. While in a man the ages of childhood, adolescence and adulthood succeed each other in a linear way, replac-ing one another, in women the three stages of development coexist independently, as it were: the attentive observer will see in them a little girl, a woman in her prime and an old crone all at once."

They turned back, and once again passed Frau Weber and Frau Brecht.

"Look at them from this angle," August added in a muted tone, almost a whisper. "It astonishes me how such a state of threefold existence is possible. It must be some unfathomable form of atavism."

Farther on, they saw four nurses carrying a coffin from the Kurhaus to the mortuary—a long, low building next to the sanatorium that was meant to be a prosectorium but looked more like a boiler house or a workshop. Dr. Semperweiss often parked his car outside it, one of only three in Görbersdorf. It was a beautiful Mercedes 37/90 horsepower, barely two years old, with a long, shining bonnet, a chassis made of exotic polished wood and comfortable leather seats. Everything about it was perfect, from the folding roof to the stunningly beautiful wheels and their pale tires. This wonder of technology radiated such overwhelming optimism that for all who came to admire it, death must have seemed an archaic part of the old order, a primordial failing from which humankind would escape as soon as it achieved its desire for modernity and a permanent trust in technology. Whatever was coming was bound to be good, because it would yield to the control of sterilized, shining instruments, appliances and utensils. These would be reparable, and thus virtually immortal.

Herr August explained that the nearest cemeteries were in Friedland and Langwaltersdorf, and the bodies were taken there to perform a decent burial, which was why Görbersdorf never saw a funeral. After all, the sight of one could lower the morale of the soldiers fighting for the health of their lungs.

"As a result, Görbersdorf is a cheerful town full of joie de vivre. Here one celebrates life, not death. We take no notice of death, do we?" He touched Wojnicz's arm with a familiar gesture.

Wojnicz smiled, amused by this game of immortality.

"So Frau Opitz will be taken away from here?"

"Yes, my dear friend, that has most certainly happened already. She has gone from here, as she did not observe the rules of the game. Here there are only the living. The dead disappear, and we have no further interest in them. We disregard death."

Wojnicz liked this too.

"Do you think one could go on like that eternally? That in Görbersdorf one is immortal?"

"In a sense, yes. Since there are no dead here. Being dead is a disgrace."

"I saw Frau Opitz lying dead on the table," said Wojnicz after a pause, without looking at his companion.

"Ah, you do not know what you saw. What did you see?"

"Her shoes, her skirts and embroidered apron, her—"

"Well, quite. Those are things, not a person."

Now they had climbed a little higher, above the ponds, where a beautiful avenue of cedar trees opened before them, with a small building resembling a chapel standing at its far end.

"I was wrong!" exclaimed Herr August at the sight of it, and he began to beat his own chest theatrically. "How could I have told you such a lie? How unreliable I am!"

Wojnicz looked at him, failing to understand.

"For that is a tomb. This is where Dr. Brehmer had himself interred, he chose this very spot for himself, so that even after death he could keep an eye on his medical foundation. Everything is beautifully visible from here."

"All right, please don't worry about your mistake—it isn't a cemetery, just a single tomb," said Wojnicz, trying to reassure him.

If ghosts can see, if they exist at all, and on top of that are interested in human life, from here Dr. Brehmer could monitor everything, every little street in the village, the huge Kurhaus building, the park, the paths within it, and Römpler's vast modern sanatorium. The hillside on which his grand tomb had been built guarded Görbersdorf from the outside world and acted as an unofficial border between the savage forest and the civilized village. Naturally the door of the tomb was bolted, but the very notion that a decomposing corpse lay behind it did not inspire conversation, so the two gentlemen turned and followed the cedar avenue back to the beaten path of the sanatorium promenade.

They started discussing the funeral, which was constantly being delayed because of police procedures, and the fact that they should attend it, perhaps by joining forces to hire a vehicle. They also discussed the service that was to be held here in the little church, just before the funeral. When they reached the guesthouse, Wojnicz asked: "What is the tune that one hears from the Kurhaus turret at noon? Somehow it sounds familiar."

But Herr August had no idea, and advised him to ask the Breslauer, Frommer.

"It must be something local."

The funeral was on a Tuesday, which Wojnicz did not regard as a good sign. At home in Lwów it was said to be a bad thing for a body to wait through a Sunday to be buried, and that if it did, the deceased would drag someone after them into the grave. But this corpse had waited through two Sundays.

His arrival at the little church was delayed by having to wait at the end of the queue for cold showers. He had managed to persuade the broad-shouldered bathing attendant that he must remain in his underwear. Then it had taken him a long time to warm himself up with a cup of hot tea. What cruelty it was to drench people in lukewarm water! It had put him in a bad mood.

The coffin was standing before a rather modest altar, covered with a wreath of autumn flowers. The Protestant service was already underway. Wojnicz found it quite strange—it felt as if some calm and serious people had come here to a sort of special administrative office, and were now indifferently submitting to some official procedures. In any case, there weren't many people, they occupied only the first three pews, and some of them were probably just random patients. In the front pew he immediately recognized the solid figure of Opitz, beside whom stood Raimund in his Sunday best, and behind them other residents of the village in local costumes with knee breeches and bright stockings. Wojnicz's thoughts slid across the plain, rough walls of the church to the flooring. His head ached. He would have to abandon the cold showers.

There were also several old women in the church, stout, dressed in black wrinkled skirts and white mobcaps tied at the back into stiffly starched white bows. There were hardly any young people, just a couple of poorly dressed housemaids, friends of the deceased, perhaps. A small group of female patients standing to one side had surely come in order to attend the service, in attire that contrasted with the rest. Their huge, fashionable hats added a bit of life to the church, just as if small flowers had grown on a toppled monument or a squadron of ladybirds had landed on a gravestone. Had they come to the funeral out of boredom? Or as tourists eager for impressions of the exotic local Silesian culture?

One figure in particular stood out: a tall, slender shape, a straight back, and strands of fair hair escaping from under a vast hat, definitely not in harmony with the restrained architecture and decor of the church. This hat seemed scandalous in this modest temple, and perhaps that was why it captured Wojnicz's attention. From his perspective he could only see the tip of its owner's nose and the beautiful line of her high cheekbones. She wore a honey-colored cape thrown over a bottle-green dress. For ages Mieczysław could not tear his gaze from this wonder. He had no idea what it was that attracted him so strongly: the slender woman or the combination of colors. Both awoke in him an intense longing for something familiar, yet impossible to define; it felt as if one day he would find the word for it, but for now it did not yet exist.

The pastor had just finished the liturgical greetings, and singing floated up to the vaulted ceiling of the church—very good singing, almost as if from a well-rehearsed choir.

His father had often repeated to him—though Wojnicz did not actually remember when and in what situations he had heard him say it; "repeated" meant that he expressed it often, sometimes without even opening his mouth—that women are by nature treacherous and fickle. Weepy. It was impossible to know what to grab hold of, what to trust in them. They were elusive, as slippery as snakes or silk (a peculiar juxtaposition, indeed); it was hard to catch hold of them, they slithered out of your hand and would then laugh at your ineptitude. There was an old saying that Uncle Emil frequently quoted, and this Mieczysław remembered well. It was to do with Gliceria, or maybe a fiancée of his uncle's, the only one, who had walked out on him and married someone else. On these occasions, his uncle—normally so well-mannered—would remove the spoon from his soup and brandish it above his plate.

"Woman, frog and devil, these are siblings treble."

The little Wojnicz did his best to fathom the meaning of this adage, but he had no idea what exactly his uniformed uncle, who usually expressed himself precisely, was trying to say.

Was there really a connection between a woman, a frog and a devil? This damp, murky threesome removed the woman from wallpapered, tidy bourgeois bedrooms and dragged her into the woods, over the forest floor and into the marshy zones of peat bogs; apparently this trio were relatives from the same abyss in the depths of the forest, where no human voice or eye could reach, and where every traveler lost their way. Oh well, there were no such forests in the vicinity of Lwów, maybe just somewhere in Volhynia, or on the slopes of the Carpathian Mountains. He found it easier to imagine what Gliceria might have in common with a frog than with a devil, though he had never seen a devil, and to tell the truth he did not believe in them. "Folktales," his father would say. As for the frog, then yes, indeed: she was fat and shapeless, and her apron-topped skirts deformed her figure even more. If she were to squat down on the kitchen floor, and if she were to raise her head the right way—yes, she would look like a frog.

After the singing came a reading from the Gospel of Matthew, the passage about the sheep and the goats, to which Wojnicz had never actually paid much attention. Along comes the Son of Man, and just as a good shepherd separates the sheep from the goats, he separates the just from the unjust. Wojnicz felt sorry for the goats—they were such wise animals; they had had a small herd of nanny goats at their manor house in the countryside. The baby goats were especially amusing, bold and inquisitive. As a child he used to play with them, and even credited them with having their own sense of humor. What did the Savior have against billy goats? The Polish Gospel only mentioned the males. Was it to do with the fact that they did not produce young or milk? So where were the nanny goats and their children? Why did the Gospel leave them out? What a bizarre story, he thought. He also wondered for a while whether Frau Opitz had been more of a sheep or a goat. And what was he? And what about the Grizzled Lion, and August, what were they? Goats? And Thilo? Now, not bridled by concentration—he was finding it hard to focus on the pastor's sermon; not only was it in German, but in the local dialect, which Wojnicz could barely understand—his imagination was playing tricks on him, causing him to envisage the people sitting in the church with the heads of sheep and goats. Curiously, there seemed to be more goats, yes, yes, they looked more distinctive and inquisitive, but the cluster of sheep muzzles was also striking, especially on the side where the women were sitting—soft, elongated little snouts and a soft, trusting gaze.

Yes, their gaze . . . For quite a while he had been sensing someone's gaze on the back of his neck. He turned around, as if to inspect the church's scanty decor. Behind him sat a boy, a teenager, with a fair, flushed face, in wire-rimmed spectacles with extremely strong lenses that magnified his gray eyes. It seemed to Wojnicz that this boy had been expecting his glance—he was strangely tense, as though trying to give Wojnicz a sign, to remind him of something. It was an unpleasant, ambiguous situation, and Wojnicz turned to face the front again, doing his best to forget about it.

He left the church early, furtively, to arrive on time for the final lunch sitting. He would excuse himself later by pleading infirmity—after all, everyone here was ill. He had noticed that others too were finding the pastor's long sermon hard going. Beneath the gateway stood three men with strangely darkened faces, as if stained by smoke. In fact they were puffing on cigarettes, and were wreathed in a bluish cloud of smoke. They were talking in whispers, clearly waiting for the families to emerge from the church.

Wojnicz did not wait for his companions but, overcome by a surge of bad temper, headed downhill, stretching his long, thin legs, and almost ran to the Kurhaus for lunch. He was suddenly animated, his hunger crying out like a bell summoning him to the solemnity of the body.

They made their way to the cemetery in Langwaltersdorf in two carriages. It was a good excuse to escape the Görbersdorf valley for the outside world. At once the sky became a little brighter, and several times the sharp autumn sun broke through the clouds, revealing an incredible pageant of colors on the hillsides. They drove along a highland river, on which the provident local people kept ponds where trout were raised.

Only now did the unusual position of the village become apparent, as one drove into it under a railway viaduct through quite a narrow passage where two horse-drawn carts could only just pass each other; if they had been the wagons that transported coal and other goods into the city, this would surely have been a major obstacle.

Beyond this gateway, Görbersdorf and the entire valley unfolded, supposedly sited on top of a large underground lake, between dense though not very high mountains. This was why Herr August had said they were living in a Leyden jar, in which various vibrations were mixed, producing an electric current.

The cemetery in Langwaltersdorf was old and crowded, certainly not designed to accommodate the deceased from the sanatorium, which did not yet exist when this necropolis was founded; soon it would run out of space. It lay beside a slender church, close to the junction of two cobbled roads, one of which led to Waldenburg while the other ran along a wide, bright plateau via Nieder Wüstegiersdorf to Glatz. The cemetery did not resemble the ones familiar to Wojnicz from Poland.

He was not accustomed to such modesty and lack of ostentation. In the East they looked quite different—the graves were grand, each one was different, and many of them were richly decorated or had statues. Since childhood he had been deeply moved by the ones with a weeping angel, perhaps because his mother's grave had been provided with such a figure. Allegedly his father had ordered it at his son's request, though in fact he had been too young to have expressed such a wish yet. Perhaps Mieczyś Wojnicz's father had thought that his son would want an angel of this kind on the grave of his mother, who had died several months after giving birth, enfeebled by the effort of producing a child and by some sort of inexplicable depression. Now Mieczysław's memory of his mother was forever linked with the gracile stone angel, kneeling in a gesture of deep despair unbecoming of a celestial creature.

The local people must have had another way of coping with the memory of their deceased; perhaps they exercised their imaginations differently, and in their fondness for the concrete they preferred to replace the dead with pictures of them, carefully framed and positioned on the furniture or hung on a wall; here in the cemetery there were only rows of similar gravestones, shrewdly arranged and modest, but very well cared for. A stonemason with a steady hand had carved the barest information necessary for sustaining the memory: first name and surname, date of birth and of death, sometimes just of death. It was hard to form an idea of the people lying under the gravestones; there was nothing for the imagination. But the future engineer Wojnicz saw the cemetery from a singular point of view, in cross section through several layers of soil. It was full of horizontal lines, like on the graphs they had produced at college: the top layer was formed by the rectangles of gravestones, under that there was a layer of grass, plants, and their roots hungrily reaching downward, a strip of earth that had settled by now but differed from its surroundings in having been artificially mixed, and below that came the large rectangle of a coffin and its contents, the irregular outline of what remained of a human body, an elongated shape encrusted with bones.

Wojnicz walked in solitude among the graves, reading the names of the dead. On the other side of the main avenue the domination of three surnames ended: Fischer, Opitz and Tilch. There beneath a soaring cross the sanatorium section began and variety appeared; each of the gravestones was significantly different. Some were engraved with an Orthodox cross while others consisted of a small slab without religious symbols, set upright in the opposite direction to the rest. And the surnames—mostly German, but also French, and then, Oh! There were some Polish names, and a good many Czech and Swedish ones. Death was decidedly cosmopolitan.

Wojnicz noticed that the cart carrying the coffin was already in place, and that the mourners were lining up around the open grave. He spotted Herr August and Herr Lukas and went to stand alongside them in silence. He also saw Opitz, with his eyes lowered, Raimund looking solemn, and Frommer, slightly to one side, closely inspecting all the mourners. The other faces were unfamiliar, though some of them attracted his attention because they were dark, with black rings around the eyes. One might well be scared of them on first sight. Naturally Frau Weber and Frau Brecht had come too, in black headgear that resembled saucepans. That was all. The funeral was brief, devoid of unnecessary words, as if it were impossible to say more about this terrible, macabre event that should be forgotten as quickly as possible. And that was what Wojnicz did—he forgot. As they were driving back to the guesthouse, perversely, or mischievously perhaps, he asked Lukas and August if they believed in the immortal soul and what happened to it after death, and thus prompted a veritable pandemonium of ideas, arguments and counterarguments, quotations and references, so by the time the carriage was passing the nursing home at the start of their village, he did not know what his companions were talking about, and his only thought was of lying down in bed.

By a twist of circumstance, as Frau Opitz's body was descending on ropes into the open grave, the exact autumn equinox took place, and the ecliptic was aligned in such a special way that it counterbalanced the vibration of the earth. Naturally, nobody noticed this—people have more important things on their minds. But we know it.

In the highland valley that spread above the underground lake stillness sets in, and although it is never windy here, now there is no sense of the faintest puff, as though the world were holding its breath. Late insects are perching on stems, a starling turns to stone, staring at a long-gone movement among the clumps of parsley in the garden. A spiderweb stretched between the blackberry bushes stops quivering and goes taut, straining to hear the waves coming from the cosmos, and water makes itself at home in the moss thallus, as if it were to stay there forever, as if it were to forget about its most integral feature—that it flows. For the earthworm, the world's tension is a sign to seek shelter for the winter. Now it is planning to push down into the ground, perhaps hoping to find the deeply hidden ruins of paradise. The cows that chew the yellowing grass also come to a standstill, putting their internal factories of life on hold. A squirrel looks at the miracle of a nut and knows that it is pure, condensed time, that it is also its future, dressed in this strange form. And in this brief moment everything defines itself anew, marking out its limits and aims afresh; just for a short while, blurred shapes cluster together again.

It is a very brief moment of equilibrium between light and darkness, almost imperceptible, a single instant in which the whole pattern is filled, the promise of great order is fulfilled, but only in the blink of an eye. In this scrap of time everything returns to a state of perfection that existed before the sky was separated from the earth.

But at once this perfect balance dissolves like a shape on water, the image dims and dusk starts to drift toward night, then night gains the upper hand—now it will be avenged for its six-month period of humiliation, establishing new bridgeheads every evening.

5.

HOLES IN THE GROUND

A few days after the funeral, two plainclothes policemen arrived from Breslau and held some interviews in the dining room. They treated Wojnicz lightly when they learned that he had only just arrived at the resort.

"Did you know the unfortunate woman?" one of the policemen asked him.

"Did I know her? No, I did not."

"But did you see her?"

Wojnicz wondered what to say.

"Yes, I did, but not all of her."

"What do you mean?" asked the policeman in alarm.

"I saw bits of her. You see, sir, in that short time she was always on the move, and I saw either a hand holding a tray or a shoe holding the door open." Wojnicz blinked, as if images of Frau Opitz were passing before his eyes.

The policemen looked at each other with barely concealed mockery. "Did you ever talk to her?"

"No, of course not. She was . . . a servant. I only arrived recently. She died the day after I got here."

"Do you know the people living at the guesthouse?"

"No, this is the first time I've met them. That is to say, we're gradually becoming acquainted. We're waiting for places at the Kurhaus."

"Ah, yes, I hope there will be vacancies soon," said the policeman, and immediately lost countenance. His lips wondered for a while whether to say sorry, but evidently they decided the faux pas had gone unnoticed.

"He tormented her," whispered Thilo to Mieczysław as they were going upstairs. "Of course I didn't tell them that. He used to make her sleep in the cellar for weeks at a time, down where he keeps potatoes and pickled cabbage. He never gave her the letters her family sent. The fact is, she was a slave. I saw him myself, the day before she died, beating her about the head with a wooden ladle because she burned the meat. That's why his food sticks in my throat. I'd much rather dine at the Kurhaus."

Wojnicz was sure Thilo had a fever again and was making things up. He was relieved when he was alone in his own room.

In the afternoon, when everyone was out for their treatments and Opitz had gone to do the shopping in Waldenburg, Mieczysław realized that this was the only moment in the day when the house was empty. At four, Raimund and the other boys from the guesthouses and villas were waiting outside the nursing home for the post, which they then distributed throughout the village; the news came a little late, but it was still current until evening. Wojnicz liked to be alone; only then did he feel he could loosen the collar placed around his neck hours ago—so stiff that it hurt his delicate skin, but he had to wear it whenever he was with others.

He was determined to inspect the loft. He did not know what to call the sounds he could hear from there at night. It was not cooing, but more like puffing, it reminded him of breathing combined with bubbling. He had heard that many old houses had martens and other small predators living in their attics, so he knew that creatures of that kind might have moved in for the winter.

A narrow wooden staircase led from the residents' floor to the loft, where in a small corridor there were doors to three attic rooms. They were very simple doors, without the decorations on the ones downstairs, just plain boards fitted with old-fashioned iron locks and handles.

Wojnicz opened the first door on the right as quietly as he could. He saw a narrow little room with a small mansard window, and under it a metal bed covered with a throw. It was pink and purple, made of many different kinds of fabric sewn together, ingeniously and tastefully harmonized. It looked cheerful and girlish. The walls were covered in shabby wallpaper, lilac with white vertical stripes. On the dressing table stood an earthenware bowl and matching jug. On a cabinet next to it lay a hairbrush, a comb and a jar of pomade. Beneath a small square mirror some carefully hung ribbons shimmered. There was also a small table topped with a crocheted doily, a carafe of water and a glass; next to it stood a chair completely covered by a carelessly flung dress—it was dark blue and a little tatty, fraying along the seams. Wojnicz opened a small, single-door wardrobe and saw several similar dresses on pegs. Below them was a pair of boots, with crumpled newspaper pushed into the uppers to prevent flopping. There was also a wicker basket filled with balls of wool, mostly purple, pink and white, and a pair of knitting needles driven into them menacingly.

Wojnicz realized that he must be in the room of the deceased, the woman whom he had seen only fleetingly. He touched the fabric of the dress, and the flounce on a petticoat. He squatted to run a finger over the neatly polished boot leather and then stealthily retreated into the corridor.

The whole house was still silent—evidently nobody was back yet. Standing by the doors to the other rooms, Wojnicz hesitated, then opened one of them and immediately stepped back a pace. It too was an ordinary attic room with a mansard window, but in the middle of the dark space, brightened only by the light falling through the thick, dusty curtains, stood a chair with wide leather straps attached to its legs and armrests, fitted with buckles. It took Wojnicz a few seconds to realize what this device was for, but then, with his mind's eye, he saw and understood.

The chair was for tying someone up.

Of course he imagined himself there. His heart began to thud in his chest. He quickly closed the door and noiselessly, almost without breathing, went downstairs to his room.

There is a pair of nearly new, high-topped hiking boots standing by the door of Mieczysław Wojnicz's room. We like inspecting boots. These are made of well-tanned pigskin, carefully polished. They have rubber soles, high cuffs and dense lacing, each eyelet finished with a metal ring. Putting them on will involve a little effort. Raimund polished them at dawn, helping himself with spit. The toes of the boots are slightly scuffed, but good polish made of soot and tallow has rendered these imperfections almost invisible. Wojnicz has received these boots as a gift from Opitz. As a gift! He looks at them in disbelief, at a loss how to thank his host for this unexpected present. He keeps repeating: "Why, I . . . why . . ." but Wilhelm Opitz declares as straightforwardly as can be: "One of the patients left them behind."

A nervous thought flashes through Wojnicz's mind—the words *left behind* have unsettled him, but he has no time to reflect, everyone is waiting downstairs, and the boots are a perfect fit. Though outside it is foggy, Opitz has promised that as soon as they go higher up, the sun will start to shine.

There were seven of them including Raimund, who drove and was then to perform the role of porter—carrying a knapsack full of provisions and some rugs on which they could rest. First they rode in a cart, sitting along the sides like peasants, all the way to the trailhead. Apparently the beginning of October was always a good time for mountain hikes. Now an endless discussion was underway concerning the best source of information in Görbersdorf about the weather. Should one look in the Viennese or the Berlin newspapers? Or perhaps those from Prague? Each of the gentlemen had his own theory. It was notoriously hard to forecast the weather here.

"I don't know how to express my gratitude," said Wojnicz to Opitz as they headed uphill, truly touched by the gift of the boots. "And you thought about me at such a difficult time. I'm eternally grateful."

He really had no idea how to thank Opitz, who was leading their expedition. Pale and serious, he was looking extremely dignified today, his rather common features ennobled by mourning.

"You have no need to thank me. My conduct is as natural as can be, for he who is in need shall receive, Herr Wojnicz."

Wojnicz told him about Dr. Semperweiss's prognosis, adding that he might even be able to go home for Christmas.

Opitz merely sighed.

The charcoal burners' settlement, which they passed deep inside the forest, made an unpleasant impression. Sticky mud full of bark, pine cones and twigs spilled around heaps of smoldering logs, as if the skin of the forest had been ripped off, leaving the wound inflamed. The charcoal burners stared at them gloomily, out of dark, sooty faces. Opitz shook hands with one of them and nodded in the direction of the hikers. They were waiting for Thilo, who was finding it hard going and kept stopping to catch his breath. Wojnicz held back with him. With humor that made light of his condition, Thilo talked about the virtues of landscape painting, but his broken sentences betrayed how difficult it was for him to breathe.

"Landscape . . . is a great . . . mystery . . . because in fact . . . it takes shape . . . in the eyes . . . of the beholder," he struggled to say.

He added that it was a sort of projection of the spectator's inner state, and that we should wonder whether what we are seeing might look entirely different in reality.

Wojnicz replied that as a child he had been bothered by the question of whether, for example, everyone saw the color green similarly, or was "green" just an agreed term for something that each person might perceive in their own way. If so, then our inner representations of the world might be dramatically different. Only language and social norms would be keeping some kind of order.

"But in fact colors are particular wavelengths, objective measures," he concluded.

"Except that they can act on the human eye in all sorts of ways. How do you see green?" asked Thilo.

Wojnicz could not answer. Green like a leaf—that was all that occurred to him. He could only talk about it through comparison, through analogy with something else.

They set off up the hill again, where everyone was waiting for them, and out of necessity fell silent. The topic evaporated.

"Have you seen . . . the cemetery . . . in Langwaltersdorf?" asked Thilo, breaking the silence, breathing heavily. "It's worth a look. It's a special map of the world of the living."

Wojnicz could not quite understand what he meant.

It was hard to describe the charcoal burners' base as a settlement—there were just some large kilns, and near them some shacks cobbled together out of wood, branches and tar paper. With what seemed to Wojnicz undue animation, Opitz told them about the work of the charcoal burners, who hung around in a scattered group, looking totally uninterested in this entire show. Their black fingers held sloppily rolled cigarettes in dirty papers, and their eyes shone out of their charred faces. Their shabby, torn clothing brought to mind some bizarre fashion, exotic and primordial. Wojnicz felt as if they had all ended up in one of the prints he had enjoyed looking at as a child, depicting scenes from distant lands where two civilizations confronted each other for the first time.

Opitz showed them the kilns and with expert knowledge explained how they were filled. Once they were loaded with good material—the best wood was beech, which was plentiful here, as were hornbeam, alder and birch—to a total of twelve cubic meters, they were lit and left to heat. You had to wait until the right temperature was reached, and then close the hole at the top, letting the fire settle evenly, while the smoke emerged from small holes at the bottom. Under no circumstances could the vents be blocked, so keeping a constant eye on them was a crucial task. The kiln burned like that for hours on end, around the clock, then just before dawn you opened the lids and checked with a long stake to see if the charcoal had carbonized yet.

"These kilns are a local invention known as retorts," said Opitz, raising a finger to call his inattentive tour group to order. "Now, as you can see, the retort is hot and the burning process is underway inside it, destroying what until recently was ordinary wood, to extract completely new and desirable, if not noble elements. These fellows know how to manage this, and how to check if the charcoal has appeared."

With the gesture of a compere he pointed at the nearest group of charcoal burners. Their faces did not change—they expressed indifference, or even, thought Wojnicz, something like contempt.

"Once you have checked that everything is all right, you wait a few hours more, until white smoke appears, and then blue. At that point you must pour water over the oven," continued Opitz.

"How much water do you need for something as hot as that?" asked Herr August astutely.

That Opitz did not know. In his verbose dialect he asked the man he had spoken to earlier. The man spat out a single word.

"About a hundred liters," translated Opitz.

Then he explained that all the lids were sealed with mud to keep the steam inside. The next day, once everything had cooled down, the charcoal was ready. You opened the door and removed it with shovels. After burning the entire stock, you obtained about half a kiln of valuable product, and whatever had not burned up was used as tinder for the next load.

"And what could happen if the kilns were left unsupervised for a while?" asked Opitz rhetorically, leaning on his hiking stick decorated with little metal badges and edelweiss flowers.

The men with blackened faces looked at him with perhaps slightly greater interest.

He answered his own question. "The entire load would be incinerated. Instead of charcoal, you'd have a kiln full of white ash. The job would have failed."

"Is it dangerous work?" inquired Wojnicz spontaneously, and immediately felt ashamed of asking.

"Oh yes," replied Opitz jestingly, ending his lecture and gesturing for them to move on. "If you let yourself be enveloped in smoke, you lose your bearings and fall into the retort."

The charcoal burners cackled.

The answer embarrassed Wojnicz, and he promised himself not to ask any more questions. Opitz let the hikers go ahead and watched with great patience as they trudged uphill. A handful of sickly men, wanting to believe they still had plenty of life ahead of them. He kept the closest eye on Thilo von Hahn. The boy came last, breathing heavily and looking down at his feet, as if thinking about another world entirely. The blood in his ailing lungs could not provide enough oxygen, so his heart was thumping; one might wonder why Opitz had insisted on his coming with them. Opitz gave a barely noticeable sign with his chin, connecting the figure of Thilo with the gaze of the charcoal burners. They replied with a faint nod, also barely noticeable. Wojnicz saw this, but, wrapped up in his own hurt pride, immediately forgot about it.

Although Dr. Semperweiss had firmly forbidden conversation during physical effort, the gentlemen paid this no mind, and carried on with the series of discussions they had started yesterday or the day before, or had been holding since time began, stopping now and then and leaning on their shepherd's staffs. One of their inflammatory topics was the disappearance of the *Mona Lisa*. Two years ago, someone had broken into the Louvre and carried the painting off like a baguette. On the anniversary of the theft, as La Gioconda was still lost without trace, the newspapers had once again written at length about this event. The company was divided into two camps. According to Thilo and Herr August, this was the irreparable loss of a special cultural symbol, one of those works of art that are the axes of civilization, around which we organize ourselves spiritually as well as socially, and which humanity has a duty to protect above all. Herr August's declamation on the topic struck a tone of heartfelt rapture that made it sound as if all the words were capitalized; striving to speak clearly but somewhat burdened by the weight of those letters, his lips swelled and became moist with spittle, so that with every *P* or *B* Herr August sprayed flecks of saliva, no doubt full of mysterious Koch's bacilli. Opitz and Lukas in turn accused them of hysteria and exaggeration, claiming that there were more important matters than the *Mona Lisa*, and that although they appreciated Leonardo as an artist, one should not raise works of art onto such a high pedestal. Besides, they said, the *Mona Lisa* was merely a portrait of someone's mistress, with a lecherous smirk to boot, arousing a certain impure pleasure in us ("Oh, no! Not in me!" retorted Herr August) and unworthy of the attention devoted to it. Works of art should educate and bring the past closer. Here Lukas grew particularly excited, and his voice became a bark. Changing the subject, he launched a crusade against modern art, which he regarded as primitive and devoid of merit. At this point the men fell into such heated debate that everyone had to stop for a rest, leaning on their staffs, for more time than they should have. But what was to be done? Thilo had to come to the defense of modern art, trying to show Lukas his own incompetence, parochialism and bad taste—and his intellectual limitation too. Of course, Thilo expressed none of this directly, but his tone took on a scathing irony, which made Lukas even angrier. Finally Mona Lisa herself took a beating—she was not even pretty. Generally the appeal of women relied on the fact that they were faking, as if hiding a mystery, which was what drew men to them. But that was just a pretense, concealing an intellectual void. At this point the emotions calmed, and it seemed that at least on this matter they were all in agreement. Opitz issued the command to march on. As they headed uphill, they had to focus on the stony path, so they walked in silence. Lukas took advantage of this:

"Woman represents a bygone, inferior stage of evolution, so writes Darwin, and he of all people has something to say on the matter. Woman is like . . ."—here he sought the right word—"an evolutionary laggard. While man has gone on ahead and acquired new capabilities, woman has stayed in her old place and does not develop. That is why a woman is often socially handicapped, incapable of coping on her own, and must always be reliant on a man. She has to make an impression on him—by manipulation, by smiling. The *Mona Lisa*'s smile symbolizes a woman's entire evolutionary strategy for coping with life. Which is to seduce and manipulate."

And soon, despite the steep path and the injunction not to talk during physical effort, the conversation had shifted onto new tracks and intensified again—on the topic of women they all had something to say.

Now Frommer took the floor. As he spoke, he often stopped to draw invisible figures on the moss with his cane. In his opinion, some singular things had happened in this part of the country. He stressed that he had found it all in an archive in Breslau, and that not an ounce of it was fabrication. He said that the local territory had been witness to the violent clash of two religious camps. The Reformation had found its bridgehead in the nearby Czech lands, but many were in favor of it in our Prussian territory too—the peasants, the townsfolk, but above all, the gentry. When the Catholics gained power, one of these local aristocrats, von Stillfried, was sentenced to the loss of his entire fiefdom and half of his inherited goods for participating in the "Czech rebellion," as it was known. A painful punishment! To save his property, he converted back to Catholicism, and as can happen in these situations, he became more papal than the pope. In his religious fervor, he began to hunt down every deviation from the true faith, every act of heresy and, above all, paganism. It was he who unleashed the persecution of heretics in this district, and although he lived in a castle in Neurode, his influence spread all the way to Waldenburg in one direction and Glatz in the other.

And so, early in the spring of 1639, this Stillfried had condemned two women to death for witchcraft, after several days' torture—Eva Bernhard and Anna Tieff. Yes, Frommer had memorized these names, and now served them up with a note of satisfaction, as if to say he was a serious, though amateur historian. Eva was interrogated in April, mainly about witches' sabbaths on Homole, a peak on the Czech side. Eva named all the women she knew in the entire district, as well as those she knew only by sight or by hearsay, from the Czech side too— Barbara Brands from Kostenthal and Dorota Meisner from Braunau, as well as women from Nieder Wüstergiersdorf and Görbersdorf.

Eva was beheaded and burned in Neurode, while Anna did not live to see the pyre—she died in prison of the wounds suffered during torture.

It seems the judges scented blood like hunting dogs, and now they thought every woman was mixed up in witchcraft. And looking at the mountains and the forest, at the moss and the stones—and especially climbing Homole and seeing that enormous hole in the earth, out of which the devil himself emerged at their sabbaths—made it clear that these places incited women, who were after all born with a moral handicap, to abort their fetuses here, to make venomous potions and cast spells on the innocent. Now the women felt the scrutiny of priests, judges and their assistants. Even a neighbor was an enemy. A brother or a husband might be too.

In summer, such terror gripped the villages on both sides of the border that the women abandoned their families and duties and fled into the mountains, as if the sound of the devil's flute had enchanted them.

"The villages were empty, the cows went unmilked, children wept with hunger, kitchen gardens were choked with weeds, clothing was frayed and full of holes"—as if in a trance, Frommer listed these degrees of the world's collapse—"ovens were cold, provisions rotted, cats and dogs went feral, sheep were overgrown with wool. In Braunau on the Czech side too, Dorota and Barbara were taken away and tortured: they were stretched on a rack and tormented with fire and brimstone. The townsfolk quailed at the sound of their screams coming from the municipal dungeons, until finally, unable to bear it, the town of Braunau made an official plea to Prague. They asked if the torture had to continue, and whether the husbands of the accused should not bear the costs of the trial (two Reichsthalers), because Braunau was a poor town, and the aforementioned husbands happened to be wealthy. Who was to pay for it all? In reply, the appeals court in Prague ruled that the torture should stop and the women should be released, and that they should not be burdened with the costs of the trial. The women were freed, but the court in Prague would not agree to restore their good names. They died in disgrace. Unfortunately, Neurode did not defend its witches," Frommer ended his account, as if in sorrow.

"A fine tale," said Herr August. "And it shows the power of common sense and the market."

"Apparently a good many of the runaways never returned," added Frommer.

Wojnicz walked quietly, glancing anxiously at Thilo, and listening to

Frommer with an attention that now and then was distracted by noises from the forest: rustling, the distant cry of a bird, the creaking of tall beech trees. Or the movement of an animal seen only from the corner of his eye, or wisps of fur torn from a body by a protruding branch. Or simply the great panorama of mountains that briefly shone through the tall trees, and then vanished as they descended and the forest grew thicker.

This story gave rise to a conversation about atavism. Panting and occasionally stopping, the gentlemen carried on a debate without in fact quarreling at all, but tossing in arguments on behalf of the same attitude. Being closer to nature and its rhythms in comparison with man, who is more civilized, woman represents a kind of atavism, stated Lukas with great self-confidence, adding emphasis by stressing each syllable of the word: *a-ta-vi-sm*. Opitz said that although he didn't fully understand what *atavism* meant, he was sure that woman was often a social parasite; yet, appropriately controlled, she was able to work on behalf of society—as a mother, for instance.

"Whether we like it or not, motherhood is the one and only thing that justifies the existence of this troublesome sex," he concluded, and they all understood that this was his way of trying to cope with the death of Frau Opitz, since, after all, she had not had any children.

Finally, as ever, Thilo spoiled the fun, by offering a curious hypothesis, apparently from France, that the *Mona Lisa* does not depict a woman but a feminized friend of Leonardo's, as it was widely known that the artist preferred the companionship of men to that of women. This theory prompted a pitiful smirk from Lukas and the mute satisfaction of Herr August. Next Lukas, clearly tired, returned to his main theme, voicing a scathing criticism of modern art that ended: "All that's good in art is whatever those cretinous maniacs obsessed with locomotives, propellers and all that futurism of theirs have not yet attempted."

He pronounced the word *futurism* with the utmost contempt.

By now they were walking at an even pace along a flat woodland road. At this time of year, the beech forest on either side of it was idyllic, the dark red leaves forming claret-colored vaults overhead. Yellow and orange splashes of birch and maple intensified the autumn carnival of colors, especially against the turquoise and golden backdrop created by the rays of the sun and the blue of the early October sky.

"I've seen all this before in the spring," said Thilo, and sighed. "We came here then too."

He and Wojnicz were at the back of the procession. A few dozen meters ahead of them walked Lukas and August. The latter was gesticulating, so perhaps they had returned to one of those topics on which they could never agree.

"I was much stronger then, I was only planning to stay until summer . . ."

Then the road became steeper again, making it hard to talk. Wojnicz was delighted by the pillows of dark green moss on either side of it and the slippery yellow caps of the larch bolete mushrooms. He could not stop himself from gathering some in his hat.

When at last they reached their destination, he felt a bit disappointed. He had been expecting something more spectacular, but Opitz proudly showed them some holes in the ground, overgrown with moss and blueberry bushes. Raimund spread out the rugs and poured lemonade into tin mugs, serving with it some small buttered rolls.

"The locals call these holes 'witches' mouths,'" said Opitz, but then, squinting comically, added that in fact they should be called witches' arseholes, because at times of extreme heat or extreme cold, whistling air came out of them.

The only one to laugh was Lukas.

"Science tells us something quite different," replied Frommer, who had dressed very smartly for the outing, exchanging his stiff white collar for a black silk neckerchief (he looked like the clerk at a funeral home). "The difference in temperature between the depths and the surface causes air to move, and to whistle and hiss as it emerges from the holes."

Wojnicz lay on his belly and peeped inside, but he couldn't hear anything; the air was at a standstill, damp, autumnal and full of the scents of the forest. He pushed a hand into the fleshy moss, as deep as he could, and felt a moist chill on his fingertips, as in the cellar where Józef used to send him for potatoes and sauerkraut. His father had devised these "Red Indian" tasks, for which the little Wojnicz received badges. Going down into the cellar meant having to conquer a sudden attack of fear and disgust that made his fingers tremble as they lit the candles. The cellar was L-shaped, leading first to the left, then the right. The potatoes lay in the darkest, dampest corner, fenced off behind some boards, in a heap that dwindled by the day and in spring sprouted white shoots, desperately seeking the light. Beside them stood barrels full of cabbage and gherkins.

Once he saw a large toad in there, sitting motionless on top of the potatoes, staring at him with its bulging yellow eyes. He screamed and raced upstairs, but despite his pleading and tears, his father told him to go back down. Luckily the toad was not there anymore. But afterward, every time he went into the cellar, he inevitably had it in mind; even now, whenever he thought about it, it was there, and would remain there forever. The idea of killing it, as he at first imagined, by taking a large stone down with him from the sunlit world and throwing it at its soft, warty body, gave him a strange thrill that made his pulse run faster. But he was afraid that the consequences of this murder would be even more terrible. Crushed by a stone, the toad would contaminate the potatoes, and he would never be able to forget about it. From then on, whenever he put his hands into the barrel of gherkins, he was afraid that by some miracle it had got in there, and he would accidentally take hold of it, lurking among the pickles, as if it had the power to change into anything damp and slimy. Yes, it was a great school of courage— he had earned those badges the hard way. So now it was nothing for him to put his hand into the Windlöcher, to explore the moss with his fingers and smell the fragrant breath of the earth's interior.

Thilo lay down beside him and adopted the same position: they both stared into the dark hole that led into the depths.

"Hey, hey!" Thilo called down into it, probably expecting an echo, but the hole was too narrow, too moss-coated, for his voice to bounce off the walls of the abyss.

And behind them a bottle of Opitz's liqueur, the miraculous Schwärmerei, was already being passed around, to fortify them, to raise their spirits in this great treacherous world, where lethal microscopic creatures attacked their innocent lungs, intent on killing them. To hell with Koch's bacilli! They raised a small toast and tucked into the treats from Raimund's basket.

Wojnicz saw that Thilo had fallen asleep. He was lying on his side with his eyes closed, breathing evenly, and his anxious face had brightened.

So Wojnicz joined the men reclining on the rugs, holding mugs full of Schwärmerei as they discussed tales about witches. The Grizzled Lion claimed that the first mention of witches was by Apuleius in *The Golden Ass*, but Herr August insisted that Aristophanes had already described them in *The Frogs*.

"*Batrakhoi*," he said, showing off his Greek. "It means frogs. With the stress on the last syllable. There's a conversation between Dionysus and Xanthias, when after crossing Lake Acheron they find themselves in the wilderness and see something strange."

Wojnicz looked at him with sudden curiosity. Removing his rather shabby woolen frock coat, Herr August stood up, moved his lips for a while, as if repeating an old lesson to himself, and began to recite. He did it superbly, altering his voice to adopt a different tone for each participant in the dialogue:

XANTHIAS: By Zeus, I can hear a noise.

DIONYSUS: Where? Where's it coming from?

Herr August put a hand to his ear.

XANTHIAS: Right behind you!

At this point, hopping comically, Herr August changed position, to express the confusion of his characters, and carried on:

DIONYSUS: So get behind me!

XANTHIAS: No, now it's gone ahead.

DIONYSUS: So get ahead of me!

Suddenly Herr August's face changed. His mouth twisted into a grimace of terror, his eyes became round and his cheeks began to quiver.

XANTHIAS: Aargh, I can see a gigantic monster!

DIONYSUS: What's it like?

XANTHIAS: Terrifying. And it keeps changing: It's a bull, no, it's a mule, and now it's a woman. And what a beauty!

DIONYSUS: Where is she? Let me at her!

XANTHIAS: The woman's gone, she's changed into a dog.

DIONYSUS: So it's Empusa!

XANTHIAS: Her whole face is one great ball of fire!

DIONYSUS: Does she have a leg of bronze?

XANTHIAS: By Poseidon, the other one's made of cow dung, I'm sure of it!

DIONYSUS: Where can I run to?

XANTHIAS: And where can I?

Herr August fell silent and bowed modestly, to make it known that this was the end of his spontaneous performance. To Wojnicz, the blush on his face made this small, reddish man look fine and handsome.

"And what happened next, Herr August?" asked Opitz, intrigued.

"Oh, I can't remember any more, I have a poor memory," said Herr August coyly; meanwhile, the awoken Thilo began to clap. Who would have thought Herr August was such a good actor? The Grizzled Lion would no longer have any advantage in this field. But he too was laughing and clapping with a look of magnanimity on his face, as if he had given his assent for this performance.

Flushed and happy, Herr August knew that he had won their hearts, at least for now, during this little trip into the mountains. At least here he had triumphed and to some extent dissipated all the digs and humiliations that he had had to bear because of his, er, diminutive stature and mental constitution (for we would not call this an affliction). He explained that it was just a translation, and that once he could have recited the same thing in the original Greek, but he had stopped reading Greek long ago and would get certain expressions wrong now.

"You're too modest," said Wojnicz, showing his appreciation for Herr August's little drama, which had made a huge impression on him.

Wojnicz would have liked to recite something himself, but all that occurred to him was *"Lithuania! My homeland!"* He had studied Greek at school, but the teacher used to hit them with a ruler across the hands, so now he associated the language with a sudden, burning pain that, though short-lived, pierced to the bone. That was how the poetry of Homer had been recorded in his flesh. He sought something interesting from his beloved Latin, but the only thing to come to mind was Cicero's grandiloquent speeches. He wished he had had a teacher like Herr August. As he reflected on his education, a sip of bittersweet Schwärmerei awoke the memories.

Their flat on Pańska Street in Lwów was cozy and sunny. The drawing room and dining room windows overlooked the street, quite a noisy one, because the cobblestones paving it changed every movement into a rumble, a drumroll. But after a few years, one's brain grew so accustomed to the noise that his father thought of their abode as quiet. Mieczyś was enrolled at a German-language gymnasium located on Governor's Ramparts. Twice a day he walked the route from home to school and back, passing the Bernardine monastery, and then looking at the shop displays on Cłowa Street and Czarnecki Street. Then he went past the fire station, feeling decidedly greater respect for this institution than for the monastery. Several times he was witness to the firemen mustering to sally forth, whether as an exercise or to attend a real fire, and the coordination of these agile men in uniform always delighted him. The terse commands, shouts and gestures reminded him of dances he had seen in the countryside, with foot-stamping and bizarre figures performed by human bodies. Here the firemen danced for a purpose, to respond to a blaze, to combat destruction, or even death. Their well-practiced movements were measured to perfection, faultlessly effective. Whatever move some of them started, others finished.

They passed each other hoses and buckets, they reported, leaped up and down, one-two-three, and the fire engine was ready for the road, ready to fight the element, while they sat motionless on their seats like lead soldiers. Then one of them set off the siren, which drew the whole world into the orbit of their service. Little Mieczyś was so awed that goose bumps appeared on his skin. In just two minutes, the fire engine was prepared for battle—wrapped in hoses, equipped with pickaxes, crowbars and hatchets, and encrusted with shining brass helmets—and it moved through the open gate into the city.

He walked on through the shady old trees in the park on the Ramparts and reached the school, which towered over the city, elevated, like the Dormition Church with its three cupolas standing opposite. In this church—he sometimes looked in there—was a painted angel that made him especially joyful. He called it the "Four-Fingered Angel," ignoring the name *Gabriel* that was written next to it, because the way the artist had depicted its hand, extended in a gesture of blessing, made it look as if it were missing a thumb, and the ring finger was slightly too short as well. Little Mieczyś felt a sort of strange relief as he gazed at this imperfection in perfection. Thanks to this minor flaw, the angel seemed closer to him, not to say human. Captured in motion, standing firmly on the ground in a green, shimmering robe (yes, there were spots of light on it), with one wing visible—not made of feathers, like a goose's wing, but as if woven from hundreds of tiny beads, and lined in red—an angel holding a reed. It looked busy, somehow preoccupied. Angels were described as "he," but it seemed obvious that the Four-Fingered Angel was exempt from these brutal divisions and had its own, separate place, its own angel's sex, its own divine gender.

Mieczyś was taught German by Mścisław Baum, a large, good-looking Jew with the physique of a Viking, and although in the lessons they constantly did their best to pronounce the words carefully, to speak the German of Goethe, something always pulled them toward Galicia and its singsong, slanting, Polonized and Yiddisher version of the language, in which the words seemed slightly flattened, like old slippers—one could feel safe and at home in it.

Wojnicz's class could easily be divided into four groups: Poles, Jews, Ukrainians and a mixed crowd including several Austrians, one Romanian, two Hungarians and three Transylvanian Germans. Mieczyś instinctively kept to the sidelines, as if he did not belong to any of these groups, and ethnicity was not enough for him to define his place in the jigsaw puzzles they were always making, changing the vectors of strength, dependence and advantage. The other children seemed to him too noisy, and he was afraid he might get into conflicts. He could not bear violence, all that rivalry, all the scrimmages and punches. He was friendly—perhaps that was too big a word—with a boy named Anatol, or Tolek for short, whose father, an assimilated Jew, was a well-known dentist. The boy clearly had artistic talents and a certain delicacy of manner that appealed to Mieczysław. He spoke softly and "appetizingly"; yes, it was in Tolek's company that Wojnicz had become aware of this concept. Sometimes he let Tolek rummage in his wooden pencil case. With his long fingers, Tolek would carefully arrange the pencils, touching the graphite points with a fingertip, and Mieczyś would feel a shiver of pleasure, from the skin on his head down his shoulders and back. Well, together they were a couple of outsiders. Today he could say of Anatol that he was Thilo's herald; sometimes he felt as if Anatol was the same being, but in another time and another body. A sort of angel too. Unfortunately, he did not know what had happened to Anatol after the gymnasium. They had lost touch when they finished school.

Wojnicz applied himself most to mathematics and chemistry, as his father wanted him to, and in the belief that his father knew better than he did. But he was fascinated by Latin, and if he could, he would have devoted most of his time to it. The Latin master, the tiny, rather comical Mr. Amborski, used to lend him his own books, of which Wojnicz's favorite was *The Golden Ass* by Apuleius. It was an old edition in the Bibliotheca Scriptorum Graecorum et Romanorum Teubneriana series, but it proved too difficult for a beginner to read. So the kind Mr. Amborski had found and gifted him a German translation by August Rode, and Mieczyś had come to know this version almost by heart, enjoying the text wherever he opened it. It was the only book he loved, and nothing else had ever made such a great impression on him. Somehow the picaresque tale of an unlucky man transformed into a donkey suited him personally. He felt a kinship with Lucius, though of course they differed in terms of courage, sense of humor and curiosity about the world. Lucius was the hero, but he smiled wryly from the pages of the book, ironically, contesting his own hero status, conscious of his own absurdity. Mieczyś wanted to be just like Lucius: cunning, cheeky and self-confident; he could even have acquiesced to his naivety, which proved to be a good quality that always led to unexpected places, down the alleyways of life, where one might experience a sudden or even a violent transformation. Where one might change and become unrecognizable, and yet still remain one's real self inside. Clearly there was both an outer and an inner existence. The "internal" one was dressed in the "external" one, and from then on was perceived by the world in that form. But why might the "internal" feel so uncomfortable inside the "external"? thought Mieczyś. Lucius's adventures were like dreadful torment, because the danger of never managing to return to his own shape was always hanging over him, the threat that he would die as a donkey, and that his real nature, his internal existence, would never be recognized! Mieczyś was deeply affected by this drama, though of course he did not confide in anyone. Lucius seemed less upset by his situation than the boy reader; with his roguish, ironical smirk, he stuck fast on the horizon of Mieczyś's world, as a donkey and as a person all at once, believing that one day he would find his rosebush, and his metamorphosis would occur by command of the mightiest goddess.

When Wojnicz began his studies, Lucius was pushed to the margins of his mind, forced out by angular mathematical models, by technical drawings, by X and Y, logarithms and tables. But Wojnicz had brought the old German translation of *The Golden Ass* with him to the sanatorium, and now it lay by his bed, though he had not yet had the time for reading.

His father had sent him to do technical studies in the belief that this would make a man of him, an engineer. But above all, Wojnicz senior was convinced that every citizen of this great superpower must be a useful part of it, because that was the best way to be useful to Poland too. "You are a Pole, you must never forget that, but you are also a subject of His Imperial Majesty and a part of his great project that unites nations." He did not believe that one day Poland would push through to independence. Why on earth should that happen? Only a large country was strong. Only a diverse country could survive difficult times. Were it to come into being, Poland was bound to be a weak country, and the scars from the partitions would make life a misery for many years to come.

There had been an idea to hand Mieczyś over to cadet school, and for some time this had been Uncle Emil's dream. He claimed this would help. But one evening, as the brothers were discussing this plan, their glances met and in embarrassment they stopped talking about it.

The sun had started to cast dangerously long shadows when Opitz gave the order to return, but before they set off, he planned to take their picture.

Suddenly the moment became festive. Willi Opitz set up the camera tripod that Raimund had carried, and now, chivvying each other, they scrambled to get in place for the photograph. Wojnicz stood up abruptly, which made his head spin; he wobbled and might have fallen if not for the strong arm of Lukas, who helped him to right himself.

As they stand there quietly, posing for the picture, it seems to Wojnicz as if total silence has fallen, as if his ears are blocked and his head is spinning because of the altitude they have reached. Willi Opitz bustles beside the camera, then runs up and aligns the hikers in an even row: first Herr August with Longin Lukas; then Frommer, stiff, intent and silent; then Thilo von Hahn, sweaty, with a look of satisfaction on his face; Raimund leaning against a tree with that crooked smile of his; and next to him, Wojnicz. Opitz calls out a command, races back to the camera and throws a dark sheet over his head. Suddenly everything dies down, and Wojnicz feels as if it is not Willi Opitz taking their picture, but the entire curved horizon that has become the edge of a gigantic lens. A short, unpleasant rasp rings out and a garish flash dazzles the people posing. For a split second Mieczysław notices an incredible phenomenon—the light of magnesium bounces off the spruce trees and firs and returns to them, briefly coating their bodies in ash; it is as if in this split second he has glimpsed beneath the jackets and sweaters not just their bare white skin, but also their bones, the shape of their skeletons; it feels as if they are standing on a stage, as if this is the overture to an opera, and the spectators in this theater are the trees, blueberry bushes, moss-coated stones and some fluid, ill-defined presence that is moving like streams of warmer air among the mighty trunks, boughs and branches.

6

THE PATIENTS

As they walked down the stony path, Wojnicz tried to keep close to Herr August, one pace behind him, to be able to have a talk with him—not yet knowing what it would be about—until finally he was granted the honor. Herr August slowed down enough to walk arm in arm with him, letting the Grizzled Lion go ahead. The discussion about the origins of human civilization, rather sluggish because of the difficult terrain, had tailed off, and now, despite having a delighted listener at hand, unfortunately Herr August had to concentrate on looking underfoot, because it was easy to trip and go flying. From this intermittent conversation Wojnicz learned that Herr August regarded himself as a writer.

"My father was an Austrian official, but he was born in Jassy," he divulged. "My mother was from Bukovina, but she was Austrian. Though what does that mean, when her parents had estates in Hungary and felt themselves to be Hungarian. And in my turn I am . . . it's hard to say. In terms of language, I think in German and Romanian. And in French, of course, like every European."

He regarded the fashion for nation-states as transitory, and believed it would end badly: the artificial division of people according to such feeble categories as the place where they were born did not suit the complexity of the question of identité.

"The concept of 'nation' does not speak to me at all. Our emperor, yours and mine, says that only 'peoples' exist, nations are an invention. The paradox lies in the fact that nation-states are in desperate need of other nation-states—a single nation-state has no raison d'être, the essence of their existence is confrontation and being different. Sooner or later, it will lead to war."

At this point he said something in French, but Wojnicz could not understand a word of it. Herr August liked to throw in French words, or even better, entire quotations. "The quotation is a legitimate literary genre," he would say. "And as a man of letters I practice this genre."

Oh yes, he could talk in quotations, but only his equal would be capable of deciphering them. It was the same with aphorisms. Whenever he entered a room where other people were already present, an aura of generalization always came with him—everything suddenly became relative, suspended, in rough outline, nothing certain, because Herr August was capable of presenting an issue in such a way that his listener ended up taking the position opposite to the one with which he had arrived. Herr August was convinced that this was wisdom.

He never appeared without a foulard, and he had several of them, in various color combinations, suitable for any season, any weather and any attire. His favorite color was snuff, and he was most often seen in a jacket of this shade, with which he wore a dark green foulard, the color of a bottle of Schwärmerei. To complete the outfit he wore brown trousers, leather shoes and a gold watch on a chain, which stuck out of the pocket of his chocolate-brown waistcoat.

He seemed to be creeping, dragging his feet as he made his way along the promenade, as if he were encountering unexpected air resistance. This is how people walk who, despite an innate lack of self-confidence, through hard work have built themselves a solid belief in their own uniqueness and value.

"My dear Mieczysław," he said, pronouncing the name softly and with difficulty, like a child, "do you agree with me that mankind exists only in language? Everything except language is bestial and indiscriminate. It is thanks to language that we are who we are. That is why I labor over every sentence; every word must have its proper place. My hobby is studying phraseological connections and a critical attitude toward them, because each of these connections is like a thickening of the muscles, like a dough that must be kneaded for the organism of our soul to be flexible and to work efficiently." And he actually showed Wojnicz a pocket-size book bound in navy blue canvas: *A Phraseological Dictionary of the German Language.*

Wojnicz also learned that August had been in Görbersdorf since the previous Christmas. He had come for the winter holidays, intending to purify his lungs and go back to work in Vienna. But during a routine examination, Dr. Semperweiss had identified a worrying spot in his left lung, so Herr August had written to ask for leave and prolonged his stay.

"So have you met them all?" asked Wojnicz, endeavoring to prompt his interlocutor to tell him stories about the Kurhaus patients, perhaps even some gossip. In fact he was interested in one person only, but nothing could have induced him to admit it.

"Many of the patients are communists, not just the Russians," Herr August volunteered. "It's an old tradition, dating back to the days of

Dr. Brehmer, who had a weakness for all manner of revolutionaries. He traveled to London to attend seminars given by Karl Marx—I wonder if the name means anything to you, my dear Mieczysław? Curious, isn't it? Brehmer himself built a large empire, not without financial difficulties and debts, but eventually it brought him some profit. We might look at it as quite a paradox that he fraternized with those subversives who advocated common ownership. Ha!"

Wojnicz did not know what to say; he had no opinion on the matter of common ownership, and he had not heard much about Marx.

He learned more about Hermann Brehmer, the founder of the sanatorium, who, he understood, had almost divine status here. He had been born somewhere in the countryside outside Breslau, the city where he had first studied natural history. "Like most Breslauers, he went away to Berlin, where he was overcome by the 'revolutionary spirit' and became such a zealous advocate of 'democracy' that his behavior prompted public outrage and got him barred from taking his exams in Breslau. So he remained in Berlin, continued his studies there, and just like Marx, dreamed of going to England, which he succeeded in doing. Though only for a short time. He came to know Marx in person and attended his private lectures. But then"—at this point Herr August folded his hands as if in prayer, as he always did when he wanted to draw special attention to what he was saying—"he was hired by the British government as a botanist in the British colonies and was all ready to embark when, the night before the voyage, his unbridled curiosity drove him to attend a talk by a physiologist he found so fascinating that he dropped both Marx and the colonies, and became a doctor. Isn't that a splendid biography?"

Wojnicz expressed his admiration. Portraits of Brehmer, bearded and serious, hung everywhere here; he was venerated.

"You see," Herr August continued, "it wasn't easy for him to return to his studies after that flirtation with the communists. But his well-connected sister-in-law persuaded Humboldt himself to give him patronage"—here again he folded his hands and repeated—"Humboldt, so that young Hermann Brehmer could go back to university, for which he later named a pavilion after that great scholar. Now do you understand?"

Yes, yes, Wojnicz had been listening so attentively to Herr August's account that now and then he slipped on the pebbles.

"As you look at me with those big blue eyes of yours, it makes me wonder if I haven't been unduly occupied by questions of politics and economics," said Herr August, stopping and gazing at Wojnicz for some time. "In fact, they're worth no more attention than today's supper."

They had to wait for a while because Frommer was far behind, and Herr August needed to catch his breath too.

"You see, young man, the tradition of treating communists for free is still in place to this day, even though the views of Dr. Semperweiss

and the sanatorium management have nothing to do with communism. Though several of those slovenly Russians contracted lung disease in Siberia, exiled there for their political views." Now Herr August lowered his voice and spoke straight into Wojnicz's ear. "A friend of our Thilo, a communist in fact, also has good connections here, and the sanatorium is treating our boy for free. He only pays for the guesthouse. Actually it's not he who covers the cost, but that friend of his from Berlin. A philosopher," he said, folding his hands again, which made it look as if he were praying to the very word *philosopher.*

Wojnicz noticed that Herr August's voice had become different somehow, throaty, and the silence that fell was bound to end in hawking.

Once August had finally coughed for a while, expectorating into his handkerchief, and cleared his throat, Mieczysław learned that young Thilo did not have much time left, and that the knowledge that death was imminent was making him very "neurotic." It was not the first time Wojnicz had heard this new, fashionable word from August's lips.

The news came as a shock to him. Just then Opitz came running up, his cheeks flushed.

"You see, I don't neglect my duty as proprietor of the Guesthouse for Gentlemen," he said, breathing heavily from effort. "Whatever happens, I do my best to fulfill my obligations and not be carried away by emotion. A man must be above all these feelings, above mawkish desperation and tears. Women revel in such things."

Wojnicz cast him a fleeting glance and instantly averted his gaze; he was reminded of the chair in the loft.

"I deeply sympathize."

"Don't feel sorry for me, Herr Wojnicz. I brought it on myself. Why on earth did I have to get married at all?"

Opitz patted him on the arm in a friendly way and they moved on together. He said he had had four wives. One had left him without a word and gone back to her mother. The second had died in childbirth, along with the baby. The third had fallen sick. He said this perfunctorily, and added nothing more. Not wanting to seem importunate, Wojnicz did not ask what else had happened to her. The fourth wife was the latest. Opitz had never understood them, nor had he really wanted to. He had not felt right with any of them. At the start they had always fought over who would be in charge, but he would not let himself be ruled over. Either they were weak and whining or they tried to take control of the relationship and manipulate him. One thing was for sure—each of them had nearly sucked the life out of him, he had had to pay for every single one with his vital energy. He said this with a surprising bitterness. They had all sponged off him, used their tricks to soften him up and put him off his guard.

"No, I shall never marry again," he said more loudly, striking his chest. "I can have the same thing by hiring a maid, one of those poor country girls from the local villages in search of a job. Or . . ." At this point Opitz paused and looked at Wojnicz. He wasn't winking, but Wojnicz felt as if Opitz were *restraining* a wink, that he would gladly have winked. Oh yes, he was convinced that Opitz was hiding something.

Wojnicz was not quite sure what to make of this, so he kept quiet.

"Unfortunately those girls are bad cooks," added Opitz once they had reached the main trail, which was far more comfortable.

Opitz took every opportunity to repeat that he was Swiss. His mother had been Swiss, but he never mentioned his father, as if passing over half of his heritage, and as if it went without saying that it was his mother who had given him his national identity. Being Swiss sounded grand, especially as the Swiss mother's brother had served in the papal guard—Opitz had a framed photograph of him on the piano, but it was blurred, and what caught the eye was not the uncle himself but his bizarre costume and remarkable headgear.

It was hard to know how to respond to these repeated assertions of Swiss origin, especially as Wojnicz had no opinion about the Swiss, but there was distinct pride in Opitz's voice as he made them: by this token he was above them all, in some way he was racially—a word that kept ever more boldly appearing in their conversations—superior. His continued claim to be Swiss frustrated poor Herr August, who was not just an internationalist but was not sure exactly who he was by ethnicity, as though such matters were not of the slightest interest to him.

Now Longin Lukas had intercepted Wojnicz. He caught the young man by the elbow and held it for a while in an iron grip, then at last informed him in a military tone in which, as usual, there appeared a note of grievance addressed to no one:

"Common sense and rationalism. Everything that's evil is derived from made-up notions and ideologies. There's no need to superimpose anything upon the world—the world is as we see it. It is as it is. There are certain laws that can be described. Their number is finite. Some we do not yet know. God exists and created the world. People are villainous by nature, so they have to be controlled and constantly taught. The rich are rich because they are capable and have good connections. It was always so, and so it will always be. Freedom and democracy are all very well, but within limits. The Ten Commandments are the standard for each European, whether he is a German, an Italian or a Romanian. There must be some kind of order."

One could tell that he was fond of his own voice. He held his head high, and his words were aimed not exactly at others but above them, over their heads; they flowed out in a broad wave, and whatever he said seemed solemnly confirmed by authority, beyond question, collectively recognized as a certainty. He tended to sprinkle his speech with anecdotes that began, "Once, when I was in . . ." followed by the name of a place, and that usually involved his high-ranking or famous and highly accomplished friends. He referred to his acquaintances by their first names, and it was only from context that his listeners could guess, with admiration and astonishment, that these were public figures, well-born, famous, or otherwise notable. On top of that, he had a manner of speaking that made him sound impatient, especially at having to explain the obvious to lesser mortals. This impatience made him raise his voice, just as he now did when he began to explain to Wojnicz the costs of supporting oneself at the health resort: "Are you aware, my dear friend, that the Kurhaus has a fair system? There are two branches, for first- and second-class patients. Treatment for the former, with accommodation, is from two hundred and forty to three hundred marks per month, depending on the room, of course, and for the latter from one hundred and thirty to one hundred and sixty marks. There's also a plan to create a third class for the poverty-stricken, but I don't know where they would find room for them. In the mortuary perhaps," he said, laughing at his own joke.

His bright, cold gaze and sharp features prompted respect, and his straight back and flat stomach reminded Wojnicz of the gymnastics teacher at the school he had attended in Lwów. At the same time, it was hard to rid oneself of the impression that Lukas despised others. This contempt was like a skeleton; without it he might have collapsed and dissolved like a melting snowman. But in spite of all that, Wojnicz thought he seemed weak, as if made of flimsy material that looked good from the outside but would not last.

Of course, Wojnicz had already heard about Lukas from Herr August, who was always well-informed and regarded himself as the model of discretion. He had also learned a little from Thilo, and the circumspect Frommer had put in his pennyworth too.

Lukas was from Königsberg. His father was a Russified Pole (apparently his actual name was Łukasiewicz), and his mother was half

Russian, half German. At home they spoke in Russian and German. His father had made a fortune on Siberian trade for a Polish company, as rapidly as he had then lost it, which was why Lukas regarded the Poles as weak and indecisive. The family had sunk into poverty, and after the wretched man's death his mother had returned to Tula and married a civil servant, who was wealthy and generous enough to send his stepson to college in Königsberg. Lukas described himself as a "philosopher," but Frommer had told Wojnicz that in reality he was a history teacher at a boys' gymnasium. He had married young and become a widower young. He never mentioned the daughter who paid for his treatment. He lived a regular and healthy life, not counting alcohol and a weekly game of cards, at which they played for such small stakes that it could not be described as gambling. As Wojnicz learned from various conversations, Lukas lived on the ground floor, in a glass-walled annex with a separate entrance. As a result, his status was a little higher, and certainly a bit distinct. The separate entrance guaranteed him a sort of freedom that the others could only envy. Even though his quarters merely gave on to a rather unattractive courtyard that offered no special view, just a wooded hillside, the Grizzled Lion celebrated his privilege. Every night after supper he sighed and tossed above the heads of the others, "Ah well, time to go *home*."

"Is it not true that a person can be best defined by his bad habits?" Wojnicz's father would say. Mieczysław could almost hear his voice in his head as he looked at Lukas, talking glibly.

Yes, Longin Lukas could have been a glaring example of this: he was overfond of alcohol and women. Apparently he had been expelled from the Kurhaus because of the latter, as he had brought them into his room (it was Raimund who told Wojnicz this story), and so he had to be content with the Guesthouse for Gentlemen, though he was still privileged thanks to the aforementioned separate entrance to his exceptional room. He consumed alcohol in the form of beer, and as Wojnicz understood it, he had a special medical dispensation, or rather he thought he had one. Raimund brought him the beer in dark bottles sealed with porcelain stoppers. Strong and heavy, it came from the Waldenburg brewery. And of course he drank Schwärmerei. After all, Dr. Brehmer's treatment regarded a certain amount of alcohol as medicinal. Weakness was cured with champagne, and insomnia with brandy and milk at bedtime. Lukas took these principles to heart. He drank every day, from noon on. In the morning he could be seen sober, but irritated. In the early afternoon it was plain to see that he was relaxing, a look of contentment appearing on his face. In the evenings at supper he was tipsy, chatty and eager for debate, in which he took a decided position. Whatever it was about.

The amount of alcohol he consumed was having an effect on his figure, which no doubt he regarded as athletic; it was erasing the sharp lines, so it could be said that Longin Lukas was becoming increasingly blurred against the backdrop of the world, and though his face must once have been beautiful, bags and a slight puffiness had appeared beneath his eyes. He shaved carefully, but there were days when he was not up to this duty, and then a white stubble instantly aged him by ten years. But despite all, he was still handsome.

He had a habit of interrupting his interlocutors. It was a sign of impatience toward others, which was fundamentally the driving force of his existence. He was impatient because everything fell short of his imagination and expectations, as if what he thought about the world came from other, higher realms of the spirit. Moreover, since his youth he had been sure he was unique, but somehow the world was unable to accept the fact.

Everything about him said: *I already know, I have long since known what you want to say.* Over the years, this was joined by the feeling that he had experienced more than others—this fact gave him great satisfaction, but also locked him inside himself, for it confirmed his belief that it was a waste of time to enter into interaction with others, as they would not understand any of what he said, and he would not learn anything interesting from them. So he remained in the highly superior conviction that he was a thoroughly tragic creature.

Before the funeral he had accosted Wojnicz in a surprising way.

"Your female compatriots are famous for their beauty," he had said. "It must be a question of miscegenation, as there's the highest probability that hybrids will produce both the greatest beauties and the vilest creatures."

Wojnicz was confused, unsure whether to regard this remark as a compliment or a reprimand.

On another occasion Lukas asked him: "Where did you acquire such perfect German? The people who live in Galicia are nothing but illiterate peasants."

And yet Wojnicz liked him. Lukas's condescension seemed purely paternal. He had no intention of fighting it and was happy to submit. This evidently flattered Lukas, and maybe that was why he sought opportunities to be in Mieczysław's vicinity and to lecture him on the world's mysteries, always in the same specific way—with a mixture of contempt and grievance.

They were approaching the end of the expedition. Their carriage was already waiting for them on the road below. Everyone stopped to take in the wonderful view for one last time before plunging into the valley. And as the horizon was high, they saw the mountainsides covered in patches of golden light, aflame with the reds and yellows of beech trees against the deep green of the spruces, with spots of white here and there that, to Wojnicz's amazement, turned out to be flocks of sheep—with the speedy dots of sheepdogs and the black commas of shepherds buzzing around them.

Here we are watching them, as usual from below, we see them like big, strong columns topped by small, chattering projections—their heads. Their feet mechanically crush the forest litter, snap the small plants, tear up the moss, and squash the tiny bodies of insects that have failed to heed the vibrations heralding imminent annihilation. For a short while after they pass, beneath the forest floor the mushroom spawn quivers, that vast, immense, motherly structure transmits information to itself—where the intruders are, and in which direction they are bending their steps.

7

WOE, WOE IS ME!

he great edifice of the sanatorium was plainly visible from every point in Görbersdorf. Its redbrick walls shone in the autumn sun, and the sharp, pseudo-Gothic turrets reminded Wojnicz of a gramophone needle, extracting concealed sounds from the record of the sky. Somewhere far away there was thunder. The huge building looked quite absurd in this deep valley, amid the modest homes of the locals and several grand villas for visitors taking cures scattered on the hillsides, erected as if in reserve for a settlement that would arise there in the future. Its tall, narrow mass and intense color made it look like a model set up just before Wojnicz's arrival for an unknown purpose, perhaps as part of the set for a performance that was soon to begin.

He walked along the main street, still empty at this early hour, and although the weather had deteriorated a little over the past few days, he strode briskly, with a smile on his face, because some men loading sacks into a cart were also smiling broadly at him. The town was so

neat and pretty that it reminded him of the drawing on a tin of gingerbread his uncle had once given him—lovely, shapely houses with lace
curtains in the windows and beautiful door handles; outside they had
little fences, flowers and signs, all spruce and clean, everything the
perfect size for a human being—the best illustration of that word a
Pole found difficult: *gemütlich*. Several of the houses had been built
with the patients in mind, so they boasted ornate balconies, bay windows and terraces, some in the Swiss style, with beautifully decorated
wooden porches and verandas. He was fascinated by the Kurhaus
buildings scattered about the park. The oldest, called the Weisses Haus,
had twenty rooms and was the first building in the naturopathic foundation established by Dr. Brehmer's sister-in-law, who had unsuccess-
fully tried to practice hydrotherapy here in the mid-nineteenth century.
Dr. Brehmer had taken it over from her as a young man, and had suc-
cessfully cured several of his first patients there. Walter Frommer had
soberly filled in Wojnicz's knowledge of Görbersdorf, and it was he
who confirmed August's revelation that Brehmer had tried to get a
state concession to expand the foundation, but was refused it because of
his communist past. Nearer the street stood the large Altes Kurhaus,
opened in 1863, with forty rooms. The Neues Kurhaus, which was built
later, accommodated patients from all over the world in its seventy
rooms, and the basement of the north wing housed an inhalatorium
and showers for therapeutic bathing in winter. The two buildings were
neatly connected by a glassed-in passage, where a winter garden and a
reading room had been established. As Wojnicz determined, the reading room stocked a wide range of periodicals in German. The one that
interested him most was *Kladderadatsch*, an illustrated satirical weekly,
which included lots of amusing cartoons; reading the jokes improved
his mood for the entire day, though he could not understand all of
them. He did not pick up the dailies, *Kölnische Zeitung* and *Frankfurter*

Zeitung—these were read by the middle-aged gentlemen, who then discussed the more important articles over coffee. Wojnicz was too young to take a real interest in politics. What was happening inside him seemed far more intense than the world's most dramatic political events. For the Poles there was *Time*, read to destruction, on top of which one of the patients had the dreadful habit of underlining entire sentences in pencil, after which the newspaper was not really fit for use. Among the books in Polish he found several by Kraszewski, and *The Heathen* by someone called Narcyza Żmichowska—this he had instantly appropriated, but a few days later he put it back on the shelf; he could not read novels. He was simply unable to concentrate on something so unreal. Anyone who donated a book to the sanatorium library wrote their first and last name on the title page. *The Heathen* had belonged to one Franciszka Ulanicka, and the Kraszewskis to Antoni Bolcewicz.

The books were lent out by a young man, not much more than a boy, named Tomášek—the same boy who had gazed at him so intently during the funeral mass. Thanks to his thick-lensed glasses he could have passed as a bookworm, and perhaps that was why he had been assigned to the library. He came from the Czech lands and was apparently a cousin of Sydonia Patek. For some reason, every time Wojnicz came for books, this dim-witted librarian stared at him insistently, and once, through his own woolgathering and inattention he had overturned a shelf full of newspapers. Wojnicz found this very unpleasant, and did his best to avoid the fellow. He would wait until Tomášek was occupied with something else, and then exchange his books and journals himself, writing down the titles on a sheet of paper.

One time Tomášek came up to him while he was examining the portraits of a dozen or more writers that decorated the walls of the sanatorium library. Most of them had beards, and they all looked very dignified. Tomášek stood to one side, slightly behind him. Then a strange thing happened that put Wojnicz off this alarming figure even more. The boy began to talk in a whisper, with a Czech accent, while also sighing and dragging out the sounds, so that Wojnicz was not quite sure if he had understood him properly.

"These old men are always waylaying the young ones," he said, and Wojnicz could not tell if he meant the esteemed authors whose portraits were hanging on the wall, or the men at the Kurhaus, or perhaps old men in general. "They bewilder us, they tell us to do things that aren't good. They turn us against each other, they get us into awkward situations so that later it's hard to back out with honor. I'm sure you know what I'm talking about . . . They tell us to be devoted, they expect total sacrifice, they force us to swear oaths. They're old, so they've had plenty of time to work it all out in their minds, but we are weaker, it's harder for us to debate, we don't have as many arguments to offer as they do. What's more, they don't lack money. We think to ourselves, 'One day I shall be just as they are, with power and money. And then I shall reward myself for everything.'"

Wojnicz turned to him with raised eyebrows. The boy was red with excitement, and there were beads of sweat on his still-childish nose.

"Don't say I haven't warned you," he said, and disappeared among the bookcases.

At the Villa Rosa, to which Wojnicz had taken a special liking during his walks, there were rooms for the patients who were only mildly unwell. This seemed to be where the woman in the hat lived. Above the villa there was a shrine in honor of Humboldt, with a bust of him; during Brehmer's lifetime, summer concerts had been held at a small band shell near this shrine. Wojnicz liked the fact that in addition to these fine, lavish buildings for the wealthier patients, Görbersdorf also had the Volksheilstatten-Abteilung, meaning the therapeutic department for the masses—lodging for the worse-off patients, at a distance from the main grounds, scattered about the village in private houses. And if he were not waiting for a vacancy in the main Kurhaus, he could have been among them.

It all reminded him to some extent of Truskawiec, where he had once been with his father to take the waters, except that it was larger and more solid. On the short promenade leading to the sanatorium he would examine the patients—bright hats, parasols, suits that fell somewhere between everyday outfits and Sunday best; perhaps that was the fashion at the sanatorium. And the people moved in sanatorium mode too, slower than the slowest walk at home in Lwów, because by walking any faster they would instantly cover the length and breadth of this village and would have to walk the same route several times. So every few paces they stopped to chat and shoot glances at their fellow patients, and thus not a single detail of the costumes escaped them, not a single new face could remain unobserved. Every novelty of couture, every gesture, every hairstyle was bound to be noticed and duly remarked upon.

The Russians decidedly kept apart, and were distinguished by their exaggeratedly festive attire. Some had brought their whole families along, for a shorter or longer stay, but in those instances they stayed in villas on the side of Buchberg, a densely wooded mountain, and led the life of healthy people. One also saw Scandinavians, tall, pale and gloomy. Several times Wojnicz heard the Polish language, but he did not leap forward to make a connection. The Poles went about in small groups, and were either unnaturally quiet or excessively noisy.

In the colorful, relaxed crowd, among whom nobody would suspect illness, Wojnicz found himself seeking out the tall figure of the woman from the church. He supposed that perhaps she walked more often in the other direction, toward the little Orthodox church, which he already had an appointment to visit with Herr August. By now he could recognize her step—a little swinging, not at all refined. It was the walk of a busy person who was lost in thought, focusing on her own goals. And she always kept a hand in her jacket pocket.

Whenever he saw her, he was struck dumb, and a gentle blush rose to his cheeks—he did his best to hide it by pretending to feel cold, and then covering his mouth with his scarf, but he could already sense the attentive gaze of Lukas or the slightly ironical glance of Herr August. He knew that his confusion would become a topic for comment and allusion in their evening debates. Once he had vanished to his room, they were sure to thrash out the question of his blushing for some time. But whatever they had been talking about earlier, later on it was bound to come down to the same thing—women. Once called forth by the absurd death of Frau Opitz, the subject kept returning, and her lifeless figure continued to disturb them. Wojnicz had noticed that every discussion, whether about democracy, the fifth dimension, the role of religion, socialism, Europe, or modern art, eventually led to women.

Wojnicz found the rest-cure hours deadly boring until he learned to make use of them as time for himself, conducive to thinking. He had noticed that when one participates intensively in life, one has no time for thinking or examining everything precisely, if only in one's imagination. So for the first few days he always lay down beside Thilo, knowing that Thilo would immediately doze off, or even snore gently. Then Wojnicz set to work, transforming his impressions into experience and constructing meaning for everything surrounding him. He never managed to finish reading a single page, though it should have been easy. But he was overcome by a strange sense of peace, in which thoughts flowed through his mind freely, emerging from who knows where and departing to who knows where, to be replaced by others. It was definitely not a state of sleep, but nor was it ordinary waking consciousness. It was as though in between these two conditions some unappreciated layers of thought existed that one could not actually control, but that one could set in motion, providing one then allowed them to follow their own paths. If Wojnicz had been familiar with the practice of self-reflection and introspection, which at their next meeting Dr. Semperweiss recommended to him, he might certainly have noticed how thoughts arise and what they are like—they are wisps of sensations carried by time like gossamer, moved by the wind, trails of tiny reactions that arrange themselves into random sequences eager for meaning. But their nature is volatile and impermanent, they appear and disappear, leaving behind an impression that something really did happen and that we took part in it. And that what we are stuck inside is stable and certain. That it exists.

In this state some individual words came back to him like an echo; taken out of context, some sentences resounded. His mind wandered to Lwów, and to the manor house in Glinna where he had spent his early childhood, as his horizontal position adopted unnaturally in the middle of the day revealed to him forgotten details of his brief life. For example, he remembered that whenever his uncle Emil was due to arrive in Lwów, special preparations were made. Józef would run to the shops and always returned with a duck in a basket, while a boy from the market helped him to bring in the vegetables and apples—apples were a must.

At the time, January Wojnicz's younger brother, Emil, was already a cavalry officer in the Austrian army, a tall, handsome, fair-haired young man with a perfect figure and impeccable manners. He wore a flaxen mustache, which gave his youthful, delicate features gravity and manliness. His blue-gray jacket beautifully hugged his slender torso and lent his skin a refined pallor. But the finest thing of all—as Mieczyś saw it—were the red breeches tucked into knee-high, wonderfully polished boots. Emil would arrive, click his heels and immediately light a cigar, in which the boy's father kept him company. Mieczyś would receive from his uncle a box of cakes from the patisserie and some military trinket or other: cartridge cases, a penknife or a mess tin. Then he would have to answer his uncle's questions, which, as he had learned it all inside out, he did convincingly and with great self-confidence:

"A cavalry division consists of two brigades with two regiments each."

Or: "A cavalry regiment includes six troops."

He also had to add that each division had under it a special horse artillery division and four machine-gun sub-units. It was from the cartridges for these guns that the cases came, though Mieczyś was not quite sure what to do with them. He simply carried them in his pocket and felt their pleasant weight.

The day before his uncle's arrival, as soon as he had done the shopping, Józef would go down to the cellar to cut off the duck's head, and then all afternoon, the bird hung tied to the metal trim above the tile stove, with the stump of its neck downward over a bowl, into which the blood dripped slowly, drop by drop.

Mieczyś had already learned from earlier pain and regret that on no account should he befriend the duck brought home from the market, he must not feel sorry for it, so he ignored the pitiful, sometimes most indignant quacking before it went to the slaughter, and blocked his ears to avoid witnessing its brief presence in the house.

But the bleeding, feathery shred tied to the edge of the stove filled him with despair and induced doleful, helpless weeping, which he was obliged to hide from his father, his uncle and even Józef. They would have said he was whining like a woman. The horrible sight of the dark red, almost brown blood congealing on the stump forced him into painful ambivalence—to feel afraid, while also feeling a strange, indescribable fascination close to pleasure, far mightier than picking scabs off his knees, or teasing an already wobbly milk tooth. His chest was racked by sorrow that could not change into weeping or relief of any kind, but just went on pushing from the inside, paralyzing his lungs. For there was a mysterious bond between him and the dead, headless duck as the blood dripped from it, a physical sensation, a feeling of faintness and weakness arising from total defenselessness. The horror was completed by the beauty of the feathers, sticky with blood but shimmering wonderfully in the light of the kitchen, dark blue and golden, inky and greenish, azure, sapphire—there were no names for them, but they unerringly reminded him of the wings of the Four-Fingered Angel. So the duck's death became blasphemy, an attack on the entire world.

But the worst was yet to come. Whenever with the help of Józef, the blood, vinegar, seasoning such as allspice, bay leaves, marjoram and pepper, prunes and dried cherries were used to produce czernina— duck's-blood soup—Mieczyś knew what torment lay ahead of him. A plate of this soup would be placed in front of him, as yet another test of maturity to be conducted in the presence of his uncle, the officer. But his father and Emil would not betray any awareness that this was an exceptional, very special situation. They would chat away to each other, usually about business or politics, not yet about whether Emil was planning to marry—this question would arise only over the liqueurs. Meanwhile Mieczyś would be sitting over the plate of chocolate-colored matter full of beads of fat, with his napkin under his chin, feeling tense inside, helpless against the saliva that was gathering in his mouth and that his constricted throat refused to swallow.

Then his father would cast him a fleeting glance, and, as if sentenced to torture, Mieczyś would pick up his spoon and plunge it into the dark goo. At this point Emil would be rolling his eyes, sighing that it was the best thing he had eaten in all his life. The satisfaction expressed by these compliments brightened the usually gloomy countenance of Józef, who would not depart for the kitchen, demanding more praise by his presence. Mieczyś knew that the two men's eyes were about to turn to him, so he negotiated with himself internally, explaining to himself that he must do it, that he could not disappoint his two favorite people, who wanted the best for him, and that to be a real man he must master himself, because they were serving him this dish out of *love*. Then tears would come to his eyes, and the spoon, shaking and spilling drops of soup, would rise to his mouth, which could do nothing else but open and receive this offering. He always hoped his memory of the taste of czernina from the previous occasions was wrong, and that now it would suddenly turn out to be surprisingly good. But once again something horrible filled his mouth, unlike anything, only barely tinged by the flavor of bay and marjoram, lacquered by a butter brush, but in fact disgusting and revolting. It was a taste that screamed, full of violence, steaming, pushing its way between his tongue and cheeks, sweet and sickly. His throat tightened, and he felt the urge to vomit again, but this time he was able to control it, to ignore it, so that after a moment of hesitation it retreated deep inside his body, disappearing in his intestines, and the helping of boiled animal blood flowed down into his stomach. His father and uncle pretended not to be watching him, but he knew they were testing him closely and coldly from the corners of their eyes. As he took the next spoonful, then another, his father would calm down and start to make jokes. Tears would fill the boy's eyes, but he ignored them too, making them vanish somewhere far down in his body.

"This is a traditional Polish soup. Only a simpleton won't try it. And how much brawn it gives you!" said his father jovially.

Uncle Emil smiled, and the ends of his flaxen mustache took on a dark red color.

It's simple, Mieczyś would be thinking as he swallowed his tears, which mingled with animal blood inside his puny child's body. To be a man means learning to ignore whatever causes trouble. That's the whole mystery.

On his way back from a walk one day, he had entered the Görbersdorf post office and bought several postcards, each showing a different scene, and some stamps, so now he was wondering who should receive them. The only people he could think of were his father and uncle.

For his father he chose a view of Dr. Brehmer's Neues Kurhaus. It was shown in a vanishing perspective, which further emphasized the monumental size of the building. He was sure this view would impress his father, that the sense of solidity would translate into faith in the efficacy of the therapy, and his father would be happy that he had managed to place his son in an establishment so worthy of respect. The redbrick walls and the beautiful arches of the cloisters brought to mind a medieval castle, as did the towers and the sloping roof. Yes, his father would think his child had got into a sort of Prussian paradise where all the boys finally emerged as men. He decided to send his uncle a view of the valley in which the settlement lay, smaller than a town but larger than a village. From a distance the buildings looked like a scar on the perfect architecture of nature, like a healing, granulating wound. On the first postcard the buildings looked truly triumphal, but on the second, juxtaposed with the power of the mountains, they just seemed comical.

There was not much space for correspondence on either. So Mieczysław merely wrote his greetings, that he was feeling well, that he admired the local food and was making a list of dishes from this Silesian cuisine. That he missed them, and that they were sure to see each other again soon.

Wojnicz was only interested in the Orthodox church because he had seen the woman in the hat who had had such an effect on him emerging from it; apparently she often went there.

He saw her again while out on a walk with August and Lukas.

She was strolling toward them with that swinging step of hers, her hand in her pocket, leaning on a frilly parasol. Suddenly everything came to a boil inside Wojnicz—the sight of her caused him immense, indescribable pleasure, it was stronger than the "appetizing" quality he kept feeling in Görbersdorf at the sight of the furniture, rugs and curtains, the chairs upholstered in soft leather and the great care with which all these objects had been arranged in the right places, with the patterns in order and devotion to detail. The appearance of the woman in the hat beat all that, because every item she wore, and the lady herself, summed up exactly what had always drawn and fascinated him— the integrity, the significance and harmony that until now had peeped out at him from various objects, but never as a whole, only ever in pieces.

The two gentlemen bowed to this handsome woman, and Wojnicz muttered something, but as he was not wearing a hat, he did not know what to do with his hands. As he looked at her, time slowed down, and in that split second he saw so many details, and so many wonders took possession of his soul that as she passed by he felt faint. He stopped, and forced a cough to hide his confusion, his admiration and his desperate yearning.

The church, which he visited a few days later in the company of the guesthouse residents, proved surprisingly small, the size of a chapel, and perhaps for this reason Wojnicz found it cozy (appetizing!), even though the walls were bare and wooden, with no ornamentation. He was accustomed to Orthodox churches that looked quite different— joyful places, carpeted and colorful if not gaudy, with icons covering the walls. The ones at home in Galicia were rural, peasant churches; Longin Lukas would have said they were infantile because of the vulgar taste that prevailed: tapestries, little rugs, flowers made of dyed crepe paper, and paper garlands—all this he remembered from the Orthodox church in Glinna. This one seemed elegant and exotic. The Silesian architect hired for the job had done his best to match the little church to Sudeten architecture, which was why it looked so odd—if

Prussian Orthodoxy were ever to emerge out of Europe's religious confusion, this building could serve as its first architectural embodiment.

He learned that the church had been built by a rich Russian patient for his compatriots to have somewhere to pray during their treatment. Now they could do that in this recently completed building, which despite its beautiful new walls of brick somehow managed to look old. Only inside did the visitor realize that the space was not large—perhaps too small for the increasing waves of Orthodox patients. But the Protestant church in Görbersdorf was not very big either, as if negating the principle that God is our refuge in times of trouble.

To prepare the interior as well as possible for its sacred function, the rich patron had employed a painter who came from somewhere in the outside world but quickly became embroiled in an affair with a patient, with whom he ran away to escape her jealous husband, leaving bare walls behind him. Soon after, the patron's wife had died, following which he fell out of love with Görbersdorf and withdrew his funds, as if to tell God: Too late, the offer no longer stands. In any case, the little building was constantly dogged by one scandal or another—either an indecently rich sponsor, or an eccentric aspect that looked out of place, or a painter, though now the topic on everyone's lips was an icon donated by an unknown person, apparently of great artistic value, which had prompted concerns that the church should be firmly padlocked, or provided with security guards. Apparently the strange icon was not a gift, but had been placed here on loan, and it was seen as a social obligation to go there on a Sunday to discuss the question of Emerentia yet again.

Herr August, insensitive to the architecture of the church, at once strode firmly toward the left wall by the iconostasis, where high above the heads of the spectators hung the famous icon depicting Saint Emerentia, and with a nonchalant gesture pointed his cane at it.

What the icon depicts is best viewed through the eyes of Wojnicz, which are, after all, innocent:

A woman with an infant is sitting on the knees of another, slightly larger and more substantial woman in a brick-red dress, with a hand raised as if in greeting. But she too is sitting on the knees of an even larger woman. This one has a dark, wrinkled face and a piercing gaze. She is spreading her arms slightly, so that her dark, almost black robe encompasses the two smaller figures and the child. The lining of her robe is dark blue, and it features stars, the moon and the sun. Behind this outspread robe the background is gold, eternal light, lux perpetua. The faces of Mary and the Infant are painted a shade of pink, they look fresh and alive, gazing boldly at the viewer; the Infant actually appears to be winking at them. The face of Anne, slightly swarthier, is characterized by tension, as if she sensed a threat in this whole situation, or were afraid to say too much. Whereas Emerentia looks like she is suffering; the painter has used a very thin brush to cover her in tiny wrinkles, which make her look plantlike.

It occurred to Wojnicz that there was something unpleasant about the wrinkled old woman's expression.

"*Brrr*," said Herr August, "do you see? Read what's written there, if you can. Of course there is no Saint Emerentia, that is a Western name, but Panagia, the Most Holy. The great-grandmother of our Savior, the mother of Saint Anne and grandmother of Mary. The line on the distaff side. Paintings depicting the genealogy of Christ in this way are often titled *Anna Selbviert*."

"I have never come across such a saint before," said Lukas in surprise, mildly put out, not by his own ignorance but by the world for failing to reveal this figure to him.

Thilo, who had sat down on the only chair in the church, certainly not intended for the congregation, addressed mainly Wojnicz: "I know

this one. In Flemish art, a tree grows from the body of crouching Emerentia, with the figure of Anne on it, holding her daughter in her embrace, and a tree grows from Mary's heart, with just one flower on it,
the Infant Jesus."

Wojnicz nodded. Suddenly he remembered how Gliceria used to
take him to the Orthodox church in the village, but he had never managed to hold out to the end of the service. His legs would refuse to obey
him, and from the surfeit of impressions he would suddenly be over-
whelmed by drowsiness. Gliceria had carried him out asleep, and then
his father had reproached her.

"And what do you think of this bizarre painting?" Herr August suddenly inquired.

"What do I think?" he asked, roused from his reverie. "No, no, I
wasn't considering it. It's very . . ." He sought words that would not
compromise him in the eyes of Herr August. "Very distinctive."

Now began the clarification, quotation and lecturing. Folded as if in
prayer, Herr August's hands became in reality a tool for pecking, they
were a superbeak with which, like a woodpecker, he drilled smooth
paths of knowledge, roads of understanding, and basic routes of erudition into the heads of his audience. Standing erect, he rocked gently
back and forth, capturing the attention of his listeners, who had been
joined by a well-dressed couple and a Catholic nun. Now and then
Thilo tried to interrupt August's speech, but knowing that he could not
possibly take control, he only put in a word or two, and thus stimulated
August to even greater displays of eloquence.

What did Wojnicz learn before he could push his way closer and
dare to turn his gaze from the sermonizing August? That it was a rare
motif in art, almost nonexistent. That in Orthodoxy this was the only
known icon of its kind (on this both August and Thilo agreed). That in
the Middle Ages it was a popular motif in the West, but with time it had

vanished, or had maybe even been removed from places of worship. That it referred to a legend, according to which, seventy-seven years before the birth of Jesus, the prophet Archos, who lived on Mount Horeb, saw a young girl of extraordinary beauty, and then had a dream in which a tree grew from her body, bearing splendid fruits, one of which was the finest of all. And he told the young woman that she would have a wonderful descendant. That August would estimate the age of the icon at about two hundred years (Thilo claimed one hundred and fifty), and that this was because of the characteristic shade of gold in the background and the way the hands were painted, or was it the ears? This Wojnicz could not entirely understand. Et cetera, et cetera . . .

To tell the truth, Wojnicz found the icon rather depressing. It was dark and crowded, as though woven from the bodies of three women, who passed from one into another with nothing but heads ringed by halos emerging from this muddle. It lacked the classic gravity with which icons were painted. There was something dramatic, excessive and unfortunate about it. Gloom and gold. Straight lines and flour-ishes. The background was gold, engraved into a sort of swirling tan-gle of leaves and pliant stems. Against this background appeared the group of people—the Infant at the center in a dark red robe, small and sickly, holding a large, ripe apple that looked too pink, as if cooked, and his Mother, actually still a little girl, was pale and haggard, as if motherhood had been too much for her. The much larger woman, whose knees she in turn was sitting on, was dignified, with a serious, mature face, and entirely dressed in dark blues and silver. But she too looked withered. These three persons sitting on each other's knees . . . there was something indecent about it, thought Wojnicz, a sort of ex-aggeration that looked like a joke. He imagined that eventually a viewer would come along and make fun of the fourfold face of this unique, tangled group of bodies, they would burst out laughing instead of preserving the proper solemnity for a visitor to God's temple. Some people were right when they said that this bizarre icon was inappropriate here, because of its peculiar fourfold nature and because of this Emerentia, who looked ugly and terrifying, witchlike even, not in harmony with anything and only here by accident or because of the artist's spite. No one wanted to look at her. All eyes were turned instead on the Infant and his youthful Mother—with concern, or possibly a growing desire to provide help and support.

Wojnicz sighed. It all seemed unaesthetic, downright ugly, shocking but also provocative—no wonder the painting was attracting attention and stirring the patients' emotions.

They left feeling chilled to the bone. It was one of those autumn Sundays, quite cool already. An intense smell rose from the ground, pushed its way into the nostrils and invaded the lungs to peep inside them and ask: So what do we have here? Will we live to see the winter?

The wind was only moving the tops of the trees, and it felt as if somewhere beyond the mountains and the forests the winter was ready to take off. Wojnicz thought of the skis on display in front of the guesthouse, which Raimund was going to grease with a special lubricant made of animal fat.

As there was no therapy on Sundays, they turned off the promenade and, instead of heading for their afternoon tea, went into the Zum Dreimädelhaus café. It was a cozy place with oak-paneled walls, decorated with mountain landscapes and pictures of deer and hunting. It smelled of coffee and mulled wine.

"How about a glass of the strong stuff?"

A polite waiter with sky-blue eyes pushed some tables together, and now they could go on pontificating. If only they listened to each other. Staying too long in a tavern was strictly forbidden by the doctors, because of the stale air and thick smoke. So they all had a sense of guilt that ruined the flavor of the very good local beer.

Thilo sat down beside Wojnicz and ordered verbena tea with honey. Wojnicz hesitated, but finally decided on the same as the other gentlemen—beer—though he was not fond of it.

"Have you been to the cemetery?" Thilo asked him in a whisper.

Wojnicz said yes, distractedly, while reading the menu, paying special attention to the section headed "Desserts."

Thilo looked at him expectantly.

"Did you see?" he said.

Mieczysław had no idea what Thilo meant.

"What did I see?"

Thilo glanced at the ceiling with distinct impatience.

"You saw nothing," he said.

They set about their beer and bread rolls with sauerkraut.

"Don't you have the feeling," asked Thilo, leaning so close to Wojnicz that his face almost touched his collar, "that we get everything in a muddle here? That we can't remember what we said the day before, and what we ended on? Which side we took, who was our adversary and who our ally?"

Surprised by this question, Wojnicz began to think about it. Yes, Thilo was right. Until now Wojnicz had presumed it was to do with being in a new place, with having so many new impressions, and days filled with tasks—surely this was why he had no time for quiet reflection.

"In my case it could just be a matter of acclimatizing," he replied hopefully.

"No, we've been here for months," said Thilo. "One sinks into a strange state of mind here."

Wojnicz did not reply. Once the waiter had nimbly woven his way between the tables to bring them a tray with beer mugs and a small tea-pot, Thilo said in a whisper: "Look around. One day all this will be forgotten, all of it. Look at it, all this will disappear."

A jolly company entered the café. The hubbub increased, stifling individual conversations. Even Herr August was drowned out. One had to raise one's voice to be audible. So they headed for the exit.

On their way back to the guesthouse they began to feel the first waves of afternoon hunger. Dusk was falling, suppertime was approaching, and from the main sanatorium building came delicious smells of roast meat. After his mug of beer, Wojnicz was feeling a little tipsy; at the back of the company, he could hear only scraps of conversation from the gentlemen walking ahead of him.

"There's better beer at Bergland . . ."

"What will Willi have made for our supper tonight?"

"Has he finally hired a cook? Will we still have to eat those navvy's dishes of his?"

"Once there's a vacancy at the Kurhaus, you'll see the suppers are better there too . . ."

"It's impossible to save a single penny here . . ."

"At the Neues Kurhaus a room with full board would cost exactly the same as at the main Kurhaus . . ."

By the time he came closer, they had resolved this debate and returned to the icon.

"It won't let me stop thinking about the fact that a woman has indeed been equipped by nature with the great power of giving birth, but is entirely devoid of control over that power. Something greater must always support her in it, some natural law, some social order, some moral code. That's what Emerentia is!" said August, jabbing the air.

"Because a woman's body belongs not only to her, but to mankind," said Lukas, a little irritated that they had not drunk a second round.

"Since she gives birth, she's public property, this capacity of hers to give birth cannot be treated as her *personal* quality," he said, stressing that word, then courteously returned a greeting to a couple passing by. "At the same time as being herself, a woman belongs to us all."

"Yes, you're right," said Frommer suddenly, leaning forward as if trying to spot mushrooms on the pavement. "Being both a subject and an object simultaneously involves her body, that's obvious. But I am thinking of a woman's intellectual and spiritual qualities."

"What do you have in mind?" Herr August asked politely.

"In the philosophical sense we cannot treat a woman as a comprehensive, complete subject of the kind that a man is. This means that a woman can only develop and retain her identity within the sphere of a man. It is he who gives a framework to her identity."

"But then she'll be treated like an object!" said Thilo in alarm.

Just ahead of them, a sudden gust of wind twisted a small heap of leaves into a tiny whirlwind, a whirl-breeze, barely a whirl-puff.

"That's true, it has to be admitted, like an object. Yet no one is stupid enough to fail to recognize a certain degree of female subjectivity. When one looks in the face of a woman, one must admit that there is in fact something separate, distinctive and subjective about her. Right? But on the other hand, her body, and thus she herself, belongs to all, since it is a vessel from which people come, so a woman's body, her belly, her womb, belongs to mankind."

"But what is meant by 'to mankind'?" said Lukas in a sulk. "Meaning to whom? That reminds me of the socialists when they talk of 'property of the state.' Of the state, meaning of whom? The civil servants?"

The whirl-breeze proved to be a harbinger of wind, which had somehow made its way into the windless territory of Görbersdorf and struck at them with considerable force. Wojnicz raised his collar and veiled his mouth with his scarf.

"Excuse me, young man," said Herr August—who was after all a socialist—holding on to his chocolate-brown hat. "A woman should have her rights, of course, but she should never forget that she belongs to society, which appoints the institution of the state to take care of its interests, so to put it logically, a woman, hm, hm, can be commanded by the state. That is true. The state may assign her social roles, tasks, but also, and perhaps above all, it can protect her rights as an individual."

"Suffrage as well?" asked Lukas provocatively.

"Well, I think the time for that will come too. I am simply thinking of the right to live in peace, without hunger, the right to medical treatment, and to liberty within the social and moral guidelines."

The wind raised leaves and twigs from the ground; it was cold and sharp. They were just approaching the Guesthouse for Gentlemen.

"You said that a man shapes a woman's individual identity, so to speak. The state in turn would shape her social roles," said August, addressing Frommer.

"And the church her spiritual life," put in Frommer with a sneer. "I stand up for the woman entirely here. I don't know if you gentlemen have heard, but one of the early ecumenical councils considered the question of the female soul. At the time, in the early Middle Ages, it was not so obvious that women had souls. Yes, yes . . ."

"Well, sometimes when I look at my housekeeper . . . ," began Lukas ironically, but he did not complete his sentence.

"At any rate, after many days of debate a secret vote was held . . ."

"And?" asked Wojnicz, impatient for the end of this story.

"And there turned out to be a difference of just one single vote. Imagine, gentlemen, just one vote!"

"But on which side?" cried Wojnicz nervously.

"That of course they have souls. Surely you don't doubt it?"

And after a pause he added: "I have often wondered who the bishop was who tipped the scales."

For three marks they hired a carriage and went to the cemetery in Langwaltersdorf. Wojnicz had to quench his sense of discomfort at abandoning his Strahlendusche—the hydrotherapy, for which he had in fact paid extra. What if his father found out about it? But on the other hand, he needed fresh air, and a trip beyond the valley; by now he was starting to get tired of its stillness and lack of wind. Besides, what a great joy it was to be with someone young, someone his own age. They started joking around on their way to the coach stop, but once they were on board and had set off in the open carriage, Thilo fell silent, probably because he always shielded his mouth with a scarf. He was afraid of the cold.

"Do you feel the same?" he asked indistinctly. "There's no greater pleasure than a trip to a cemetery, is there?"

Thilo's sarcasm impressed Wojnicz, who was fascinated by his constant changes of mood. Today Thilo seemed to be in excellent form, maybe because it was warm and dry. The leaves smelled intoxicating, and they were surrounded by the scent of fir trees and pine sap, which always reminded Wojnicz of the happiest moments of all the Christmases in his life. That was what they were talking about, but Thilo did not share his enthusiasm for Christmas. For Thilo it was a time of family onslaught, thanks to his mother's poor physical and mental state and the constant presence of his stepfather, which was hard to bear. His stepfather got drunk each evening and bore grudges against everyone. Sometimes he made Thilo appear before him in his pajamas to be questioned about history, or he would tell him to stand to attention, which he called "making a man of him." His mother was incapable of sticking up for her son, and only showed her maternal side when his stepfather had to go away on business, which happened quite often. Then they would be on good terms, letting each other go about their business during the day and spending the evenings together. His mother treated him like an old friend from childhood who by some strange chance had ended up at her house. She had given up her acting career when she met Thilo's father. After his death, when Thilo was little, a friend had encouraged her to try morphine. Now she took the drug regularly. Thilo related this without resentment.

"I understand you," said Wojnicz, laying a hand on Thilo's similarly gloved hand.

"You're an odd creature, so completely unaware, so innocent," said Thilo, giving him a look of curiosity. "I don't know who you are. Where on earth have you come from?"

"From Lwów. They grow us in greenhouses there," joked Wojnicz, and Thilo laughed long and heartily.

The carriage drove through the village and finally stopped at the gateway to the church, beyond which lay the cemetery. From here a view unfolded of a beautiful, undulating plateau full of autumnal shades. Somewhere below was Waldenburg.

Droplets of water hung on the cobwebs slung between the gravestones; the air was the color of the Tokay they had gorged on the day before, and it tasted the same too—invigorating. Thilo went first, slowly, leaning on an old-fashioned cane. They passed Frau Opitz's freshly dug grave, and then left the main avenue to walk across the grass, which was still sharp and springy, as if not expecting the approaching winter. Now and then Thilo paused and breathed heavily, looking at Wojnicz apologetically.

They stopped at a small section of the cemetery in the farthest corner, on a hillside. This was the oldest part of it, and although the graves here were laid out in even rows just as everywhere else, it was plain to see that the order had soon slipped out of control, so there were lots of curving paths and blind alleys, and the gravestones had little in common in terms of style. Some were grander, others less so, some of the tombs were tall and others squat, some had crosses while others suggested that their owners were from far off and refused to fall in line with the local customs. At a steady pace Thilo led him to the back gate, where beyond the stone wall russet pastures stretched away.

Wojnicz cast his companion an inquiring glance.

"Take a good look at these graves. Learn to see at last," Thilo urged him.

So Wojnicz went in among the graves, and the first thing he saw were of course the names, which were not so very different from those in the main part of the cemetery: Fischer, Opitz, Kluge, Tilch, nothing but men, most of them young; when he calculated the differences between the dates of birth and death, the result was never more than forty years. He looked at Thilo questioningly, and at the gravestones again. First name, surname, date of birth and of death. Usually just of death. And something else. Underneath the name and dates on other gravestones there were almost always some words: expressions of grief or regret, references or quotations. But not here. On all the gravestones in this part of the cemetery there were just a few small letters, almost invisible, forming the inscription: *Weh mir, o weh!* He did not know what it meant; he felt there was no reason why he should know these particular German words, as graveyard inscriptions were rarely taught at school. He had a vague association with poetry, but he did not know what it could be. Something from a ballad? They had come to the end, to the stone wall, where stood a grander tomb with an eye-catching, quite fresh inscription: Rudolf Opitz, 1889–1908.

"His brother," said Thilo. "Nineteen years old."

Thilo turned and headed for the exit. Wojnicz cast a final glance at the gravestones.

Rudolf Opitz
21 Sept. 1889–11 Nov. 1908
Weh mir, o weh!

Only now did he notice the full scale of what he was looking at, without understanding. *Nov.*, meaning November. Those three letters, *Nov.*, featured on every single headstone in this section. All these people had died in November.

"Thilo!" he cried, wanting to be sure, but Thilo had already boarded the carriage and covered his knees with a rug.

Wojnicz ran after him, feeling as if there were an empty space in his brain that he had to fill, or else he would have no peace.

They were late getting back, and as Nurse Schwartz handed out the blankets in the rest-cure area, he gave them a reproachful look. They occupied the two farthermost deck chairs on the upper terrace, from where there was a stunning view of the orange-and-green mountainsides. With Schwartz's assistance, they wrapped themselves in the blankets, even though it was not cold. The weary Thilo immediately dozed off, while Wojnicz slowly gathered his thoughts in his favorite manner: systematically and—one could say—appetizingly. This way of thinking, neither cold nor orderly, was like a game, and it was meant to be nice and comfortable. So Wojnicz imagined the whole of Görbersdorf to be like a fairy tale—a fairy tale taking place within the image adorning a box of gingerbread. He could think up anything he liked without being afraid of seeing something unpleasant or unacceptable. Wojnicz thought this game was a bit like making an herbal: it involved drying each experience, gluing it into his collection and examining it like a specimen. Something had to happen here each year in November, it must be some sort of dangerous sport. He had seen skiers descending pell-mell down steep trails. And acrobats who used lianas to jump from tree to tree like Mister Jig, an imaginary figure from his childhood. Or muscular, half-naked swimmers, who leaped headfirst into ponds. He must ask Opitz, or even better, Dr. Semperweiss—he would know best. Yes, he would do that, because Thilo seemed very concerned about it. He would do that for him. He imagined the two of them skating on a frozen pond. Thilo's scarf is fluttering, Wojnicz is wearing a hat with a pom-pom. Suddenly the ice beneath Thilo breaks, he falls into the water and just his scarf is left on the surface . . .

Wojnicz felt a wave of tiredness and opened his eyes. He saw Thilo sleeping peacefully, and then his gaze wandered past the wrought-iron railings toward the part of the rest-cure area where the women were relaxing. He hoped that by some miracle he would spot that huge hat trimmed with artificial flowers and tulle. But of course she would not be wearing it here, where the sickly cleansed their poor lungs with marvelous mountain air, full of mysterious ingredients with the power to kill those mysterious tiny creatures to whom they had done no harm, and whose fierce hostility they could not understand—Koch's bacilli.

8

A SYMPHONY
OF COUGHING

e shall not say any more about the many minor obligations of a patient, padding off each morning to the hydrotherapy Wojnicz found so loathsome, about the towels, the changing rooms, the stethoscopes put to chests—all those things that filled our hero's days to the brim. We shall not describe yet another walk along the promenade toward the Orthodox church or beyond, to Humboldt's shrine, as Herr August called the pavilion on the hill. By now Wojnicz knew how many boxes of pelargoniums hung outside Albynsky's café, apparently named Zum Dreimädelhaus in honor of his daughters, and how many spittoons filled with sawdust stood along his route to the Kurhaus. We shall not quote the laconic content of the postcards sent every second day to his father and uncle. Or list the names of all the patients to whom he bowed along the way. We shall not report on the weather—this in fact was done by the observatory, which meticulously noted the air temperature and humidity, and also the wind force (which was always below average). Nor shall we endeavor to cite the topics of all the conversations the gentlemen held on their walks, or to summarize the ones they carried on each evening over the Schwärmerei. Suffice it to say that Mieczysław Wojnicz felt well here, his cough was no longer as intense, and his fever had stopped bothering him as it had in Lwów. On top of that, he was sleeping well, if he managed to block his ears with wadding to avoid hearing the coughing from the other side of the walls and the suspicious warbling from the attic. And yet somewhere underneath this well-ordered, regular life he felt a gnawing anxiety; a discomfort had settled in his soul—he could not put a name to it, but it never left him. Just as the other day, when he woke suddenly in the night and lay there with his eyes open, staring into the darkness. He had awoken because somehow in his sleep he had remembered that the late Frau Opitz had a mole on her upper lip, just above the corner of her mouth, a slightly raised brown mark the size of a pinhead. This discovery had shaken him, and he lay motionless, full of unexpected sorrow.

The guesthouse windows looked onto a densely overgrown mountainside, as if Görbersdorf had done a deal with nature that granted it special permission for its location, on condition it did not move away from the stream. At first Wojnicz thought the dark wall of forest looked like a black stain, an indiscriminate, enigmatic space of no interest to him at all. Yet ever since voices and rustling noises had started to emerge from there (if he left the window open, these sounds became unbearable), he had come to perceive it differently. One night in early October he heard a monstrous voice coming from out there. Horror-stricken, he sat in bed, too scared to move, but then, with trembling heart, he put on his slippers and, quivering with fear, slipped out into the corridor.

"It's a stag. Please don't be afraid, just go back to bed!" shouted Willi Opitz from downstairs, as though anticipating his question.

Wojnicz was embarrassed. Ah, yes, it was just a stag. The rutting season.

Yet in the course of the next few nights, when the animal gave its concert with admirable punctuality, he found it hard to accept that it was the voice of a common animal, all part of nature. It was *natural*. To him it was as if these theatrical, bombastic noises were being made by a wounded, drunken Galician woodcutter who had been beaten by his rival and was now in his death throes. But once he had told himself that it was just a mindless animal, subject to the force of its own instincts, he was overcome by emotion, he felt stirred—the sound was mighty, the stag awakened visions of a great strength concealing both might and desperation, despair at being caught in the grip of a superhuman force, trapped in this call that was determined by sexual destiny, a call that bid one to wager everything on a single card and drew one to danger-ous places where one could easily lose one's life. The stag's noises con-tained a madness, a readiness to leave the familiar paths and go beyond all the rules, to cross the borders of safety, or even to abandon one's own existence.

The roaring stag went beyond the night, beyond a dream, beyond its usual realm and route, and loomed like a phantom within the bounds of the health resort, appearing in its dark, damp, narrow courtyards like a monster overcome by its own lust, a male fiend. And this poor animal was the victim of inner sexual forces that put everything before its own life—an endless need to go beyond itself, to multiply its spe-cies, even at the cost of its own existence. Wojnicz listened to the mon-strous noises with a sort of smoldering embarrassment, because they cast light on things that should be hidden, they drew the veil of silence from things that should remain mysterious, revealing them like clutter hidden behind a drape, like the soiled underwear Gliceria pulled from the basket and sorted before it was taken to the laundry. All those sweat-soaked collars and dirty underpants with stains on the white cloth, all the nastiness of bodily functions that Wojnicz's father was always warning him about.

The gentlemen laughed at the roaring of the stag in search of a female partner, while making highly insinuating jokes that, to tell the truth, Wojnicz did not entirely understand, despite which he blushed, suspecting that they involved obscure corners of life that were scrupulously concealed and full of hidden meaning.

He liked the suppers that dragged on into the night and inevitably ended in debate. The subjects recurred, vanished and returned. Does man have a soul? Does he always act selfishly? Monarchy or democracy? Is socialism an opportunity for mankind? Can one tell whether a text was written by a man or a woman? Are women responsible enough to be allowed voting rights?

When Wojnicz arrived one evening, they were still talking about the extraordinary air crash that had occurred here in Silesia a few days earlier.

It gave the gentlemen occasion to argue at table about whether mankind really needed technological progress, and the victims it claimed were the necessary price to be paid (August), or perhaps human hubris was at work here, unfortunately in league with chaos, and bound to cause mankind to collapse one day (Lukas).

"People are always going to pay for their curiosity and their desire to improve the world, that is inscribed in our destiny," said Frommer, "but progress must be accompanied by the development of the human spirit."

Here he showed a newspaper, from which one could learn that someone named Roland Garros had flown a plane across the Mediterranean Sea. Or that a man had succeeded in making a parachute jump from a moving plane and landing safely. This sort of news made Wojnicz feel anxiety, an inner itch—there was so much going on in the world, while here he sat, confined and sick. But he regarded his confinement at the Guesthouse for Gentlemen in the company of these men, and in the Görbersdorf valley in general, as a lesson in patience that would be useful later on when he returned to normal life. The debates held over Schwärmerei between Lukas, August and (less often) Frommer (who had moments of total stupor and silence) could be highly instructive for him. After all, his father and uncle never held forth intellectually to this extent; at most they discussed current events and what the newspapers said about them, especially all manner of speculation on when the heir to the throne would take over, and whether the old emperor would abdicate or die. And they were always interested in the conduct of Russia, that unpredictable neighbor, which was treated with mistrust, with the suspicion of hidden motives in every political move.

He liked listening to August (whom he always thought of as "Herr August"), who, along with his characteristic way of jabbing the air with his folded hands, sometimes in his excitement made a gesture that simulated tearing one's hair out. Whenever he did it, an ironical smirk of pity appeared on Lukas's face.

However, Wojnicz had noticed that even their most heated debates often ended rather abruptly, without any conclusions. The gentlemen would suddenly fall silent, as if tired by the very act of talking; at most one of them would venture something like, "Yeeees, so that's the way it looks" or "Yes, quite so," which was meant to end the dispute at a point of recapitulation, after which their gazes would turn inward, as if they had remembered some important personal concerns, worries that till now they had pushed into deep shadow. At this point Lukas usually stood up, folded his hands behind his back and began to stare out of the window. August would drum his fingers on the table, as if playing an invisible piano accompaniment to the soft *param, pam, pam, param, pam, pam* coming from his lips. Frommer would freeze on the spot, like someone caught red-handed. Opitz would disappear into the kitchen. At first Wojnicz had tried to restore the flow of the conversation with a question, but they had ignored him. It was a strange stalemate, and at such moments he felt very uneasy, as though the normal course of life had been interrupted. It was like twisting the electric light switch he so admired here—one click and it was dark.

Then he would toss and turn in bed for ages, unable to fall asleep. The warbling from the attic was a constant reminder of something he did not wish to remember. He would get up and look past the curtains at the promenade lit by modern gas lamps that emitted a greenish light, always deserted at night. He would splash water on his face. He would try to read.

Sometimes his sleep was disturbed by coughing from the other rooms. Unbearably irritating at first, with time this sound had become part and parcel of the house, its sonic architecture. Soon Wojnicz had learned to distinguish whose throat produced which individual hacking noise.

August's cough, for example, was deep and powerful, entirely at odds with his puny physique. It seemed to come from the tube of his body, from the deepest spot, sounding baritone, cavernous, as if leaving an echo behind it. In the way of an engineer, Wojnicz often wondered how Herr August's feeble lungs could produce such strong resonance, as if his small but well-proportioned body were like a guitar on which the illness played its chords.

From the room opposite, Frommer coughed dryly, like barking. These sounds cascaded around the building, as though someone had torn a string of beads from a neck and thrown them to the floor—first they filled the corridor, then they parted ways, going down the staircase into the sitting room, and up it into the loft. They forced their way into Mieczysław's room in short volleys so emphatically that he could not help waiting for the next series. This, a so-called dry cough, further dehydrated by cigarettes, quite devoid of any juice or moisture, was just like Walter Frommer's entire body. Sometimes when Frommer moved he seemed to rustle, as though underneath his neat, black, outmoded frock coat he had oakum instead of muscles.

Poor Thilo coughed in a completely different way. From his room came a bubbling noise, the sound of rotting matter, age-old fermentation, as if the boy's body were being boiled in retorts by damp miasmas, as if some primeval substance the consistency of mud, from which millions of years ago life had emerged, were making itself heard. Thilo coughed up masses of phlegm, while Wojnicz rooted for him through the wall, because it was not easy. Sometimes Thilo tried again and again to rid himself of the mucus filling his sick lungs, and finally succeeded when hope seemed lost. Then Wojnicz would hear a tearing sound, like cracking, then a splash, followed at once by groaning full of relief. Several times Wojnicz had seen bloodstained wadding in the metal waste bin that Raimund brought out of Thilo's room, to mix its contents with sawdust and burn it, according to sanatorium instructions; this combination of red and white was always shocking, a sight that felt like a blow.

Longin Lukas could still be heard from his annex, because on top of his cough he always made a sound as if he were having to perform hard labor and suffering from the effort. It was quite high-pitched, shrill in fact, with a vague note of grievance in it, so that anyone who heard it was bound to feel guilty.

Opitz coughed too, and even Raimund—though not as often and not as violently—which may have been to do with the fact that the kilns had started up, and wet, rarefied smoke often rose over the valley, permeating one's clothing and causing one to long impatiently for the feeblest breath of wind.

As a result of this symphony of coughing Wojnicz suffered restlessly in bedclothes that always felt slightly damp with the cold that increasingly filtered through the chinks in the wooden house.

He quickly learned that the only person who could receive him at this hour was Thilo, who slept in the day rather than at night. Mieczysław would put on a sweater and trousers over his pajamas, then take a seat on Thilo's shabby green sofa, from where he could view the landscapes spread out on the floor and against the walls, and the picture on the easel.

They tried to play chess but soon found it boring. In any case, Wojnicz did not like chess. His father had tormented him with it too often. He must have been hoping that learning to play chess would organize Mieczyś's foggy, unruly mind. After all, chess was played at court, and the emperor himself had shown great fondness for it. This was the entertainment of well-born men, requiring both the intelligence essential for playing it and an ability to see ahead. Wojnicz senior believed that moving around the chessboard in keeping with the rules would introduce an element of automatism into his son's life that would make the world safe for him, if not friendly. So every day after lunch, just as the body was digesting and a gentle afternoon somnolence was suffusing it, they sat down at the table and set out the chessboard, and his father would let Mieczysław make the first move. Whenever the boy made a mistake, his father came over to his side, stood behind him and tried to steer the child's attention in a cause-and-effect chain of potential next moves. But whenever Mieczyś was resistant, or "dull," his father let himself be carried away by anger and left the room to smoke a cigar, while his son had to sit over the chessboard until he had thought up a sensible defense or attack.

Little Mieczysław Wojnicz understood the rules and could foresee a lot, but to tell the truth, the game did not interest him. Making moves according to the rules and aiming to defeat your opponent seemed to him just one of the possible ways to use the pawns. He preferred to daydream, and to see the chessboard as a space where the fates of the unfortunate pawns and other pieces were played out; he cast them as characters weaving complex webs of intrigue, either with or against each other, and linked by all sorts of relationships. He thought it a waste to limit their activity to the checkered board, to leave them to the mercy of a formal game played according to strict rules. So as soon as his father lost interest and went off to see to more important matters, Mieczyś would move the chess pieces onto the steppes of the rug and the mountains of the armchair, where they saw to their own business, set off on journeys, and furnished their kitchens, houses and palaces. Finally his father's ashtray became a boat, and the pen holders were rafters' oars, while the space underneath a chair turned into a cathedral where the wedding of the two queens, black and white, was taking place.

Among this race of chess people, he always identified with the knight, who delivered news, made peace between those who were at odds, organized the provisions for expeditions or warned of dangers (such as Józef's entrance, carpet cleaning or being summoned for lunch). Then, when chided by his father, or sent to his room without supper as a punishment, he would head off with the dignity of a knight—two steps forward and one to the side.

"My father wanted me to be a soldier," said Wojnicz, as he examined his friend's works.

"You're joking! Uniforms always make me laugh," said Thilo, watching the movements of his brush as it painted cubes and circles: this was his favorite motif for his "abstractions." "All those epaulets and medals, that whole system of symbols to remind us what heroic deeds their wearer performed, or how important he was. All those ranks and hierarchies, and then the discomfort of the uniform, the con-tradiction of clothing, so stiff and uncomfortable. And the dirtier the war, the grander it is. All those accessories, right down to the buttons. National emblems on buttons—can you imagine? If you shift your viewpoint a short way, just a touch, from the absurd toward common sense," said Thilo, starting to move his head comically, "a uniform is an absolutely astonishing disguise. What exactly do those men in uni-forms do? They kill. What do they take pride in? Violence."

"You're a pacifist."

"Yes. Who in their right mind would want killing?"

"I've always liked uniforms."

"Oh, especially in your Austrian army, the dress ones. Ours are more modest. It's true, the uniform gives a man a shape. Without a shape a man is comical. In his underwear, for instance, or in nothing but socks."

Wojnicz smiled to himself and glanced at his pajama legs sticking out of his trousers. He remembered the time he had got up in the night to have a pee and, still half asleep, had come upon his uncle in the lavatory. Emil had a band stretched over his mustache that bisected his face, flattening his features in the process, and making his handsome countenance look grotesque and funny, like the face of a puppet. His trousers were down around his ankles, exposing his hairy legs and the brownish gherkin hanging between them; somehow it seemed to Mieczysław unworthy of a military man to be carrying such a wilted fruit in his trousers.

"Shouldn't women dress up in some sort of uniforms too, and wear medals according to how many children they've had, how many dinners they've cooked, or how many patients they've nursed? That would be both beautiful and fair. But if you like uniforms, weren't you attracted to the army?" asked Thilo.

"My father wanted it, but as you know we don't have our own army or our own country. I'd have been fighting for the emperor."

Thilo nodded.

"So he thought he'd be sending me to the invader's army, just as he had sent his younger brother, and if Poland were ever free, we'd simply change our uniforms and instantly become the well-trained army of a free, young state. But I turned out to be weak and sickly."

"Your father must have been disappointed, eh?"

"Indeed he was. Then he forged a new plan. He decided that if his son couldn't join the army, not even a phantom one, he should sign up for another service. He chose my course of study himself. From then on I was to study for the Fatherland, to raise its state of civilization to a higher level, because the present one is primitive and backward. He would say that until things are put in order, until the cities are modernized and the countryside civilized, until ignorance and illiteracy are wiped out, it won't be possible to build a healthy society."

"He's right."

"So I went to study what he wanted in Dresden."

"Did you like it?" asked Thilo, looking at him closely and, so it seemed to Wojnicz, with sympathy.

"I felt lost there. A city like Dresden is not conducive to technical studies. I'd have been better off studying art, like you, but as you know, it's not appropriate for citizens of nonexistent countries to take up something so nebulous."

Thilo closed his eyes and said: "I'm sorry for you, Wojnicz. You're so sensitive and good. I'm afraid someone will take advantage of you. But you have great strength that you don't yet know how to bring to the surface."

Wojnicz blushed deeply at this compliment.

"But I am an expert on sewage systems, and I even know how to construct a water closet."

Wojnicz had fallen sick in the final year of his studies and had then spent twelve months at a house in the country, where there were certainly no water closets or anything resembling one. Instead there was a privy, a wooden hut behind the house. In winter, when he had a fever, he had not left the house at all, but had relieved himself in a bucket, which the servant then emptied. During this year of lying inactive he had become interested in beekeeping, having found a book on the subject in his father's small library. That summer, with his father's assistance, he had managed to set up a small apiary, and as this enthusiasm for beekeeping had greatly improved his health, his father had accepted that studying water closets should go to hell in favor of patriotic beekeeping.

"Don't ask me any questions, or I'll go on and on and on about it," he warned Thilo.

If the Poles took up beekeeping, they could become a major economic power, because honey was a valuable raw material, suitable not just for immediate consumption, but also for producing other comestibles, cosmetics and medicines, not to mention the natural wax to be sourced from the hives. The benefits of beekeeping were the first thing he and his father had ever agreed about. Both saw the advantages of promoting beekeeping, of apitherapy, the production of honey liqueurs and of beeswax ointment for rheumatism. January Wojnicz observed that, rather than becoming beekeepers, the Poles would be better off becoming bees. Bees—what a splendid society, what harmony and joint responsibility. This was an instinct that the Poles lacked, and that was why they had let themselves be torn into three parts and were now stuck in slavery like flies in amber, with mouths agape, a lifeless race. If only they had a queen, and if only she could establish eternal order, in which thrift and industriousness were the greatest virtues!

And there was something else that Mieczysław would never have dared to say in front of his father, of course, for Wojnicz senior was always serious when he spoke of Poland or the Poles; every time, his face clouded and his brow wrinkled with worry and concern. But Wojnicz junior thought they all needed sweets, a luxurious pleasure, something "appetizing" that melted in the mouth and that tasted of herbs, flowers and sunlight. If he had not lacked the boldness, he could have told his father: If the Poles ate more honey, the whole country would change for the better.

Whenever his nocturnal visit to Thilo came to an end, instead of going straight back to his room, he usually went barefoot upstairs to the attic, for a brief visit to Frau Opitz's room, while the others were still asleep (he could hear snoring from Frommer's room and August coughing in his sleep). He also went there during the day, once he was sure that Raimund and Opitz had driven to Waldenburg or were out of the house on business of their own. He did not do anything in particular here. As he sat down on the bed, the mattress sagged under him;

despite the discomfort, he would gradually feel inertia sweeping over him, like a stupor. He would cover his shoulders with the fringed table-cloth and then simply sit and stare.

Here on the bedstead lies a neatly folded nightshirt made of faded linen, trimmed with silk-twist lace. In one place the threads are broken and pilling. Wojnicz leans over the shirt and inspects the wound in the lace at close quarters. Suddenly he remembers an impression from that first day when he entered the dining room and saw what he saw. The details of that afternoon have been gradually fading from his memory, but now a concrete scene comes back to him, like a picture lost from a file and by chance recovered. A cheek, the outline of the jaw, peach-like skin covered in fine down, and the corner of the mouth, a dainty line the shape of a comma, ever so slightly curved, as if those lifeless lips were just about to smile.

Wojnicz is surprised by this memory. He was not expecting to re-member this image. He was not even aware of having looked at it.

From mid-October, fine, sunny days set in. A few cold nights had caused the trees to turn red and yellow, and in the second week of the month Wojnicz suddenly awoke to an entirely altered setting—now he was surrounded by every possible shade of yellow, orange and red, still interwoven here and there with retreating green. The frenzy of colors, highlighted by the blue chill of the sky, was intoxicating, and Wojnicz even felt like asking Thilo for some paints so that he could document this astonishing transformation. Colored leaves were falling onto the cobbled streets, as though some force were trying to carpet the hard surface in a mosaic pattern. How much the world had softened, how much it had mellowed! Masses of swallowtail butterflies as big as sparrows, suddenly awakened by the sunlight, were bouncing off the windowpanes as they sought shelter from the approaching cold, only to die helplessly on the sills. Their crumbled, faded wings would be swept away with the first spring cleaning.

After four weeks' treatment, each patient went to see Dr. Semperweiss for a thorough examination.

After auscultating Wojnicz's lungs at length, an extremely boring examination, the doctor seemed entirely satisfied.

"Could you please undress fully?" he asked.

Wojnicz was standing before him in nothing but his drawers, which came down to his knees and were of very thin, soft cambric. His father had bought him a dozen pairs, as well as some cotton underwear, four new shirts and a very smart russet-colored morning coat, possibly not the height of fashion, as he had now confirmed. His underwear too seemed rather outmoded when he compared it with that of patients from all over Europe during the hydrotherapy devised by Father Kneipp.

"I must refuse," he replied with a determination that showed on his face.

Busy arranging his tools for examining the throat, Dr. Semperweiss spun around in amazement.

"What did you say?"

"That I must refuse."

"But why on earth? You're at the doctor's!"

"For—for religious reasons," said Wojnicz, stammering.

"But you're a Catholic, and Catholics undress for the doctor."

"It's complicated."

"Savages," retorted Dr. Semperweiss after a pause. "I haven't the strength to deal with you. How can you be treated the modern way if you refuse to uncover your own arse?"

Wojnicz listened to this calmly, as if accustomed; one might even have thought he shared the doctor's indignation.

"I should throw you out of here. Go and be cured by quacks and witches."

Wojnicz remained silent.

"So how do you cope with the baths, you prudish youth? You have to undress there, don't you?"

"I keep my vest and drawers on."

"What a good little Catholic you are! Well, I'm not going to fight against prejudices and I'm not going to examine you either. I'll make a note of it in your records. Ha, I'll put that he refused to undress," quipped Dr. Semperweiss, and changed the subject, his mind already elsewhere. "Five proper meals a day, don't forget. Plenty of milk and butter. It must all be hot. Daily walks and rest cures. The best friendships are formed in the rest-cure area, and who knows what else. Is there anything more to say, young man with the unpronounceable name?"

Wojnicz dressed in haste.

"No. No."

"How does that Opitz fellow feed you now that his cook has died?" the doctor suddenly asked with concern, as if feeling a surge of guilt. "You can transfer to us with full board. You'd like our chef, he's from Italy."

"I have breakfast and lunch at the Kurhaus, and I value the chef's talents highly. I have supper at the guesthouse and I can't complain. There are always fresh cheeses. The proprietor goes to Friedland for goat cheeses. For now we're coping, and Herr Opitz is looking for a woman to do the cooking."

Semperweiss folded his arms across his chest and sighed.

"A woman to do the cooking. Do you know that it's our mothers who bear the blame for our failures? They're the ones who shape our attitude to the world and to our own bodies. These are the latest discoveries of the science known as psychoanalysis."

Wojnicz was already at the door, but Semperweiss gestured to him to come back and sit down.

"What I have to say might interest you. It's the mothers," he went on, "who infect the child with excessive emotionality, which eventually leads to all sorts of illnesses and feebleness of spirit, and above all inner effeminacy. Women are volatile and fickle, quite incapable of shaping a child's awareness that the world is our challenge, that its rules are tough, and its order requires us to have a solid attitude, to stand firmly on our feet and not give in to any delusions."

"You talk the way my father would if he . . ." Wojnicz hesitated; Semperweiss cocked an ear.

"If he what?" he asked with curiosity.

"If he talked about my mother at all."

"Doesn't he? I'm sure you have a close relationship with your mother, hence your—so to speak—ladylike fragility."

In a few sentences, Wojnicz explained his family history.

"Oh well, it's a pity she died," said the doctor, "but that doesn't mean she's blameless. She left you when you needed her most! But I can tell you, dear Herr Wojnicz, I too was raised almost entirely without women. That's to say without other women, because I am very close to my mother. She's coming up to her eightieth birthday. But she is an extremely special woman. Yes, yes . . . sometimes I think . . ." Here Dr. Semperweiss paused, then changed the subject. "A man can get to know himself thanks to psychoanalysis, this new science. These days the psychology of the unconscious is the only way to gain real answers to real questions. Do you analyze your dreams?"

Wojnicz blinked in amazement.

"I don't dream much. And I don't dream at all here, because there are pigeons cooing in the attic all night."

"If you were to dream of water, or frogs, wet things, and, oh, caves for example, it could mean that you have a complex to do with your absent mother . . ."

Wojnicz remembered the toad sitting on the pile of potatoes. He flinched imperceptibly.

"Then you would have to fortify your virility, stand up to this softening energy. That's what you need, Wojnicz! You must kill in yourself your mother who abandoned you—"

"She died, I don't have to kill her," Wojnicz corrected him.

"Even so, she abandoned you, and that is taking strength away from you. To make up for her absence, you identify with her in a dangerous way, hence this ladylike effeminacy, this softness."

Wojnicz shrank inside himself.

"Now, now, my lad," said Semperweiss, who must have noticed this change, "don't snivel, don't capitulate. You must get a grip on yourself. Even the toughest men melt like jelly when they're subjected to women's tricks. And that includes women acting from beyond the grave."

For a moment Wojnicz felt as though it were his father talking. He could even see him—standing against the patterned wallpaper, against the windows and the asparagus ferns, cigar in hand, as the smoke formed beautiful swirls in the air, meandering threads that never repeated the same shape. Now he should go up to him and kiss his hand, as he usually did. And say: "Yes, Father." His father seemed to relish his subordination, this gesture of submission calmed him down, at least for a while. Mieczyś could then leave the room and see to his own affairs: the chess pieces, his herbal and his beloved Latin. His father would remain outside his son's closed door, unaware that his control and influence did not reach beyond it and had no effect on the fern leaf pressed between sheets of tissue paper and its regular, standard spirals.

"We could actually get by without them. Without women, of course. If we were only capable of being strong," concluded Dr. Semperweiss, and gave Wojnicz a friendly clap on the back, enough to make him wince with pain.

At the door, Wojnicz asked quietly about Thilo, but staring out of the window, the doctor replied, "Don't get attached to him, my boy. He hasn't much time left."

Wojnicz spent ages watching a sluggish fly that was roaming around the table, closely inspecting the dried plants. It was plainly living on reserve energy, perhaps only because Raimund had stoked the stoves today, and the pleasant warmth was reminding every living thing of the sunny days of summer. The fly's fellows lay dead on the windowsills, like black crumbs. With disgust, Wojnicz tried to pick them up by the leglets and throw them out, but his fingers were too clumsy, so he had to use the postcard he had just written to his father.

That night the cooing from upstairs drove him to despair, so he went to Opitz's medicine cabinet in the corridor and took out a small bottle of valerian drops.

Not bothering to measure the correct amount, he poured half its contents into a glass, watered it down, and drank it.

Now we can see Wojnicz sitting on the bed of the late Frau Opitz again; he places his hands on his thighs and stares ahead, the crossed pattern of the window reflected in his blue irises. He is breathing calmly as waves of fragrance meet in his nose—an herb to deter clothes moths, some very cheap perfume, dust, starch, and the indeterminate odor that human beings leave behind after they die.

He sits like that for a quarter of an hour, maybe a little longer, and now he is sure that the cooing ceases entirely whenever he comes in here.

9

THE TUNTSCHI

illi Opitz and Raimund were standing in the courtyard be-hind the house, dressed in rubber boots, hats and capes. They were holding light wicker baskets. Wojnicz was on his way out for a solitary walk when he bumped into them. From the sitting room he had taken a hiking stick with a spiked tip; it was covered in badges from the local mountain hostels. He had thought that if he went out through the courtyard he would not encounter anyone, and now he tried to conceal his disappointment and surprise.

"Ah, gentlemen, you look as if you were off to pick mushrooms!" he said with a laugh, aware that it did not sound quite natural.

The glances the other men exchanged seemed to forge an unspoken agreement between them, as though they had hit upon an excellent idea at the same moment.

"Indeed we are off to pick mushrooms," they said simultaneously.

Then, as if this remark, uttered spontaneously and sincerely, was to have consequences in the material world, Willi Opitz added: "Perhaps you'd like to come with us?"

Wojnicz could find no reason to refuse. He had not planned his walk in detail, he had considered that "anything might happen," and now it had. So he nodded and joined them.

Before entering the forest, they fortified themselves with a few swigs of Schwärmerei from a bottle Opitz suddenly pulled from his bosom, and at once they were filled with excitement, because they discovered that there at the edge of the woods they were standing right in the middle of a patch of wonderful yellow chanterelles. Once Wojnicz's eyes had grown accustomed to the subtle differences between the leaves and the mushrooms, he was carried away by such elation that he fell to his knees and began to pull chanterelles, one after another, from the soft carpet of moss. He was moved to the point of tears by their abundance. From the corners of his eyes, he could see the two other men moving around on their knees, and it looked as if their baskets would soon be full to the brim. It was impossible to gather all the mushrooms. Finally Opitz sat down, took another slug of liqueur and handed the bottle to his companions.

"We'll have a splendid supper," he said. "Nothing more, nothing less. All we need is cream."

They started chatting in their dialect, and Wojnicz did not even attempt to understand them. He reached out to pick the most beautiful specimens. Soon the higher they went, the thicker the forest became, and marvelous velvety bay boletes began to emerge from the forest floor, and in among the beech trees there were cèpes too. These fabulous mushrooms prompted only moderate delight in Opitz and Raimund. It was Wojnicz who kept jumping up and down with excitement, emitting high-pitched shrieks, until finally he stepped aside to remove his vest to use as an extra receptacle for his harvest. As he picked up leaves with the tip of his walking stick, he realized that he was looking for morels, the mushrooms of his childhood—in those days he and his father would wander the groves for hours in search of those beautiful, mysterious fruits of the forest, which tasted like no other on earth. Afterward, he always wanted to help Gliceria peel them, clean their bodies of dry leaves, pine needles and soil, and peep under their crumpled caps, but his father was against it. They would leave the basket in the kitchen, and then his father would make him copy entire passages from Sienkiewicz's *Trilogy* to practice his handwriting. Gliceria was to take care of the mushrooms.

Having dropped behind, from afar Wojnicz saw the stooping figures of the two men picking something in a clearing. Excited, they had fallen silent.

"What wonder is this?" he asked as he approached.

They did not answer. Between finger and thumb, they were carefully taking hold of some tiny mushrooms on spindly stalks, miserable, uninteresting-looking things. Wojnicz squatted to examine them more closely—they were wretched little creatures with grayish Phrygian caps.

"For the liqueur," said Opitz, without looking at him. "Schwärmerei."

So that's what it is, thought Wojnicz, and leaned over to join them.

"What are they called?"

"There are various names," replied Opitz. "Spitzkegelige Kahlköpfe, our local sweet liberty caps," he said, smiling, and for the first time Wojnicz saw his teeth, large and widely spaced.

Wojnicz was happy to join in this harvest, and soon they had filled every empty space in the baskets with these fragile oddities on their long, thin stalks, the jewels of the fungus world, delicate and very valuable as an ingredient in that illustrious drink. Wojnicz sat down on the soft moss without worrying about getting his trousers wet or dirty, and once again closely inspected these inconspicuous items. In comparison with the fat, sumptuous cèpes or the elegantly upholstered bay boletes, the little liberty caps looked quite insubstantial. Frail and brittle, they seemed to quake at the mere sound of human footsteps, and a careless grip could easily destroy their fragile little caps, no, they were more like hoods, the kind that are put on infants' heads; even the freshest specimen was already damaged, its little hood going black from the bottom, as if aging were a special feature of this species. And yet once you grasped it by the stalk, you could feel its surprising elasticity, the resistance of matter that only appeared to be fragile and easily destroyed—yes, in it lay that strength of the weak, so common in nature, camouflaged and deceiving the senses. If not for this quality, the world would consist of nothing but strong, delicious, perfect specimens, nothing but the noblest cèpes.

With his less than agile fingers Opitz grabbed a mushroom below the cap and carefully pulled it from the ground, then placed it in the basket as if it were very precious. Wojnicz did his best to copy him. He asked how much liqueur this number of mushrooms would produce and how Schwärmerei was made, but Opitz was so engrossed in what he was doing that he gave only perfunctory answers, and Mieczysław learned nothing specific.

Once they had picked this beautiful glade clean, they went back into the forest and set off toward home—at least so it seemed to Wojnicz, who had lost his bearings. They walked downhill along the edge of a young spruce wood, passing on the right a lovely beech forest carpeted in bright green moss.

"Look over there," said Raimund suddenly, in a strange, husky voice, and gave a cackle. "It's over there. What a big one."

Wojnicz did not immediately understand what he was referring to, and it took him a while to spot a worrying, strangely familiar shape on a small rise in the forest floor. They went closer—Raimund giggling the whole time—and then Mieczysław could make out that it was indeed a human shape. An unpleasant shiver ran through him, and he felt the alarm of seeing a fellow creature in danger.

But it turned out to be a puppet made of moss, sticks, dry pine needles and rotten wood, overgrown with a fine lace of mushroom spawn. The head, quite deftly made spherical, had a face formed from a bracket fungus, with pine cones driven into it for eyes, and an opening drilled into its softer part for a mouth. Thin twigs imitated long hair scattered all around. The figure's arms and legs were thrown to the sides, and between the legs—instantly attracting an onlooker's attention—was a dark, narrow hole, a tunnel into the depths of this organic forest body. It also had breasts made of stones, with nipples painted on them in some sort of sap, and wide hips. The belly was coated in soft moss.

Wojnicz felt a sort of inner commotion in his whole being; he was overcome by a strong impression of being outside reality that rose to his throat, forcing him to swallow his saliva several times, though he did not yet know what he was looking at. Raimund laughed hoarsely, and he and Opitz exchanged knowing glances. Wojnicz gazed in fascination at this mid-forest anomaly, at this contravention of the usual order of things. It had taken someone a good deal of time to create this figure, not quite human and not quite vegetable. They must have spent ages considering and preparing the materials. The stones on the chest had been imported from somewhere; they were pebbles, so they must have come from a stream below.

"It's the charcoal burners. This is their handiwork," said Willi Opitz. "They wanted to enjoy themselves. Let's get out of here."

He picked up the baskets and set off downhill, and Wojnicz followed. Raimund dallied a little longer, looking around, as if to remember the spot, but finally he caught up with them, and fifteen minutes later they were in the village.

Willi was reluctant to answer questions, but by the time they reached the Guesthouse for Gentlemen Wojnicz had managed to extract the entire bizarre story.

The charcoal burners whom he had seen before at the clearing, the men with blackened faces and gloomy expressions who occasionally came down to the village to get drunk, had an ancient custom that they never mentioned, but everyone knew about it anyway. They came to work for the whole season from far away. Deprived of women for such agonizing periods of abstinence (and many of them were not married in the first place), they made themselves these recumbent Puppen, or dolls, to relieve themselves.

The dolls were known as Tuntschi, that's what people called them, and to soften what he had said, Opitz added that such practices existed wherever there were men, because men need gratification and they cannot wait, or they become sick and dangerous. Male desire must be instantly satisfied, otherwise the world would collapse in chaos. So it was, the world over. Because men's desire was so strong that it could destroy them, they had to have a means of relief. Anyone should understand this and find it normal. Similar Tuntschi were also made in the Alps, where the shepherds were away in the mountain pastures for the entire season and were thus entitled to seek this form of gratification. But it happened on the distant steppes too, where men tended to herds of animals. And among gold prospectors.

"Wherever men are deprived of women," cackled Raimund, who had rejoined them.

So the Tuntschi were a part of life, and the fact that Wojnicz had never heard of them meant merely that he was still wet behind the ears and should finally become a man. As he said this, Opitz grabbed him by the shoulder and with a rough gesture shook him, hugging him to his hard, manly chest. Several chanterelles spilled from the young man's vest.

As Wojnicz was changing for supper, picking pine needles out of his socks, brushing cobwebs off the woolen sleeves of his jacket and combing seeds, bits of twigs and God knows what else out of his hair—everything that the forest leaves on us—he thought about it all. Did he ever feel the sort of desire Opitz had been talking about? Had he ever experienced anything so overwhelming?

When he entered the dining room, everyone turned toward him with curiosity and barely concealed but friendly smiles.

For supper, baked zander was served, and a heap of potatoes with a chanterelle sauce, thickened with cream and sprinkled with parsley. No one failed to ask for a second helping. Wojnicz scrupulously recorded this menu in his diary.

Everyone talked about how, as soon as a place became free, they would move into the Kurhaus, from which one might assume that they were living at the Guesthouse for Gentlemen temporarily. Wojnicz was intelligent enough to understand that a sort of game was being played that suited each of them, and in which he too had started to take part without even noticing. For in fact nobody believed a place there would ever be vacated. He too refused to believe it. Perhaps he did not really want this mythical place to become free—because then he would have to fulfill his promise and move to the main sanatorium building, and that would be disastrous for his wallet. While at the Guesthouse for Gentlemen one paid a monthly average of 150 marks, at the Kurhaus one had to lay out twice as much. Of course it would be far more convenient to live there, because everything was right at hand, the rooms were more comfortable and the cooking decidedly better; sometimes delicious aromas floated all the way to the park.

When seen on the promenade, the Kurhaus patients looked taller and cleaner, and their shirts were whiter. They were like well-fed poultry, even if they were as sick as others—the women wore the "pigeon breasts" that had been in fashion for several years, a frilly ruffle of cambric or silk on their chests that made it look as if they had just boiled over the top of their tight, narrow skirts, while the men's heads protruded from stiff collars, as if they were being served on a tray for afternoon tea, and their frock coats were like the plumage of male pigeons. The patients dressed carefully for their walks, as though they were not languishing at a sanatorium but taking part in a national holiday. Heard from afar as they strolled along, their voices were like the cooing of pigeons, and they made little holes in the pavement with the tips of their canes and parasols.

The mere fact of having rooms at the Kurhaus ennobled and gave them a distinct advantage on the promenade—it guaranteed them the right of way and seats on the benches, the upper hand in debates, and priority in telling jokes. The daily walk was part of the triumph they celebrated here, within the sad reality of their illness, merely because by reason of their wealth they managed to be sick in better circumstances and in a more civilized way.

The patients from the guesthouses and rented rooms in villas walked at a different pace, which was hastier, let us even say pragmatic, because it led to a goal, which is always a feature of the lower born. And the poorer patients who lived at the Volksheilstätten-Abteilung strayed about the grounds of the sanatorium, as it were exchanging expensive medical treatments for the simplest and perhaps most effective fresh-air therapy.

Quite often Mieczysław heard Polish being spoken on the promenade. Or during the rest cure, from the other end of the veranda words reached his hearing that seemed rounder, friendlier; they instantly caught his attention, not like ordinary sounds, but complete meaning, which meant they crowded into his brain and refused to leave it. In this calm environment that was supposed to be curing rather than upsetting him, they were like treacherous roots sticking out of a flat surface, easy to trip over.

Wojnicz did his best to avoid encountering his compatriots at all. In the first place, he thought it better to practice his German than waste energy on chitchat. Secondly, the Poles irritated him. He was annoyed by their herdlike way of clinging together in a social clot that shifted this way and that along the promenade, self-absorbed, outwardly self-confident, but in fact full of complexes and a shameful sense of incongruity. They formed a mobile hub of the universe, concerned only with itself, blind to everything around it. Sometimes as they passed him, always in a group, he heard words and phrases that made him feel disconcerted, even though they were perfectly innocent: *albeit, Good day, madam, Do forgive me, sir.* They took him back to Lwów, when he had managed to get so far away and was almost free. He was annoyed by the Poles' carefully hidden insecurity, masked in every possible way, poised to shift into bravado rather than let itself show.

Most often he saw three men of a similar age who always walked together, dressed a little carelessly but well. Their accent implied that they could be from Warsaw. The oldest, a slightly corpulent, balding gentleman in spectacles, looked like a teacher, and that was how Wojnicz thought of him. The second—not much older than Mieczysław, emaciated and coughing—could have been anything: a student, a clerk, a poor relation living at a manor house owned by a rich family . . . And finally the third was a small, bearded man who always leaned on a cane while gesticulating violently with his free hand. Sometimes they were joined by two ladies, both in ugly jackets of a nondescript color, and then the company became noisy, if not truculent. One of the women had a pearly laugh that drew the attention of all the other promenaders. On occasion they were accompanied by an elderly married couple, well dressed and highly dignified, whose trademark was the gold monocle each of them wore, symmetrically placed in the left eye of one and the right eye of the other, as if they used them as a sign of their eternal marital bond instead of wedding rings.

One day the trio approached Wojnicz in the dining room as he was finishing his lunch, scraping the final teaspoonfuls of vanilla pudding out of the cup. They stood over him with a look of triumph on their faces, as though they had just hunted down a rare animal.

"We are pleased to meet a compatriot in foreign parts at last," said the one with the jovial expression, who went on to introduce himself as engineer Mroczek.

Confused, Wojnicz could not answer because his mouth was full of pudding that he could not swallow. He felt pinned to the wall, hunted down.

"And we thought you were a Kraut," added the second fellow reproachfully.

Mieczysław put down his napkin and stood up, as if called to an exam. The gentlemen invited him for postprandial coffee at another table, under a large palm. Wojnicz did not know how to refuse, so he headed after them in a cross fire of questions: whence, where, how, et cetera.

They gave him a thorough interrogation, to which Wojnicz replied routinely, if not evasively, which aggravated his questioners. They wanted to know where he was from, what he did, how old he was and whether he was married, what he was studying and who was his professor, and what he had done for a year in Dresden. And why was he so pale, how advanced was his illness and what was his father's annual income. And what he was planning to do afterward. And whether Dr. Semperweiss offended him too. And finally: Who were his co-residents and what did he think about the prices in the village. How much did his room cost and did he know of cheaper accommodation. Who was Sydonia Patek, did she have a husband or was she perhaps a "maid of Lesbos." Once they had finished asking questions, and the coffee had been drunk, they moved on to singing their own praises. Engineer Mroczek for example was the ultimate authority on modern threshing machines, while one of the ladies painted on silk. They talked through their noses, lengthening their vowels, while looking over the heads of the seated company as if somewhere over yonder lay the true motherland from which they drew their strength.

So no wonder that as soon as Wojnicz saw them approaching and realized that their paths might cross, he turned aside, onto the nearest little bridge, and crossed the stream, heading for the forest, or went the other way, to the upper village, or even ducked into the patisserie or the post office, just to hide from them. This was the most serious threat he encountered during his walks.

Why was our Mieczysław so afraid of them? Did he fear that they would peel away his carefully constructed image of a person who is on good terms with himself, who feels all right about himself and is sure of his own opinions? That they would take him back to Lwów, to face all those persecutors—at school, in the street, in doctors' consulting rooms, in his own home? All those physicians who tsk-tsked over him with such concern? That they would drag him into those low, hot kitchens where czernina was constantly being made? Into the cellars where toads sat on piles of potatoes sprouting in the darkness, and his uncle's boots could be seen through the windows—rapping away, one, two, at a marching step, while his hand squeezed little Mieczyś's shoulder?

He preferred to belong to this world, which did not yet know him and in whose eyes he still had time to define himself. He would rather take the risk that one day this world too would disappoint him, and he would have to run away again, escape to yet another, more distant location to avoid falling into the arms of that familiar, hopeless state in which one was simply a bother to oneself and others. By this point he had just about adopted the idea that his illness had come upon him at a very good moment in his young life, giving him a chance to reformulate himself, and that he should actually be happy to have ended up here, in this little Silesian health resort, built on the waters of an underground lake.

Of all the treatments prescribed for him, Wojnicz had an immediate, intense hatred of the Regenbad, a shower at a temperature of six to eight degrees centigrade, to which his half-naked body was subjected for up to a minute, to stimulate the body's defenses. From the start he did his best to avoid it, complaining to the doctor of a raised temperature or of feeling "weak"; another reason was that the appliance was deployed by Herr Schwartz, an elderly man with a military figure who showered his wretched victims with his sadistic pleasure as the icy water made them shudder. With one hand Wojnicz held on to his bathing drawers, while shielding his tender nipples with the other, as Herr Schwartz passed the hose and showerhead over his poor, shivering body. Herr Schwartz always tried to shame him, shouting as if at a cadet: "Come on, boy, don't snivel! Steel yourself! Be a man, not an old woman!" And: "Stand to attention, soldier!" Wojnicz also had to submit to treatments known as Strahlendusche, which meant having cold water poured over the back of the head twice a day. The aim of this was to invigorate the skin, to toughen up Wojnicz's feeble body, and above all to immunize his body against bad weather.

Sometimes Mieczysław would be close to tears, filled with deep loathing for Herr Schwartz. Besides him, there was a Bademeister, known simply as Oskar. Large, fat and muscular, with a clean-shaven head, he was usually placid and reticent. When the frozen Wojnicz was finally released from the grip of the torturer Schwartz, Oskar would rub him hard with a rough towel, knead his poor body like dough and smear warming oil on his back.

At the start of his stay, Wojnicz had complained of mild diarrhea and gastritis. It must have been the effect of switching to a new diet and adjusting to the local climate and water. Dr. Semperweiss had recommended a dose of pepsin to enhance the work of the stomach, and at night, Dover's powder, which they were very keen on here: it was a mixture consisting of one part opium, one part emetic powder and eight parts milky sugar, which had both a diaphoretic and a soporific effect.

Wojnicz's favorite place at the Kurhaus was the winter garden, which one entered from the dining room with its six enormous tables that could feed all the patients, in shifts. For Mieczysław, lunches there were quite stressful, and he wondered whether to give up on them and fully rely on Opitz and Raimund's cooking.

He was served in the final sitting, when the dining hall was already practically deserted and—most important—there were none of those Poles, because they were among the first to eat. He usually sat in the company of an old couple from Switzerland and two elderly Russian women who spoke hardly any language but their own, so he did not have to go out of his way to make conversation. The lunch was always extremely good. For example, today there was fried trout in almond sauce, a local specialty, with baked salsify and potatoes roasted with bacon and plenty of onions. And fried egg too, very yellow, sprinkled with chives. For dessert there were sorbets in several flavors. His favorite was blackberry. Wojnicz had soon learned that after such a large meal it did him good to drink a cup of coffee in the winter garden, at an openwork metal table with a view of the park. He would sit where nobody could accost him, and look through the German newspapers, in which with genuine interest he read the advertisements and articles about fashion.

Some large philodendrons with split leaves grew here, and also palms, trying hard to open the large windows with their splayed fingers and get outside. In the sunniest spot there were some cacti, one of which was more than two meters tall, and beyond them some plants whose names he did not know. There was always more moisture in here than anywhere else, producing a wonderful aroma of aerated soil and something like ozone. The wicker armchair in which he settled comfortably creaked gently with every move—this faint sound reminded him of the good times long ago, when his father and uncle had taken him to Zaleszczyki, where they sat in wicker beach chairs by a cold, shallow river, and his uncle brought ice creams in wafer cones. The taste of it had set the standard for all ice cream forever after.

As he sat in the wicker armchair in the winter garden at the Kurhaus, he was beset by memories. He was unaware of having so many of them; after all, he was a young man, and had never given himself so much thought before. He found himself remembering petty incidents of no importance, such as the time his uncle had given him a few small coins, so he had gone down to the colonial store to buy himself some praline sweets. When he reached the counter, he discovered that there was no money in the pocket where he had put it shortly before. His surprise was immense, he fingered every cranny of his clothing, trying to feel the shape of the coins, but the money was gone. Mr. Mincer, who had already handed him the little bag of sweets, watched him with rising impatience, until finally he lost his temper and asked the next customer to approach the counter.

Little Mieczyś left the shop and burst into tears in the gateway to his home. Later, he carefully searched the entire route from their apartment on the first floor to the little shop on the corner, centimeter by centimeter, but found nothing. To this day he had no idea what could have happened to those coins. But at home he said he had eaten all the sweets, which made his uncle laugh and his father scowl. He had preferred to be suspected of greed than of being such a hopeless loser.

He was also reminded of childhood baths. There was always something nervous about them. His father would take a long time to test him on his prayers before reluctantly handing him over to Gliceria. He would lead the child to her kingdom, the kitchen, where a tin tub full of hot, steaming water would already be waiting on the floor. The scent of soap and clean towels was a festive smell, the fragrance of Saturdays. Wojnicz could not remember his father ever being present at bath time. Gliceria would receive him in her plump hands, with her sleeves rolled up to the elbows, ruddy from the heat and smiling, and from that point on little Mieczyś became a participant in the ritual of undressing, being immersed in the water, and being scrubbed with a washcloth moistened with the scented soap that Gliceria kept specially for his delicate skin and that nobody else used.

Throughout the bath she twittered away to him in Polish and Ukrainian as nobody else ever did. He was her "little pearl," her "baby soap bubble," her "buttercup," her "little gem" and her "wee angel." The profusion of names intoxicated the young Mieczyś, who could not absorb all the images magically revealed by these words: jewels, churches, forests, gardens—an entire world was contained in them and other worlds too, that he did not know from his own experience, but the shape of which he could imagine. The parts of his body were his "handies," his "tootsies," his "leglets," his "wee chest"; addressed this way, he felt pleased with himself and somehow even proud of his existence, a feeling he never had when communing with his father. As he gazed at his protruding stomach it was a "tummy," and the hole in it was his "belly button." Gliceria would coo over him with sweat pouring from her brow, the entire kitchen now a steam bath.

Then she would pull Mieczyś out and onto the table, where a towel was spread, and rub the boy dry, tickling him under the arms or pretending she wanted to bite off his "wee toes." Mieczyś remembered not to laugh too loud, for fear of alarming his father, who would probably race in here, trailing the cold from the corridor and halting this delicious game, so he just giggled quietly.

The freshly laundered flannel pajamas were stiff and unpleasant, but Mieczyś knew that next morning, after the first night, they would be the same as ever—nice and soft. The passage of time smoothed out the creases and roughness, making the world a friendlier place. Once he was sitting in his pajamas, Gliceria would fetch a comb and run it through his fair hair, cut in a pageboy, and could never resist trying to braid it into little plaits.

"It's so strong, so thick," she would say.

It was wonderful to find that the repertoire of valuable things he had at his disposal included his hair. Of course she quickly unplaited it, but she would comb it in curls on his brow, which his father instantly ruffled when he came to say good night, as Mieczyś lay in the cold room in freshly starched sheets, with a bedwarmer at his feet, reflecting on those weekly moments of bath-time endearments.

One day, on his way back to the guesthouse, Wojnicz went into the patisserie, Laugers Konditorei und Café, where he bought a box of pistachio macaroons—he thought their willow-green color looked refined, promising a flavor that would be hard to define precisely and that he was curious about. Later he would write in his diary: *The actual cake is very light, the shell crunchy. Not as sweet as our macaroons from Zalewski's. But the filling is flavorless, and the color may have been added artificially, made of spinach.*

Just outside the guesthouse, hearing someone shout from far away in Polish: "A capital joke! You have quite an imagination!," he instinctively quickened his pace to reach the shelter of the building as soon as possible.

How did he come to be at the edge of the forest that same afternoon? A light drizzle had scared off all the walkers, and a good thing too—nobody saw him leaving the guesthouse, and instead of walking the usual route under an umbrella like a good boy, he turned aside.

He doggedly climbed uphill—thank goodness he had put on his old shoes—occasionally struggling to catch his breath. Now and then he stopped and looked around carefully, trying not to miss a single detail of the forest floor. He was looking for a sign, sticks arranged in a cross, pine cones set out in a particular order, unusually shaped roots, something to imply that he was close. The moist air, bloated with fragrance, was as meaty as food. Wojnicz's head was spinning, he kept having to stop and hug a tree. He felt feverish—perhaps his temperature had risen sharply—so he promised himself he would head back in a moment, as Dr. Semperweiss would be horrified by this escapade. And he knew perfectly well that he had already crossed the boundary of common sense, that Holy Grail of Herr Lukas, who would certainly not shove his way through the bushes to climb the hill. Or perhaps he would do just that? Maybe he went there too, when nobody was looking? And maybe Herr August appeared there, gasping and perspiring, wiping beads of sweat from his brow with the hem of his foulard? And what about Opitz? Did he go off pretending to be picking those little liberty cap mushrooms of his, when in fact they were just an excuse to come out here? Because Raimund—Wojnicz was in no doubt about this—definitely went there.

Where the brush ended and the beech forest began, Mieczysław slowed down. He found a huge cèpe and hesitated before picking it because he had neither a knapsack nor a string bag to put it in, but he could not ignore such a great gift, so he carried it in his hand.

No woods are lovelier or more intoxicating than a beech forest. At this time of year the leaves were already dark red, spreading a purple vault overhead that separated Wojnicz from the gray of the autumn sky. Silvery tree trunks supported this colossus, creating naves and chapels. The light that fell in here was mottled by the stained-glass windows of the treetops, where every leaf was like a piece of crystal playing with the light according to its own rules. Wojnicz walked along a central nave toward an altar in the distance, not yet visible, but everything foretold it—this was a church full of labyrinths, side naves, crypts beneath the stones, tabernacles hidden in holes in the trees, altars materializing on the mossy trunks of toppled beeches. This church was not at all definite, like a man-made church, but a place of constant change: of water into life, and of light into matter. Everything here was rustling, swelling, gathering, growing and multiplying, budding and trilling. The green moss and gray lichen made the forest seem carpeted in Persian rugs—in velveteen, sheepskin, woolly felt and soft flannel. Why on earth hadn't he come here sooner?

He came to a glade where numerous spruce trees had been planted in disciplined ranks—imported from Bavaria in the belief that they would take root in Silesia too, they were an alien element. The spruces reminded Wojnicz of Prussian troops, but what about the beeches? Those he associated with a colorful, exotic army that never went into battle but proudly flaunted its costumes, its plumes and the golden glints of metal on its helmets, and then stood immobile, to be admired rapturously for years on end. This was an army for the opera, not for war.

He almost trod on it.

He was in a clearing where there were several birches and a small oak, and plenty of stones and moss that had already covered the mouths of the boulders, muting them. It was another Puppe, not the one he had seen with Opitz and Raimund, but slightly smaller. It was lying in the moss, in fact it was moss, its body was drawn clearly and abundantly, the breasts were two stones, and this time the face was made of birch-bark on which someone had painted a pair of charcoal eyes. Moisture in the air had already blurred them, so they looked like two dark stains. The entire body culminated at a single point below the "hips," where the legs parted; a hole yawned between them, like a mouse's shelter or the entrance to a mole's den—a frequently used path, smoothed and polished.

Wojnicz stepped back cautiously, staring underfoot in fear of tread-ing on something *live*. With a mixture of horror and fascination he gazed at the effigy, carefully made of whatever was to hand in the forest—stones and moss, twigs, bark, mushrooms, leaves and loam. All he could hear was his own rapid breathing; the forest seemed to have fallen silent, and to be watching this encounter between human being and something not human, but boldly pretending to be. Yes, ev-erything was staring at him. He felt as if some ultra-vision were seeing through his hand-knitted sweater, his linen shirt and his cotton vest. It was an extremely unpleasant sensation, similar to the way he felt while Dr. Semperweiss was examining his body. He took a step backward, ready to return to the village immediately. But he had not yet had his fill of looking at this would-be creation of nature. He knew it was the work of those charcoal burners with the sooty faces. Involuntarily Wojnicz imagined them copulating with the Puppe, in his mind's eye he could see the violence of male desire, its impatience and overpowering force. He had only seen something like it once, in a barn in the countryside—the steadily moving buttocks of a nameless village boy whose body was covering the maid who milked their cows. It was like a vague portent of violence and bloodshed. He felt a hot wave of fear rising from the pit of his stomach before it surged right through him, to the tips of his ears. Then it was as if the shape on the forest floor were groaning and moving its hips, as though an underground force were pushing it upward. He stared with his eyes wide open, but the illusion vanished.

The horrible feeling that he was being watched had reached its zenith. He began to sweat. And felt terrified by the rapid speed at which dusk was falling. Gradually, trying not to make a noise, he backed out of the glade, and then, stretching his long legs, he virtually ran down to the village, swearing never to come here again.

10

THE CULMINATION
OF GEOMETRY

ll the curtains in Thilo's room had been drawn wide open to let in as much light as possible, and only now could one see the red patches on his face caused by fever. His fair hair, damp with perspiration, was twisted into little curls, and he looked like a small boy who has overheated while playing an intense game. A painting covered with frayed muslin stood on a rather primitive easel, probably knocked together by Raimund, or else bought from a local craftsman, while some chromolithographs interleaved with tissue paper lay on the table. Against the wall there was a large, flat cardboard portfolio, in which Thilo kept his treasures.

"Have you been to see Dr. Semperweiss?" asked Thilo, with hope in his eyes.

"Yes."

"Did he say anything about me?"

"Well, yes, he did, he said you're going through a worse period now. But that it's normal."

"Normal?"

"That it works like amplitude, now better, now worse."

This explanation plainly reassured Thilo.

"Didn't he urge you to move into the Kurhaus? Didn't I hear that some rooms have been vacated?" he asked suspiciously.

Wojnicz was arranging pistachio pastries on a small plate, removing them from the cardboard box with his long fingers.

"I think we're better off here, and the daily walk to the Kurhaus does us good," he replied. "Besides, as you know, I'm trying to save money . . ."

"Take a seat," commanded Thilo, pulling a chair up for his friend. "He hasn't been receiving me since last week, so maybe I'm doing badly."

"What are you saying?" Wojnicz scolded him, aware that he did not sound convincing enough.

"Have you ever seen a swamp on fire? That's how I feel. As if the moisture I have in my body were burning inside me. I'm choking on the smoke."

They were looking at reproductions and prints. Thilo talked of his good friend György, whom he missed—that is what he said: "I miss him badly." Virtually deprived of contact with his family, Thilo had to cope on his own and take advantage of the help of others. György had also made sure Thilo could have his albums and reproductions here, in order to work on his doctoral thesis about the significance of landscape in art, with particular reference to the Flemish painter Herri met de Bles. The work was demanding and difficult, because de Bles's paintings were scattered about minor collections, and his authorship was in many cases uncertain.

"We rarely notice what a painted landscape is really like. We fix our focus on the horizon and look at the depicted image. There we see the lines of hillocks and hills, woods and trees, the roofs of houses and the course of roads, and because we know what they are, and we know their names, we see everything in these categories, all separately. Ah, we say, the road winds through a valley. Or: The forest is growing on a hillside. Oh, there are some bare mountaintops. That's how we see."

He glanced at Wojnicz with glittering eyes.

"But I tell you, there's another kind of looking too, total, complete and absolute. I call it *transparent looking*." He repeated these words twice, as if Wojnicz was to drum them into his head forever. "It goes beyond the detail, it leads, as Herr August would say, to the foundations of the view in question, to the basic idea, leaving out the minor features that continually scatter a person's mind and vision. If you look this way," he said, squinting, and even crossing his eyes a little, or so it seemed to Wojnicz, "and shift yourself here as well"—at this point he tapped his head—"you would see something else entirely."

Once again the blush appeared on his cheeks that made him look like a child. Wojnicz was infected by his passion but still did not understand.

"Do you know this? Have you ever played it?" He opened a drawer and took out a very precise geometric drawing, showing some cubes joined together into a sort of cluster.

"Look," he said, pressing the drawing into Wojnicz's hands. "First find the distance and keep looking until you see three-dimensional movement."

Wojnicz did not fully understand what he was meant to do. Copying Thilo, he squinted and crossed his eyes a bit; his vision doubled strangely and went misty, but after a while, to his astonishment, the cubes were moving! How hard it was to maintain that eye position, as if looking consisted of strips, as if he had just hit upon one of these thin paths, and now that he was following it, he was seeing the cubes in a

completely different way than before. This involved heightened attention, a new kind of concentration in order not to lose this mode of looking, but he was not quite in control of it yet. Just a slight movement of
the head and the spell was suddenly broken; once again he saw an ordinary drawing, a flat collection of squares and rhombuses. So out of
pure curiosity he started looking for the way back onto the path; it
eluded him, but finally he caught sight of it again and saw the moving
blocks. This change of perspective gave him great intellectual rather
than visual pleasure—it was a bit like discovering a new drink or a
new dish, as though this unimaginable capacity, until now hidden and
rendered idle by inactivity, had been in him since birth. He amused
himself with it for about a quarter of an hour.

"Do you have any other drawings?" he asked.

Thilo said yes.

"But it's not about entertainment. It's a deadly serious matter."

Thilo shifted the easel to face the window.

"Why should I refuse you this? Let's not wait, take a look!"

He presented Wojnicz with a small oil painting of a mountain landscape. It was hard to say which part of the world it depicted, because
the mountains had a slightly fantastical, exaggerated shape, as if they
were built out of air. There were also some impossible buildings tower-
ing on them. At the center there was a swirling green olive grove, but
Wojnicz's sight was instantly drawn to a group of colorful, dramatic
figures.

"That's Abraham. And there's Isaac. Any fool would recognize it,"
said Wojnicz, sure of himself.

"The people don't matter. Narrow your eyes."

Mieczysław smiled hesitantly. He looked once, and again. He was
expecting to see movement in the picture, as in the case of the cubes that
had suddenly started to dance, but here there was nothing going on.

"Look, don't jabber," Thilo admonished him.

The painting was of Abraham's sacrifice and everything that the average person raised in the Christian religion knew about those events from the remote mythical past. To test his faithful servant, God had demanded that he sacrifice his beloved son. And so Abraham had taken Isaac off into the wilderness, to a place where sacrifices were made, and there he intended to take his son's life with a sword. God was so highly satisfied with the man's obedience that at the last moment he sent his angel to stay both the hand and the sword. The picture that Thilo had now shown him caught the most dramatic moment—steered by the father's hand and the forces of gravity, the sword was already aiming for the boy's nape. Quite oblivious, the child was waiting humbly for what would happen next. Hovering in the air, with all its angelic might, the angel was trying to stay the father's hand. Judging from the position of its body, this was not easy, because Abraham's hand had already gathered impetus and the blade was just about to strike the child's delicate neck with great force. One could have learned a great deal by looking at the angel's face, but it was hidden behind golden angel hair, in a shadow that seemed unexpected on the face of a heavenly creature; it could have been mistaken for the face of a bearded man, though angels did not have genders, let alone beards. Behind the father's back a gaping hole in the vegetation attracted Wojnicz's attention—there was something going on in this dark patch, something was glittering or shimmering, or some eyes were looking out of there.

He moved the picture closer to his own eyes, which were tired but focusing hard enough to make them water—the scene blurred a little, and the landscape changed into spots of ocher and green, brown and diluted gray. The image converted into its essential components—spots and streaks, brushstrokes and tiny flecks that grouped into vague, imprecise shapes. And once the viewer's attention was well and

truly put to sleep, a new sight loomed out of the picture, the old contours arranged themselves into something completely different that
had not seemed to be there before, but must have been, since now he
could see it. Wojnicz cried out in horror and turned to look at Thilo,
who was gazing at him with satisfaction.

"What did you see?" he asked.

"Something like . . . I don't really know. A face . . . a body? Something alive?"

"Everyone sees something different. A projection. That's Herri met
de Bles for you," said Thilo.

"What was it?" asked Wojnicz, shocked.

"Not *was*. It's still there. It's an illusion, don't be afraid."

"But the picture . . . Which is the real one?"

"Both are real, this one and the other one that's there inside it when
you change your way of looking, when you narrow your eyes."

"Where did you get it from? Is it a copy?" asked Wojnicz, moving
his face close to the canvas and tracing every detail of this peculiar
painting. He would have liked to pick up a magnifying glass to study
the third and fourth planes, for strange things could be seen there, a
figure rising in the air in the golden glow, a human shape hidden in the
tangle of greenery, or two glowing eyes in the chasm of the under-
growth. Streaks, misleading patches of unexpected depth, brushstrokes
that were in fact a labyrinth. Startled, Wojnicz shifted his gaze onto
Thilo with a question in his eyes. Naturally Thilo did not answer. He
was amused by Wojnicz's intense reaction. He slid down his pillows
and lay on his back.

"It's not a copy," he said a little later, staring at the ceiling. "I stole
that painting."

From his reluctant monosyllables Wojnicz learned that the picture
had been in the possession of Thilo's family and that it was the one and

only thing he had taken from home, with no intention of ever going back.

"I regard it as the dowry that was due to me," he said, while Wojnicz observed that his friend's lips were shut tight and his eyes had glazed over. "Every day I check to see if that raised hand with the sword has fallen yet. One can imagine looking at this whole situation a second later, as the blade plunges into the boy's neck and blood spurts from it, splashing the rough surface of the sacrificial stone, and human blood mixes with animal. It would be a sort of relief, don't you think? Anyway, that's the truth. Abraham killed his firstborn son, because that's what God wanted him to do. In the Bible it's clear. It says that Abraham returned from Mount Moriah alone, with just his servant. There's no mention of Isaac. He killed Isaac. And the one who appears later in the Bible is someone else, a substitute. God officiates on Murderer's Mount. He still takes hostages and is happy to accept human sacrifices. We think of sacrifice as a dreadful, barbaric thing, but it's we who think like that, we who are living today. In the past, people needed sacrifices to have a sense of their own causality in the face of God. And they still need sacrifices, so they never stop looking for opportunities and justifications for making them. After all, making a sacrifice is an expression of one's own strength and power over the world. You share the world with God, you let him nip off a bit of it, and in doing so you undermine God's greatness and strength. Why should God want sacrifices when he can take whatever he likes? Why should he be given something when he possesses it all anyway?"

Then things became even stranger, because Thilo claimed that a landscape is capable of killing a person. That it has immense strength, because it is a concentration of various energies, the culmination of geometry. And this happens here too, in Görbersdorf, once a year the landscape takes its sacrifice and kills a man. He said it is a great mistake to have ended up here, because now they have all become potential victims of this place. And they are constantly being watched by the local landscape.

"Look out of the window, it's as if everything has a face, do you understand?"

Wojnicz was aware that his friend's temperature must have risen, and he was considering calling for a doctor from the Kurhaus. Yes, Thilo was raving. But just then, Opitz entered the room without knocking, and with a serious look on his face placed a hand on Thilo's brow.

"Please go and fetch Raimund," he said to Wojnicz. "Have him bring some ice."

That night Wojnicz had a weird dream. He was in the consulting room of Dr. Semperweiss, to whom he handed some test results written on a page torn from the Guesthouse for Gentlemen's register. The doctor glanced at them and said: "With results like these, you've been dead for the past three days, my dear sir."

Wojnicz had a nasty feeling. He did not know how to react to the doctor's categorical tone. "For patients like you I have a special passage," said the doctor in an amicable tone. "Please come this way." And he showed him a narrow little door in the corner of the room, right by the floor. "Please hurry up. There's no point in thinking about it," he added, and pushed Wojnicz inside. He found himself in total darkness, where all he could hear was the cooing of pigeons. He woke up in terror.

Now he was lying in bed with his eyes open, listening—somewhere above the ceiling he could hear that strange noise again, quite a pleasant sound at this point, because we tend to like things we have grown used to. Then he realized that it was the middle of the night. He glanced at the watch, a gift from his father, which was lying on the bedside table, and saw that, yes, it was eleven minutes past one. It could not be birds. He felt a wave of heat wash over him that quickly changed into beads of sweat. He kept very still, afraid to lick his chapped lips. He wondered which room was located above him; he had not been in there yet. Next to it, above Thilo, was Frau Opitz's little room, but farther on?

Now he could hear shuffling noises in the corridor, as if someone were dragging something heavy across the floor. Then there were footsteps, and a feeble streak of rusty light flowed into the gap underneath the door. It twinkled, faded and then flared again, as though it was in motion. Petrified with fear, Wojnicz forced himself to sit up on the bed and feel for his slippers with his bare feet. A sudden chill ran through his entire body, as though a wind had pierced his cotton pajamas. His sweat dried in an instant, leaving a nasty sense of cold. There was no alternative. He had to find out what it was. The tension was unbearable. Trying not to make the faintest noise, he went up to the door and, silently repeating the words of the prayer: "Hail Mary, full of grace . . . ," slowly began to open it. Luckily Raimund had oiled the hinges, which did not squeak at all. Then, crossing himself, he put his head out into the corridor and turned the ebonite light switch. At once the electric bulb flashed on close to the ceiling, shielded by a mushroom-shaped glass shade.

A bizarre, stooping figure was creeping along, barefoot in a long garment. It took him a moment to realize that it was August. In a shabby, old-fashioned nightshirt he did not look like himself, on top of which, without its usual ingratiating smile, his face seemed closed and unapproachable. Wojnicz had noticed this before—when August was sure nobody was looking at him, he dropped his customary faint smile and his good-natured, mild expression, then a sharp vertical furrow appeared between his eyebrows and a shadow around his eyes. In a flash August became older and less friendly. Wojnicz found this change startling.

August turned toward him abruptly.

"Who the devil's there?" he asked in a voice hoarse with terror.

"It is I, Herr Professor, it is I, Mieczysław Wojnicz. I heard a murmur. I gave you a shock too." He sighed with relief.

In a split second August's face changed as he did his best to adopt his usual expression, kindly and a little ironical; the attempt was not entirely successful. His cheeks wobbled comically as his lips tried to utter something that made sense in this situation. All he managed was a sort of *uff, uff.* Suddenly Wojnicz felt sorry for Herr August. He tried to talk away the awkward moment.

"I heard noises, and as I couldn't sleep, I decided to see what was going on. Do you hear that cooing from upstairs too? I find it very disturbing. Does Herr Opitz breed pigeons? Don't they fly away for the winter?"

August straightened up, and thanks to the time Wojnicz had given him to pull himself together, he could now say in his usual tone: "Pigeons don't fly away for the winter." Then he added with dignity: "I was going to have a drink of water."

An uneasy silence fell.

Then Herr August said: "As we're already up, why don't we go downstairs for a glass of Schwärmerei?" And without waiting for Wojnicz to answer, he added: "You go down while I go back to my room for my smoking jacket, rather than traipse around in my nightshirt. The shot glasses are in the piano."

Fully awake now, Mieczysław welcomed this proposal. His heart had stopped racing and was demanding some small pleasure as compensation. On his way down the stairs, he stopped at a painting he had noticed before. It was a well-painted still life of a hare hanging head downward, with its throat cut, blood dripping into a bowl. On the table below lay a loaf of bread, a knife and a piece of cheese. Some plums, dark purple and gleaming, swollen-looking, were scattered around.

As he continued down the stairs, he saw a dim, brownish light, and soon after, a candle in the living room illuminating Frommer in full costume, not in his typical frock coat but in an old-fashioned one that buttoned up to the neck. He must have got here just before Wojnicz. Certain that no one could see him, he had taken a shot glass from his pocket and, trying not to make any noise, was pouring himself a drink from the green bottle of dark, almost black liqueur. He relished the first sip, smacking his lips, then threw the rest straight down his throat, all in one go. Wojnicz gave a warning cough and casually entered the dining room. Their gazes came into contact. Mieczysław could not see Frommer's face clearly, because it was hidden in the gloom of the dining room, lit only by the candle, but he could tell that Frommer was not in the least embarrassed at being caught having a drop of Schwärmerei.

"I am reading," said Frommer, pointing at a book lying open on the table. "You see, sir, I am interested in geometry, l'esprit géométrique, Engineer."

"I am not an engineer yet. I haven't completed my studies because of my illness," said Wojnicz, but Frommer took no notice of this at all.

"At any rate, not for the sort of reasons that attract precise minds to geometry. Instead I regard geometry as a cognitive project, in other words the consideration of a vision of the world that would be its reconstruction based on all points from which the world can be seen. Can you imagine that?"

"That would be something mystical," said Wojnicz timidly, unsure if putting the matter that way might not offend this austere man.

But Frommer seemed flattered by this analogy.

"Our senses impose on us a particular kind of knowledge of the world. And they are limited, aren't they? But what if the world around us is entirely different than our imperfect senses try to convince us? Have you ever thought of that?"

"Yes, I was just talking to Thilo about it."

With no shyness at all, Wojnicz peeped into the piano, where he saw several thick-stemmed glasses standing in a disciplined row. He took one and poured himself a shot of the famous liqueur.

"All I know is that, in reality, it seems impossible to coordinate the viewing points," he added.

Then he smiled, as if something had occurred to him.

"Doctor, are you familiar with the counting song the trumpeter plays here? Quite out of tune, in fact."

This melody had been plaguing him from the start. The children sang it as he was on his way to the Kurhaus. Raimund hummed it. The clock at the doctor's had it as a chime.

"I am not a doctor, Herr Wojnicz. Just as you are not an engineer. I study science out of passion."

Frommer went up to the piano, opened the lid and clattered on the keys. Then surprisingly competently played the trumpeter's tune. And sang:

Habt Ihr noch nicht lang geschlafen?
Die Uhr hat eins geschlagen . . . tü, tü, tü.
Habt Ihr noch nicht lang genug geschlafen?
Die Uhr hat zwei geschlagen . . . tü, tü, tü.

It looked as if Frommer would go on singing ad infinitum in his re-markably well-trained, even pleasant tenor, but he stopped after the fourth couplet:

Ist der Jakob noch am Schlafen. Jakob, steh auf.*

Pleased with himself, he closed the piano lid and said: "It's an old Silesian counting song. I knew it as a child."

He began to describe the complicated rules of the game it accompa-nied, and poured himself another glass of Schwärmerei.

The bottle of liqueur always stood on the sideboard. It was a modest-looking bottle, with a slender neck that leaned slightly to one side, as if inviting one to raise it to one's lips. The dark green glass must have had to be melted by hand before being blown at the glassworks in Petersdorf, not a simple process. There was no label or anything to ad-vertise the contents. Beside it, a carafe of water and a tumbler stood on a silver-plated tray. There were no shot glasses for the liqueur, which might suggest that the contents of the bottle should not in fact be drunk. The lack of a suitable glass was a clear sign that different rules were in force here, to which one must conform, waiting for the appro-priate moment when one would be initiated.

As he came in for meals, Wojnicz's eyes had often run into the green bottle quite provocatively displayed on the sideboard; it was actually the first thing one noticed in this heavy room full of wood and hunting trophies. It was only after supper, when Raimund brought in the requi-site number of beautiful little liqueur glasses on a tray, that the bottle was passed around. It seemed inexhaustible, filling glass after glass

---

* (German) Haven't you slept for long enough? / The clock has struck one. / Haven't you had enough sleep yet? / The clock has struck two . . . / Jakob is still asleep. Wake up, Jakob.

with a sort of dogged munificence, prompting smiles on the faces of the beneficiaries. Its strange flavor and smell made Wojnicz think of the word *underground*. It tasted of roots and moss, mushroom spawn and licorice all at once. It must have contained aniseed and wormwood. The first impression on the tongue was not good—it seemed to smell bad, but only for a split second. Then warmth flooded the mouth, and the sensation of an incredible wealth of flavors—like forest berries and something entirely exotic. It occurred to Wojnicz that this was how ants tasted. Yes, it was the flavor of ants. He knew that, because as a child he had once tried to eat an ant and its flavor had stayed with him for good, but that was the extent of his experience as a taster; he had gone no further than this surprising discovery.

He too poured himself another glassful, then decided to question Frommer on the thought that was occupying him.

"You've been here longer than I have. Did you hear about the terrible death in the forest last year? Apparently a body was found torn to pieces."

Frommer's oval face tensed visibly.

"So you already know," he said.

"It's true?" said Wojnicz, worried.

To tell the truth, he had brought up the topic to lighten the atmosphere and to gossip. He had thought it was the product of poor Thilo's feverish delirium.

"I don't know if I can talk to you about it. I'm not sure how you'll take what I have to say."

"I was brought up in the spirit of rationalism to believe there's always an explanation for the strangest things," said Wojnicz.

Frommer looked around, and then suddenly spoke in perfectly good Polish. "There are things that we do not yet understand. It's hard to pass any comment on them, all the more because they're not rational.

Since they exist, they must *fit* into the logic of the world somehow," he said, and fell silent.

Wojnicz stared at Frommer with his eyebrows raised in total astonishment.

"You speak Polish?"

"My mother's maiden name was Wawrzynek," said Frommer, pronouncing the difficult surname with surprising grace; he had clearly practiced it all his life.

"But this is wonderful, I can talk in my own language here."

"Let us not overindulge this secret understanding. But I shall tell you the truth: Unfortunately your question is legitimate. Yes, it's true. People are constantly perishing here. Dying a terrible death. That time is now approaching."

"What time?"

"The first full moon in November. Close to Saint Martin's Day. Sometimes around All Saints'."

Unable to utter a word, Wojnicz gazed at him.

"You're joking," he said at last.

Now Frommer told him the same story that Thilo had, but far more coherently, in a much more systematic way.

"In late autumn, usually around the Catholic Saint Martin's Day, one person dies in the forest, a shepherd or a charcoal burner. A person, meaning a man. Young or in his prime. The remains are found, and this is the worst part of it: bloody human body parts spread about the forest that have to be gathered up and buried. It has been going on since long ago, and it's a wonder this population hasn't dwindled considerably. But in recent years the victims haven't just been local people, that is to say, local men; this cruel slaughter strikes visitors too."

"Patients?" asked Wojnicz in alarm.

"Yes, indeed." Frommer seemed lost in thought, rubbing his smoothly shaven chin. "Mainly patients. One person a year is not so many for such a population. After all, people die here more often than anywhere else. Statistically speaking . . ."

Frommer expatiated about death as though it were a quite dispassionate, clear-cut phenomenon, akin to building a railway line, where one had to establish the frequency of supplies of rails and ties. He presented some statistics for the region, comparing it with other places. With a bony finger he drew a graph on the table, on which his damp fingertip briefly left a mark.

"You know, there are plenty of explanations. It may be wild animals. Apparently wolves come up from the south, from the Czech lands. Maybe a bear from Saxony has ended up here. Or perhaps it's dogs that have gone feral? On top of that, this is a special time of year. In highland regions, there's a day that is celebrated as the close of the farming season. That's when people finally bring down the livestock from the pastures and shut them in barns for the winter. They fatten the geese for Christmas and get ready to butcher the pigs. It's the start of the bloodletting season, my dear fellow."

What exactly are you trying to tell me, Herr Frommer? Wojnicz wanted to ask, but just then a figure appeared on the stairs.

"Would you like a drop of Schwärmerei?" asked Frommer as Herr August came down to them, wearing a beautiful shiny smoking jacket the color of red wine. "We're talking about geometry."

"I'm happy to join in, though I am a humanist to the core."

"But have you heard of the fourth dimension?" asked Frommer quickly, pouring August a generous dose, and without waiting for an answer added: "We live in three dimensions—length, width and depth."

It was evident that the theosophist from Breslau was gearing up for a long speech.

"But one can easily imagine creatures known as Flatlanders, who live in a place called Flatland, as if on a sheet of paper, two-dimensional, where there is no depth. Can you see it? Please activate your imagination. They have no concept of us three-dimensional creatures. We only appear to them when we cut through their two-dimensional, sheet-of-paper world, and even then they can see us only as if in cross section. Do you know what I'm talking about? They don't see our entire figure, but only whatever bisects the plane of their flat land, so to speak. Take a three-dimensional figure, a cube, for instance, with one of its vertices aimed toward Flatland. When it cuts through a two-dimensional plane—try imagining a simple sheet of paper—first the Flatlander will see a single dot, which will at once change into a section of increasing length, which at some point will start in turn to diminish until it is just a disappearing dot. If you, my dear young man, were to dive head-first into Flatland, to put it in a nutshell, first for a split second the Flatlanders would see a dot, then a section the length of the diameter of your head, which would suddenly change into a larger section, just like the width of your torso with the arms pressed against it, and then finally turn into two slightly narrowing sections representing the diameter of your legs that will vanish as soon as your body passes Flatland. No one there could possibly guess what you really look like." Frommer laughed with satisfaction.

"Allow me."

He grabbed Wojnicz's forearm in an iron grip and drew him toward the sideboard, where the bottle of Schwärmerei was standing, then re-filled Wojnicz's glass and lit a cigarette for himself.

"My point is that we may be similarly disabled inhabitants of a world that consists of three dimensions, and we shall never know what a four-dimensional world is like. Do you see? We have no tools or senses to introduce us to a world with an extra dimension, let alone a fifth, and a seventh, and a twenty-sixth. Our minds cannot conceive of it."

It was a very strange speech, because the topic had appeared out of nowhere, and no one else was particularly interested in it. Wojnicz tried to interrupt the speaker, but Frommer was in an odd state of excitement and refused to give up the floor. August meanwhile sipped his drink with his eyes closed, sitting in an armchair, as if Frommer's lecture were of no concern to him at all.

"You know of the Möbius strip, don't you? It's from topology—have you heard of it? The famous strip is a flat piece of tape, the ends of which have been stuck together after being twisted one hundred and eighty degrees. The Flatlanders, inhabiting its surface, live de facto in a two-dimensional world, though they are not aware of this, and think their world has no limit. But what if people, like us here, are also locked inside our three dimensions, entirely unconscious of genuine reality, which takes place in four dimensions?"

"Naturally, you are taking time into consideration too—" said August, trying to interrupt him, but Frommer ignored him.

"Now imagine a cylinder, like this cigarette tube. You glue the ends together, but before that you twist them through a fourth dimension. The result is a strange figure, a bit like a trumpet and a bit like a mushroom. Can you imagine something of the kind?"

Wojnicz was not sure.

"A torus," said Herr August suddenly, as if he had found a long-lost treasure in his capacious memory.

This pleased Frommer.

"It looks as though the humanists know a thing or two," he said approvingly, and addressed Wojnicz again: "Our world may be nothing but a shadow cast by four-dimensional phenomena onto the screens of our senses."

Then he presented them with a theory he had read in the work of some Englishmen, stating that perhaps that extra dimension is a world of thoughts, which have a concrete, material form there, but only reach us as phenomena. A collective mind brings them down here to us, and in doing so creates "thought-forms," forms on the border of the spiritual and material world, created by collective hopes and fears.

"Something like gods?" asked August, with an innocent look on his face, as Longin Lukas appeared, in a coat thrown over a pair of rather grimy pajamas.

"God exists objectively," he said, heading straight for the piano to fetch a shot glass.

Straight after him Thilo arrived, also in pajamas, over which he had thrown a blanket. He looked quite pitiful.

"I can't sleep," he said. "And I can hear your voices, so I decided to join you."

He was given a glass of liqueur—everyone else filled their own glasses too—and as soon as he had become acquainted with the topic of conversation, he was eager to hold forth a bit. The gentlemen began to lecture each other, each presenting his position as though pulling the topic over to his side, like a too-small quilt. It was a good thing Wojnicz had absolutely nothing to say and did not have to speak. But as a result, they addressed themselves to him, as if he would have to judge their eloquence and knowledge afterward.

"That is how art thinks nowadays," began Thilo. "It holds that a depicted object is only our mental projection of it, what we *know* about the object, whereas in fact we have no access to what it *really* looks like or what it actually is. In other words, even traditional representational art creates objects rather than rendering their truth in reality. By doing so, it closes our minds instead of opening them."

"Well said, young man," said Herr August, livening up. "In other words, our agreed-upon projections paralyze our cognition."

"But modern, progressive art, the twentieth-century kind, has far greater ambitions. It wants to go beyond these limitations, to stage a revolution in perception, it wants to see things in a new way, from many viewpoints simultaneously, even ones that seem impossible. Cubism, futurism. These currents do not reach backwaters like this one."

Speaking with such conviction, Thilo was beautiful, despite the dark, feverish flush in his cheeks. Then he started listing figures whom he called great painters, who would change the history of painting forever: Delaunay, Kandinsky, Léger, Feininger. Those were Thilo's favorite artists. Unfortunately, the names meant nothing to anyone else.

Only Lukas had any comment on this ardent speech, and his was ironic.

"What was once called progress is now called decadence," he said.

And then he began on his own tack: "We must have a foundation in the one thing that will last for thousands of years—faith. Without faith we are like animals. Like beasts." Whenever he spoke the word *beasts* Lukas moved his head violently, and his cheeks quivered, making him look like an angry rodent. "Only Christianity protects us from flying at one another's throats. Even the nonbelievers should make a mental effort and at least pretend to believe, not sow atheistic or deistic ferment. Man is at base an evil, licentious creature. He is made up of instincts, amoral by nature. Christianity has turned us into people, and as soon as its standards are gone, we shall be left with nothing, and pure nihilism will take over."

As he made his speech, he purred with satisfaction, as if enjoying this apocalyptic vision.

"It's already happening. The end is nigh!" he prophesied.

At this point August took the floor, folding his hands as if to pray.

"In a way, I agree with you," he said. "Faith in the continuity of culture will save us, our faith in myth, which is a platform for mutual understanding. This myth also includes Christianity, but naturally, not only! The sphere of Western civilization is more than that, my dear sir, it involves overcoming man's egoism and acknowledging that he is at base good, but the world spoils him. If every man were given the opportunity of a decent life, neither the police nor the army would be necessary. Whereas one should regard religion just as one regards mythology, as a collection of instructive tales that help us to live."

It turned out that Herr August had brought with him his own container for the consumption of Schwärmerei. In a moment of abandon, he took a plain shot glass out of his pocket and automatically reached for the liqueur to fill it. Lukas took advantage of this brief instant to bring up arguments that he had used many times before.

In Lukas's ideal world, everything had its place, and he was most sensitized to the place of women. According to him it was women, with their unbridled biological behavior, with their disturbing proximity to nature—they were the factor that destabilized social order. Yes, they should be pushed into the private sphere entirely, from where they would not threaten the order of the world.

Their hats obstructed him in the street—he snorted at the thought of this annoying aesthetic ostentation, which he compared to the way chimpanzees and other primates displayed their sexual organs. Their high-pitched chatter disturbed him in cafés. They should not be allowed into cafés. As he said this, Longin Lukas reverently cited the person of Otto Weininger.

Here August butted in to remind them that a few years ago a café had been opened in Vienna, the Kärntner Bar, which did not admit women, and that this had stirred protests. August took no position on the subject, but he praised the fine interior decor—everything was designed to be "very masculine." He lowered his voice and addressed Wojnicz, as if he alone could appreciate it: "Just imagine, marble, onyx, mahogany, real leather. A black-and-white floor, minimalist, very masculine, it reflects warm, but, God forbid, not sentimental light from the backlit Bakelite tables . . ."

But Thilo, Lukas and Frommer were talking politics now. Only one sentence got through to Wojnicz, shouted by Frommer in a high, screeching voice: "Oh, nothing bad will happen now, the Balkan crisis has been seen off, Turkey has asked for a truce!"

The liqueur has a wonderful taste, it flows over the tongue like pure bliss. What else does Opitz add to it? Wojnicz promises himself that he will ask about it tomorrow, but right now he is seized by great somnolence, and a delicious, tempting vision of his bed appears before his eyes, with its cool sheets and large pillow. And then there are tomorrow's duties toward his own health to be considered. And so, inebriated, he gets up, feeling as if every movement is divided into small pieces, made up of individual pictures. They are all standing in a streak of light flowing from the electric bulb, but in the recesses of the dining room floats a dense, swirling darkness. From the corners of his eyes Wojnicz can see sparks glinting out of it—as in a painting by de Bles—or maybe eyes, or perhaps Abraham's endless sacrifice is happening over there. He shakes his head, and a strand of hair that is usually brushed back falls over his eyes; for some unknown reason Mieczysław clicks his heels before Herr August, and mumbles: "If you please, I am going off duty, sir!"

Surprised and disappointed, Herr August gazed foggily at Wojnicz's saluting hand, and then asked to be escorted to his room. But they did not get far. They sat down on the landing on two chairs beside a small, round table, where there was always a carafe of water and two glasses. First they treated themselves to the rather stale liquid, and after a brief silence August began to acquaint Wojnicz with his life story, employing a narrative full of sighs, coughing and incomplete sentences. They were sitting so close together that Wojnicz could smell August's breath— it was as sour as curdled milk that has been forgotten for a long time. Mieczysław proved a rather insubordinate confidant, because he was already feeling distracted and tired by having to converse in German all the time, and the drink was forcing him to focus on the words, consequentially discovering their new, unexpected meanings while ignoring their main thrust. August was telling him about the city of Kronstadt, where he had grown up, located somewhere in Europe's Romanian borderlands, so Wojnicz could not fully understand why they had spoken Spanish at home. August became emotional when he mentioned that his father—who seemed to have been a tradesman of some kind— had subscribed to the Viennese newspapers. Over the coffee that he drank with a passion, he had read the *Neue Freie Presse*. At this, Wojnicz too was overcome with emotion, because his father had read the same newspaper in Lwów. In a surge of drunken familiarity, Mieczysław and Herr August embraced in a manly way that soon made Wojnicz feel uneasy, because it was as if August did not want to let go of him but was trying to trap him in his sour breath, in his stuffy Viennese atmosphere.

Once Mieczysław managed to get out of his grip, August described how his family had moved from Kronstadt to Vienna, where he, little August (it was hard to imagine him as a child!) had attended the Theresianum, the city's best private school, which had permanently infected him with a love of the ancients by showing him those noble worlds that existed somewhere here and now, but in another, better dimension, and continued to exert an influence on us though we did not know it.

For a while they were lost in thought about the existence of those worlds, even here, in this damp guesthouse in Silesia.

"Did you know that in Plato's *Symposium* Pausanias says that there are two Aphrodites: the first is the heavenly one who has no mother, and whose father was Uranus himself, and the other is the wanton daughter of Zeus and Dione. Only this wanton Aphrodite is a woman and has a female element. The first, heavenly one, has nothing female within her, and is in essence the most masculine of men, and is also the most perfect love, namely the kind that makes boys its object . . ."

He fell silent with a smile full of anticipation, but after a pause he added hastily: "It is not I who say that, but Plato."

But when Wojnicz did not react to this revelation, August said: "Greek civilization is the universe of man liberated from nature, from his worst instincts, it is, it is . . ." As he sought the word, tears began to trickle from his eyes.

Good God! August was crying like a child!

Wojnicz had absolutely no idea how to behave as the old man in the wine-red smoking jacket went on sobbing quietly, so he stood up and bowed solemnly, this time without saluting, then went to his own room.

Now we shall make an exception and leave Wojnicz to return to his room on his own. Let him go. Let him ignore the strange noises that are bubbling away in the attic, although in fact there is nothing there that could explain their origin. As if creatures made of dust were arguing among themselves up there, conducting mysterious polemics, some voices try to persuade others, at first they do not agree, they conflict, but now another one offers new arguments in the form of that *coo-coo-cooing*, and the exchange of opinions starts all over again. And it is led by the deepest, most resonant voice, which cuts short excessive, bombastic talk with a single coo—then briefly everything falls silent, only to start up again a little later.

Let us instead follow Herr August upstairs to his south-facing room with two windows at the top of the house, where this idle man of letters has been living for almost a year, and where he is not writing his history of the world, a book that—it goes without saying—by not existing, is not going to throw this world to its knees.

There is nothing original to be expected in his quarters here, all the rooms are alike, furnished in a cozy, bourgeois way, full of little patterns and details.

Here is the bed, covered by day in a dark green patterned bedspread, and here is the wardrobe, with his aforementioned foulards hanging on the door, a round table with a soiled crocheted cloth and two chairs, while under the windows there is a small writing desk piled with papers and books, including volumes of poetry by Rilke and Werfel. The light gray-green walls have been decorated with the help of a roller in a golden botanical design, and as the room is sunny during the day, it evokes a clean and homelike atmosphere. From the windows the inhabitant of this room sees a boundless landscape consisting of supple, undulating lines and soft patches in various shades of green. Herr August is short-sighted, a fact we have not mentioned before, so only now, as he puts on his spectacles in gold-wire frames, can he appreciate the mountains reaching up to the sky and the view of the town's final houses lying at their feet.

Now, when it is dark, Herr August carefully draws the curtains and sits at the desk covered in papers. He looks at them rather helplessly and unwinds his foulard, removes his spectacles and wipes the lenses. Squinting, he observes a mouse that has stopped in the middle of the floor, surprised by the return of its enormous co-resident. For a moment they stare each other in the eyes. Then the mouse vanishes, and Herr August is no longer aware of any other eyes watching him. He slowly undresses, with the occasional sigh. Then, in nothing but his long johns and vest, he washes his face and hands in a bowl of water, without using soap.

With his left hand he strokes himself, slowly and gently, until his penis hardens, and then the gestures become more violent; finally, a little later, his right hand skillfully opens the safety pin it has been holding until now, apparently quite by chance, and viciously stabs the point of the pin into his buttocks several times, causing tiny drops of blood to appear on the pale skin flecked by heat rash—only then does gratification come, and a sharp, irresistible spasm throws his body onto the pillows.

Wojnicz was always surprised that after drinking a certain amount of the oddly savory alcohol, at first everyone was very talkative, but later on, the more of it they drank, the shorter their sentences became, and the more of them were left unfinished, as if some force were snapping off their endings, rendering their words incomprehensible. A person was overcome by a sort of stupor, as though he had gone into the most far-flung pastures of his mind, whence the view was incredible and made the need for words vanish. At such moments Mieczysław often felt as if they all understood one another perfectly, that a glance was enough for everything to become obvious. There were even situations in which the gentlemen sat in silence, simply gazing at one another, as if the discussion that had been so lively had shifted into some collective inner world. This occurred only after imbibing a copious amount of the liqueur, let us say a third bottle, which in fact was not such a rare event. Then, gazing at each other, they would sigh knowingly, and Herr August would fold his hands into a prayer beak, as if trying to remind them all of something; for a while they would struggle to focus on this sign, in the absolute, wordless belief that something important existed within the cosmos that could never be forgotten, that there was a foothold being indicated by Herr August, and in the fullness of time this foothold would change into a pivot, an infinite pivot, painfully vertical, and around which a carousel would turn, carrying them all, soaring into the sky on separate little seats. Now and then, unfortunately, someone would break free of the chains and fly solo into the air, vanishing in the silver glow of the earth.

Wojnicz thought the Schwärmerei brought on visual effects too. Whenever he lay down after boozing (promising himself not to drink so much of this demonic brew!), under his eyelids he saw flares, or figures that seemed to be made out of little mirrors reflecting each other and their surroundings from various angles, sending his vision into a truly agonizing frenzy. Another world was storming his body, trying to get inside his brain, by sending out flashes and illusions.

It was happening right now. Back in his room, he felt totally drained. He had trouble keeping his vision in one place—it kept escaping him, like Mister Jig in his train-journey game. And when poor Mieczysław laid his head on the pillow, he felt the world turning great circles around him. He was feeling sick. His languages got muddled. He sat up on the bed and lit the candles that were standing on the bedside table in case there was no electricity.

"Am I going to die?" he asked one of the candles.

It did not immediately answer. Its flame flickered, as if unsettled by this question. "Only very small or very large things are immortal," it said cautiously. "Atoms are immortal and galaxies are immortal. That's the whole mystery. The range of death is very specific, like a radio wave."

At these words Wojnicz was flooded with sorrow. Through the candle flame his father was looking at him, his stern gaze full of disappointment.

"Father, you would have preferred me to die," he said, and he wished that right now his father, January Wojnicz, the engineer from Lwów, a pragmatic and extremely masculine man, could hug him, even in an awkward, military way, by clapping him on his slender back in a gesture designed to raise the spirits of a soldier who had broken down on the battlefield. Or even stiffly, like Herr August, with a sort of dramatic determination. He longed for his touch and his physical presence, and was even aware of his father's scent, which had flown to him from afar before, the fragrance he could smell on passing by him or on entering his bedroom: the scent of that English cologne of his, like old leather rubbed with lemon, smooth from long use, polished by the touch of hands. Poor Father, he thought. He's like an object, like a worn-out tool.

WHITE RIBBONS,
DARK NIGHT

very day, the Grizzled Lion and Herr August conducted the
same ritual, having a joke over which of them was to let the
other go through the door first.

"But, Herr Professor, you go ahead, there's no question, I will follow you."

"Allow me, today it is I who shall wait, out of respect for your
knowledge and erudition."

"No, I cannot allow someone of such great merit for the humanities
to enter after me. Please go ahead, my dear sir."

"But it's unthinkable! I shall follow you."

And so on.

Finally they would somehow manage to enter. They would sit down
at table and carry on their debate like actors on a two-man stage, each
dogged in his efforts to come out on top and to dishearten his interlocutor, though outwardly they were as polite as they could possibly be.
Sometimes Frommer played the role of moderator, feeding them topics

that seemed entirely innocent but in conversation suddenly became critical, of vital importance, to be settled without delay. At the same time, they were happy to jump from topic to topic, treating them as little more than an excuse to show off their eloquence and erudition; they dropped them without regret, consenting to a lack of resolution, though each was convinced that he had succeeded in defeating his opponent, especially as they did not listen to each other very carefully.

"Democracy, my dear friend, does better within polytheistic systems," said Herr August.

"And why is that? I do not understand the connection."

"Because polytheism prepares our minds to look at the world as being diversified, full of different energies that coexist. Monotheism is more suited to feudalism because of its hierarchical structure of superior and inferior beings."

Lukas nodded approvingly.

"A curious idea," he said, "yet it cannot be proved."

"Unless we turn to ancient Greece, it worked there," said August, eager to draw his opponent onto his own territory. There he was invincible. But Lukas was not born yesterday.

"I, my dear sir, believe that democracy is a sham system. It always has an element of theater, and inherently tends to bring out a strong leader who will push toward building an autocracy. Fortunately, outstanding, talented individuals are always going to be born who will not find a place for themselves within a democracy; at most they will take advantage of its mechanisms to assume the lion's share of power and subordinate the democratic community to themselves. That is how it works, such is the law of the development of societies. Therefore democracy is a transitional system, impermanent by nature. Ours is a hierarchical world, so it was established by God. There is no clearer confirmation of this hierarchy than that recorded in Genesis."

"If we lived within polytheism, dear friend, you would think differently. Democracy is a horizontal system, it assumes that many people may potentially have an equal influence on the world."

Lukas smacked his lips for a while and looked up, as if a definitive answer were to be found there that would knock August into a cocked hat.

"We must regard polytheism as a primitive, culturally inferior order. It is thanks to monotheism that we have become civilized, thinking individuals with a unique, distinctive nature. An individual god is a guarantee of our own individuality. A resemblance to God, that is the point, not man's outer features, but his essence; he is one of a kind, singular . . ."

"Yet one can imagine a flat, horizontal world, without all those hierarchies that eventually lead to injustice . . ."

"You socialist!" exclaimed Lukas, for whom August had just overstepped the limits of decent behavior. "How about a matriarchy? A system where sexual urges and emotions set the rules, not the pure spirit of rationalism."

"Allow me to interject," said Opitz, who had just brought in some roast meat, potato salad and salted herrings—the best, so he said, in all Silesia. "But in the history of mankind there has never been a civilization based on matriarchy, has there?"

They all looked at him with interest, but they were distracted by the herrings—spongy, reddish, arranged in rosettes, with some capers and pickled garlic at their centers.

"Women," he added, "are incapable of creating a national organization, or even a tribal one, because by their nature they submit to those who are stronger."

Here the discussion was dispelled by the wonderful scent of fish, and then "Silesian Heaven" arrived on the table too, one of the few dishes that Raimund knew how to make, consisting of potato dumplings with pork cutlets in a strange prune-and-mushroom sauce (did the cook add his favorite liberty caps to this as well?). This dish was served to them at least once a week, and here its name was pronounced as "schleschis himraich," which made it hard for Wojnicz to guess what it meant. He ate up the dumplings and meat, but he found the sauce quite unpalatable, a fact he scrupulously noted in his diary.

"I read some literary criticism in the local papers that was written by a woman," said Lukas, continuing the discussion interrupted by the herrings. "So here too the suffragists want to have their say. It is truly grotesque."

"As far as brilliance in literature is concerned, dear gentlemen," said August, picking up the topic, "the surest sign of an outstanding work is that women do not like it."

He fell silent, casting his gaze over his companions' faces, pleased to have formulated a neat and well-rounded thesis that surprised him as much as it did the others.

Nobody disagreed. They were busy with their food.

"What a pity we can't test that—we have no women here," muttered Frommer, and pushed away his plate, disappointed that Raimund was now serving compote for dessert; Frommer did not regard compote as a proper dessert.

August had already finished too. After a while he moved to an armchair, and as he waited for the ritual glass of Schwärmerei, he puffed on a cigar, then began to cough, so he regretfully put it down on the edge of a heavy cut-glass ashtray. He sighed, drummed his fingers on the table and said: "Do an experiment. When you have the opportunity, mention the name of a writer who is important to you in a woman's presence, and ask what she thinks of him. The higher you value someone, the lower women will rate him, and that's because what women seek in literature is an excuse to arouse their emotions. They are a long way from making use of ideas. Women are inclined toward literature that safely revolves around interhuman affairs, especially relations between ladies and gentlemen"—here a quarter smile flashed across his face, or a mere eighth of a smile, raising one corner of his mouth like a nervous tic—"focused on a sentimental and sensual exchange. They always describe the dresses and the patterns on the wallpaper in great detail. They are drawn to the lower classes, and they take pity on animals. They often yield to the attraction of all manner of oddities: ghosts, dreams and nightmares, but also coincidences and other chance circumstances, with which they try to conceal their lack of talent in sustaining a consistent plot."

"Please give us an example," asked Frommer. "You are generalizing greatly."

"It is hard to provide examples because on the whole few women write. And if they do, we do not read their work."

"Indeed," agreed Frommer.

"Language itself interests men as the most perfect communication tool, as the greatest achievement in the development of the species homo sapiens. Honing sentences, studying the depth of meanings, playing with connotations. Why have the greatest poets always been men?" asked August rhetorically, and emptied his glass of liqueur, closing his eyes as he did so to convey his bliss.

"You are right," Lukas agreed with him. "There are no women in the history of literature, just as there are none in science. There are only isolated cases of females who, as a result of the unfathomable mysteries of inheritance, have received from their grandfathers and fathers a modicum of the male spirit, the gift of Apollo."

"Dionysus is not a woman, and he too belongs to the heritage of men," said August.

"But by nature he is the masculine personification of everything feminine: the madness of oblivion, sexual impulses, sensuality and ecstasy, the natural urges that are so strong within the seemingly weak female body," stressed Lukas, and thus shifted the discussion into the realms of Greek mythology.

And so it went—first a declamation by August, then another tirade about the collapse of civilization from Lukas, followed by some incomprehensible allusions made by Frommer, until the disputants' tongues were slowed by the effect of Schwärmerei and once again they were all overcome by a sort of thickening feeling, which made it hard to move because of weakness or disinclination. As if the world were built of plywood and were now delaminating before their eyes, as if all contours were blurring, revealing fluid passages between things. The same process affected their ideas, and so the discussion became less and less factual, because the speakers had suddenly lost their sense of certainty, and every word that had been reliable so far now acquired contexts, entailed allusions, or flickered with remote associations. Finally they sank into dreadful fatigue, and one after another floated off to their room, breathing heavily on the stairs.

On one of these busy autumn days, when the light was steadily losing its minutes, like a careless miller whose sack full of holes is spilling grain, Longin Lukas ran into Wojnicz outside the house and invited him to his "refuge," as he put it, in the annex. He sat his guest on the bed and handed him a large glass of the local beer. As Wojnicz was not fond of beer, while Lukas knocked the drink back as though extremely thirsty, he merely wetted his lips, looking around the glass-walled room that his host rented, in fact a veranda with a small room attached.

There was a sloppily made bed covered with blankets, which were needed because it was cooler here than in the main guesthouse, thanks to the veranda. There were some ties hanging on the door of an oak wardrobe, and a washbasin half full of dirty water. A well-worn rug speckled with stains made a rather poor impression. Below the window, next to the passage onto the veranda, stood a solid armchair, and beside it, a curious piece of furniture—a small revolving bookcase full of books. The veranda was graced by a large writing table covered in newspapers, documents and broken pencils. All this was in disorder, out of control, as though the person who lived here always interrupted himself in midstep and never finished what he had begun.

With great enjoyment Lukas soliloquized, first on the topic of Christianity, then on the strong state that would forcibly introduce strict standards and would be built on religious and cultural unity. Then he managed to move on imperceptibly to Dr. Semperweiss and "that health resort," which allowed communists to be treated for free while decent people had to pay through the nose. Once his tongue had loosened a bit and his face had gone red, he brought up the subject of "poor August," as he put it. Although tipsy, he tried not to betray any emotion, and in his own opinion was being extremely objective.

"August is quite simply a Jew, but he hides it. That's why he pretends he's not concerned about *race*."

Lukas liked this word; it explained a great deal, could be used to sum up cultural, political and economic issues simply and neatly, it suited every purpose and was also becoming increasingly fashionable.

"There's something feminine about him too," Lukas continued, "a weakness, a sort of readiness to fall into line. Even when he's playing the philosopher, he does it like someone *racially* inferior, like a woman or a Negro."

Then he opined that people "of this type"—which clearly meant inferior—were demanding their rights, the same ones as ordinary citizens, in the belief that they could have these rights, ignoring the biological obstacles. He also suspected Dr. Semperweiss of being a Jew, because he was interested in some Jewish psychological theories known as "psychoanalysis." Lukas had an opinion on this subject too.

"You see, dear boy, reducing the nature of man to some primitive impulses actually means the collapse of all philosophy and science. In any case, Freud's entire discipline is only applicable to Jews."

Unfortunately Wojnicz could not pick up the prompt to criticize this newfangled field, because he knew nothing about it. Nor did he have much to say about impulses, as—to tell the truth—so far he had had little interest in sex. He knew that this interest was bound to appear one day—everyone talked about it and dropped hints—but for some reason he regarded himself as still immature. Sometimes he felt a little excluded from this community of sex, allusions and jokes, as if others had a talent that he lacked.

Once Longin Lukas had finished criticizing psychoanalysis with his usual note of rancor, he shifted to a more familiar tone, moved closer to Wojnicz, and nudged his arm before starting to talk into the empty space between them.

"If, my boy, you wanted, as I do, to . . . you know . . . If you ever do want to, then tell me. I am in a position to arrange it for you. At a reasonable price, and for you they might even do it for free," he said, laughing raucously. "The girls are from Waldenburg, clean, well-looked-after, robust—in short, in pure good health."

It took Wojnicz a while to understand what this was all about, then he blinked, not sure how to respond to the offer. Lukas nodded encouragingly. And suddenly Wojnicz felt sorry for him, for those sagging cheeks and that slicked-down hair, and for his entire figure, which only looked strong but was as though made of cotton wool. He felt pity for Lukas's "refuge," this dirty cubbyhole, and for his entire life. His throat tightened at the thought that Lukas would soon die. So he asked about the price, and made a face as if he would consider it. He said he would be sure to think about it, and was grateful for this generous masculine information, and then—maybe a little awkwardly—he returned Lukas's familiar nudge, embellishing it with a knowing glance, and took his leave.

In Brehmer's method, an enjoyable life was of crucial importance for allowing the patient's recovery to proceed harmoniously. Thus, one of the resort's long-awaited attractions was an expedition to the nearby tavern beside a pond, where a special dish was served at this time of year that was not be found anywhere outside Görbersdorf. Groups of patients reserved tables there, and as the tavern was quite small, one had to wait one's turn.

On the penultimate Saturday evening in October they all set off for the tavern, unfortunately without Thilo, who was no longer getting out of bed. As it was not far to the pond, they went on foot, eager for some excitement and made merry by the frosty air that turned their breath into great clouds of steam, distinctly marking their presence. Leading the way, Opitz shone a carbide lantern that gave off an ugly gray light, while at the back of the procession Raimund carried an ordinary paraffin lamp. A corroded moon lorded it in the sky, made to seem cold and unfriendly by the rapidly moving clouds now shielding, now revealing its face. On the way, each drank a shot of Schwärmerei as an aperitif. Wojnicz, who had not refused the liqueur, was conscious of its effect: a pleasant mist descending on the mind, the waning of one's usual level of attention—a pleasant state that took away everyday anxiety, while the fears it added seemed so fantastical that they were not worthy of notice.

Wojnicz did not actually know how it happened or who started it, but the gentlemen's topic of conversation had turned to him. Lukas appeared to have suggested it. They were making fun of him, saying that on the promenade he looked round after the women, and was especially interested in Frau Large Hat. Wojnicz went red. Fortunately it was dark, and nobody could see his blushes. He felt embarrassed because they were talking about him, ascribing feelings to him that he did not have, though in fact he wished he did. Yes, they were talking about the gap inside him, about the empty space that his life had yet to fill. So perhaps their conversation full of cackling was opportune.

"Women are always at odds with probity," said Lukas. "If only our young man would give it a try, it'd all be over and done with. He'd be sure to think they have some sense of guilt, some principles. He'd probably be very disappointed, or maybe it has already happened? There's nothing there, no depth."

He laughed merrily, as if he had discovered the truth.

"Yes, yes," said Opitz, "women have no depth. Watch out, Herr Wojnicz. That minx has probably set her cap at you already. And don't be fooled by the fact that she's a Slav. They're still pagans."

To respond to this, Herr August found a quotation, as he did for everything. At the rear of the group, lit from behind by Raimund's lamp, he looked mysterious, his fluffy hair forming a sort of halo.

O! why did God,
Creator wise, that peopled highest Heaven
With Spirits masculine, create at last

This novelty on earth, this fair defect
Of nature, and not fill the world at once
With Men, as Angels, without feminine . . .

They were just passing two hooded female figures who moved out of their way, probably maids or cooks from one of the guesthouses. Once the men were a little farther away from them, Herr August spoke again:

"It's possible that here we are in a northern version of Thessaly, and all the local women are witches."

"Definitely those two toads who sit outside their house, what are their names, Frau Brecht and Frau— I've forgotten," muttered Lukas, but loud enough for Wojnicz to react, joining in with the male choir at last:

"Sydonia Patek is definitely a witch. I'm afraid of her."

"Oh no, excuse me, but please don't mix her up in this, she isn't a woman at all. And what's more, she's on our side. Anyway, whenever she gives me an injection, I bare my backside without any shame. I tell you: she is not a woman," joked Lukas.

"The doctors' punishment for breaking the rules should be a short tête-à-tête with Sydonia Patek," put in Herr August, with a spiteful smirk on his face.

Lukas scowled.

"I think I'd rather do it with a goat than with that horror."

"She has as much charm as a scarecrow," added Opitz.

Suddenly Frommer, silent until now, spoke up from the front:

"She reminds me of a hare put out in the frost to be seasoned."

Wojnicz too was truly terrified of this person, not because of her particular charm, or rather lack of it, but her lifeless face, on which no emotions ever showed, and her taciturnity. She replied in monosyllables, never looking at her interlocutor but aiming her gaze somewhere down and to the left. Her spectacles, in tortoiseshell frames, were the color of dirty water. Her white uniform, a gown buttoned at the back and tied with a belt that had a bunch of keys attached to it, deprived her of characteristics. She was a medical functionary, an agent of the Kurhaus. One time he had seen her giving some unfortunate fellow an injection—stooping over the man as he lay on his belly, reduced to his exposed buttock. She reminded him of a predatory harpy bending over a chunk of succulent meat, just before sinking in its beak and tearing it to shreds.

"I can bear spiritual communion with women only in small doses. Even if the girl is not as limited as a suffragist or as deprived of taste as a so-called artiste," said Lukas, rounding off the topic with a neat synthesis.

The defective moon was entirely hidden behind the dark slush of wet autumn clouds.

"That old story I told you, about the women who ran away into the mountains. Apparently some of them left behind children and husbands, and took care of them from afar in some magical way, dropping food or medicine outside their doors," said Frommer. "To this day they live in the forest, but they've gone completely feral, they attack charcoal burners and men they happen upon."

Lukas burst into loud laughter, but at once it was replaced by a fit of coughing. They stopped for a while.

"It's an old ailment, but it has only been given a name lately—women without a man suffer from hysteria," he said, wiping his lips on a handkerchief that looked gray in the gloom. "Dr. Semperweiss is studying it. Sexual urges that go unsatisfied turn women into lunatics."

"What do you mean, they live there to this day?" asked Wojnicz soberly, returning to Frommer's previous statement.

"That's what the villagers believe. That somehow they have survived in these woods. In the holes we saw."

Here Lukas intervened, making a short speech against superstitions. There was a note of superiority in his voice, and the whole time he addressed himself almost exclusively to Wojnicz. As soon as they set off again, he began talking about hysteria, and what Hippocrates understood by it. As he spoke of the womb that wanders around a woman's body in search of moisture, Wojnicz was aware that he was blushing deeply.

"But when a woman has intercourse," Lukas patiently explained, "the womb is moistened and no longer needs to roam about her body. That is why a woman needs intimacy; it's a vital remedy. Even if she's unwilling, she has to be cured in this way to guard against that terrible illness."

"There must be some truth to those rumors. Maybe someone really did run away to the forest once upon a time, a madwoman, and that was how the whole story began," said Wojnicz, trying to resuscitate the topic, but a moment later Opitz stopped and turned to face them. In the light of the carbide lamp his face looked quite ghostly. His bushy eyebrows cast large shadows.

"Gentlemen, we have reached our destination," he informed them.

It was hard to see the locally famous pond in the darkness, but when the moon briefly emerged from behind the clouds, its brilliance spilled out like mercury, and then they saw the sheet of water hidden in the forest. On the shore stood a small, very pleasant-looking tavern with a wooden pier leading straight into the water. The light in the windows instantly reminded Wojnicz of the pictures from fairy tales, or from the labels of various sweetmeats—a fairy-tale cottage that promises peace and a return to the happy land of childhood.

Two figures had just tied a boat to the jetty and were starting to haul some flat baskets, sure to be full of fish, into the tavern. A marvelous aroma of something smoked and hot floated on the air, mixed with the smell of burning beechwood.

A new spirit entered the nocturnal wayfarers as they went inside the tavern. They pushed their way brusquely to the table and chaotically took their places, with no concern for order or the basic rules of courtesy. They threw their coats and jackets on the chairbacks. Wool exuded the dampness, carbide and paraffin with which it was saturated, the odors hidden among the fibers of the fabric now brought to life by warmth. The scent rose on the hot air in the Tyrolean tavern, enhanced by a pleasant smell of wood burning in the fireplace and the rough but subtle scent of the stone walls.

The tired men communicated in grunts, impatient for their food. The other tables were packed too—plainly the fame of the specialité de la maison was widespread. Opitz had done well to bring them here. Hungry and irascible, at once they ordered a round of the local beer, which gradually calmed them down.

For now we can smell the distinctive scents of their bodies, rising off their sweaters and blending. Frommer gives off an odor of dust, a touch musky, papery, dry, as if rustling—the smell of old, desiccated leather, like a shabby wallet. Lukas smells sharp—it is the odor of fear and readiness to fight, the invisible halo of a would-be warrior who, having lost his physical strength, takes part in the war from a distance, shouting out commands and passing comment on the strategists' moves. The smell of August is completely different—he emits organic fumes of rancid matter that will shortly be corroded by putrefaction, the decomposition of particles of flesh; he is surrounded by the sour-milk, larder smell of forgotten provisions, a smell that is already out of control, but is still being stifled by eau de cologne and refined shaving soap. Whereas Opitz is wreathed in a cloud of carbide—a smell that makes one's teeth grind, and that causes saliva to gather in the mouth. Nothing can escape from under it. But Wojnicz is bursting with his own scent, though he does not know that. It pushes all the other odors into the background, it dominates them, though the person emitting this aroma feels lost and unsure of himself. His pheromones are as if electrically charged, overwhelming, like the smell of a fox's fur, or of a billy goat fleeing from hunters.

Next day, during his rest cure, the memory of supper brought back to Wojnicz a nasty sense of nausea. First, beer had been served, then there was praise for a local liqueur, possibly similar to Schwärmerei, and when at last the famous main course was served, they were all so hungry that they wolfed it down at high speed, then asked for second helpings. It consisted of a special kind of ribbons that resembled noodles, long, quite thin and off-white, stringy, as if not as fully cooked as they should be. The sauce proved similar to béchamel, just a bit hotter and spicier. The food crunched in the mouth and was altogether very tasty.

Wojnicz asked numerous unnecessary questions about the details, wanting to record this food in his notebook, where he referred to it as "white ribbons." Finally, while the gentlemen were discussing the Balkan crisis and each of them was delivering his prognosis, the landlord, a Herr Kudlik, took Wojnicz to the kitchen, where the aforementioned baskets had already been emptied, with just the leftovers from preparing this "macaroni"—some shapely whitish gristle—filling a few small pails.

There is no point in hesitating to reveal the origins of this delicious dish, though Wojnicz had spent some time wondering how to put the whole matter into words so that both his father and his uncle Emil would believe him: Should he refer to the biology of how invertebrates reproduce, or should he present this thing in entirely conventional culinary terms? (After all, was czernina really any better?) It turned out that, once a year at around this time, the reproductive cycle of a certain parasite of freshwater fish reached the stage where the individuals that had multiplied in the bellies of the fish burst them open and made their way outside. Islands of live ribbons floated on the surface of the pond, in a sort of ritual of fervent exchange of sperm, of mutual fertilization, squirting each other with semen. This was the time when in huge nets the local fishermen fished out these "white ribbons," as they were euphemistically called, and made them into the famous dish.

The following afternoon Wojnicz was finding it hard to continue resting quietly, feeling nauseous as he imagined what those creatures looked like in his stomach now. The whole act of human consumption, the idea of stuffing one's body with alien matter, seemed so absurd that he had serious doubts about continuing to keep his notebook full of recipes. He decided to take a short walk along the back streets and alleys, but he had come to know them so well during the month that he had been here that he quickly grew bored. Therefore he headed rapidly along the promenade toward the forest, passed the sanatorium and went out beyond the Orthodox church. Trying not to think about anything, he counted his steps until breathlessness made him lose track. He reached the forest and went deep inside it, following a track that led uphill. He was met with the sight of moss, moss-coated branches, and small mushrooms, definitely inedible, whose names he did not know— all this improved his poor frame of mind and dispelled the nausea. The scent of pine needles had a similar effect. Now he felt a weight gathering on his chest, a good weight, full of love, full of vital juices. Oh yes, life cannot be light, one must feel it, it is like good ballast. He went on walking until he glanced at the watch from his father, which always showed that he was already late for something; and so it was now—lunch!

Hurrying back for the meal, Wojnicz was stopped by a strange sight. As he passed one of the courtyards, his eye was caught by a man leaning over a piece of furniture, as though to repair it. Wojnicz went a few more paces, then suddenly stopped and froze. He backed up cautiously, to avoid startling the man, and saw a chair exactly like the one that had been standing in the attic at the guesthouse—a solid piece of furniture with straps attached to the armrests and legs. The man was nailing something on with a hammer; he must have fetched out the chair after a long period of neglect, in order to restore it. At some point their eyes met, and Wojnicz gave a slight nod, reaching for the hat he was not wearing. The man did not return his greeting but went back to his interrupted work.

On the little bridge just before the guesthouse he bumped into Frommer, stiff and buttoned up to the neck as usual. He was looking pensive, smoking a cigarette and flicking ash into the stream below the bridge.

If people can be described in terms of their addictions, then in Walter Frommer's case it was cigarettes, which had turned him entirely yellow and withered. He smoked avidly, holding the cigarette between his middle and ring fingers, crushing the long filters flat, which meant having to suck in the smoke harder, with more energy—and then his cheeks caved in and his noble face bordered by carefully trimmed graying hair acquired an unexpectedly predatory look. Anyone who otherwise appeared so nice and inconspicuous should not smoke. His figure conveyed a strange tension between bluster and reserve, as if he had to keep himself constantly in check, for if he were to loosen his grip, something unspeakable, insane and terrible would be released from his dried-up, smoke-wreathed body, like a genie that would fly out of his mouth and deny everything that Frommer had ever said or done.

They exchanged the usual niceties, criticized the fickle weather and expressed hope for its speedy improvement, supporting the faction that favored Berlin newspapers for their forecasts. They passed over yesterday's supper in silence. Wojnicz was rather reluctant to stop and talk, because he was already late, but now they were gazing at the stream together as it flowed beneath them. Suddenly Frommer spoke:

"You know what, I can clearly sense the influence of the underground lake. Don't you get the feeling that the underground water washes away our thoughts here? Right now it's hard for me to find a single one to describe what's been going on."

"You think so?" asked Wojnicz hesitantly.

"I also know why there's such a fondness for planning and all sorts of routine here. Without them, everything would dissolve. We'd be carried away by the mist, we'd talk without making sense, as in a dream. The mortar between the bricks of our houses would rot and the seams of our clothes would come apart."

Wojnicz cast him a look of surprise.

"Yes, it's a strange place. Full of some kind of mystery . . . ," he said, and paused, ready to tell, or at least hint at, the cooing, the attic, the chairs, the hat, and Frau Opitz's room.

Frommer gazed at him piercingly, as if demanding that Wojnicz give him a sign, wink in a knowing way.

"Is there something you want to tell me, Herr Frommer?"

"You must swear to keep total and absolute discretion," he said, sounding utterly indifferent in his stiff but correct Polish, as though talking about the weather.

Naturally, Wojnicz agreed, and suggested they sit down on the little bench outside the house.

"No, that will attract attention. Let's walk. I shall escort you to the Kurhaus for lunch."

They headed back to the promenade.

"I have talked to you, but I have not told you the whole truth." Frommer paused and then admitted: "I am a policeman, Herr Wojnicz. I came to Görbersdorf last autumn after the dreadful crime that took place here in November. And as I am in poor health, my superiors allowed me to take a cure while also conducting an investigation. They are not hoping for much, because the case has been known to the police for years and is impossible to solve."

Wojnicz did not understand.

"What do you mean, 'impossible'?"

"The same event has been recurring for a number of years, but it has probably been happening since long ago; in the past, nothing was said about it, especially as the murder victims were charcoal burners, shepherds and local people of low status. But for the last few years the victims have been patients, and so the case has taken on color in Breslau."

"Why are you telling me this, Herr Frommer? Can I help with the investigation in some way?"

"Well, I shan't beat about the bush—I am afraid for you."

"For me? Afraid? What on earth do I have to do with it, for the love of God? Do you think I believe in all that nonsense about the revenge of the forest Tuntschi? First of all, if that were really the case, all the newspapers would be writing about it. Secondly, if it has been going on for many years, the murderer must be as old as Methuselah."

"Or immortal," said Frommer, but instantly switched to a very matter-of-fact tone. "You are from far away and you have no relations here. Whatever you do, you'll always be a bit of an outsider. I've been watching you, you're the type. Nobody would take much notice if something happened to you—"

Wojnicz halted in his tracks and turned his entire body toward Frommer.

"You are joking, aren't you?"

Without stopping at all, Frommer slipped past Wojnicz and went up to a café window, where cakes were displayed on beautiful trays.

"In conducting an investigation I take a close look at everything," he said. "I've made many observations, and gradually I'm starting to see the whole picture. At the right moment I shall tell you what I have discovered. For the time being, please be on the highest alert."

"What have you discovered? You can't elude me now. First you rouse my curiosity, and now you're trying to brush me off."

"All I can say is that I can't exclude supernatural causes."

Frommer turned around, leaving Wojnicz in utter astonishment.

12

MISTER JIG

No, it was not that Dr. Semperweiss's patients in Görbersdorf spent all their time on expeditions and at supper. Our account passes over the monotonous autumn days that consisted of nothing but therapy, rest cures and examinations. And of boredom, which was as ubiquitous here as the damp. The days sprawled far and wide, boldly extending beyond dusk and carrying their existence on into the evening. At the Kurhaus the lights sometimes burned until midnight, although silence was obligatory at night. Shadows would flit among the buildings, and Lukas would sneak off somewhere and come back, in what seemed a very tipsy state, his body fired up by a woman, downy goose feathers clinging to his dark brown overcoat.

One could understand the Görbersdorf residents' affinity for geese, because there were ponds, streams and lakelets all over the neighborhood, as if the underground water were pushing upward, constantly reminding people that it was there, that it existed. There may even have been a mild threat in this abundance of water—what would happen if it ever decided to pour out onto the surface of this Leyden jar of a valley?

The omnipresent geese benefited from this. Twice a day they decorously migrated from the sleeping quarters they shared with the hens to these bodies of water. The gander always led the way, ruffled and alert, sporting an ample crop, followed by his harem of ladies in white, gaggling away, as if passing comment on everything they met along the path. Occasionally the gander liked to intimidate the patients, stretching out his neck and threatening to nip them. The female patients would run off, squealing, which introduced an element of variety into the tedium of the sanatorium day. There were goose feathers lying around everywhere as well, not just the large ones one could use to write down our history, but also the small fluffy ones that came off the birds while bathing or were plucked out during frenzied grooming. The wind lifted them above the promenade, over the bridges across the stream, and some were carried high above the rooftops, whence they observed the human world. They liked to catch on people's clothing too, and picking feathers off one another's arms was a universal gesture here, an expression of mutual tenderness, even, born of the sense of solidarity that exists between people who are sick and doomed to die.

Unfortunately, an equally tragic time was approaching for the geese. They were destined to die this autumn, like every year. Grown strong, fat and confident on the plenitude of summer food, they were at the close of their lives.

Opitz was sharpening his knife, and Frau Weber and Frau Brecht were no longer shelling broad beans or runner beans, but stitching together thick canvas to make pillowcases.

The beautiful, proud geese were soon to be transformed into jars of schmaltz, confit, stews and pâtés. Coming straight toward the dressed-up patients in their stately fashion, they had no idea how defenseless they were, or how firmly their fate was sealed. The human advantage over the condemned birds lay in the fact that the people were aware of their murderous intentions. So they simply smiled to themselves as they watched the retinue of geese moving through the village with the gravity and self-assurance of immortals.

It was harder and harder for Wojnicz not to admit that visiting Frau Opitz's room had become a sort of addiction. He only did it when he was sure Opitz was out of the house, and the omnipresent Raimund, as quiet as a shadow, was not bustling around in the yard but had gone off with a basket to fetch eggs, or to collect the post. Mieczysław would climb to the top floor on tiptoes, in just his socks. It was entirely innocent. He simply could not refrain from peeping in there every couple of days. He told himself it was for the sake of order, to check that everything was in its place, that nothing had changed—though it would be hard to imagine what might not be in order in the dead woman's room. First, he simply stood in the doorway, absorbing every detail of the cozy but modest room. The faded pastel colors, the pale blue wallpaper, the linen runner with its grubby fringes. Then he would go inside and quietly close the door behind him. For this moment he would willingly have sacrificed all his treatment, all the most interesting conversations, even coffee and cakes at the Zum Dreimädelhaus. Once he was there, the whole house fell silent, as though struck dumb; even the cooing in the loft died away, and he could hear his own heartbeat. He would sit down on a chair with a worn-out back, inspect his surroundings, and always notice a new detail: a hairpin wrapped in a cloud of dust lying in a crack under the window; or a long, fair hair on the bedspread, thick and healthy, almost down to the floor. That the pom-poms on the slippers were coming off, and the paint on the iron bed was peeling in one spot, he already knew; gazing at these tiny imperfections gave him great pleasure, as if Frau Opitz's room had been inside him forever.

After about fifteen minutes he would get up and leave, just as quietly as he had come in, stroking the bedspread on the way, and the scarf hanging on the door peg. As he descended the stairs, he would recover his usual shape, becoming Mieczysław Wojnicz again, a student at the Lwów Polytechnic, aged twenty-four.

He often saw Dr. Semperweiss about, showing the patients his Mercedes during the lunch break. He would raise the bonnet and tell them eagerly about its horsepower, range and fuel consumption. The patients, most of them men, would lean over the complicated machinery, all those pistons, pipes and ducts, grunting in admiration and seeing the inconceivable future in this vehicle. The doctor would also set out beyond Humboldt's shrine with his rifle to shoot at birds. Wojnicz once joined him, and saw that Semperweiss only aimed at the birds, then turned on his heel to chase them in flight with the barrel. He never heard a shot.

"Is your rifle loaded?" he asked the doctor with a laugh.

"Ah, it's you," said Semperweiss, and beckoned him to follow. "Of course it is. I'm going hunting, after all. But you know what, the point is to have a choice: to shoot or not to shoot. I don't want to kill the birds, I'm not hungry." He laughed out loud at his own joke.

It occurred to Wojnicz that this was another version of his own "pheasant distance."

It was one of those rare, beautiful autumn days. The whole place radiated a sense of abundance and fulfillment. After the walk, a warm room, a cup of afternoon coffee and something sweet were waiting for them below.

"Please tell me, Doctor, what do the graves at the cemetery mean?

They all have the same date of death, always in November," said Wojnicz, looking the doctor straight in the face.

"What on earth can I tell you? Human credence often latches on to absurdity. Indeed, accidents happen here, and somehow, as you rightly note, they occur regularly each year—er, in autumn, in early November, when it's my ritual to take a holiday and go to visit my mother near Hirschberg, where we have a small estate."

From the account that followed, Wojnicz understood that "we" meant the old mother and him. The doctor had no siblings but was a much-loved only child. His father had died long ago, so his mother had transferred all her attention to her clever son. Semperweiss had completed a doctorate in pulmonary diseases and regarded his job at Görbersdorf as practical research, intending eventually to return to the university and give lectures. Wojnicz also learned that the doctor was there on an extremely advantageous contract, and his diligence allowed him to work at the hospital in Waldenburg as well. At his mother's home near Hirschberg, in early November there were two family jubilees—her birthday, and the anniversary of the doctor's father's death. Each year his mother invited her sisters and their families for these important family gatherings. This year the doctor would drive there in his wonderful Mercedes, which was sure to impress them all.

"Did you know that Mercedes is a woman's name?" he remarked. "So should I refer to this car as 'she,' in the feminine?"

On their way back to the village, Wojnicz plucked up the courage to ask about Thilo. The doctor said nothing, but merely shook his head in sorrow.

"Is it that bad?" said Mieczysław in alarm.

"He's dying. We've already written to his family."

Wojnicz took a deep breath.

"Perhaps something can still be done, Doctor?"

"Perhaps, perhaps. If there were a substance that one could swallow or inject and that would storm its way through the human organism, killing all those Koch's bacilli on the way, all those lethal internal civilizations that unwittingly infest the body and consume it from the inside, I'd give it to him immediately. But nothing of the kind exists."

After a short pause he continued:

"You must understand, you oversensitive youth, that a consumptive's fever eats away at him nonstop, bringing anxiety and physical agitation. Your friend does not have much life ahead of him, he came here too late. There was too much delay, in the belief that he was young and could overcome the illness on his own. What's more, his friend and guardian, a well-known philosopher, was always traveling and refused to part with him."

Here Dr. Semperweiss smiled rather oddly, meaningfully, as though expecting a reaction from Wojnicz. But there was none.

"People live too fast these days," he went on. "There are too many temptations. Too many philosophical ideas have set that boy's imagination on fire, and his sensitivity has become hypersensitivity. I'm telling you this in confidence, so you won't have any inflated expectations where he's concerned. He's in a very bad way. The local climate helps when the body and spirit are strong. Many people are condemned to confinement here. Fear of death confuses them, and they yield to false hopes, illusions and pipe dreams. So it was he who took you to the cemetery?"

Wojnicz admitted that it was.

The next day, when Wojnicz came to be examined, they resumed the conversation about old wives' tales. He was hoping to be pronounced healthy by now. He sat stripped to the waist, while first the doctor auscultated him at great length and very precisely, tapping his back here and there. Occasionally Dr. Semperweiss sighed, which alarmed Wojnicz, and then scribbled some symbols on a sheet of paper. It must have been a map of Wojnicz's lungs. He wanted to know what the doctor could hear in them, but after putting down his shiny modern stethoscope, Semperweiss made a few notes, then sank into a chair and began instead to talk of Opitz.

"Please don't forget that Herr Opitz is civilized only on the surface. You're smart enough to have noticed it. Underneath, he's a primitive man. Possibly he's the one who disseminates those folktales. It's quite simple: the local population are rough and uneducated. When the charcoal burners and shepherds finish their season, they come down from the mountains, drink themselves unconscious and get into scraps, and there's always a victim. Someone either falls off a bridge onto stones or freezes to death, because sometimes it's very cold by then, or they fight over a girl. This is not your world, young man. You're here for therapy, not to listen to fairy tales. If they believe in some sort of forest spirits, monsters that tear innocent youths to pieces, that's their right. That's how they understand the world. This is a poor area, and the local men have always derived a great deal from the forest and the mountains, either as shepherds grazing their flocks on the highland pastures, or as charcoal burners working the whole season in the forest. They're thirsty for women, but they're also afraid of women, with whom they don't know how to behave. No wonder their heads are full of fanciful stories."

He got up and approached Wojnicz.

"Would you open your mouth, please?"

He brought out a metal spatula and spent a long time inspecting the patient's throat.

"Each of us is a potential lunatic, young man. Fantasizing is the norm. Each of us sits astride the border of our own inner world and the outer one, balancing dangerously. It's a very uncomfortable position, and not many succeed in maintaining their equilibrium."

He sat down and set about making notes on what he had seen in Wojnicz's throat.

Wojnicz questioned him about the women who were said to have run away to the forest centuries ago.

"By now one could write a complete history on the basis of these facts: their crazy descendants are now murdering the descendants of the persecutors of their antecedents . . ."

"Ah, I see you have already yielded to the indoctrination of Frommer. He is not an untrustworthy person, but rather sees the world as a system of conspiracies. It's a specific kind of madness, though innocent. Women's madness is a very different thing, its nature is entirely different from that of men. This has been observed and proved at many hospitals. Men go mad as a result of various kinds of physical disorder, such as a rush of blood to the head, contamination of the blood by reason of an inappropriate diet, or yes, yes, unfortunately, syphilis. In women it's nothing like that, because the female psyche is weaker, with a thinner layer, so to speak, covering the instinctive, animal element that's inside her. By making holes in that cover, mental illness allows all those primitive instincts to emerge and gives them power over the fragile, delicate psyche."

Once he had finished the examination, he started to wash his hands. Lost in thought, Wojnicz slowly did up his buttons.

"And as for your host, Opitz," said the doctor, returning to the conversation, "he went to conquer the world by visiting his uncle in Rome, and that's where his illness appeared, so he hurried back, got married and began to live at an appropriate pace. Thanks to the local climate, the illness stopped progressing. Do you think any of us would have chosen to shut ourselves away in this damp, tragic valley, where Dr. Brehmer has built this expensive modern prison for us? And for many others . . ."

"But that does not concern me. Will I be going home for Christmas?"

"If only you would let me examine you, my dear, bashful young man, I'd inspect your body more precisely, and I'd check your lymph nodes—"

"I've told you, it's a religious matter," Wojnicz interrupted him. "Besides, I've been examined over and over again, without gaining the slightest protection against this illness."

"You are a philistine, and that's that. Just like Opitz. All you Catholics are the same, you have only a thin veneer of civilization on the surface."

"Why are you always insulting me, Doctor? Have I done something to deserve it?"

Dr. Semperweiss stopped in his tracks, surprised by his young patient's boldness.

"Aren't we just sick bodies to you? After all, from your perspective there's nothing to show that I'm a Catholic or a Pole, because there are no signs of nationality or denomination in the lungs, nor in the sinuses or anywhere else in the body. Can you tell from Herr Frommer's sick lungs that he's a Protestant? And that his mother was Polish?"

"Was she?!" exclaimed the doctor. "For the love of God, you fiery young Pole, you can't see a joke. I'm teasing you." He gestured for Wojnicz to finish dressing. "I'm just trying to get your blood moving."

"But you don't know that it hurts me. It really does hurt me."

"It shouldn't."

"Perhaps I don't feel self-confident. You are a doctor, and I am a sick patient. I'm talking to you in a language that's not my own. I feel isolated and alone here." Wojnicz's voice began to tremble. "My lungs are real, but my nationality is not. It belongs to a sphere of which Herr August would have more to say. A mythological one, perhaps?"

"But that doesn't mean nationality has no effect. It's plain to see as soon as one crosses a border—in the architecture, in the state of the farmyards. Am I not right?"

Wojnicz was standing behind a screen, buttoning up his shirt.

"You know what," the doctor continued, "I am a doctor, and I believe in science. And science favors simple statements that can describe the vast majority of the world's complexities. Like this or like that, if A, then B, and not C."

"But you submit to prejudices too," retorted Wojnicz, emerging from behind the screen fully dressed and ready to leave.

Once he had closed the door behind him, Dr. Semperweiss sank into thought, and he spent a long time rubbing his chin, which was covered in two days' growth of beard. In the silence of the consulting room, he could hear the pleasant rasp of the thick stubble. Then he reached for a small brass bell to summon Sydonia Patek, who soon entered with the usual solemn look on her sallow face.

Still a little infuriated, Wojnicz dropped in at his favorite café and ordered a cup of chocolate. He squeezed into a corner, where he had his own table by now, and consumed the delicious thick drink with a teaspoon. Then he ordered a second one. Its taste reminded him of childhood, when Gliceria was still with them. She used to make him a mug of cocoa for his afternoon tea, followed by something even better—kogel mogel. Gliceria would blend it smooth and white, so that all the sugar crystals melted into heavenly sweetness. When she left, the cocoa and kogel mogel vanished. And the doctors began.

In his short life, Mieczysław Wojnicz had met a very large number of them.

On his medical mornings, his father would wake him very early and, pointing at his watch, would stress that they were already late. The sleepy Mieczyś would keep sinking into torpor and had to be hurried, because the train would not wait, would it? His father would clumsily do up the boy's jacket and smooth down his hair. At such an early hour his stomach was usually still asleep and refused to open for a sip of hot chicory coffee, let alone a sandwich.

"All right, all right, we'll eat later, now make haste."

Overnight, Mieczyś's shoes seemed to have forgotten the shape of his feet, and he had to struggle with them. He only became fully conscious once they were outside and a droshky with an equally sleepy driver was taking them to the station.

Wojnicz could still remember the feel of his father's rough, hot hand as he tried to keep up with it while racing onto the platform. The odor of grease, fuel, metal and steam instantly took possession of them, and for some time to come the boy's little coat retained that special railway-journey smell: nasty, unnatural, alien and full of anticipated violence.

On the train, just past the bounds of the city, the little Wojnicz would suddenly wake up, feeling hungry. His father would take out the sandwiches that Józef had made for them the night before. Eating on the train was a separate pleasure, not sullied by anything. The sour rye bread coated in butter melted in his mouth like the most refined savory. Mieczyś would gaze at the large, wide fields just beyond Lwów, where the trees were few and far between, as if in this land trees were not respected but thought to spoil the stunningly straight horizons. The sun would be rising somewhere behind them and chasing the train as it headed west. The villages were at a standstill, like lurking, terrified animals, with only the towers of Catholic and Orthodox churches daring to protrude into the sky.

First his father would read the newspapers that he had bought on the run at the station, and then—ever prepared—he would open a very precious German thermos flask, from which he poured hot tea into a metal mug and shared it with his son. The tea had a metallic aftertaste, as did the entire journey. Mieczyś would watch as his father nodded off, then cast only the occasional glance at his mustache to settle his vision, set dancing by the moving landscape.

The boy had thought up a special game for train travel. It involved visualizing a small, dark figure whom he called Mister Jig, shifting him from point to point with his gaze. Mister Jig could rest only on sharply projecting elements of the landscape—trees and towers, tall fences or chimneys. He could never, ever be allowed to fall to the ground. The game was especially hard in this flat scenery, so the boy was forced to concentrate. He always thought that if he managed to convey Mister Jig to Kraków without touching the ground, nothing bad would happen to him there and he would not have to suffer the usual emotions— shame and a sense of guilt. But he never succeeded. Maybe if the train had gone through more heavily wooded terrain, or industrial zones where hundreds of chimneys stuck into the sky, maybe if it had gone through large cities, Mieczyś would have been safe. But not here.

In Kraków they took a droshky from the station and drove to yet another doctor. Once they had stopped for the night in Alwernia to visit a famous professor. But he had not been able to help either.

Every consultation was roughly the same. First his father talked to the doctor, then Mieczyś was asked to come in and told to strip naked behind a screen. It never occurred to him to protest. Both of the gentlemen knew what they were doing, they had concerned faces, and all of this was meant to be for his good.

Mieczyś would undress reluctantly, and often had to be hurried, unless the gentlemen were carried away in conversation. He took off everything that he had put on at home a short time ago, but in reverse order: jacket, shirt, vest, shoes, trousers, stockings. There was something perverse about it—a person hides beneath his clothes, clothing is a safe hiding place, and now he was being forced to get out of it, to submit to examination yet again. For as long as he could remember, he had constantly been examined, his body constantly an object of wonder, the sight of it constantly prompting an expression of concern on the faces of its observers, most of whom were old gentlemen, doctors and specialists, with mustaches and clean-shaven jaws, exuding a smell of eau de cologne, unmade beds and shabby wallet leather. They would bring their wise, ugly heads close to the boy's body, assisting themselves with spectacles or monocles. Sometimes they touched him. His father allowed this, and the child was not asked.

Every time he hoped there would not be any touching. He believed that this time there would not be. As he stood before the two men in his underwear, he felt a chill rising from the wooden floor, from the gaps in it, from somewhere.

"And your drawers."

That was what they said in Kraków to describe the lower part of his underwear—drawers.

"Please take off your drawers."

He knew that it mattered greatly to his father, so he turned his eyes away from the man examining him and tried to find a very remote spot on which to latch his vision. Sometimes he chose the top of a tree seen through the window, and sometimes simply a spider in a corner of the ceiling on the opposite side of the room.

Well, he was as he was. He couldn't help it. He thought of himself as normal. He once tried to explain this to his father, but he could not find the right words. Then he thought about the mysteries of yeast cake rising, or about a pigeon that had laid a sad egg in the recess of a blank window.

His father called these visits consultations. He constantly believed that a cure existed somewhere. When he gradually began to understand that there was no cure, the idea of an operation arose in his mind, a time when a scalpel could be used to cut everything into the right shape.

Once Wojnicz was a teenager, the examinations had acquired a different character, becoming more and more fraught, if not fierce, as if his affliction prompted impatience, or even—medically justified, of course—violence.

In Vienna, having first smeared his fingers in Vaseline, a Dr. Kubitschek tried to push them into the hole down there, the result of which was pain, dreadful and excruciating, so that despite the efforts of the muscular assistant who was holding Wojnicz down, the doctor was hit in the face and his wire spectacles landed on the floor with broken lenses.

That was how it looked. There was no helping it.

13

GHOSTS

On these rather gloomy, rainy days in late October, Thilo lay in bed covered up to the chin, assailed by sweats and shivers alternately. By the bed stood a spittoon, which Wojnicz tried not to look at when visiting his friend; it was filled with balls of white wadding stained with blood. He could not help being reminded of the Sunday-best pocket handkerchief that his father wore on solemn occasions, such as funerals, weddings, national holidays or anniversaries of the Third of May Constitution—a scrap of red-and-white material, a contrast of colors that could only prophesy trouble.

Now and then a large male nurse appeared, hired by Thilo's mysterious guardian; he emptied the wretched vessel, administered medicine and gave Wojnicz—the patient's so-called friend—reproachful looks for being incapable of helping him with all this. Unfortunately, communication with Thilo was becoming increasingly sporadic. Sometimes he was delirious, and then he repeated those terrifying words, saying that "the landscape kills," or shouting out threats aimed at someone who plainly wanted to do him harm. At these moments Wojnicz would sit beside him, wipe the sweat from his brow and moisten his lips. He also stroked Thilo's hands, which clearly soothed him, and even sang to him softly, almost in a whisper.

Wojnicz would sit in Thilo's room for hours at a time—for this purpose he exempted himself from some of his treatments, especially Father Kneipp's baths, which he regarded as barbaric. Here, in Thilo's room, he had a quiet time, his presence at his friend's bedside evoking a sorrowful state of peace—a mood that Wojnicz had liked since childhood. It was a sort of everyday melancholy that he knew well, and which had the "appetizing" quality that he sought in every situation. This melancholy had cosmic dimensions, but he only experienced a little bit of it, a tiny, microscopic part. Whenever he cast a glance at Thilo, his throat constricted and his chest ached, as if someone had placed a great weight on it that was just about to crush his heart. There were no tears. Wojnicz was quite incapable of crying—his father had knocked that out of his head early on. It was one of the basic lessons: don't snivel, don't be a sissy. So his body had found other ways to endure sorrow.

He spent most of his time in Thilo's room holding a large magnifying glass, which he slowly moved across de Bles's canvas, unable to stop admiring it.

How is it that from tiny strokes of a brush dipped in paint an entire world with many depths comes into being? De Bles's painting seemed fathomless—when he magnified it, he saw even more details, minute spots of paint, very light brushstrokes, indistinct patches and mysterious flaws. As he wandered about the clouds, supple, rounded lines emerged from them, resembling figures, faces or wings. But when he moved down toward the vegetation, among the leaves he saw eyes and noses, bits of hands and feet, elusive bodies that existed fleetingly, only when his vision brushed against them for a single, unrepeatable moment. In the aerial castle windows, he spied the corners of chambers, and semi-transparent creatures inside them, each connected with a tragedy, a regret. Maybe Abraham's sacrifice was being performed there too, but in slightly different configurations and with different actors? De Bles's canvas seemed to be full of messages, like a detailed map using a language of simple signs that carry branching meanings, a world that proves infinite once one goes deep inside, where one keeps discovering new things.

The weaker Thilo became, the more intriguing Wojnicz found the black patch marking the cave. He shifted his magnifying glass to that spot and grappled with the darkness. At those moments he was silent and, reassured by Thilo's breathing, leaned over the painting armed with his lens. Gradually he learned to discern shapes there, though he could not easily say what they were. Two feebly glowing sparks. Eyes, perhaps? Maybe those of a large animal, or of some living thing that was watching us all the time, without us knowing it? Or maybe it was God, wanting to see at close range if Abraham would carry out his order?

"You have such amazingly long fingers," said Thilo one day, and reached out to take Mieczysław's hand in his cold palms. Mieczysław had been looking through his herbal, where on each page the carefully dried plants affixed with tiny strips of paper would remain in perpetuity.

"Look, here's lily of the valley, *Convallaria majalis*," he told Thilo. "It looks so ordinary, doesn't it? You've seen it many times in your life, but you could only describe it very generally from memory. Am I right?"

Thilo leaned over the flower, pleased that his attention was needed. There was something deeply moving about his zeal, his interest in a plant that, though dead, still preserved its unique and wonderful structure, the neat little veins, the beautiful shapes, the baroque edges and recurring patterns.

"What a pity it's autumn, I could have collected some local specimens here too," said Wojnicz.

"You can wait until spring. The winter goes by quickly."

"Oh, no," countered Wojnicz. "I'll be home for Christmas. So will you."

"I'm staying here. In the graveyard where Frau Opitz and all the others are lying."

Wojnicz put aside the herbal and cast Thilo a disapproving look.

"Hug me," said Thilo quietly.

And without hesitation Wojnicz hugged his slight, fevered body. It was a strange feeling, as he had not hugged anyone, or been hugged, for a long time. This sense of another person's presence through just a few layers of clothing, the fragility of the bones and the delicate softness of the body, flooded him with a nice warmth, as if he were back in Gliceria's kitchen, eating kogel mogel. It was the best place he had ever been, and if he only could, he would have taken Thilo there. Stunned by this sudden sensation of pleasure and calm, he closed his eyes, and he felt Thilo's heart beating against his chest, a tiny section of the great factories of nature. He had no idea how it came to the point when Thilo von Hahn, a young but talented expert on landscape art, took his face in his hands and planted a long kiss on his lips; Wojnicz did not know how to return it, so he simply accepted it, feeling moved but also brimming with wonderful serenity.

"When I die, take the de Bles. It's yours. I'm giving it to you."

It had been a very long time since Thilo had come to supper. At first his chair stood empty, but then it disappeared, and everything looked as if it had always been that way. Wojnicz usually waited until the last moment to go down, when the gong rang out from below. He liked being on his own awhile, especially as he was spending most of his time with Thilo. In these rare moments of solitude, he sat in his room poring over the herbal, pensively looking through his collections.

In any case, after noon he started to feel unwell. It often occurred to him that formerly he had not been ill at all. He had ended up here by a twist of circumstances, and only then had Dr. Semperweiss discovered an illness in him, which was now making its presence known—some peculiar ailment, with no name or description in the medical textbooks. Some mysterious processes were taking place inside him, the maps were changing, the continents were shifting. The rivers were leaving their beds, and mountains were erupting from the lowlands. All this absorbed his inner energy, making him feel weak and sleepy. Then he would lie down on the quilted counterpane on the bed clumsily made by Raimund and fall into a doze.

During supper the usual discussions went on, but Wojnicz hardly spoke at all, not even when Lukas or August accosted him. For several days they had been talking about the decline of history, and the end of the world, which Lukas was convinced was nigh—the less the others said, the more strength his orations gathered. He claimed that mankind as produced by Western civilization had reached the limit of its development. The end was plain to see in human diseases—we did not have enough air. Tuberculosis was a symbolic as well as a physical disease.

"The great epoch of mankind is drawing to a close, can nobody see that?" he would shout through his napkin as he wiped tomato sauce off his chin.

In response, from the end of the table Frommer would repeat that every culture was a process that had its beginning, matured, reached its zenith, then withered and never returned again. And, at its close, ghosts were bound to appear, because the fight shifted to the borders between worlds as well.

"Something new will soon come along and give a voice to the ghosts," he added in a quavery voice.

Wojnicz thought him very theatrical. He learned that Frommer regarded himself as the last of the people who were still capable of understanding the mechanics of the apocalypse.

At the same time, meat-filled dumplings coated in dark sauce and other tidbits such as small peppers stuffed with mince, gherkins and fried mortadella croquettes were disappearing from their plates—in view of Raimund's culinary helplessness, Opitz was now ordering the meals from some women in the village. The best dish was rice pudding with apples, as fluffy as a cloud.

After supper the gentlemen sat around the table, sprawling in the sort of pose that a sated, well-fed body usually adopts. The stove was well-stoked, so the room was nice and warm, especially compared with the extremely bad weather outside—it was pouring, and the wind, the first real autumn gale, was lashing the windows with streams of rain. Only their faces looming out of the darkness were reflected in the panes. The table was still covered in breadcrumbs, and the tablecloth was stained by a large drop of sauce.

Yes, now the suppers dragged on, and Wojnicz was unsure whether it was the effect of the noticeably shorter days on everyone, or if a shadow had been cast over the whole guesthouse by Thilo's ever worsening state, causing them to seek one another's presence to raise their spirits. Somehow a large bottle of Schwärmerei would appear from nowhere, and Herr August would light the one and only cigar allowed him that day, puff on it a few times and then cough hard enough to produce tears.

One evening Lukas drummed his fingers on the tabletop, unintention-
ally copying Herr August with this gesture—or maybe mocking him?—
until, scowling with distaste, he said:

"I see that certain irrational ideas are cluttering your minds in a
most unhealthy way. You are making yourselves anxious and fearful."

To which Herr August replied:

"That is in the nature of autumn. One thinks of death, which is always alarming. Especially a violent death, like the one here. It's no
wonder people are susceptible to fairy tales and mythology when they
don't understand what's happening around them."

Raimund, who was bringing in some Schwärmerei, stopped in the
doorway and leaned against the frame.

"Ghosts," he said curtly, and Opitz glanced at him reprovingly. Lukas snatched up the topic with gratitude.

"We are moving on to the terrain of demonology, in other words a
line of thought typical of the early stages of the development of the human spirit. When the transcendent, one and only God appears, all demonology vanishes. It goes up like a puff of smoke. When we submit it
to inspection, modern man is bound to regard it as a form of atavism
and childishness, is that not so?" he said, looking at Herr August.
"There are no devils. Ever since the Son of God sacrificed himself for
us, the devils have had nothing to say."

"Nothing to say," Herr August repeated pensively, very slightly ap-
ing Lukas's Baltic accent. "And yet devils do exist, simply because
we're talking and thinking about them. Because epic poems and stage
plays have been written about them. And because people believe in
them—here in the countryside they're in deadly fear of them."

To this, wreathed in a haze of smoke, Frommer replied:

"There's too much proof of their existence for one to sweep it all under the carpet. I know people who have experienced communion with ghosts. I myself have seen some unusual things," he said mysteriously.

They all waited to see if Frommer would say more. Would he present one of those shocking, silly little stories that kitchen maids were so eager to tell each other? But of course he fell enigmatically silent and vanished in clouds of smoke.

It was impossible for August not to respond:

"I agree with you, sir. That is the only form in which they exist, as our inner, subjective experience. As illusion and mirage."

"Oh, excuse me, but a mirage is certainly not a subjective experience. It is the reflection of an image that appears as a result of meteorological phenomena," said Frommer from behind his smoke cloud.

At this point Lukas intervened. He was in one of his irritable moods:

"Devils are a synonym for chaos, negation and falsehood. Devils are always a multitude against God's unity. Man's greatest enemies. They do not exist, although we are constantly having to fight them."

"Excuse me, but how can one fight a nonexistent enemy?" Wojnicz ventured to ask, surprising himself with his own boldness.

"A multitude against a unity," said Lukas, ignoring him. "Chaos against order. Nature against the Logos. Paganism against the One and Only God. Those are the devils. Demonology shows us a world that is closed within itself, without any transcendence, because devils act within the world, devils act within nature, and in the vision of the world in which devils exist, God is something beyond nature, while man is a prisoner of nature."

With evident regret, Herr August carefully stubbed out his smoldering cigar.

"I see a bit of a contradiction here. We could all establish that devils exist as symbols, as images in our heads. And because we believe in them."

At this point Frommer spoke again. He loomed out of the shadow and the smoke to take a glass of Schwärmerei from the lamplit table.

"For me, devils are a sort of guarantee of life's continuity. What would things be like if there were a large hole between the world and God, pretty much a yawning abyss, not filled, but ethereal? The devils cover up this hole in existence. They're like the saints in Catholicism— they are a kind of demon too, but they appear to be helpful. If you have room for the saints, you must make room for the devils. He who believes in Saint Anthony is bound to believe in the devils that persecuted him—that's logical."

Everyone was looking at Lukas, knowing he was a Catholic, and so this was his concern, but just then Wojnicz spoke up.

"Are devils capable of speaking? Do they have voices?"

"In *The Enneads*, Plotinus says they knew how to use human speech, but over time, the fathers of the Church insisted they did not. They said devils have no power of speech. The Church took away their voice, so now they're up to mischief," said Herr August, smiling to himself.

To which Lukas replied:

"In my view, one should ritually deny the reality of devils, and if that's impossible, one should exorcize them. Only God and the world exist, there is nothing in between. The spirit and matter. Philosophy and science. The sacred and the profane. The mind and the body. This is the foundation of our entire civilization, this is how our minds work. One or the other."

"That's quite enough radical dualism; Asiatic, I would say, straight from Zoroaster," said August in response. "We, meanwhile, brought up as we are within Greek tradition"—at this point he looked around the company, as if wanting to make sure all of them without exception really did attest to their affiliation with Greek tradition—"must refer to Plato and the ideas of his intermediate world. This third sphere performs the function of mediator between the transcendent God and the immanent man. Between spirit and nature. Between the empirical and the metaphysical. Paradoxically, being an intermediary, this in-between world contributes to the preservation of differences between those two. Think about it, Herr Lukas."

"Plato was a pagan. We have Aristotle!" protested Lukas, none too logically.

"Indeed, the old world was pagan, as was Aristotle too, but that doesn't change the fact that it was our world just the same, and we are greatly indebted to it. I postulate acknowledging the rationale for this world that's in between either-or; it would be something like a gray zone between the one and the other," said August.

"Apparently you're an atheist, yet you defend the gray zone where devils reside," Lukas accused him.

"I am seeking a place for them, so that you can chase them out of it and exorcize them. I am only speaking as if all this were to exist, as if there were to exist— The existence of devils is elusive. Devils are the army of Proteus, always changing shape and returning in new bodies, in new episodes."

"I'd say that it is rather nothingness that has the power to adopt various shapes, more or less sinister," parried Longin Lukas. "It's nothingness that tempts and seduces, commits corruption, and always acts in this strange way, as if existing and not existing at the same moment. It's built out of our projections, our anxieties, it readily feeds on our fears."

"As I said: here are your devils, all these local Tuntschis and Empusas."

Herr August pointed at his own temple, but just then the wind struck the windows so hard that one of them opened and a pot of arte-misia, one of many deployed throughout the house, fell to the floor.

Opitz, who had said nothing until now, hastily cleaned up.

After the brief commotion, Wojnicz spoke again.

"Herr Lukas, on the one hand you deny the existence of devils, but on the other you recommend fighting them. How can that be? Which side are you on?"

"I believe one should push them out of the sphere of human reason, one should cause them to cease to exist at all. Humanity must rid itself of its devils."

"How is it to do that?"

"Take control of them, eradicate them . . ."

"You know that is not possible," said Frommer suddenly. "These are creatures that employ other laws than earthly ones."

"There are no other laws than earthly ones. There is only God."

For several days our Wojnicz beat simple paths—he went from the guesthouse to the Kurhaus, and took two daily walks. He also made two daily visits to Thilo, who was getting worse and worse, so that fin-ally a telegram had been sent to Berlin, but whether to fetch his parents or his close friend Wojnicz did not know. Each morning Dr. Semper-weiss came into the room that smelled of paints and left it in an ever more solemn mood. There were thoughts of transferring the patient to the Kurhaus, where he would have better care, but somehow the idea was eventually dropped. A second male nurse was hired, and now the smell of soap and disinfectant filled the air upstairs; this sturdy figure in a gown with the sleeves rolled up would be seen standing outside the guesthouse on the courtyard side, smoking cigarettes.

Once again Opitz proposed a little outing to relieve the guesthouse residents of their negative thoughts and get some air into their lungs. One must do one's job, one must live, he kept repeating. After all, there was always someone dying here.

Herr August was often waiting in the dining room for Wojnicz to appear in order to take possession of him, at least for the time it took to walk to the Kurhaus. Always slightly inclined toward his interlocutor, with his hands folded as if to pray, he delivered lectures embellished with Greek quotations that Wojnicz did not understand, but he was afraid to admit it.

On the afternoon preceding the outing to the Heuriger, a rural restaurant, Herr August visited Wojnicz in his room. He slipped in, freshly shaved and scented with eau de cologne, the smell of which immediately flooded the room. From under his snuff-colored smoking jacket he fetched a green bottle.

"I have brought a small aperitif," he said with a warm and friendly smile. "Just enough for two shots. Let us drink to friendship."

They sat down at a small table where Wojnicz had been writing postcards to his father and uncle. He pushed them under his herbal, even though August did not know Polish. At least he had that advantage over him. They talked about various things—about the virtues of an herbal, about Thilo's health, and the imminent onset of winter. Suddenly August leaned confidentially toward him:

"I have found you out, you beautiful creature, Mieczysław," he said, uttering Wojnicz's first name as if he had spent a long time learning it. "I know who you are. If Jupiter and Venus bear witness simultaneously, a chimera will appear that is respected and nice-looking . . ."

The first thing that occurred to Wojnicz was to do with the hole in the wall: perhaps he had not blocked it properly, or maybe he had failed to notice others in the walls or door. Suddenly he missed his father—he would have known how to respond, how to behave. He felt his body stiffen, and to give himself more time to respond he reached for the glass of Schwärmerei and—despite his resolve to drink less—gulped it down. August eagerly poured him a second.

During the few seconds while the drink was flowing down his throat into his stomach, shortly to mix with his blood, a sense of calm swept through Wojnicz.

"We should be getting ready now, Herr August. We must dress warmly," he said, standing up and going over to the wardrobe for his coat. "I didn't know you were interested in astrology as well. There'll be something to discuss with Herr Lukas."

August watched him over his shoulder, without moving from the spot.

"And this is from Plutarch: 'Does he prefer female delights, or a boy's charm?,' 'Wherever he sees beauty, he is ambidextrous.'"

Wojnicz was standing by the door with his back to his visitor. He merely let his head drop.

"Cicero talks about it," said August enigmatically, and added: "Do you know that those like you were drowned in the sea?"

They traveled in a bizarre coach of local devising, with benches running lengthwise, so they sat opposite one another like firemen, more in silence than not, merely making isolated comments here and there, because the whole cart kept rattling and creaking. Wojnicz was gazing at this world burning with autumn fires through half-closed eyelids, which was a new exercise in looking—he was doing it just as Thilo had advised. It made the world seem flat, composed of nothing but spots and lines, some of them totally unexpected. Whenever his eyes stopped looking in the old way, in which one is already familiar with the object of one's vision, surprising figures came into sight. The road they were now traveling, which led through large, open mountain pastures to Langwaltersdorf in the Reibnitz direction, was like a triangle with soft lines, surrounded by streaks of brown, sienna, olive green and rust. These streaks toyed with symmetry, recurring around each successive bend in the road and teasing the fuzzy edges of the triangle with the unexpected texture of the verge, into which the thick, dark lines of trees were rooted. The sky was sinking its teeth in between the mountains visible on the horizon, gnawing at the earth. Red leaves spilling from the beech trees were like claw marks bathed in blood.

"Are your eyes sore?" Frommer questioned him, and in his gaze Wojnicz saw genuine concern.

As they drove up to a small but very pretty mountain refuge, the sun had hidden behind the ridge of a high crag, but on the other side it must still have been casting a golden glow across the lowlands. Here it was very dark, velvety.

The innkeeper, dressed Alpine-style in lederhosen and thick socks, invited them inside the warm cottage, where they were regaled with homemade wine (not very good), and then a liqueur made with seven local herbs, the recipe for which was a strictly guarded secret. The refuge's special feature was one of the local tarns that were said to be formed by the underground lake coming to the surface in the shape of large, deep ponds whose water was always cold and crystal clear.

Opitz addressed the innkeeper with great deference, while Herr August and Herr Lukas, once the mixture of alcohols had made everyone a little bolder, began to argue again. From the kitchen came a wonderful smell of stew—all the guests were hungry, and they were impatient for the moment when they could finally eat their fill. This time the conversation was about tradition, and from what Wojnicz could hear with half an ear, Lukas was insisting that tradition should be taken seriously and literally, as therein lay the wisdom of entire generations, whereas August claimed it was the stiff outer armor that keeps a better grip on a community than religion does, but in the liberated world that was sure to arise, not a trace of either would remain.

"November the third is our Kaninchentag," said the innkeeper, interrupting these arguments while arranging the plates and cutlery. "This is the day when we eat a dish known as Angstel."

Wojnicz took out his notebook and wrote down this information, paying close attention to the appearance of the dish, which was served in cast-iron cocottes. At the same time, once he was sitting on the other side of the table he avoided August's gaze. Earthenware bowls filled with mashed potato, and pumpkin of a beautiful golden-yellow color appeared, as well as pickled gherkins and fried beetroots. They all dug into the stew with gusto. At first Wojnicz turned the irregular chunks of meat on his fork mistrustfully, but finally gave in, and when more wine was served, his appetite awoke with the force of a tornado.

Following the question of tradition, over their stew the gentlemen turned to considering the topic of the daimon, but their conversation was soon dominated by the innkeeper, who brought a bottle of another liqueur of his own making and noisily praised it:

"Well, tell me frankly, who makes the better Schwärmerei, is it Herr Opitz, or is it me?" he shouted, and then began to pour the familiar drink into some beautiful cut-glass tumblers.

Wojnicz tasted it with curiosity. Yes, the flavor was different— sweeter, less spicy—but the innkeeper's liqueur also had a stronger taste of moss, the damp forest floor, softened fir, needles and ants. He asked for more—he could feel the liqueur dissolving in his stomach and storming his nervous system. He felt the familiar animation, the sharpening of his attention, and that sense of being entangled in minutiae—he had no idea how to describe it.

"The stew was splendid! I've never had anything like it before," said Herr August, reaching for his daily cigar. This time he did not light it, but merely rolled it between his fingers in a sensual way.

"What an aroma," enthused Lukas, slightly tipsy by now. "It must be the local seasoning. Why not tell us what you put in it? Allspice, for sure . . ."

The innkeeper eagerly agreed that nothing so good was made anywhere. He sat down on the edge of a bench, plainly gearing up to tell more. As he smiled, his face blurred miraculously.

"The preparations for this dish have been underway since the spring. You need at least three dozen rabbits of a similar age." He leaned his arms on his widespread knees, and they turned their chairs to face him, which made it look as if he were telling a hunting yarn. "They're such cowardly animals! The night before Kaninchentag you go to their cages with a loaded shotgun and fire in the air a few times, to make plenty of noise." He threw up his hands. *"Bang, bang, bang!"* he shouted. "Most of the rabbits die of a heart attack. We say their hearts burst out of fear."

Silence fell, and the innkeeper realized that perhaps he had not been understood.

"That is the main ingredient of the stew, my dear gentlemen!" he exclaimed, addressing them as though they were children. "That's exactly what you've been eating. The terrified hearts are flushed with blood and taste delicious. That is our Angstel. We make the carcasses into terrines, and once they've been tanned, the skins are made into furs for the ladies."

He burst into effusive laughter, and in the process his face lost its features entirely.

Wojnicz went outside and was instantly embraced by the strong velvet arms of the mountains, which were illuminated by a dull yellow glow that evidently came from Waldenburg. He felt the uttermost disgust and despair at the thought that he had been caught in a trap and would never be free of it, that once again he would be living in fear and with the feeling of being a counterfeit, a cheap imitation. Full of terrified rabbit hearts, his stomach contracted with horror and revulsion. He leaned a hand against the warm wooden wall of the house and vomited at length.

A narrow flight of stairs led up to the door into the attic. The steps were toy-size, as if made for children, and the door itself was distinctly smaller than all the others in the house. Moreover, it had been sloppily coated in dark brown paint, with other colors showing through it, as if the door were old and had been painted again and again for centuries. Wojnicz looked around and listened for a while, to be sure no one was coming, then he went up the stairs and grasped the door handle. He had to push it hard, because it looked as though nobody had opened it for a long time. In the gap under the door a strip of dust had gathered, in which he could see the remains of dead insects, some hairs and crumbled leaves. As Mieczysław stooped and entered the attic, he had to hold his breath for a moment because of the intense smell of earth, decaying wood and mold that prevailed in there. He had been expecting a chill, but—quite the contrary—he was met by moist, humid air. The entire floor was covered in conifer needles and clumps of moss, which also partly coated the walls, as well as the wooden rafters. The tiny windows were wreathed in pale gray lichen, or perhaps it was some very old cobwebs. Wojnicz took a few steps forward, but soon had a strange feeling that his feet were sinking in the conifer needles, so he withdrew to the threshold in horror. In one corner stood a rather large piece of furniture—Wojnicz recognized it as a chest of drawers covered in lush moss, its long stamens ending in spherical spore cases hung downward, like whimsical jewelry.

He squatted down and sank to his knees, then leaned on his hands and crawled toward the chest of drawers—in this position he could spread his weight more evenly and avoid sinking into the conifer needles—until suddenly he touched something cold and slimy. As if scalded, he tried to retreat to the threshold, but then he noticed that he had come upon a colony of larch boletes; the mushrooms grew boldly, their honey-gold color almost shining in the gloom. After a few seconds of boundless astonishment, he instinctively began to pick them but had nowhere to put this fungal bounty. He decided to sacrifice his handkerchief, which very soon proved inadequate. The sight of the mushrooms had pushed his sense of danger to the margins. He took off his shirt and, semi-naked, advanced far into the room, picking the golden boletes, while the springy fruiting bodies of the moss brushed against his chest. The air in here was damp and stuffy. He did not even notice that a very soft wheezing noise was coming from his throat, rapidly becoming more and more like the cooing he knew so well, which no longer irritated but pleased him, sounding personal, friendly, like a mother's familiar voice. By now his shirt was full of mushrooms and he had to withdraw from this Aladdin's cave. It was hard to go backward on all fours, and at the same time he knew there were still plenty of little golden heads among the fleshy conifer needles. I must leave them for later, I'll come here again, he promised himself with great excitement, feeling truly happy. How sorry he was to leave this place! And once again his throat emitted that sound: *coo-roo-coo*, as if Wojnicz were complaining, *coo-roo-coo*, or as if he were summoning someone.

From the corner of his eye, he noticed a faint, rapid movement, but he thought it must be the pigeons that lived here, or maybe some other birds of a kind that did not fly away to Africa for the winter. What riches that Opitz fellow had in here! Did he know about it? Wojnicz wanted to boast of his discovery, but then suddenly he felt he had no desire to share this treasure with the others. Why should he tell them what he had found in here? Did they share their secrets with him? No, he would not tell a soul.

He made his way to the stairs and, holding the bag made of his shirt with one hand while shielding his chest with the other, he quietly tip-toed back to his room.

14

A TEMPERATURE CHART

ince the bizarre and gruesome evening when they had gone out for rabbit hearts at the inn by the pond, Wojnicz had decided to stop drinking Schwärmerei. There was something wrong with this thick, tasty and strangely addictive liqueur. Its bitter sweetness prompted bliss, but later on the drink disturbed one's nerve function and concentration. Wojnicz felt as if his normal reality as a patient at the sanatorium was suddenly being invaded by an entire system of offshoots of time, its potential side pockets and pleats. Time was gathering into folds, minutes kept disappearing into seconds or extending into quarter hours, making it easy to lose one's bearings within it. Something similar had happened to space. It felt as if the whole of the attic had not yet been explored, as if new doors kept on appearing there. Sometimes the guesthouse suddenly became too large as well, as though it had swollen in the night, as though new spaces had burgeoned within it. He often dreamed that the corridor had doubled in length, and that farther down there were some more little rooms, from which he could hear cooing or the roar of an enamored stag. Sometimes after drinking the liqueur Wojnicz failed to reach his room without stopping on the stairs to scrutinize the smoke-stained still lifes. He started carrying the magnifying glass about with him, the one he had used to examine the de Bles, thanks to which he discovered that the stair rail was badly eaten away by deathwatch beetles. Long years of work by these insects were gradually turning the rail into a fragile skeleton that would crumble with a crash one day under someone's hand. He tried to look at some kitschy landscapes through the magnifying glass, but it was too dark in the guesthouse, and the feeble glow of the electric light bulbs, sporadic and buzzing, merely inflamed the views hidden in these canvases without revealing much. But he nervously bypassed the picture of the hanging hare by stretching his legs and skipping over a few steps. Schwärmerei made him feel like that hare, as if he were suspended above the table of a giant, and he even felt as if he were seeing everything upside down.

Next morning he would be bothered not so much by a hangover as a feeling of having lost something, of being unable to remember his own words, of having holes in his memory through which a vague murmur would force its way into his brain. He decided to fake his drinking, and once he even managed to pour away the contents of the glass without being noticed.

The beginning of November was particularly damp. It rained for days on end, now as disagreeable streams of water, now as a warm spray from the sky into the air. The brook below the Guesthouse for Gentlemen swelled and began to wash away its banks, rinsing off the remains of summer dust and goose feathers, and tearing out small plants that had rashly moved too close to the current. People could hear the constant hum of water, possibly coming not just from the brook; sometimes Wojnicz felt as if it were omnipresent, emanating from underground as well, from beneath the foundations of the houses, from the cellars, or from under the surface of the park. It escorted the cobbled street, accompanying people's footsteps, the rattle of carriages and the growl of the few car engines. Moisture settled like a thin layer of icing on the leaves, which had gone red and yellow long ago but still held on to life, not yet ready to divorce the trees. In the heavy, humid air each leaf fell theatrically and astonishingly noisily. Splat, splat, and it was glued to its companions that had already started to upholster the pavements and flagstones.

Wojnicz was still managing to elude Herr August, who kept looking at him meaningfully and seemed to be following him all the time, and to escape Lukas, who always greeted him with a knowing smile, like a partner in a future crime, and also the disturbing Frommer, who saw him as an insider, privy to the secret of his real profession; to avoid them, he would go out beyond the one and only road, turn off the high street and instantly head into the mountains, passing some small, well-tended gardens along the way. Unless he had a fit of breathlessness, he was able to climb quite high up, and then he could see that to call the settlement below a town was a major exaggeration. It was an open space with some houses built on it, where as soon as the sun set (and every day there was visibly less light), piercing cold immediately moved in from somewhere in the mountains, a damp chill that blended with the rather bitter smell of smoke from the chimneys and permanently waterlogged wood. A pan in which a dish unknown to the world was being made.

This was when Wojnicz had time to think. As he did not like to do it on the move, he would find himself a fallen tree, or even one of the benches, where he would sit—gazing at the village and the vast, monstrous Kurhaus building that was always in sight—and think. But not ahead, to the future. He only knew how to think backward; his thoughts were memories, because his mind was not yet free, and he had to keep on grappling with what had happened to him in the past.

These memories were of individual moments, fairly trivial ones, and he did not really know why he remembered them. The smell of cooking wafting from the kitchen, which annoyed his father so much that finally they had taken to ordering meals from restaurants. His own sense of shock the one time he saw his father drunk and in tears; he must have been little, because he had felt the strong hand of Gliceria, who took him out of the room and made sure he forgot about the situation for a long time. Or his solo expedition to the village at the age of five—to this day he could not imagine what had prompted him to go there. He had not come home until evening, when his father, in a frenzy of worry about him, had slapped him in front of everyone.

But gradually he was abandoning that long-ago place inside himself, and increasingly often he felt that it had happened not to him but to someone else, someone called Mieczyś Wojnicz from Lwów. Viewing these scenes was like looking at postcards, and he could have added greetings to them. But what he liked to do was to ask himself: "How is it that . . . ?"—and here he would insert all the paradoxes, all the injustices and sufferings of this world. It was like a new version of Mister Jig, the game he had played with such abandon on every journey. And this new amusement was well-suited to the rest cures, walks around the park or lying in bed waiting for the clock on the tower to start waking Jakob.

For example: "How is it that someone can die so young without having lived through anything yet?" Or: "How is it that in the face of a terrible illness like consumption, each person finds their own strategy for coping with it?" Or else: "How is it that people who look at the same thing see something different?"

Naturally, he found no answers to these questions. He promised himself he would ask Longin Lukas or Herr August about it all, but somehow they always retired into realms of interest to them alone, and rarely let him get a word in. Moreover—or so he suspected—they would be incapable of furnishing him with simple explanations, without quotations, without paraphrasing or lecturing, so that he would understand.

After his solitary walk he would return to the guesthouse, make sure that apart from Thilo and his nurse smoking outside no one else was there and go straight upstairs to visit Frau Opitz's room again. Every morning he looked forward to it, and was only afraid that some unexpected event would obstruct him.

These visits were now rather different from at the start. As soon as he entered the room, his breathing quickened. First he would stand still in the middle of the room, taking shallow breaths. His body would remain tense, ready for something that was not yet happening, but was just around the corner. The cooing from the attic was more distinct in here, but no longer stirred the old anxiety. Far from it—now he thought he could recognize individual syllables in those rounded, feathery sounds, partly human and partly avian, pleasant to the ear.

Then he would sit on the bed and stroke the nap of the soft, faded coverlet. Next he would take off his shabby shoes, and with a steady hand he would reach under the bed, where the dead woman's slippers were lying; with a decisive movement he would put them on, and they fitted him perfectly. He felt a tremor run through him as he pulled off his thick sweater and donned a cambric camisole. At first clumsy, his hands had soon gained proficiency in coping with the tiny buttons and little straps. He sat there awhile, tense as a bowstring and shivering with cold, before tying on a wrinkled Silesian skirt with petticoats and tightening the bodice. He would stand up straight, keeping still, as if to give the world a chance to grow used to this version of Wojnicz—in a flared skirt. His heart would stop thumping, he would feel very calm and—one could say—entirely free of thoughts. After one of these quiet moments of total focus and intensity, he would undress and return to his former appearance. He would carefully fold the pieces of clothing, put them back in place and quietly go downstairs.

Thilo was lying in bed with his eyes closed. He looked greatly changed to Wojnicz, no longer a young man, but as if devoid of age or gender. Wojnicz found this sight so chilling that in the first instance he felt like retreating. But he got the better of himself on seeing that Thilo had opened his eyes and was looking at him, waiting for him to come closer.

"Look," said Thilo, taking hold of Mieczysław by the sleeve. "This is my temperature chart. You see? Examine it."

Wojnicz picked up a clipboard with a sheet of paper attached to it, on which the temperature was recorded. It showed a broken line, not very jagged.

"And now look over here," said Thilo, pointing a finger at the line running along the crests of the mountains outside.

His face flushed for a moment, maybe from effort, because he was trying to raise himself onto his elbows. The color spread right up to his brow.

"The line is identical, can you see that? It's just the same. How is that possible?"

Wojnicz shifted his gaze from one to the other, and indeed, by some miracle the two lines, of the fever chart and the mountain peaks, looked very similar, almost a perfect match.

"I told you—here the landscape kills. This is the sort of place, one of very few in the world, where the landscape kills," said Thilo with patent difficulty. "They don't cure here at all, they kill, but they don't know it. How? Perhaps this place produces some sort of energy, topographic force fields or something. Ask Frommer. And swear to me you'll send a telegram for György to come."

"It has already been sent. He'll be here any day. Maybe your parents too."

"No, not my parents. I don't want them here. They didn't love me and they were ashamed of me. Anyone but my parents—I have nothing in common with them."

He was silent for a while, as if needing to digest the satisfaction arising from this confession. Then he started up again:

"The landscape has cornered us, and now it's slowly killing us, tearing us to pieces. It's the landscape that's the murderer. Tell Frommer. I know who he is, I'm not stupid."

"Thilo, why should it kill us?" asked Wojnicz, trying to reassure his friend. He sat down on the bed beside him and took him by the hand. "Who would want to kill us and why? Have we done something wrong?"

"It's enough that we've been born," he replied.

He went quiet, the flush vanished and the pallor returned. Blood appeared on his lips. Wojnicz listened closely to Thilo's breathing. When there was no reaction and it looked as if he had fallen asleep, he stood up and tiptoed toward the door.

"Don't forget about the picture," said Thilo, as Wojnicz pressed the handle. "I stole it from my parents and I don't want it to go back to them. Make sure it doesn't get lost if they take me away to the Kurhaus."

Wojnicz saw a small package leaning against the wall, messily wrapped in the local newspaper and tied with ordinary hemp string, just as postal parcels are tied to make it easier to carry them. No one would have guessed what it contained.

In the armchair where Frommer usually sat, a thirty-something-year-old man was now dozing with his arms folded on his belly. He had a bushy black mustache and a storm of curly hair. His wire-framed spectacles were at a comically crooked angle on his rather prominent nose. A traveling coat was draped over the back of the armchair, and a suitcase rested at his feet. Wojnicz kept very still, but the man plainly sensed his presence, because he opened his eyes and mumbled:

"I'm waiting for him to wake up."

Wojnicz immediately guessed who the newcomer must be.

György—whom Thilo referred to as "Kai"—appeared to be frightened, like someone who finds himself in the wrong place and has no idea how to behave. His intelligent eyes swept over Wojnicz, trying to place him. Mieczysław introduced himself.

They exchanged a few perfunctory courtesies; in fact the man did not seem interested in anyone's company.

"I'll show you the way, he's not asleep now."

When they entered the patient's room, the guest's small spectacles steamed up.

"Kai, Kai," whispered Thilo as they came in, trying to raise his head.

It looked tiny, like a child's. His hair had acquired a touch of gray, as if coated in dust, and was dull and stiff. His cheeks were red from the fever burning him up from the inside. Now and then a wheezing noise emerged from his lungs.

"My God, my God," repeated the philosopher and communist from Berlin.

He knelt by the bed and held Thilo's hand.

Wojnicz could not look at this. He retreated outside with the nurse, who at once lit a hand-rolled cigarette.

"*Schwule,*" said the nurse with distaste.

On waking next morning, Wojnicz realized that Thilo had died. When he peeped into the corridor, he saw strangers and their coattails, as black as a raven's wing, disappearing down the stairs. One of them was carrying Thilo's clothing, and another had his boots. Wojnicz sat on his bed, petrified. Everything in him shrank and turned inward, everything in him sought refuge at the hypothetical center of his body, where there surely lived a soul in direct contact with the world beyond, with time without end, with the galaxies and with God. By now the tears had reached the top of his throat in the form of ephemeral bubbles, but his eyes remained dry.

Today he was incapable of simply getting up and going to his treatments; he could not bear to look at August's ingratiating face or Lukas's disdainful countenance, he could not stand the sight of Frommer, even less Opitz, and he would probably have flown at Dr. Semperweiss's throat. He pulled the quilt over his head to avoid hearing the movements in the guesthouse, the footsteps on the stairs, the clink of cups, the whispers—in such a boring place even someone's death was a popular attraction.

He remembered the painting. In nothing but pajamas, barefoot, he went to Thilo's room, where the rumpled bedclothes were streaked with blood. He picked up the package wrapped in newspaper and hugged it to his chest, remembering what he had once seen there. In his own room he unwrapped it, and with the magnifying glass in hand examined the black stain amid a sea of greenery, the spot where two mysterious dots were shining. But the magnifying glass did not reveal any more than that; even the brushstrokes disappeared. All he could see was a great big nothing.

"Seeing is what matters most," Thilo had once stated. "It's not just a question of the eyes we have, we must see with our other senses too, though this has not yet been proved." So he had said. "Close your eyes and look. You can see the same room, can't you? You can see where the pieces of furniture are, you can see their solid shapes. I'll put out the light because we don't need it now."

He had been right. From that day on, Wojnicz had practiced this way of looking as he fell asleep, and he always saw something in the dark gray light whose source he could not identify—because it was not dark or black beneath his eyelids, as one would expect in a place where there was no light. He had no idea where this feeble, diffuse, dark gray glow was coming from. Beneath his eyelids it re-created the entire room, everything was in its place: the wardrobe, the dressing table, the patch marking the curtains, the windows, even his shoes scattered on the floor. Curiously, he did not know if he was really seeing it or imagining he could see it—or maybe, even worse, was he seeing something imagining itself? Or perhaps his eyelids were partly transparent? Maybe they were a filter, through which the lunar nature of the visible light was now seeping, identical in character, but not the same thing. What on earth was the source of the threadlike streaks of light that came winding like smoke from the cracks in the floor? From behind the frames of the pictures of mountains hanging on the wall? From the fringes of the rug by the door? From the wardrobe keyhole?

"I can see," says Wojnicz to himself, and hastily gets out of bed to go up to the windows and look outside with his eyes closed.

He can see the distinct contrast between earth and sky—the sky is darker than the earth, it is the earth that is shining with this phosphorescent, ashen light, the kind with which the darkness is gleaming. He can see the street, and the shapes of houses on either side of it, though they do not stay upright but seem to wobble unsteadily, the roofs coming down low, making the buildings look like overgrown mushrooms; the trees, spreading and proud by day, now project pitifully into the sky like broomsticks; the paving stones, so clean and shiny by day, now seem to be strewn with pine needles, spongy and soft as a carpet, stifling footsteps.

"This is all because of the Schwärmerei," says Wojnicz, and goes back to bed.

And now, lying hidden under the quilt, he again closes his eyes, just as Thilo taught him, to catch sight of that ashen world. He sees the coffin being carried across the bridge and carefully, expertly loaded into the hearse. He sees Opitz, giving orders as usual, György with a sunken face, Herr August holding a handkerchief to his cheek and Frommer standing stiffly by the door. Lukas is at the entrance to his annex, swaying gently on his feet. He even spots Frau Weber and Frau Brecht beyond the bridge, in the street, looking grim and ugly.

The coffin is standing on one of three catafalques in an elegant mortuary. That same night a patient at the Kurhaus has died too, and perhaps it gladdens Thilo to have company at this final stop before going into the ground. Now they are both lying there—strangers in life, united by a common fate, colonized by Koch's bacilli.

Under his eyelids Wojnicz can also see that Opitz and Raimund, who escorted the coffin from the guesthouse all the way to the mortuary, are back now, and are standing by the front door. They are talking, leaning toward each other, and now and then they cast glances at his windows. This frightened him and he opened his eyes.

At around noon he dressed and went outside. He raced around the entire village, crossing the length and breadth of it at a rapid pace, without returning the bows of the smug, well-fed patients, who had managed to forget that in a short time the same fate as Thilo's awaited them. Finally, avoiding the Polish group who were hunting him down to pay their condolences, he chanced upon the Russian church, and as there was nobody in it, he went inside, closed the door behind him and hid in a corner beneath the strange icon. The group of painted figures suddenly seemed close to him, as if it were a family portrait—he gazed into the women's solemn faces, and in the Infant he saw poor Thilo. He did not find Saint Emerentia's robe as cheerless as the previous time; now it seemed protective, like the lining of his mother's fur coat, which was so valuable that his father had not given it away to anyone. It still hung in the wardrobe at their apartment in Lwów; the scent of the perfume sprayed on it had long since evaporated, leaving nothing but the smell of mothballs. In his father's absence little Mieczyś used to go into the wardrobe and stroke its dear hairs, put his hands in the pockets and, without removing it from the hanger, wrap himself in it, so that he could feel its smooth, cool lining. He preferred it, cool and silky, to even the softest fur of a slaughtered animal. This was exactly what came to mind now as he gazed at the face of Saint Emerentia—she must surely be the protectress of wardrobes, the matron saint of mothballs, hiding places, narrow passages, dark corridors and fox dens.

On his return he was assailed in the sitting room by Herr August, who was unusually excited, with flushed cheeks. He had just seated the pale and indifferent György at the table and was telling Raimund to serve him coffee, biscuits, and of course—just to try it—Schwärmerei. Distractedly, the philosopher downed a glass of it, while talking non-stop about Thilo, and what he had learned from the doctor. He had a strange accent, harsh, though not from Berlin, but some other place abroad. Wojnicz had never heard one like it before. He kept half-heartedly repeating: "Oh well, one could say there was no chance anymore."

Then he addressed Wojnicz.

"Thilo had a certain object, very valuable, in that its value is . . . sentimental. A family keepsake, you know. Did he leave something for me? I'm asking because you befriended him."

It was one of the more difficult moments in Wojnicz's life. As soon as György began talking, Wojnicz knew what he was going to ask. It was fortunate that this handsome man with curly hair could not read his mind, or he would plainly see the picture by de Bles sitting in Wojnicz's room, wrapped in newspaper and stuffed between the wall and the cupboard. Before György had finished his question, Wojnicz had had time to consider his answer. Everything in him wanted to say: *But of course, Thilo left a painting. It's in my room, I'll bring it down for you.*

But he did not say that at all. Some other voice spoke in his throat, a voice he was not expecting, though for the past few weeks he had suspected it was there. It was like a new point of balance inside him, around which everything was now reorganizing itself.

"Unfortunately I haven't a clue about that. Thilo didn't pass anything on to me."

And after a pause he added:

"I'm very sorry."

15.

THE WEAKEST SPOT
IN THE SOUL

ojnicz stripped and lowered his gaze. Once again he had encountered what he hated most—looking, judging, comparing with what ought to be, what must be, what there is
elsewhere, not here, but there, among "everyone." He turned his head
away and felt exactly the same as when his father took him to see all
those doctors—separated from his own body. Mister Jig was back too,
a nimble creature that jumped from object to object, capable of racing
against trains. He had already been on the glazed cabinet, then on the
windowsill, then the coatrack, where the doctor's white gown was
hanging, then he had made his way outside, onto the tip of a spruce tree
and then the cornice of the building next door. Yes, Mister Jig had acquired the energy to take Mieczysław away from himself, and was
probably ready to jump onto the mountain peaks or the soft borders of
the clouds. Just then the little tune about sleepy Jakob suddenly resounded from outside, and Mister Jig burst like a soap bubble, while

Mieczysław found himself back in Dr. Semperweiss's consulting room, undressed, defenseless and pale with shame and cold. The edges of medical equipment were pressing into his harmonious, beautiful body, all those scales, syringes and sterilizers turned against him, even Dr. Semperweiss's pen, which was about to write down the diagnosis and reduce Wojnicz to an anomaly. But Dr. Semperweiss came up to him, handed him his vest and underpants and even threw his sweater over his shoulders, which might have been a gesture of affection.

"Well, then. Please get dressed."

As Wojnicz dressed behind the screen, he peeped out through a crack. He thought the doctor would sit down to write, but he stood gazing out of the window with his hands folded behind him. Once the patient was sitting in front of him, as he had sat so many times before, waiting for the verdict that in precise medical terms would express the hopelessness of the situation, Dr. Semperweiss said:

"People have their fictions and believe what they have mutually agreed upon. But you know, it's not necessarily true that things are only like this or that. It's simply helpful in navigation, in practice, to say consumption or syphilis, one or the other, but you know best that most of our experience does not yield to such simple divisions." Here he cast Wojnicz a penetrating glance. "I urge you to create your own fiction, one that says it's you that's perfect, for instance."

What Semperweiss had said was terrifying and alluring all at once. Feeling the burden of this truth, Mieczysław hunched up on the metal stool he was occupying, but he also wanted to spur on every word that fell from the doctor's lips, to make them fall straight into his ears more rapidly.

"*Yeees*," said Semperweiss, drawing out the word. "Inside all of us there's a feeling of not being of standard value, the belief that we lack something that everyone else possesses. All our lives we must come to terms with this sense of inferiority, overcome it or harness it to the cart of our ambitions and our ruinous pursuit of perfection. But what is perfection, does anybody know?"

"As you can see, I am not just anyone. I am an anomaly," said Wojnicz, taking the sweater from his shoulders and pulling it on.

After a short silence the doctor continued:

"You should treat it in the same way as the minor ailment you have in your lungs, as something we must learn to live with, without letting it destroy us. This is the cosmos of the body. Here anything can be an anomaly that will later become an advantage, and will allow us to win in the race of evolution. It's simply a matter of looking."

"I have learned to hide it. Nobody will see it. Just you. And it's a secret. You have a right to know this secret because you're saving my life. But you are obliged to keep quiet about it. My father cannot find out that you know. No one can find out that you know."

The doctor leaned back comfortably on his chair and folded his hands as if to pray.

"You see, Herr—Fräulein— You see," said Semperweiss, getting confused, and a smile suddenly appeared on his face. A smile is an understatement—he began to laugh, and Wojnicz stared at him in amazement, blackly at first, but somehow the doctor's laughter made him feel better too.

"As soon as I get back from Hirschberg I must take you for a ride in my Mercedes. My car that's a female. I'm told there's another one like it in Pless, owned by a prince," said the doctor once he had regained his composure.

That was nice, and now they both relaxed, though Wojnicz was still trembling. Semperweiss said he communed with imperfection on a daily basis, and that this entire place was a land of imperfection, the last stop for defective specimens doomed to gradual destruction. After years of working here he had learned to think that each person, each human organism, possessed a point of least resistance, a weakest point, this was the famous Achilles' heel, and it was like the law of the pearl: just as in a mollusk the grain of sand that chafes it is neutralized by mother-of-pearl, ultimately forming a jewel that we find valuable, so all the developmental lines of our psyche will arrange themselves around this weakest spot. Each anomaly, claimed Semperweiss (for he certainly did not want to use the word *defect*), stimulates a particular mental activity, a particular development, and collects it around itself. We are shaped not by what is strong in us but by the anomaly, by whatever is weak and not accepted.

"If you, young person, were to ask me what the soul is, I would answer like this: The soul is the weakest thing within us. Your soul is in your morbid symptoms."

But Wojnicz refused to listen to this.

"All my life I have believed that one should focus on what is strong, healthy and powerful. That's how my father brought me up. But you're telling me the soul is a dustbin."

"I did not say 'dustbin.' Please look at it from another angle. Our entire culture has grown out of a feeling of inferiority, out of all those unfulfilled ambitions. And yet it is the other way around: That which is weak in us gives us strength. This constant effort to compensate for weakness governs our entire lives. Demosthenes had a stammer, and that was exactly why he became the greatest speaker of all time. Not *in spite of* it, but *because of* it."

"You're wrong, Doctor. Culture involves striving toward perfection," said Wojnicz, trying to defend himself.

But Dr. Semperweiss was sure of his own idea.

"A sense of inferiority affects one's whole life, especially one's thinking. Did you know that? Because we lack confidence, we think up a very stable, rigid system to keep us upright. To simplify what seems to us to be unnecessary complication. And the greatest simplification is black-and-white thinking, based on simple antitheses. Do you understand what I'm saying? The mind establishes for itself a set of acute opposites—black and white, day and night, up and down, man and woman—and they determine our entire perception. There's nothing in the middle. Seen like that, the world is far simpler, it's easy to navigate between these poles, it's easy to establish rules of conduct, and it's particularly easy to judge others, often reserving the luxury of obscurity for oneself. This kind of thinking protects us from any uncertainty, crash, bang and it's all clear, like this or like that, there is no third option. Aristotle or the golden calf." Here he laughed so jovially that Wojnicz almost joined in with him. "This protects us from reality, which is built up of a multitude of very subtle shades. If anyone thinks the world is a set of stark opposites, he is sick. I know what I'm saying. It's a powerful dysfunction."

"But what is the world like?"

"Blurred, out of focus, flickering, now like this, now like that, depending on one's point of view."

Wojnicz found it all too complicated, too far away from himself. Could one live in such a world? How would one design sewage systems in the city of Lwów? What could one rely on? Or believe in? He couldn't understand what Semperweiss was saying. After all, this doctor had led him up the garden path several times before. He thought he could out-talk him and turn all the attention away from him, to generalize his problem, so that Mieczysław Wojnicz himself would disappear under these generalities. He was already familiar with these methods of invalidating him, of pushing him into a dark corner.

"I am not normal," said Wojnicz with sudden despair. "And it'd be better if I died here. I hope that will happen. It'll relieve everyone, especially my father. That's why he sent me here. So that I'd die."

His final words were stifled by the sobs that burst from his throat and that he could not control. Feeling awkward, the doctor gave a slight cough.

"The only consolation I can offer you is that there are lots of people like you," he said earnestly, as if he had realized that for this young person a drama was being enacted here. "You can escape this primitive, stark division. Don't forget that the binding vision of the world is highly conventional, and it's built upon the personal lack of confidence of those making the judgments. Someone like you will prompt antipathy and hatred, because you will be a clear reminder that the vision of the world as black and white is a false and destructive vision. You, Herr Wojnicz—or however I should address you—represent a middle world, which is hard to bear because it's unclear. This vision maintains in us a peculiar irresolution, and does not let any dogma take shape. You treat us to a land 'in between,' which we'd rather not think about, having quite enough of our own black-and-white problems. You show us that it is greater than we thought, and that it affects us too. *You are a bomb*," he said, articulating the words emphatically. "The worst thing possible is to feel fully valued by others, and particularly—as I would put it— to be considered of standard value. It means we become literalized, and we come to a halt in the development that a lack of full appreciation prompts us to strive toward. When a person recognizes that he has become perfect and fulfilled, he should kill himself."

They sat for a while in silence. Wojnicz had settled down and was staring at his shoes. They were quite useless by now; both soles had come partly unglued, and the toes were completely scuffed. The familiar sight reassured him. Somewhere at the very bottom of his body, somewhere far away on its periphery, he could sense a sort of gentle vibration, something small and happy, something exciting. He glanced at the doctor and realized why he had fallen silent—he was lighting a cigar. Soon he was surrounded by clouds of aromatic smoke, like an oracle.

Wojnicz coughed.

"Every society has two pillars of activity: hypocrisy and conformism," said Dr. Semperweiss, and raised a finger to the height of his nose, then started moving it left and right. "While I'm about it, you young and unusual creature, I'll tell you that you have a slight squint, nothing to be worried about, but please be aware of it. So, hypocrisy always cites high-flown ideas that build a community. One should believe in them and show that one believes in them, but at base nobody takes those ideas entirely seriously. They are for others, and should be in force for them. Whereas conformism is a mode for moving about within this imaginary world that tells us to ignore everything that sticks out and doesn't fit. And forgetfulness serves this purpose."

Then he added:

"I think you'll be home for Christmas."

Wojnicz returned to the guesthouse in a state of elation. He jumped across the whitewashed curbstones and was quite unperturbed by the fine drizzle that had just begun to fall. He was mentally composing a card to his father, but he could not get past *Dear Father*. As he passed the café he decided to stop economizing, since his stay would be over soon, and went inside to buy some colorful macaroons for his afternoon tea. There were only a few people in the café, including Frau Large Hat. Wojnicz looked the woman right in the eyes as they passed each other in the doorway. As she went out, carrying a box of cakes before her, she smiled encouragingly, but Wojnicz ignored this smile.

With his long finger he pointed out the cakes, first four, but then he decided on six. They were quite expensive. He was always imagining that once he became a well-established sanitation engineer he would buy himself a whole tray of macaroons, a heaped plateful—the cakes would be arranged in a pyramid, by color, from the darkest purple, probably dyed with blueberry juice, through the willow-green ones to the jolly red ones.

Only when leaving the counter with his package of cakes did he see Frommer, sitting stiffly in a corner of the café and watching him. Barely cracking a smile, he made a gesture inviting Wojnicz to his table. It was impossible to refuse.

"You should get away from here as fast as you can," said Frommer in Polish, and looked at Mieczysław in a strange, imploring way.

Surprised, Wojnicz said nothing, considering his situation—he had rashly let himself fall into a trap and now he was caught in it for some time. Finally he said:

"Why should I do that, Herr Frommer? What are you trying to tell me?"

"I want to save you."

Inclined over an empty, coffee-stained cup, he looked sick with anxiety. He took out a wad of documents carefully filed in a gray binder, on which was written in a very fine hand:

Case
Görbersdorf, 1889–1913.
Facts and Hypotheses

He wetted a finger and opened it to a page with a table that specified where, when and who had perished.

"I've been seeking a common denominator, perhaps I have been overtheorizing. If I myself were ever to perish, though I may be too old, I would finally learn what it's all about. You know, sometimes I think I could sacrifice myself, if only to find the solution to the enigma at the very last moment."

"It occurred to me you should occupy yourself with how Frau Opitz died instead. More and more often I think there's something mysterious about her death," said Wojnicz. He was wondering how to find an excuse to go back to his room and unpack the cakes. "That's a real task for a detective."

"That we shall never know, though the police autopsy showed older and newer evidence of violence. She must have been beaten. I know the case fascinates you, I have seen you visiting Frau Opitz's room on several occasions."

Wojnicz blushed and quickly said:

"I suspected as much, and also that her suicide is convenient for all."

He summoned the waiter and asked for coffee and a plate for the cakes. Then he undid the package.

"So what are you driving at, Herr Frommer? Do you have another interesting theory?"

"We must be open to other dimensions of human experience," said Frommer in his slightly incorrect Polish. "Open to things that have been forgotten and abandoned as childish and unworthy of modern man. Our ancestors were right: They are still with us, they are present, they speak to us, they demand attention. All the wrongs that happened in the past have not ceased to exist, they continue to resonate and make us tremble inside."

He stopped talking while the waiter served the coffee. Wojnicz

M. BEUCHLERS
Heilanstalt am Buchberg
für Lungenkranke

GÖRBERSDORF
in Schlesien
Höhenluftkurort 561 m

Die Anstalt ist 1890 gegründet und bietet Aufenthalt für 44 leicht lungenkranke Patienten. Sie liegt abseits der Dorfstraße, von einem zwei Morgen großen mit Nadelhölzern bewachsenen Garten umgeben. Infolgedessen ist sie vollkommen gegen Staubentwicklung geschützt und selten ruhig gelegen. Wegen der kleinen Patientenzahl ist der Verkehr ein geselliger; dadurch wird dem Kranken die Trennung von der Familie und den heimatlichen Verhältnissen nach Möglichkeit erleichtert. Ein geräumiges Gesellschaftszimmer mit einem Klavier, Radio, Tageszeitungen, Zeitschriften, einer guten reichhaltigen Hausbücherei, sowie verschiedenen Unterhaltungsspielen steht den Gästen zur Verfügung. Unmittelbar an die Anstalt schließen sich bequeme Wege zu nahegelegenen, ausgedehnten Nadelwaldungen mit herrlichen Aussichtspunkten an. Im Jahre 1928 wurde 2,5 km vor Görbersdorf in Schmidtsdorf ein Sanatorium mit 24 Betten, im gleichen Sinne wie die beschriebene Anstalt geleitet, angegliedert. Zu dieser Anstalt gehört eine Landwirtschaft mit Weidebetrieb unter tierärztlicher Aufsicht, die die Kranken beider Sanatorien mit bester Milch versorgt, ebenso eine eigene Gärtnerei, die Frischgemüse liefert. Ein ausgedehnter Fichten-waldbesitz, zu Spaziergängen einladen, schließt sich dem Sanatoriumsgarten unmittelbar an.

Kurmittel. Vollkommene Ausnützung der klimatischen Reize des Mittelgebirges. Strenge individualisierende ärztliche Behandlung, unter Berücksichtigung aller, in der Praxis bewährten Heilmethoden. Freiluftliegekur, im Wechsel mit ärztlich dosierten Spaziergängen, Anwendung von Abreibungen, Packungen, Duschen, Bädern im Sinne einer allmählichen Abhärtung. In geeigneten Fällen Behandlung mit künstlichem Pneumothorax, Nervenschnitt. Größere Eingriffe (Plombe, Plastik) in ständiger Fühlungnahme mit einem namhaften Lungenchirurgen. Künstliche Höhensonne, ärztliche Belehrung und Erziehung zu einer gesunden Lebensweise. Gute und reichliche Ernährung.

Die Beköstigung ist folgende: **1. Frühstück** (½ 8 Uhr) Malz- und Bohnenkaffee, Weißgebäck, Butter, Fett und Milch;
2. " (10) Brot, Weißgebäck, Butter, Milch;
Mittagbrot (1) Suppe, Braten, Gemüse oder Salat, Kompott (Sonntags Nachspeise);
Kaffee (4) Schmalz, Milch oder Suppe, Aufschnitt,
Abendbrot (7) wie 1. Frühstück;

Die Mahlzeiten werden an gemeinsamer Tafel eingenommen. warme und zweimal wöchentlich kalte Küche, Tee oder Milch.

Kosten. Der Gesamtpreis für ein Zimmer mit Verpflegung, ärztlicher Behandlung, Bedienung, Benützung der Liegehalle, Liegebett und wöchentlich ein Bad beträgt täglich 7,10 RM. Hierzu 2% Trinkgeldablösung. Für Bettwäsche, Mund- und Handtücher 0,20 RM., für Heizung und Beleuchtung 0,30 RM. mehr. In einem Zweibettenzimmer ermäßigt sich der Preis um 0,50 RM., sowie 40% der Heizung und Beleuchtung. Für die erste Untersuchung mit Sputum- und Urin-Untersuchung werden 10.— RM. berechnet, desgleichen werden Injektionskuren, Röntgen-Untersuchungen, sowie außergewöhnliche ärztliche Bemühungen, wie Pneumothoraxanlage, operative Eingriffe an Kehlkopf, Nase und Ohren, besonders angesetzt. Als Aufnahmegeld zur Erhaltung der Gartenanlagen, Unterhaltungsspiele und dergl. werden einmalig 2 RM. in Rechnung gesetzt. In dem Sanatorium

Beuchlers Sanatorium Schmidtsdorf
Post Görbersdorf Schles. — 520 m ü. d. M.

encouraged his companion to help himself to a cake, and Frommer absent-mindedly chose the first one to hand—a red one. Wojnicz himself had already eaten a crimson macaroon, and now he reached for a violet one.

"You know that I am a theosophist, I believe in spiritual beings that live in a different dimension and are watching us from that dimension."

As soon as Frommer started talking in Polish, Wojnicz thought everything he said sounded childish.

"They certainly have a different value system from ours," continued Frommer. "I don't know what they see, and I don't know what they look at, but I know they are there, here, all around. 'All around' should be understood in quotation marks."

As he leaned over the table again, Wojnicz could smell his odor: dry, dusty, slightly stale, papery, like a cardboard warehouse.

"It's not a force from this or another world. This force comes from here. I think it is demanding balance. I do not believe it knows that it's committing a crime."

Now Wojnicz reached for the yellow cake, and almost sighed with bliss—it was lemon-flavored. Frommer lowered his voice, and Mieczysław felt ashamed of his own behavior.

"You see, sir, the soul escapes from a tortured body in panic and will never want to return to material form again. It makes an alliance with nature—ultimately, everything comes from nature. So I understand it, Herr Wojnicz. The Tuntschi are sure to have noticed you already. They want young men."

Wojnicz blinked. He was not sure he understood what Frommer was saying. It felt as though he were drinking Schwärmerei, not coffee.

"I . . . ," he began, and did not finish.

"Yes, yes, you've understood me correctly. You're intelligent. The locals understand this too, and they feed the Tuntschi on whatever they have to hand—you, the weak, sick men who are here in large numbers. It's simple: In the past the Tuntschi took members of their families, they killed men from around here, and so the locals learned to deceive them. For the past fifteen years or so only young patients have perished, unless something goes wrong—like a few years ago, when Opitz's brother died, or someone careless happens along, like one of the charcoal burners two years ago. But they have refined this method to perfection—they offer the victim to the Tuntschi themselves. I am quite sure of this: They thought that this year they would succeed with poor Thilo, but he died too soon. So now they are casting hungry eyes at you, Mieczysław. You must leave this place immediately."

"But there are plenty of young men here, why me in particular?"

"Naturally, I would advise all young men of 'conscription' age, so to speak, to get out of here."

Wojnicz's sugar-filled mind could not entirely focus on what Frommer was saying. He took him to be an old crank and fabricator who derived pleasure from disturbing people's equilibrium. Dr. Semperweiss's words, which had put Mieczysław in such a state of elation, were still ringing in his ears. Frommer's strange speech was preventing him from celebrating. As he sat with him and reached for the last cake—a green one that Frommer had politely refused—he felt like a child who had finally managed to return to the very instant when he had eaten Gliceria's kogel mogel, and he realized that this special moment was the epitome of the appetizing quality he was always seeking. Everything is in its place, safe, objects come alive at the touch of Gliceria's hands, their usefulness is thrilling, as are the damaged, knife-scarred tabletop in the kitchen and the clean tea towels embroidered with the letter *W*, and his whole life, right from the start up to now. He himself is a part of this world in which for a certain period time and space have been reserved for him, and he must take advantage of it.

It occurred to him that he could start afresh from this point. All over again. From Gliceria's kitchen.

From his briefcase Frommer produced a tin sandwich box with his first and last names engraved on it and put his uneaten cake in it.

"For later," he said, without looking at Wojnicz. "I just wonder how it is that nobody can see all this, nobody notices it all happening quite casually, as if the death of these young men were an ordinary event. A sort of occasional sacrifice. I told you I'd be ready to give my life to find out the whole story, that's all I have left. For how long does one live with tuberculosis?"

At this point he glanced at the youthful Wojnicz and suddenly realized his faux pas. There was no helping it, so he lowered his gaze.

They both lowered their gaze.

16

A PERSON IN ONE SHOE

J ust a bit more," mumbled Raimund. They were climbing uphill, Raimund in front, wearing a cotton-drill raincoat with tails that swished before Wojnicz's eyes, shielding the entire view. Suddenly struck by a sense of absurdity, Wojnicz stopped and filled his recovering lungs with cold, moist air, which definitely contained some microscopic amounts of moss, pine needles and particles of mud.

"I'm not going farther," he said.

Raimund turned around to face him with an ingratiating grin, a smile lined with vexation.

"Just a bit more," he repeated half-heartedly. "Willi wants to show you something very important."

"I'm not going anywhere." Wojnicz was out of breath, and to tell the truth, he had no idea how on earth he came to be here. It was the afternoon. He'd been sleeping when Raimund had come to see him and told him to get dressed. Wojnicz understood that Opitz had some shoes for him, though the word was not spoken. Or maybe it was about something else, something important, as if they'd arranged to meet. Dazed by his nap, he had donned his half-dead shoes and thrown on a jacket. At the last second he had also grabbed his gloves. And off they went.

He wanted to know where they were heading in such haste and what exactly Opitz had to show him. No, this was absurd. Where on earth had he ended up? What for? Had he gone mad, to race after this boy, who was telling him something in a lively tone in his dialect, which Wojnicz could not understand? All he recognized was the name *Willi*, and . . . well, he had been brought up to be courteous and obliging, not to cause trouble, not to stick his neck out but to wait in the shadows until it was clear how matters stood. What had got into his head to go out so lightly dressed? By now they were beyond the village and were entering the forest. He was feeling cold and had no desire to go any farther. Soon it would be dark, and how would they get back then?

It was impossible to argue with Raimund, who was glowering at him suspiciously, as if expecting a surprise move. Wojnicz turned around and started going down toward the village; from here he could see the roofs of the houses and the great hulk of the sanatorium.

Just then Raimund whistled, and in seconds, before Wojnicz had managed to take a few steps downhill, several of the charcoal burners appeared out of nowhere, burly lads whose eyelids were soiled with black dust. They did not need telling, but plainly knew all too well what they were to do—in a few leaps they had surrounded the astonished Wojnicz. He knew that look. He had been in this sort of situation many times; whenever his father left him at a new school, his attempts to get on with the boys in his class had always ended in much the same way. Sometimes it took longer to reach this point, and sometimes it happened faster. Occasionally he had been regarded as "one of us" for several months, until finally someone hit upon a trail and discovered Wojnicz's anomaly; there are highly talented people of this kind who can sniff out anything that is different. Now too the charcoal burners were looking at him as a victim, like a hare caught in a snare. Wojnicz struggled desperately, but strong hands, hard and ruthless, had already grabbed hold of him from all sides. They're going to kill me, he thought, and he knew how he had sinned, he knew why he was in line for this punishment. In a way he had always been expecting it, and now he saw his life as patient preparation for this very moment. He caught a glimpse of his father and his uncle, who must have known long ago that this would occur, and who had primed him for it with love and concern. They had taught him to hide, to avoid confrontation, to be cautious, to check the thickness of fully drawn curtains, and to block the keyholes in doors. Yes, they had done their best. But they knew that one day this would happen.

The charcoal burners seized him firmly by the arms, and when he started to kick, two more grabbed him by the legs and carried him, panting and cursing. Raimund walked alongside, giving them orders in that strange dialect, which here in the forest sounded like snarling. Wojnicz kept lashing out until one of the men kicked him in the belly—the pain was so dreadful that from then on he surrendered, utterly paralyzed by fear.

No, he probably had not done anything to offend. Nothing of the kind occurred to him. He had behaved moderately and politely. He had not entered into conflict with anyone. He had concealed his emotions. On the whole he had hidden away, just as his father had always taught him. "Keep your distance," he often said. He had other advice: Whenever you come close, they'll do you harm. Don't fraternize or they'll regard it as weakness, and they'll try to take more liberties. Don't talk to men for too long, they can be dangerous. Keep away from women, they're unpredictable. Never drop your guard. Yes, perhaps Wojnicz's one and only sin was that he had dropped his guard. Why Raimund? Who was he?

The charcoal burners carried him up the hill for about a hundred meters and then stopped, tired. They put him on the ground and, breathing heavily, they rested, but first they bound his hands and feet. They told him to drink from a bottle, but when he recognized the characteristic smell of Schwärmerei and shook his head, they grabbed him by the chin and poured a mug of the bittersweet liqueur into his mouth. Now he was completely disarmed.

They had ended up on a piece of flat ground in the forest, not far from the spot where Wojnicz had seen a Tuntschi for the first time. They pulled off his jacket, which one of the men evidently planned to appropriate for himself, because he hung it gently over his arm. They also began to tug at his sweater and shirt, and once his rib cage was bare, white and totally hairless, with those wretched enlarged nipples too, they cackled for quite a time. Wojnicz closed his eyes and felt himself float away into some other realm; it was as if he had risen above the ground and were hanging in the air, just about to take off into the sky like a balloon, but the charcoal burners' strong, ruthless hands dragged him down onto the cold, damp forest floor. They had leather straps hidden in their pockets which they used to tie him very deftly to a fallen beech trunk, causing the coarse bark to cut into his back painfully. They were in a great hurry, darkness was falling, and in the east a very bright glow was starting to emerge—he could see that they were anxiously looking in that direction.

They were still trying to pull off his trousers when Wojnicz felt the tree trunk trembling beneath him, and the forest floor quivering under his foot (one of his shoes had fallen off), and he could hear a sort of buzzing sound, a low vibration that grated on the ear. From somewhere far away, from the top of the mountain, he could hear noises, growing louder by the second: a clank, a clatter, a dull thunderclap and—could it be?—that familiar cooing, but now much louder, wild and chaotic. The faces of his oppressors had gone stiff and pale, discolored by unimaginable terror. They let go of him and in panic started running down toward the village, dropping their straps and axes, losing their hats and gloves.

"They didn't take him. They didn't take him," they were shouting. "Run for it!"

And then also:

"The chairs, the chairs!"

Wojnicz struggled, but every movement rubbed the skin on his back raw and hurt his spine. The sound was rising, but Mieczysław could not tell if it was coming from the outside or if its source was inside his head—it was like the ringing one hears when one has a fever, or when one dives deep and there is pressure on the eardrum.

Wojnicz is blinking, because he is seeing everything in blue and green, as though he were suddenly underwater—like the time in childhood when the ice broke under him and he almost drowned in a pond. The sky looks hard and solid, so very tangible that if he jumps up he might hit his head on it. From the tangle of branches, leaves and tree trunks his blinking eyes are picking out shapes they could not see earlier. Yet they were here all the time. Now he can see them—the slender bodies of supple figures, part human, part animal. Something he had taken for a pile of leaves is now a shape, a brown face veined like a leaf, a face that turns toward him; the eyes are dark, but soon those eyes become two acorns and there is no face anymore. But just a moment— now that face is floating in another spot.

Here we are, slightly changed, but just the same as before, warm but also cold, both seeing and blind. Here we are, here are our hands formed from decaying branches, our bellies, our nipples that are puffballs, our womb that blends into a fox's den, into the depths of the earth, and is now nursing a fox's litter. Can you see us at last, Mieczysław

Wojnicz, you brave engineer from the flat, woodless steppes? Can you see us, you frail human being who likes to dry leaves to paste in a book and save them from decay and death?

"Help, Hilfe!" he cried, but oddly, his voice seemed to get stuck somewhere near his face; totally deafened, he could not even hear himself. With an immense effort he managed to free one of his hands from its bonds. It was covered in blood and shaking. Trembling, he tried to untie the other one, but his fingers could not reach the right spot. All he could see were some pine cones rolling down, as if set in motion by a gust of wind.

Something was coming from above, something was sliding, pushing its way downward. Poor Wojnicz feverishly disentangled the cruelly tight straps binding his feet, but he froze still when he saw us.

Right beside him he caught sight of a mossy face and the flash of a pair of moist eyes, dark green like an underground lake. He was looking at a compact torso formed of sticks interwoven with pine needles, moss and wet earth. Warmer air swept over him, like breath that smelled of a heap of rotting foliage, and the large dark eyes were staring at him—with curiosity, but he could not sense any thought in it, this curiosity was certainly not human. The face came close to him, and from a short distance it scrutinized the pores of his skin, his eyelashes, lips and brows. It was joined by a second face, and then one more. Almost ceasing to breathe, he gazed at us with terror that gradually faded, for we wished him no harm. The poor human being could sense this, and with its free, bleeding hand touched our cheek, and felt that it was alive, that underneath there was a sort of body, not like its own, because our bodies have an experimental consistency, they are occasional, dependent on tides and air pressure, underground currents and transpiration.

Our eyes penetrate deep inside. We can see the skeleton, the beating heart, the peristalsis of the intestines, the esophagus working away as it endeavors to push down the saliva that has gathered out of fear. We can see the tongue, arranging itself to utter some word. The diaphragm rises and falls, drops of urine flow from the kidneys to the bladder. The uterus clenches like a fist, but the member swells with blood.

The straps fell off, and with stifled sobbing Wojnicz began to wobble his way downhill, catching hold of trees because his eyes were full of tears. His torso was bare, one foot was shoeless, and his messy fair hair ringed his head in an ash-gray halo. In the waning twilight the valleys were fading before him, but the darkness had not yet acquired its proper hue, because the show was only just beginning, and over in the east the sky had started to brighten with a different, not solar tone, until finally before Wojnicz's eyes a lurid clipping of light appeared among the trees, and then the entire pitted face of the full moon. Below he could see Görbersdorf and the tiny figures of people. The paved high street was reflecting the moonlight and looked like a stage, and the modern electric lamps were shining too.

Wojnicz pushed on home, convinced that the most vital thing he must do was to hide under any sort of clothing, cover his exposed body—he was fully focused on that.

Stained with blood and earth, he appeared on the promenade, hobbling shakily in one shoe. It was surprisingly empty; instead of intensifying, the dusk was being diluted by the moonlight that was flooding everything. The scene he saw was like a black-and-white drawing on a gingerbread tin. It's the Schwärmerei, he thought. He felt unwell, his legs were starting to collapse beneath him and his throat tightened: he was about to be sick. The one thing he had to do was reach the guesthouse and hide there, under the bed if need be. By now he was at the back of the sanatorium, next he had to cross the well-lit street and then run a few hundred meters. But he saw something moving by the side entrance to the Kurhaus. Limping, he ran into a courtyard and continued his journey along the back streets, parallel to the main one, from where he could hear conversations growing louder and the shuffling of feet. He peeped cautiously at the street and in total amazement saw a crowd of patients being herded along by Sydonia Patek, wielding a white cane—silvered by the moonlight, her medical gown looked like metal. The people at the front of this group were moving at a slow walking pace uphill toward the end of the village, toward the forest and the mountains where the charcoal burners had their encampment, but it could not be described as a march or a procession because there was no order in it—the small crowd teemed along in a bewildered manner. They were all in a good mood, judging by the individual voices that emerged from the multilingual chatter. He even heard someone cheerily exclaim in Polish: "No, my dear sir, I'm certainly not joking!" The bugle call sounded from the Kurhaus tower because it was suppertime, but it sounded rather sluggish, and on the second repetition it suddenly broke off, as if the trumpeter had had a moment of doubt and given up playing. Among the crowd in the distance he saw Lukas and August, deep in conversation as usual. He also spotted Frommer, standing slightly apart from the others, absorbed and pensive, holding an unlit cigarette. The entire throng was babbling, debating, joking and arguing about something in various languages, when suddenly Wojnicz realized that apart from Sydonia Patek in the form of a quasi-shepherdess with a cane, herding this human flock, there were no women at all. Wojnicz went back into the courtyard, and, still afraid someone might see him in this state, tottered as fast as he could to the guesthouse, passing the bench where this time

Frau Weber and Frau Brecht were not in evidence, nor were there any lights burning in their windows.

When he finally reached his destination, it was not cold that he felt, but shame and fear that somebody might see him like this. He dashed into his room, tore off the bedspread and covered himself with it. Only now did he feel a chill and how very tired he was. With numb hands he managed to put on some warm vests and a wool sweater, and to change his trousers, which were ripped and soiled. The sock on his unshod foot was muddy and torn to shreds. He threw it away in disgust and wiped his dirty foot with a towel. He was shaking all over, no longer with cold but with the indignation that is always prompted by incomprehensible, totally unjustified violence. No, he could not say that he was unfamiliar with it. Somewhere on the edge of his consciousness, though reluctant and weakened by a continued effort to displace them, some memories of similar experiences lingered. He let out a loud sob, but quickly restrained himself from weeping. If he had let himself cry, he would instantly have been flooded by his old unhappiness, his great alienation. If he had yielded, he would inevitably have brought back the suffering from which he had saved himself. Or from which he had been saved.

Suddenly he heard a clatter overhead, as if something heavy had fallen to the floor. He held his breath and looked out into the corridor— silence reigned, clearly there was nobody at the guesthouse. Downstairs an oil lamp was burning, one of those that were always left alight to avoid wasting electricity, in case somebody wanted to go down to the sitting room. He heard the clatter again, this time accompanied by a dull moan.

Still in one shoe, but now with the other foot completely bare, Wojnicz went into the corridor and, listening intently, moved up the stairs as quietly as he could. The dim light of the November full moon was falling through the little windows, but here inside it was quite dark. The disturbing noises were coming from behind the closed door of the small attic room with the mansard window. As soon as the floor creaked under Wojnicz's shoe, total silence fell. Wojnicz noticed that he could not hear the usual cooing in the attic either.

"Is anyone there?" he called hesitantly.

"Wojnicz? In here, here, come here!" He heard Opitz's voice from behind the door. There was a note of feverish impatience in it.

Mieczysław opened the door, and in the moonlight falling into the room he saw the proprietor tied to a chair, trying to pull free of his bonds, but in vain. Wojnicz could see how tight they were.

"Untie me," demanded Opitz in a fractious tone, addressing Wojnicz informally, as *du*, not *Sie*. "Come on, untie me."

Wojnicz was so amazed that for some time he could not understand what Opitz actually wanted him to do. He stood as if spellbound, staring at the man writhing on the chair.

"Come on! What are you waiting for, muttonhead? What are you staring at? Untie me!"

Wojnicz continued to stand there. He was thinking.

"How the hell did you get here?" shouted Opitz. "You were meant to be gone! How do you come to be here?"

"Herr Opitz, please calm down," said Wojnicz, squatting before the captive.

He tried to loosen the buckles securing the straps, but they had been pulled so tight that he could not shift the clasps, especially as Opitz was thrashing about furiously in the chair. He tried to stand up, but toppled over onto Wojnicz, and they both fell to the floor.

"Who tied you up? Who did this to you?" asked Mieczysław, scrambling from under the heavy, angular, chair-bound body.

Opitz cast him a wild stare. The whites of his eyes were bloodshot with effort.

"Raimund," he wheezed. "Raimund tied me up."

"But why?" inquired Wojnicz, while starting to manipulate the straps immobilizing the prisoner's arms. They were doubly fastened, so tightly that poor Opitz's hands had gone blue. As Wojnicz grappled with the pins he looked around for a tool to help him. He thought of going down to the kitchen for a knife to cut the diabolical bonds.

"But why? Why?" he repeated.

"What do you mean, why? I told him to do it," mumbled Opitz angrily.

Wojnicz froze, but then something clicked into place in his mind and he understood. He suddenly went pale and backed away on his knees toward the wall; he could hear roaring in his ears.

"You tie yourselves up so you won't go out! You tie yourselves up so that frenzy won't come over you!"

"Untie me, you fool. Immediately," jabbered Willi Opitz, with madness in his eyes.

By now Wojnicz knew he would not set Opitz free until he had told him the whole story. He started with a simple question:

"Why me?"

The man howled furiously and tried to kneel down with the chair on his back, but the chair legs prevented him from straightening his back, so he bent forward before Wojnicz, wheezing with rage.

"Why you?"

In his forced bow Opitz panted, possibly gathering strength before a final attempt to free himself of his bonds, or perhaps he had realized that Wojnicz deserved to hear the truth. He spoke incoherently, through his teeth, struggling to control his trembling, his nervous lockjaw and his body's great impatience to join the procession of men.

It was meant to be that boy from Berlin. It was meant to be Thilo. But he had died too soon. Yes, sometimes the marked men whom they took to the forest and tied to a tree were the sickest. They'd have died anyway, so what was the harm in condemning a terminally sick person to death to save the fit ones? Wasn't it perfectly reasonable thinking? Pragmatic? Yes, Wojnicz had to agree—the sick instead of the healthy, outsiders instead of locals, the old instead of the young . . . Opitz gasped out that for as long as he could remember someone from the village had been killed, so when Dr. Brehmer's sanatorium opened up, they decided to take advantage. They selected somebody in September or October and kept an eye on him. This patient's state of health was no secret, and after a glass of Schwärmerei Dr. Semperweiss and the others forgot about medical confidentiality. "A nice fellow, but he's dying." So then they had to lure the wretch into the forest and put him on display for the Tuntschi.

Wojnicz laughed nervously. He leaned back until he was looking into Opitz's bloodshot eyes.

"What are the Tuntschi?"

Opitz glared at him with genuine hatred.

"Untie me this instant," he hissed through his teeth. "Untie me, I've got to go."

Wojnicz could not understand his meaning.

"Why do you want to go? What's going on out there? Why must you?"

Opitz wheezed horribly, as if suffocating.

"You've got to release me, Wojnicz, I've got to go there."

"Do I understand correctly that right now I am saving your life?"

Willi Opitz started to speak chaotically, as though the paradoxical nature of his own situation had not got through to him. The great cause, the sacrifice that saves the whole village. The ancient order. The law of nature. God and the devil. Afterward, as Wojnicz tried to assemble the pieces of his broken speech and make sense of it, what emerged was that Frommer had been right, at least partly.

As he could not tackle the straps on Opitz's legs, he tried to release his arms. As soon as he managed to undo the first clasp, Opitz immediately began to grapple with the second, and then with one that bound a leg. When both buckles had given way, he tried to leave the room with the chair still attached to the other leg. Wojnicz screamed at him so shrilly that his own voice frightened him:

"Opitz, come to your senses!"

For a brief moment Opitz seemed to regain consciousness, and stood there breathing heavily, but then he pushed Wojnicz to the back of the room, only saying:

"Out of my way."

Moments later, Wojnicz heard a clatter and his footsteps on the stairs. Without delay, Wojnicz followed him. Downstairs he put on his heavy boots, took someone's coat from the rack and went outside. He saw Opitz staggering his way out of the grounds of the guesthouse, finally freeing himself of the chair and then crossing the bridge to join the parade of men. There he suddenly stood upright again, as if new strength had entered him, his face relaxed, his brow brightened, and to Wojnicz, who was watching him, Opitz had even grown handsome. He joined the end of the procession, but boldly pushed his way to the front, passing his friends on the way, but there were not many of these; two or three of them had broken straps on their arms or legs. Men from the sanatorium were in the majority, but there was also the new postmaster, some male nurses and Tomášek in steamed-up spectacles. Almost at the very end, not counting an obese patient and Herr Ludwig, a crippled artist from Hamburg in a wheelchair, came Frommer, flourishing a walking stick.

Wojnicz shouted to him:

"Herr Walter!"

Frommer looked at him almost unconsciously, muttering something under his breath, and then spun around on his axis in an utterly un-Frommer-like move that looked as if he were dancing.

This alien motion horrified Wojnicz. In long bounds he raced to the Kurhaus, then up the stairs to Dr. Semperweiss's consulting room, where the rifle was leaning against the desk. Wojnicz took hold of it and checked to see if it was loaded. It was.

The boom of the gunshot rolled right across Görbersdorf, echoing several times off the surrounding mountains, off Hohe Heide, Floste, Trattlau and Gross Storch Berg, like the beating of a gigantic heart, but this made no impression at all on the men taking part in the strange procession, not even halting their advance for a second. Why not me? thought Wojnicz. Why wasn't he submitting to the frenzy, why was he thinking so clearly, frighteningly clearly? He felt as if he were watching the preparations for an open-air event, as if they were off on a picnic or to a concert, perhaps—oh yes, all that was missing was a brass band and some bunting. But the crowd passed the concert shell and strode onward, to the trailhead; some had already gone into the forest, ignoring the fact that their shoes were unsuitable, and that instead of overcoats they were wearing smoking jackets. They walked along in high spirits, discussing the price of grain on world markets or the situation in the Balkans. They moved in harmony, making way for each other on the narrowing path or pushing straight through the forest off the trail, insensitive to the stones and the spruce branches. Opitz was telling a portly townsman from Breslau about his uncle who had served in the Swiss Guard, while Lukas and August appeared to be discussing ancient warfare, or perhaps modern philosophy. For some time Wojnicz followed them in unutterable amazement, with Dr. Semperweiss's rifle beating against his legs, but at the edge of the forest he stopped, and the procession passed him by indifferently. Frozen to the bone, he gave up and almost ran back to the village.

He was just about to go inside the Guesthouse for Gentlemen when he changed his mind, entered the courtyard and peeped into the annex that was home to Raimund, whom he had not spotted in the procession. He caught sight of him, firmly chained to a chair. At the foot of the wall opposite lay the key, which Raimund had thrown away after securing himself. His face was red and his eyes bloodshot, with a beseeching look, but Wojnicz slammed the door shut and went back to his own room.

He was fortunate not to witness what happened after the procession had plunged into the forest. The mist adored these places. The bright, joyful moon, which had been illuminating all these happenings until now, had misted over and was flooding the forest with a light like diluted milk, in which everyone had a pale, corpse-like face. The walkers were straying among the trees, pushing forward with set expressions, each going it alone, following his own fate. The streaks of viscid mist disoriented them even more, introducing further confusion into the ranks of this bizarre raggle-taggle army, this chaotic, irreligious procession. Soon its participants were scattered about the vicinity, each in solitude confronting the mist, the rustle of twigs, the crunch of moss, the scribble of bark on the trees and their splayed branches.

Opitz stood alone at the edge of a small clearing, stooping a little, as if preparing to toss a weight onto his shoulders. He was breathing heavily, and each breath chilled his ailing lungs—after all, he was as sick as the others—before escaping in a little gray cloud into the frosty air, for the full moon had brought the winter with it.

There was nothing violent about it—just a fast, almost imperceptible motion, which left poor Opitz hanging above the ground. The expression painted on his face was one that we had never seen before: sorrow. He must have known what was going to happen.

The rest, the few who were close by, watched it all from among the trees as if awakened, with distinct relief: *So it isn't me!*—and undoubtedly this was cruel on their part. Many of them had seen this dreadful mystery before, but just as for women with respect to giving birth, enough time had passed for them to forget the pain and fear; the Schwärmerei was working its magic too. *Yes, it's possible*, their faces seemed to be saying. Yes, this is really happening. The thing we feared most and tried to push away, to cheat, to ridicule and fool. It really has returned in the same dreadful form, and here it is, taking its prey.

Opitz's body fell to the ground in pieces, showering the moss and the bushes in bloody shreds.

Finally snow began to fall, and by daybreak it had covered everything, so that nothing spoiled or dirty, no single glove, no sodden newspaper, no chipped paving stone, was now visible. At once the world cheered up and put it all out of mind—what is the sense of remembering the stuff of one's failures, one's disturbing shadow?

Nor could anyone remember how they got home, or whose hands had released those strapped to chairs.

That morning, as though nothing had happened, wearing winter coats and wrapped in fur collars, the patients poured onto the little streets of Görbersdorf, treading their prescribed routes in the fresh snow, and only a few of the men showed traces of the night: a scratched cheek, a spruce needle in the hair, a ripped overcoat. At around noon, once the sun had fully forced its way into the valley, they abandoned the treatments their doctors had recommended to throw snowballs at one another, and to blunder down the church hill on hired sledges.

All day Raimund had been greasing the skis.

Wojnicz dressed his injured foot. Of course his shoe was gone forever, but a good thing too—it was not fit for use anymore. With trembling hands he washed the blood from his wounds and wrapped his foot in a handkerchief, a present from his father that had a beautiful cream-colored monogram, *MW*. He no longer cared what was going on outside; through the window, from the corner of his eye he saw the large wet flakes flying from above like manna and clothing the entire earth in a festive white robe. At dawn frost had come out of nowhere, making the snowflakes more compact. In the course of the morning they had covered all the roofs, streets and parks. Gradually the entire village lost its contours, changing into a fairy-tale picture before his eyes. At once some children had appeared whom Wojnicz had not noticed before, and fitted skis carved by their grandfathers to their boots. As he stood in the window, he saw patients who, after a filling breakfast at the Kurhaus, with no memory of the night before, were fighting battles with missiles made of snow. He also saw a doctor from the sanatorium in a coat thrown over his medical gown, heading somewhere with Sydonia Patek, looking troubled and serious. There could be no doubt that life was carrying on as before, as in a well-oiled machine, and the law of 75 percent was still working to the patients' advantage. One should live in hope.

Mieczysław went up to the attic, in search of shoes more than for any other purpose. Finding himself in Frau Opitz's room, he boldly opened the wardrobe and saw several pieces of clothing hanging on pegs. Slowly he undressed, folded his clothes neatly, then shoved them under the bed, while tossing his jacket onto it. Now he stood naked opposite the open wardrobe. A small, cracked mirror above the washbasin reflected his body divided into pieces, as if this image were part of a larger jigsaw puzzle that each of us has been given a lifetime to assemble.

Finally he reached for the leather lace-up boots standing on the bottom shelf in the wardrobe. They were the right size. He felt only brief discomfort; the boot was a snug fit, gently pinching his instep, but in a short while his foot grew accustomed to it. He put on the second boot and began to look around for the rest of the outfit.

As in the windows of a huge room, in his mind's eye he could see the shapes his future would take. There were so many possibilities that he felt strength gathering within him, but he could not find the words; all that entered his head was the German phrase *Ich will*, but this was something greater, that went beyond the usual *Ich*. He felt plural, multiple, multifaceted, compound and complicated like a coral reef, like a mushroom spawn whose actual existence is located underground.

Oh yes, he could stay here after everything that had happened, or even, in view of Opitz's irrevocable absence, he could take on his function—he could easily learn to run a guesthouse, and he had noted down all the suppers in his diary, a pretty good menu that merely had to be sent for, night after night. He and Raimund would go and pick hood-shaped mushrooms, soak them in alcohol and make Schwärmerei. Although with some resistance, Dr. Semperweiss would have to recognize that the illness was gone, that the breath of the Tuntschi had blown it away like a handful of dust.

Or else he might return to Lwów, to his father and uncle, and make his own living there, in sanitation and hydroengineering, while devoting himself to collecting something, to raise his spirits.

It all fitted him, both the underclothes and the dress. He grabbed his old jacket, which was now to serve as a short coat.

Everything was decided in the space of a few steps as he went downstairs and caught sight of himself in the only large mirror in the house. Essentially, he remained the same person, but differently prepared; one could say differently served, differently garnished. Now he resembled the woman in the hat who had stirred such emotion in him and whom he had hankered after.

The passport he found in the dead woman's room confirmed that from now on he would be Klara Opitz, of Czech nationality, a citizen of the district of Friedland in Niederschlesien, who packed her suitcase and, without saying goodbye, made her way to the promenade, to the usual stopping place for the droshky that took patients to the station in Dittersbach. In her other hand she carried a rectangular parcel wrapped in newspaper and tied with string. A kind gentleman helped her into her seat. She was mildly hindered by her hat and had to tie it on with a headscarf.

As the droshky was passing a house in the middle of the village, she saw them again, Frau Weber and Frau Brecht. This time they were sweeping the snow away from their front entrance with besoms. Seeing her in the carriage, they interrupted their work and leaned on their brooms, solemnly bidding her farewell with their eyes. For a moment she thought she had glimpsed the shadow of the third woman, or at least her thick finger on the doorframe, and she was reminded of what she had seen in de Bles's painting.

Remembering something, Klara reached into her jacket pocket, where at once she found the broad bean she had picked up at the very start of her time in Görbersdorf, right here, outside the old women's house. She must have entirely forgotten about it—apparently she had quite unconsciously been carrying it around throughout her stay. Before the droshky moved off, with a sort of mischievous joy she threw it up in the air, letting it fall straight into her mouth.

EPILOGUE

othing like the incident we have described here ever happened again. The war satisfied our cravings.

Tuberculosis practically ceased to exist thanks to the BCG vaccine that has been administered since the 1920s.

Klara Opitz settled in Munich, where she worked in a hospital kitchen. In 1917 she was sent to the front in Belgium, where she served in a field hospital. After the war she moved to Berlin and all trace of her was lost. Somebody insisted that they had seen Mieczysław Wojnicz at his father's grave in Lwów in the late 1920s, however. And that he was dressed in English tweeds.

Dr. Semperweiss was called up for the army but was killed right at the start of the war near Kraków, and his celebrated Mercedes was requisitioned.

Raimund took over the Guesthouse for Gentlemen and succeeded in running it for several years, until he was brought down by an addiction to alcohol, which told him to go into the mountains one day, never to return. The guesthouse was leased out and functioned tolerably well, but after the Second World War it was nationalized and converted into apartments for four families. It stands to this day in Sokołowsko, as Görbersdorf was renamed after the war.

After defeating tuberculosis (though it may be true that he was never ill), Walter Frommer lived a long time, but died of cold and hunger during the siege of Breslau in 1945. His burial site is not known.

August August departed this life in Görbersdorf on the 11th of July, 1914, and was buried at the cemetery in Langwaltersdorf.

Longin Lukas died in Görbersdorf on the 3rd of September, 1914, and lies close to August. One can visit them there, best of all in winter, when the lush vegetation is not overgrowing their decaying gravestones and erasing the stone inscriptions.

And what about us? We are always here.

GLOSSARY OF
PRESENT-DAY PLACE NAMES

Breslau—Wrocław

Friedland in Niederschlesien—Mieroszów

Glatz—Kłodzko

Görbersdorf—Sokołowsko

Hirschberg—Jelenia Góra

Langwaltersdorf—Unisław Śląski

Lwów—Lviv

Neue Rode—Nowa Ruda

Nieder Wüstegiersdorf—Głuszyca

Waldenburg—Wałbrzych

AUTHOR'S NOTE

All the misogynistic views on the topic of women and their place in the world are paraphrased from texts by the following authors:

Augustine of Hippo, Bernard of Cluny, William S. Burroughs, Cato, Joseph Conrad, Charles Darwin, Émile Durkheim, Henry Fielding, Sigmund Freud, H. Rider Haggard, Hesiod, Jack Kerouac, D. H. Lawrence, Cesare Lombroso, W. Somerset Maugham, John Milton, Friedrich Nietzsche, Ovid, Plato, Ezra Pound, Jean Racine, François de La Rochefoucauld, Jean-Paul Sartre, Arthur Schopenhauer, Semonides of Amorgos, William Shakespeare, August Strindberg, Jonathan Swift, Algernon Charles Swinburne, Tertullian, Thomas Aquinas, Richard Wagner, John Webster, Frank Wedekind, Otto Weininger, and William Butler Yeats.

The following quotations appear in the book:

Aristophanes, *The Frogs*, lines 285–296

Milton, *Paradise Lost*, Book 10, lines 888–895

Plutarch, *Moralia*, The Dialogue on Love, 766–767

Many thanks to Jerzy Marek and Ula Ososko for their help in the most precise re-creation of Görbersdorf.